Australian Affairs: Tempted

CAROL MARINELLI

AMY ANDREWS

AVRIL TREMAYNE

MILLS & BOON

First Published in Great Britain 2019
By Mills & Boon, an imprint of HarperCollins *Publishers*
1 London Bridge Street, London, SE1 9GF

AUSTRALIAN AFFAIRS: TEMPTED © 2019 Harlequin Books S.A.

Tempted by Dr Morales © 2014 Carol Marinelli
It Happened One Night Shift © 2015 Amy Andrews
From Fling to Forever © 2014 Belinda de Rome

ISBN: 978-0-263-27527-8

0319

MIX
Paper from
responsible sources

FSC
www.fsc.org

FSC™ C007454

This book is produced from independently certified FSC™ paper to ensure responsible forest management.

For more information visit: www.harpercollins.co.uk/green

Printed and bound in Spain
by CPI, Barcelona

About the Authors

Carol Marinelli recently filled in a form where she was asked for her job title and was thrilled, after all these years, to be able to put down her answer as 'writer'. Then it asked what Carol did for relaxation. After chewing her pen for a moment Carol put down the truth—'writing'. The third question asked—'What are your hobbies?' Well, not wanting to look obsessed or, worse still, boring, she crossed the fingers on her free hand and answered 'swimming and tennis'. But, given that the chlorine in the pool does terrible things to her highlights, I'm sure you can guess the real answer!

Amy Andrews has always loved writing, and still can't quite believe that she gets to do it for a living. She loves to hear from her readers. Drop her a line at www.amyandrews.com.au

Avril Tremayne read *Jane Eyre* as a teenager and has been hooked on tales of passion and romance ever since. She has spent a good chunk of her life travelling, and has more favourite destinations than should be strictly allowable.

Check out her website: www@avriltremayne.com Or follow her on Twitter: @AvrilTremayne and Facebook: www.facebook.com/avril.tremayne

Australian

AFFAIRS

TEMPTED BY
DR MORALES

CAROL MARINELLI

With love to Fiona McArthur
I love our chats
C xxx

CHAPTER ONE

'SORRY, JUAN, I didn't mean to wake you.' Cate Nicholls
stopped twisting a long brown curl around her finger
and cringed at the sound of Juan's deep, heavily accented—but clearly sleepy—voice when he answered
the phone.

'It is no problem. Is that you, Cate?'

'Yes.' She blushed a little that Juan had recognised
her voice. He had only done a few locum shifts at the
Melbourne Bayside Hospital emergency department,
but the tension between them sizzled. Cate had tried
everyone she could think of before finally accepting
Harry's suggestion and phoning Juan to see if he could
come in. A fully qualified anaesthetist from Argentina,
he was travelling around the world for a year or two and
was as sexy-as-sin as a man could possibly be and still
remain popular. 'I'm really sorry to have disturbed you.
Were you working last night?'

'No.'

'Oh!' Cate glanced up at the clock—it was two p.m.,
why on earth would he still be in bed? Then Cate heard
the sound of a female voice and cringed again as Juan
told whoever the woman was that he took three sugars
in his coffee. Then his silken voice returned to Cate.

'So, what can I do for you?'

'Sheldon called in sick and we haven't been able to get anyone else in to cover him.'

'Does Harry know that you're calling me?'

Cate laughed—Harry, one of the senior emergency department consultants, went into sulking mode whenever Juan was around; he was still annoyed that Juan had knocked back his offer of a three-month contract to work in the department. 'It was Harry who suggested that I call you.'

'So, what time do you want me to come in?'

'As soon as you can get here.' Cate looked out at the busy emergency department. 'It's really starting to fill up…' She paused for a moment as Harry said something. 'Could you hold on, please, Juan?' Cate called out to Harry, 'What did you say?'

'Tell Juan that even though we really need him to get here as soon as possible, he can stop for a haircut on the way if he feels so inclined!'

Juan's shaggy long black hair, unshaven appearance and relaxed dress sense drove Harry crazy and Cate was smiling as she got back to her conversation with Juan. 'I assume that you heard that?'

'I did,' Juan answered. 'Tell Harry that he loves me really.' Cate listened as Juan yawned and stretched and she tried not to think about him in bed, naked, at two in the afternoon. 'Okay,' he said. 'I'll just have a quick shower and I'll be there as soon as I can.'

'Thanks, Juan.' Cate hung up the phone and wrote his name on the board. Harry glanced over and gave a quick shake of his head.

'If ever there was a man inappropriately named, it's Dr Morales,' Harry said, and Cate had to laugh. Juan had quite a reputation, and even just writing his name down would have a few staff scurrying off to check their make-up and hair.

Cate refused to.

Washing her hands before heading back out to the patients, she saw her reflection in the mirror. Yes, her shoulder-length hair could do with being re-tied and her serious hazel eyes might look better with a slick of mascara, but she simply refused to make that effort for Juan.

She wasn't about to play with fire.

With three older brothers who had all been wild, to say the least, not a lot shocked the rather sensible Cate, but Juan managed to at times—either with his daredevil sports or with the endless women he briefly bedded. He raised more than a few eyebrows when he happily regaled his colleagues with tales of his trip around Australia, but what shocked Cate most was the internal fight she was having to put up to not simply give in to that sensual smile and dive headfirst into his bed.

They had hit the ground flirting but then Cate had backed off—soon realising that Juan and his rather reprobate ways were far more than she could handle.

Cate had returned from two weeks' annual leave, newly single after breaking up with her boyfriend of more than two years, and her stomach had turned over at the very sight of Juan. She'd never had such a violent reaction to anyone and, foolishly, she had told herself she was just testing out her flirting wings on the sexy locum, just indulging in a little play flirt the first time they had met.

Cate had never really thought he'd ask her to join him for a drink that night, though his eyes had said bed.

She still burnt at the memory of their first meeting—

the rush that had come as she'd met his grey eyes, the desire to say yes, to hell with it all, for once to give in and choose to be reckless. Instead, she had refused his offer politely and, in the few times she'd seen him since then, Cate had played things down—denied the attraction that sizzled between them and tried her best to keep things strictly about work.

'Juan is a very good doctor, though,' Cate reminded Harry, because even if Juan was a bit of a rake, there was no disputing that fact.

'Yes, but his talent's wasted,' Harry said, but then sighed. 'Maybe I'm just envious.'

'I've never met a more talented emergency doctor than you,' Cate said, and she meant it. Harry was a fantastic emergency doctor as well as a highly renowned hand surgeon, only it wasn't Juan's medical talent that Harry was referring to.

'I meant maybe I'm envious of Juan's freedom, his take-it-or-leave-it attitude. He actually doesn't give a damn what anyone thinks. It would be lovely just to work one or two shifts a week and spend the rest of the time kicking back!' Harry gave a wry smile. 'But, then, Juan doesn't have four-year-old twins to worry about. Make that, Juan doesn't have anything to worry about.'

'Are things not getting any better?' Cate asked. She liked Harry a lot and had been devastated for him when his wife had been brought in last year after a car crash. Jill had died two weeks later in ICU, leaving Harry a single father to his young twins, Charlotte and Adam.

'The nanny just handed in her notice,' Harry said. 'Another one!'

Cate gave a sympathetic groan but Harry just rolled

his eyes and headed back out to deal with the patients. 'It will sort itself out,' Harry said.

'Ooh!' Kelly smiled when she saw Juan's name up on the board. 'That just brightened up my afternoon! With a bit of luck Juan will come out for drinks with us tonight after work.' Kelly winked.

'I'm sure that he will,' Cate said. 'I can't make it, though.'

'Come on, Cate,' Kelly pushed. 'You said that you would. It's Friday night, you can't sit around moping about Paul...'

'I'm not moping about Paul. When I said that I'd come out, I didn't realise that I was working in the morning,' Cate lied.

'But you said that you'd drive,' Kelly reminded her. 'It's still a week till payday.'

Yes, Cate thought, she had said she'd drive but that had been before she had known Juan would be working into the evening—he wasn't exactly known for turning down a night out.

Juan worked to live rather than lived to work—that had been his explanation when he had irked Harry by turning down his job offer. Juan had told Harry that he would prefer to work casual shifts at various Melbourne hospitals rather than be tied to one place. And, given he only worked one or two shifts a week, it had been thanks but, no, thanks from Juan. Cate had been surprised that Harry had even offered him the role.

He was, though, an amazing doctor.

He was amazing, Cate conceded to herself as she went to help Kelly make up some fresh gurneys and do a quick tidy of the cubicles.

Juan was also the last complication she needed.

Still, she put his impending arrival out of her mind, just glad to have the doctor shortage under control for now.

'Where's Christine?' Cate asked as she stripped a gurney and gave it a wipe down before making it up with fresh linen.

'Guess,' Kelly answered. 'She's hiding in her office. If you do get the job, please don't let that ever be you!'

Cate was soon to be interviewed for the role of nurse unit manager and it was fairly certain that the position would be hers. Lillian, the director of acute nursing, had practically told her so. Cate was already more hands on with the patients than most of the associate nurse unit managers, and if she did get the role she had no intention of hiding herself away in the office or going over the stock orders to try and save a bean. It had also been heavily hinted that, after Christine's haphazard brand of leadership, the powers that be wanted a lot more order in Emergency—and it had been none-too-subtly pointed out that the nurses were not there to babysit Harry's twins.

If she did get the job, Cate knew there was going to be a lot to deal with.

'Is this cubicle ready?' Abby, who was doing triage, popped her head in. 'I've got a gentleman that needs to be seen.'

'Bring him in,' Cate said. 'Kelly, if you could carry on sorting out any empty cubicles, that would be great.'

Kelly nodded and headed off and Cate took the handover as they helped the painfully thin gentleman move from the wheelchair to the gurney. His wife watched anxiously.

'This is Reece Anderson,' Abby introduced. 'He's

thirty-four years old and has recently completed a course of chemotherapy for a melanoma on his left thigh. Reece has had increasing nausea since this morning as well as abdominal pain.'

'He didn't tell me he was in pain till lunchtime.' There was an edge to his wife's voice. 'I thought the vomiting was the after effects of the chemo.'

'Okay, Reece.' Cate introduced herself. 'I'm going to help you to get into a gown and take some observations and then we shall get you seen just as soon as we can.' Reece was clearly very uncomfortable as well as dehydrated, and there was also considerable tension between him and his wife.

'The heat has made this last round of treatment unbearable,' his wife said. 'We don't have air-conditioning.' She looked more tense than the patient. 'I'm Amanda, by the way.'

'Hi, Amanda. Yes, I'm sure the heat isn't helping,' Cate said as she looked at Reece's dry lips and felt his skin turgor. 'We'll get a drip started soon.'

Melbourne was in the grip of a prolonged heat wave and more patients than usual were presenting as dehydrated. Cate had been moaning about the heat and lack of sleep herself, but to imagine being unwell and going through chemotherapy made her rethink her grumbles.

'Why don't you go home?' Reece suggested to his wife as, between retches, Cate helped him undress. 'I could be here for ages.'

'I've told you, I'm not going home. I don't want to leave you till I know what's happening.' Amanda's response was terse.

'You have to pick up the kids from school.'

'I'm going to ring Stella and let her know what's going on. She can get them...'

'Just go home, will you?' Reece snapped.

Cate looked over at Amanda and saw that she was close to tears.

'Just leave,' Reece said.

'Oh, I might just do that!' Amanda's voice held a challenge and Cate guessed this wasn't the first time they'd had this row. 'I'm going to ring Stella and ask her to pick them up.'

Amanda walked out of the cubicle and Reece rested back on the pillows as Cate took his baseline observations. 'I can't believe I'm back in hospital. Amanda should be sorting out the children, not me.'

Cate didn't comment; instead, she headed out and had a brief word with Harry, who was working with Kelly on a critical patient who had just arrived. He said he would get there just as soon as he could but, given how long the wait might be, Harry asked if Cate could take some bloods and start an IV.

Reece was pretty uncommunicative throughout but, as she went to leave, finally he asked a question. 'Do you think it's the cancer spreading?'

'I think it's far too early to be speculating about anything,' Cate said. 'We'll get these bloods off and a doctor will be in just as soon as possible.'

While she had sympathy for Reece and could guess how scared he must be, Cate's heart went out to Amanda when she found her crying by the vending machine.

'Come in here,' Cate offered, opening up an interview room to give Amanda some privacy. The interview rooms were beyond dreary, painted brown and with hard seats and a plastic table, but at least they were private. 'I know you must be very worried but it's far too early to know what's going on.'

'I can deal with whatever's going on health-wise,' Amanda said. 'We've been dealing with it for months now. It's Reece that I can't handle—his moods and constantly telling me to leave him alone.'

'It must be terribly hard,' Cate offered, wishing she could say more.

'It's nearly impossible.' Amanda shook her head with hopelessness. 'I'm starting to think that maybe he really doesn't want me around.'

'I doubt that,' Cate replied.

'So do I.' Amanda took a drink of coffee and slowly started to calm down—all she had needed was a short reprieve. 'You know, if that really is what he wants, then tough! I'm not going to walk away,' Amanda said, draining her drink and screwing up the cup as she threw it into the bin. 'Like it or not, I'm not going anywhere.' Amanda wiped her eyes and blew her nose then walked back to be with her husband.

Cate was wondering if she should try and find the intern to see Reece, though she did want someone more senior; then she considered calling in a favour from one of the surgical team and asking them to come down without an emergency doctor's referral, but then she saw Juan walk in.

He really was the most striking man Cate had ever seen. His tall, muscular frame was enhanced by the black Cuban-heeled boots that he wore. Today he was wearing black jeans with a heavily buckled belt and a grey and black shirt that was crumpled. His black hair was long enough that it could easily be tied back, but instead it fell onto his broad shoulders and, fresh from the shower, his hair left a slight damp patch on his shirt.

Cate's first thought on seeing him wasn't relief that finally there was an extra pair of hands and she could get Reece seen quickly.

Instead, as always, he begged the question—how on earth did she manage to say no to that? He was sex on long legs certainly, but more than that he made her smile, made her laugh. Juan just changed the whole dynamics of the place.

'You made good time!' Cate said, as he came over and she caught the heady whiff of Juan fresh from the shower.

'I got a lift.'

Ah, yes, Cate reminded herself, he'd had company when she'd called. Juan didn't have a car, he wasn't in any one place long enough for that, so instead he used public transport or, more often than not, he ran to work and treated everyone to the delicious sight of him breathless and sweaty before he headed for the staff shower.

'Where would you like me to start?' he asked. Juan was always ready to jump straight into work.

'Cubicle four,' Cate said, giving him a brief background on the way. She saw Reece's and Amanda's eyes widen just a fraction as a very foreign, rather unconventional-looking doctor entered the cubicle, yet Juan was so good with patients that within a moment he had Reece at ease.

Juan put one long, booted foot on the lower frame of the gurney and leant in and chatted with Reece about his medical history and symptoms before standing up straight.

'Can I borrow your stethoscope?' he asked Cate.

'There's one on the wall,' Cate said. There usually wasn't but the rather meticulous Cate had prepared the cubicle herself.

'I can't hear very well with them,' Juan said. 'I prefer yours.'

'I know! You took it home with you last time you *borrowed* it.'

'I brought it back,' he pointed out, but he took down one of the cheap hospital-issue ones and started listening to Reece's chest.

He cursed in Spanish and even Reece gave a small smile. 'They are useless. I should have brought mine but you said it was so busy that I was rushing to get here...' He winked at his patient and then Juan's full lips twitched into a small smile of triumph as Cate handed over her stethoscope.

'That's better,' Juan said.

Reece was soon back to feeling miserable as Juan examined him. He reduced Amanda to tears again when she tried to answer a question for him. 'I can speak for myself.'

'Okay,' Juan said, 'I am going lay you down and examine your stomach.' He turned and smiled at Amanda. 'Could you excuse us, please?'

Juan carefully examined his patient's abdomen as Reece tried to hide his grimaces.

'Reece...' Juan looked down. 'How long have you been sitting on this?'

'Since this morning.'

'Reece?' The doubt was obvious in Juan's voice.

'Last night...' Juan raised his eyebrows but said nothing, simply waited until Reece changed his story again. 'I woke up in pain the night before.'

'Is that one true?' Juan checked, and Reece nodded. 'Okay, I have to do a rectal examination.' As Cate helped Reece roll to his side, he was weary and close to crying. 'I'm sorry, Reece,' Juan said. 'I know it must be awful. It won't take long.'

He was so good with the patients. He never told them not to feel embarrassed, or that he'd done it a thousand times before; he just quickly examined him and as Reece was rolled onto his back again, Juan thanked him for his co-operation.

'Good man,' he said, and Reece nodded.

'What do you think is going on?' Reece asked, and this was where Juan was different from most doctors. This was where he was clearly senior because he gave Reece his tentative diagnosis.

'Your history makes things more complicated, of course...' Juan said. 'But I think you have appendicitis. I am going to ring the surgeons and get you seen as a priority.'

'Can I have something for the pain?'

'They don't like to give analgesia without first seeing the patient for themselves so they can get a clear picture.' Juan repeated what Cate had heard many times before, but again he showed just how experienced and confident he was as he continued speaking. 'Still, I will try bribing them by ordering a quick ultrasound while we wait for the bloods to come back. Hopefully I can give you something for the pain.'

It was still incredibly busy out in the department. Juan rang the surgeons and had a long discussion, then as he wrote up some analgesia he rang and arranged an ultrasound.

'Give Reece this for the pain and vomiting,' Juan said. 'I'll ring the lab and get the bloods pushed through. If we can get him round now for an ultrasound, the surgeons should be here by the time he comes back.'

'Sure.' Cate sorted out the drugs and then rang Christine and told her that she was taking a patient for an ultrasound and would she please come out of her office and work on the floor.

'That will go down well,' Kelly commented, picking up the constantly ringing phone.

'Do you know what?' Cate answered. 'I really don't care.'

Kelly held out the phone for Juan. 'A call for you.' He went to take it. 'Martina,' Kelly added.

Both women shared a look as he said a few terse words in Spanish and then promptly hung up. 'I spoke with Christine.' Juan looked at Cate. 'Did she not pass it on?'

'Pass what on?'

'I have had to speak to the nursing managers at the other hospitals where I work. Could you ask the nursing and reception staff not to put through certain personal calls for me?'

'Certain?' Cate checked.

'From Martina.'

'But if it's your mum or the girl you met last night…' Cate tried to keep the edge from her voice, but she felt like a secretary running his little black book when Juan was on call—women were ringing all the time '...then we're to put them through?'

'Okay, for *all* personal calls, just ask the staff to say they are not sure if Juan is working and that you'll take a message and leave it for him. I am just asking if the staff can be a bit more discreet.'

'The staff are discreet, Juan, but there's a difference between being discreet and rude. When it's clearly a personal call...' She took a breath. 'Fine, I'll speak to everyone.'

Juan got back to his notes and did not look up. It would simply open up a can of worms if he explained things.

He didn't want to explain things.

That was the reason he was travelling after all, no need for explanations, no past, no rules—just fun. Except Cate didn't want fun. She'd made that clear, even if not quite from the start.

He was going to do this shift and then go home.

Juan had just over two weeks to go in the country.

Had Cate said yes when he'd first asked her out they could have had an amazing few months.

Instead, she had made it very clear she wasn't interested in a brief fling with him.

She was interested, though.

Juan could feel it, he could smell it, he could almost taste it, but Cate refused to give in to it.

He wasn't going to try again.

Cate was a serious thing, a curious thing, and she was quietly driving him insane.

'Are you coming out for drinks tonight, Juan?' Kelly asked.

'Not tonight,' Juan said, and he heard Cate's small exhalation of relief.

Oh, well, Juan thought as he carried on writing up his notes.

She could relax soon.

He'd be gone.

CHAPTER TWO

'How are things?' Juan came in to speak with Reece soon after he came back from ultrasound. The surgeons had examined him there and had ordered antibiotics and changed his IV regime, and Reece was now being prepared rapidly for Theatre.

'You tell me,' Reece said. 'They said that appendicitis was serious in someone with my immune system.'

'That's why they're starting you on all these antibiotics. We need to get you up to Theatre before it perforates,' Juan said.

'I shouldn't have left it,' Reece said. 'I thought it was cancer.'

'Of course you did,' Juan said, 'but it is an appendix flare-up nevertheless. I had a pregnant woman just last week...' He didn't continue, there was a lot to be done.

Cate was trying to sort out the antibiotics that the surgeons wanted. It had been incredibly tense during his ultrasound, Reece telling Amanda over and over that she should just go home. Cate had, on her way back from Ultrasound, suggested that Amanda wait in the interview room, just to have a break from the snipes from her husband.

'Cate, can I see Reece's IV regime?' Juan asked,

and then spoke to the patient. 'Though you need to be operated on, I want you to have a bolus of fluids before you go up.'

He was so direct he overrode the surgeons' IV regime with a stroke of his pen.

Juan saw Cate's rapid blink—not many people would have changed Jeff Henderson's plan. 'I just spoke to him and discussed some changes,' Juan said. 'Reece needs to be better hydrated before he's operated on.'

'I bet that went down well,' Cate said, repeating Kelly's sentiment from a little while ago.

'Jeff was fine.' Juan shrugged. 'And, like you, I really don't care if I offend at times. This is better for the patient.'

He handed over the chart and then spoke to Reece. 'I'm going to put another IV in you so that we can push fluids in and then I shall speak with your wife.'

'Can you tell her that there's no point hanging around?'

'She's not going to want to go home while you're in Theatre,' Cate pointed out as she added the medication to the flask.

'I just don't want her here,' Reece snapped. 'I don't want to be a burden.'

'Then stop being one,' Cate said, and Juan's head jerked up from the IV he was putting in. He'd heard a lot of straight talking—emergency nurses were very good at it—but hearing what Cate had to say to Reece made him falter momentarily.

'The illness and the treatment you are on must be awful, for *both* of you,' Cate continued to Reece, 'but I can think of nothing worse than loving someone who is sick and being repeatedly told that they don't want you there, that you'd be better off without them.'

'I think she'd be happier—' Reece attempted, but Cate didn't let him finish.

'I'm quite sure Amanda would be happier if you graciously accepted her love and affection and her need to take care of you, to help you *both* get through this.'

Juan headed over to the sharps box. He could feel his pulse pounding in his temples, feel the roar of blood in his ears, and, for reasons of his own, he wished he hadn't heard that, yet he felt compelled to respond.

'She's right.' Juan's voice was husky and he cleared his throat before continuing. 'Cate is right, Reece. If your wife didn't want to be here for you then she'd have gone long ago.'

'You don't know that.'

'Cate...' Juan turned '...could you go and speak with Amanda and let her know what is happening and then bring her in?'

'Sure,' Cate answered. 'Reece, are you okay with me letting her know that you have appendicitis?'

Reece nodded. Clearly Cate's words had had an impact on him because he let out a sigh and lay back on his pillows, but as she walked out of the cubicle he met suddenly serious grey eyes. Only then did Reece realise that there was more to come.

'Right,' Juan said to his patient. 'While we've got a moment, I'll tell you *exactly* what I do know.'

By the time Cate returned from taking Reece to Theatre, the critically injured patient had been moved as well and the place was settling down. All the staff worked hard to clear the backlog and at six Juan looked up at the clock and spoke to Harry.

'Why don't you go home?'

She saw Harry hesitate. There were other doctors on but no one particularly senior.

Except the locum just happened to be Juan.

'Go and have dinner with your children,' Juan said. 'I'm sure we'll cope.'

Juan would more than cope.

Everyone knew it.

'You're sure?' Harry checked. 'Dr Vermont won't get here till ten.'

'Of course,' Juan said. 'Anyway, the nightclubs don't really get going till midnight.'

Harry gave a wry smile and headed for home, and Cate did her best to avoid the six feet three of testosterone who sat and worked his way through a huge bunch of grapes between seeing patients.

Relieved that Juan wouldn't be joining them on their night out, Cate had relented and agreed to drive her friends, but before she headed off to get ready she did have a question for Juan. He was sitting writing up his notes before handing over to Dr Vermont.

'What did you say to Reece?'

'Reece?'

'The appendicitis.'

'I'm not with you,' Juan said, still writing his notes.

'He was a whole lot nicer to Amanda when we came back in. He even thanked her for being there for him when I took him up to Theatre.'

'He must have listened to what you said to him.' Juan shrugged and Cate walked off with a slight frown. Yes, she had been direct while talking to Reece but *something* had happened while she'd been speaking with Amanda. She was sure of it, because they had returned to a very different man—and Cate was positive Juan had had something to do with it.

She just had no idea what.

The night staff came on duty and Cate handed over the patients, then headed to the changing rooms, where there was a fight for the mirror.

'I thought Christine was coming?' Kelly said. 'She said she was a little while ago.'

'No.' Abby laughed. 'When she found out Juan wasn't coming, Christine changed her mind, of course. He's made it obvious that he's no longer interested—you'd think that she'd have taken the hint by now.'

Cate changed quickly, moaning that her strapless bra dug in and gave her four breasts before pulling on a black halterneck she had bought the previous weekend.

'Is that new?' Kelly asked as Cate pulled on a pale lilac skirt.

'Yep.' Cate smiled. 'And so are these!' She held up the most gorgeous pair of wedges—they were nothing like her usual choice, and had been an absolute impulse buy.

Her first.

Cate did up the straps around her ankles and blinked back sudden tears. She was still in that wobbly post-break-up stage, still trying to work out what had gone wrong, what *was* wrong.

She'd been happy with Paul, just not happy enough. She had loved him in so many ways, but she still hadn't been able to give Paul the answer he wanted. The answer everyone wanted! Her parents had been equally shocked when the rather predictable Cate had made a rather unpredictable choice.

Why had she ended it?

'Because...' had been her paltry response.

Even Cate didn't really know why.

Juan tried not to notice when the late staff all emerged from the changing rooms, changed and scented, like a noisy flock of butterflies floating down the corridor— but there was only one who drew the eye.

She had make-up on, not much just enough to accentuate her wary eyes, and her mouth should not be allowed out, unescorted by him, when it shimmered with gloss. A lilac skirt showed off her tanned legs and he did his best not to notice, as they walked past the nurses' station, her back, which was revealed in a halterneck.

'I'm not staying long,' he heard Cate warning her friends as they said goodbye and headed out. 'I've got to be back here in ten hours.'

'Are you sure you won't change your mind, Juan?' Kelly called over her shoulder.

And he should leave well alone. Cate wasn't, Juan guessed, up to what he had in mind.

Except he couldn't get her out of his head!

Her words to Reece had lowered his defences, and the scent of her as she walked past, the sight of her bare skin...it was surely worth one more shot?

Juan wanted their time.

'I might see you there,' Juan called out to the departing group, and watched her bare shoulders stiffen, watched as she very deliberately didn't turn round.

As she, still, denied him.

CHAPTER THREE

THE BAR WAS hot and crowded but it was equally hot outside; there was just no escaping the heat.

There was no escaping Juan.

She was terribly aware of him when, about an hour after they'd got there, he arrived.

He came over and bought everyone drinks, but Cate told him that she was happy with her soda water.

'When are you working with us again, Juan?' Abby shouted above the noise.

'I don't think I am,' Juan said. 'I have some shifts already booked in the city.'

'So this is your leaving do!' Kelly said.

'It might be…'

Cate stood there, watching her friends get louder, flirtier and more morose as they realised they might never see him again. By midnight, the night had turned into Juan Morales's unofficial send-off. So much so that there was now going to be an impromptu party back at his home.

Impromptu might just as well be his middle name, Cate thought as everyone asked her to come along.

'I'm working tomorrow!' Cate said it three times, not that anyone listened.

'It will be fun,' Abby insisted. 'Everyone's going back.'

Half the bar, it would seem, was lined up outside to take taxis to Juan's as, sober, fed up, tired and with her strapless bra digging into her, Cate headed out to her car.

'Thank you for this,' Juan said as he lowered himself into the passenger seat, far too tall for her rather small car. 'I really should get there first to let people in.'

'It's no problem.' Cate gave a slightly forced smile and then tried to turn it into a friendlier one as a couple of her colleagues and friends climbed into the back seat.

'You don't mind giving us a lift, do you, Cate?' Kelly checked, though not until she'd put her seat belt on.

'Of course not,' Cate said, and put the air conditioner on. The blast of cold air was especially welcome a moment later when Juan said, 'Cate, if you want to have a drink, you are very welcome to stay the night.'

Stay!

At Juan Morales's apartment for the night!

Cate turned and gave him the most incredulous smile she could muster, before starting the engine. 'Don't they have taxis in Argentina, Juan?'

He gave her a shameless smile back and then answered with his deep, heavily accented voice, which had Cate's stomach flip over on itself. 'I'm just letting you know that the offer is there.'

The offer had been there for a while now.

'I'm working at seven tomorrow morning.'

'You're staying for a drink, though,' Juan checked, but Cate answered him with a question of her own.

'Can you give me directions?' she said as she pulled out of the car park.

'Left ahead and then you go down...' He even managed to give a sexual connotation to the simplest directions, Cate thought, or was it that she was just incredibly aware of him sitting next to her?

Cate glanced over and caught a glimpse of his strong profile. His grey eyes were framed by dark lashes, his nose was straight and he had full lips that smiled easily. There was an exotic streak that seemed to run through every inch of him.

'Have you had your interview?' Juan asked.

'Not yet,' Cate said, surprised that he'd remembered. 'There are some external applications as well that they're going through.'

'So you would be the unit manager if you get it?'

'The nurse unit manager,' Cate corrected as she sat waiting for the traffic lights to change.

'Wouldn't you miss working with the patients?'

'I'd still be working with the patients,' came Cate's rather tart response, not that Juan seemed to notice the nerve he had just jarred, or, if he had, he chose to pursue it.

'Christine doesn't.'

She turned and met eyes that were more than happy to meet and hold hers. 'I'm not Christine,' Cate said, because rumour had it he'd been sleeping with Christine when he'd first arrived and Cate could well believe it. When Cate had come back from annual leave, she'd found Christine in floods of tears in the changing room and it hadn't been hard to work out why.

'No,' Juan said slowly and with a tinge of regret that made her throat tighten at the implication. His next loaded sentence seemed to insist she acknowledge the denied desire that simmered between them. 'You're not Christine.'

'The lights have changed,' Kelly called from the back.

As the car moved off Juan fiddled with her sound system and Cate cringed in embarrassment as a rather tragic break-up song came on.

'You should be listening to happier music,' Juan commented. 'All that will do is make you feel more miserable.'

'I'm not miserable at all.'

'Have you spoken to Paul since the break-up?' Abby chimed in from the back seat.

'Of course I have,' Cate said. 'It's all civil.'

'Which means that it was long overdue,' Juan commented, and Cate pursed her lips. It was the problem with being the so-called designated driver—you had to listen as things were discussed that generally wouldn't be.

'It doesn't have to be all smashing plates and tears,' Cate said, but didn't elaborate. Trust Juan to hit the nail on the head, though. Paul had been upset and uncomprehending at first, yet she had been calm and matter-of-fact once her decision to end it had been made.

Oh, she'd waited for the tears, for torrents of emotion to invade, for all the drama that seemed a necessary part of a relationship break-up to arrive—but they hadn't. She'd sat in her garden, sipping wine with her neighbour, Bridgette, with more a sense of relief than regret.

Juan was right, the break-up had been overdue.

'How much longer are you in Australia?' Kelly asked, and Juan turned a bit in his seat to answer and to chat with the girls in the back.

'Just over two weeks.'

'You should stay longer,' Kelly said.

'I can't,' Juan said, 'my visa expires the day after I leave.'

'Would you, though, if you could?' Kelly persisted.

'I think it's maybe time to move on.'

'Where now?' Cate asked, and Juan turned back to face the front.

'Turn right along the beach road and my place is about halfway.'

As she turned, the car jolted and Cate frowned. The car was not responding as it usually did, she could feel the groan of the engine.

'There's something wrong with the car,' Cate said, having appalling visions of breaking down a few metres from Juan's and, yes, ending up staying the night. The complication of a fling with Juan was something Cate did not need and frantically she looked at the dashboard. 'It's in manual…' Cate frowned but Juan had already worked it out—their hands met at the gearstick and Cate pulled hers away.

'My fault,' Juan said, 'my legs are too long.' He slotted it back into drive. 'My knees must have knocked the gearstick.'

God, he was potent. Cate's fingers were still tingling from the brief touch as she pulled up at his apartment. 'You are coming in?' Juan checked as she sat with the engine idling and there was a moment when she wanted to be the taxi martyr and drive off—but rather more than that, yes, she wanted a further glimpse of his world.

'Sure.'

Juan let them all in and it wasn't quite what Cate had

been expecting—it was a furnished rental apartment but a rather luxurious one with stunning beach views and a huge decking area outside. It was everything the well-heeled traveller needed for a few weeks of fun, Cate thought. Yet, despite the expensive furnishings and appliances, there was an emptiness and sparseness to it—a blandness even, broken only by his belongings.

Temporary.

Like Juan.

'This is the type of music you should be listening to,' Juan said, slotting his phone into some speakers. The room filled with music that under different circumstances Cate might want to dance to. Taxis were starting to arrive and, as more hospital personnel filled his home, Juan opened the French doors so that people could party inside or out, and then went to sort out drinks.

'What do you want, Cate?'

He made no secret that his interest was in her.

'I'll get something in a moment,' Cate said, and asked if she could use the bathroom.

'Straight down the hall,' Juan said. 'And to your left.'

She followed his directions but straight down the hall was his bedroom—the door was open, the bed rumpled and unmade, and for a wild, reckless moment she wanted to give in to his undeniable charm, could almost envision them tumbling on the bed, a knot of arms and legs.

Cate pushed open the bathroom door and let out a breath.

This wasn't like her at all.

She hadn't ever really envisioned herself that way with anyone, not even Paul. Bloody Juan had her head going in directions it wasn't used to. A part of her wanted to stop being sensible, ordered Cate and just give in to the feelings he ignited—to be a little wild and reckless for once. She knew that she was sending him mixed messages, that at times she found herself flirting with him in a way she never had with anybody else.

Cate washed her hands and had to dry them on her top because, of course, he didn't have hand towels, just a wet beach towel hanging over the shower.

Whoops, there went her mind again, imagining that huge body naked on the other side of the glass shower door.

'Go home, Cate,' she said to herself. She was about to do just that, but when she got back to the lounge Juan handed her a large glass filled with ice and some dangerous-looking cocktail.

'I'm driving,' Cate reminded him.

'I know, so I take care to make you something nice—it is right to take care of the designated driver.'

It was fruity, refreshing and delicious, yet she didn't want to be singled out for the Juan special treatment, didn't want to be the latest caught in his spotlight, but she knew that she was.

Cate danced a little, chatted with her friends, finished her drink and, having stayed a suitable length of time, when she saw that he was safely speaking with others, she said goodnight to Kelly.

'Stay for a bit longer,' Kelly pushed.

'I'm going to go.' Cate shook her head and slipped quietly away and headed out to her car.

He really had chosen a lovely spot to live—there were views of the bay to the front and behind was hillside. It all looked so peaceful, it was hard to imagine that across

Victoria bush fires were raging, Cate thought, dragging in a breath of the warm, sultry night as she went into her bag for her keys.

'Cate.'

She jumped a little when she heard Juan call her name. Had she not lingered that second she would have been safely in her car; instead, she had no choice but to turn to him.

'Where I come from…' he walked slowly towards her, his boots crunching on the gravel '…you thank your host and say goodbye…'

'I didn't know you were such a stickler for convention.'

'I'm not,' Juan admitted, still walking towards her as she backed herself against the car. 'Just when it suits me.'

'Thank you for a lovely night.'

'And in my country,' Juan continued, 'the host would try to persuade you to stay for one more drink, would be offended that you were leaving so soon…' It was all very casual, except his hand had moved to her cheek and was moving a lock of her hair behind her ear.

'I'm good at offending people,' Cate said. 'There really is no need to take it personally.'

'Don't go.' He smiled. 'I only asked everyone back to get you here.'

She laughed.

She doubted it.

Actually, no, she didn't, she believed it. Anything was possible with Juan.

'I might not be called in to work again,' he said. 'So this could be it.'

'It could be.'

'I'd have liked to get to know you some more.'

She gave him a half-smile, but it wavered. Cate wanted to get to know him some more too, but for what? He made no secret that in a couple of weeks he would be gone. Juan seemed completely at ease with a brief fling, whereas it just wasn't in her nature.

Except, yes, she wanted more of Juan.

'Stay.'

'Juan…' Cate just couldn't do it and she tried to make a joke. 'I've got three brothers and they've all warned me about guys like you.'

'What?' He frowned.

'Come on, Juan.' She loathed how indecent he was. 'Won't whoever you were in bed with this afternoon mind?'

'What?' he asked again as the frown remained, but then it turned into a wicked smile. 'That was my cleaning lady,' he said. 'I fell asleep on the couch, watching daytime soaps.' He looked down at her, realised fully then that he hadn't had sex since he'd dumped Christine, since a certain Cate Nicholls had stepped into his life—how with one turn of his head he'd been very turned on. 'I love daytime soaps in Australia,' he said. 'They are filthy.'

Cate let out a small laugh.

She wasn't sure she believed him about the cleaning lady, but did it matter?

She wasn't his mother.

She wasn't anything and, yes, very soon he'd be gone.

She turned to go, only half-heartedly because he had moved in to kiss her, and not on the cheek.

One kiss couldn't hurt, Cate told herself.

It was time to have kissed someone else by now, Cate decided as his mouth met hers. Except she'd never known a kiss like it.

It was everything a kiss should be.

It was very slow and measured, his lips light on hers at first, nudging hers into slow movement. His hands crept around her waist and his tongue slipped in and slid around hers, slowly at first, letting her acclimatise herself to the taste of him, and she did, so easily. He tasted of raspberry and vodka and something else too, which Cate couldn't quite place.

He took things slowly, but not for long. Just as she started to relax, just as she thought she could manage a kiss goodbye with Juan, he breathed into her, shed a low moan into her, pressed into her, pushed in his tongue more deeply, and Cate found her missing ingredient—it was a dash of sin that he tasted of, because no kiss had turned her on so much. The press of his erection made her push her mound into him, the feel of his hot hand on her back had her skin turn to fire.

It wasn't just her first kiss after Paul, it was the first kiss she'd ever had that could propel her straight to the bedroom. She was kissing him back and with passion; it was still a slow kiss but their tongues danced with suggestion. His hand moved to her breast and how she wished she wasn't wearing a bra that was too tight and digging in, but a moment later she wasn't—as easily as that, Juan had undone it. Cate let out a small sigh of relief as her breast fell into his palm and then a moan of bliss as his hand cupped her and stroked.

'I want you…' He was at her neck and trailing his mouth down, she was stone-cold sober, yet almost top-less and drunk on lust. He kissed back up to her mouth and she could feel the trail of wetness he had left on her chest—and how she wanted him. Her hands moved to his head and she felt the thick, long, jet-black hair that he refused to cut, felt the wedge of muscle of a man it would be so easy to be immoral with, understood exactly why women lost their heads to him, for she was losing hers.

She moved her hand down to his shoulder, her fingers sliding to his neck, but Juan's hands halted hers and moved them onto his chest. It jolted her, just a little, for in that moment not a fraction of their bodies had seemed out of bounds. Cate had been utterly lost but she returned to common sense and he felt it, their eyes opening together, and she saw the regret in his as she pulled her mouth back.

'We could be so good together...' His forehead was resting on hers and she was struggling to get her breath.

Yes, they could be so good together but he would be so bad for her.

Cate wasn't looking for forever but neither was she looking for one night, or one week.

She simply couldn't do the casual thing, never had and never could. Could not walk into work tomorrow with everyone knowing she had succumbed to Juan's undeniable charm.

How she wanted to, though.

How she wanted to give in to the urges that were pulsing through her as much as the music coming from his home, how she wanted to just say, yes, I can handle this. Except, stupid her, her body came attached to a heart that was already a bit bruised and did not need to be shattered by him.

Oh, it would hurt to have him and then not. That much Cate knew.

'Get over him, Cate!' Juan said.

She was so over Paul, not that he knew it. Cate did not dare reveal the truth, so she made a wry joke.

'By getting under you?'

'No,' Juan said. 'I want you on top. I want to watch you come.'

He was bad.

He was dangerous.

He was everything she wanted and yet everything she didn't.

'Thanks for a lovely evening.'

'Would you like to go out tomorrow?' Juan offered.

'No, thanks.'

'Cate…'

So she took a breath and told him, 'I'm not what you're looking for.'

'You don't know what I'm looking for.'

'I don't know what I'm looking for either,' Cate admitted, 'but it's not…' she tried to think of the right word and she didn't know how best to say it '…you.'

'Ouch.'

Cate smiled and climbed into her car and caught the lingering fragrance of Juan from when he had been in her vehicle, the expensive note that overrode others.

She knew that she hadn't hurt him.

Ouch would be sitting in the staffroom in a couple of weeks' time, hearing who he'd slept with next, or, if they did last the little time he had left in Australia, ouch would be waving him off at the airport. Ouch would be having had him and then trying to move on.

Cate had just ended one serious relationship—a

rebound with the name Juan attached to it was heading
way too far in the other direction.

She reversed out and waved to him, and, yes, she regretted it plenty. She could see them alone in his bedroom. Many times she had envisaged him kicking those
boots to the floor and letting herself be a notch on his
temporary bed; many times she had wanted to let loose
and be as superficial and as laid back about things as
Juan.

So clearly she could see it now, could still taste him
on her mouth as she drove off, her bra around her waist,
her cheeks burning, her hands willing her to turn round
and return to him.

Instead, Cate chose safety.

CHAPTER FOUR

JUAN WOUND UP the party and did not invite anybody else to stay the night.

As the last taxi pulled off, he didn't even look at the clock or tidy up, he just undressed and headed to bed and tried to get Cate Nicholls out of his head.

She was way too serious for him.

Usually, he didn't want to hear about promotions and brothers and parts of the woman's history but with Cate somehow he did.

He thought about her hand on his neck, her fingers about to meet the thick scar and, no, he didn't want her knowing, would far prefer Cate thinking that he was shallow than to open up and confide in her...

That wasn't what this trip was about, he told himself as he lay there. Caught between awake and asleep, Juan was unsure if the kiss with Cate had been a dream, unsure even if his time in Australia was a mere figment of his imagination. He even wondered if Cate's words to Reece would disappear the second he awoke and he would find out it was all just another dream—because he was back there again, back in his head, trapped in his mind with a body that refused to obey even the simplest command.

In Juan's dreams he ran, his feet pounding the warm pavement as he dragged in the humid air.

In dreams, he threaded his beloved motorbike through lush Argentinian hills and made love to every single woman who had ever flirted with him—and there were many, perhaps Cate was one?

In his dreams, Juan jumped off bridges and felt the sting of icy-cold water as he plunged in.

In his dreams, he skied down mountains and did all the things he had never had time to do—Juan's focus had always been Martina, family and work.

He could hear the nurses, doing the two a.m. rounds, approaching the four-bedded ward, and Juan tried to haul himself out of the memory, tried to get back to kissing Cate, except he couldn't dictate his dreams and he couldn't erase his memories, and as the REM stage deepened a very natural reflex occurred.

'Hey, Juan.'

'I apologise.' Juan didn't need to look at the mirrors placed over his bed to know the sheet was tenting and that he was erect; instead, he stared at the ceiling as Graciela tried to catch his eye. 'Juan, it's natural,' Graciela said. They spoke in Spanish, Graciela, as always, practical—she was nearing retirement and had worked on the spinal unit for years. Graciela was more than used to young men finding themselves paralysed, used to the strange sight of a beautiful, fit body that might never move independently again and the humiliation a new spinal-cord injury patient faced regularly.

Yes, Graciela was kind and practical, it just didn't help now as she and Manuel rolled him onto his side. Juan was burning with shame in a bed in the Buenos Aires hospital he worked at.

Had once worked at.

Juan didn't want that part of his life over. Yes, he played upbeat for Martina and his family, insisted if there was a little improvement he could lecture and teach; but tonight the future, one where he could function independently, let alone hold another's life in his hands, seemed an impossibly long way off.

'Juan…' Manuel tried to engage with Juan. 'We still don't know the extent of your injury. You have spinal swelling and until…'

Juan closed his eyes. He didn't want hope tonight, he felt guilty that compared to his roommates there was a thin hope that his paralysis was not permanent; he just wanted to close his eyes and go back to his dreams but he knew he would not get back to sleep, knew that this would be another long night.

'You need a haircut,' Graciela commented as she washed his face. 'Do you want me to arrange one for you?'

'No.' Juan made a weak joke. He had been on his way to get his thick black hair trimmed when the accident had happened—it grew fast and he had it trimmed every couple of weeks. Always he had prided himself on looking immaculate, dressing in exquisitely cut suits and rich silk ties. Tonight those days seemed forever gone. 'I'm not risking that again.'

'How's Martina?' Graciela tried to engage Juan as they started the hourly exercise regime, moving his limbs and feet and hands. Martina had been here until eleven and Juan had pretended to be asleep the last two times the nursing staff had come around. It was important to know what was happening in the patients' lives as they adjusted to their injuries. 'Is she still worrying about moving the wedding date?'

There was a long stretch of silence before Juan finally answered, 'We broke up.'

'I'm sorry, Juan.' Graciela looked over at Manuel, who took over the conversation.

'What happened?' Manuel asked. He wasn't being nosey—the mental health of their patients was a priority, and he chatted as he moved Juan's index finger and thumb together and apart, over and over—as they did every hour—and then moved to rotating his wrist. Both simple exercises might mean in the future Juan could hold a cup, or do up a button, or hold a pen.

'We just…' Juan did not want to discuss it, still could not take it in, could not comprehend how every aspect of his life had now changed. 'It was mutual.'

'Okay.' Graciela checked his obs and shared another look with Manuel. 'I'll see you a bit later, Juan. Hopefully you'll be asleep next time I come around and I won't disturb you.'

Asleep or not, the exercises went on through the night.

Graciela moved on to the next bed, leaving Manuel to hopefully get Juan to open up a bit. Since his admission Juan had remained upbeat, insisted he was dealing with it, refusing to open up to anyone, and Graciela was worried about him, especially with the news of the break-up. Relationships often ended here; patients pushed loved ones away, or sometimes it was the other way around and the able-bodied partner simply could not cope with a world that had rapidly altered.

'Hey, Eduard.' She smiled down at the young man,

who gave her a small grimace back and moved his eyes towards Juan's bed. 'Is he okay?'

'He'll get there.'

For the first time Juan didn't think he would.

There was one thing more humiliating than a massive erection in full view of the nurses. It was starting to cry and not being able to excuse yourself, not being able to go to another room and close a door, to thump a wall, not even being able to wipe your own snot and tears.

'Let it out, Juan,' Manuel said as he covered Juan with a sheet and saw his patient's face screw up and tears fill Juan's grey eyes.

'I...' He didn't want to let it out, he had held it all in and he wanted to keep doing so. There was young Eduard in the next bed. He'd only been here for three days and Juan didn't want to scare him—Juan had been trying to cheer him up today.

He just couldn't hold it in any more.

The sob that came out was primal, from a place he had never been.

'Good man,' Manuel said.

Juan lay there sobbing as Manuel wiped his eyes and blew his nose. He was in hell and humiliated and scared and everything he'd tried not to be.

'Good man,' Manuel said, over and over.

He'd been a good man, Juan thought. He'd done everything right, everything had been in place—an amazing career, a loving fiancée. He *had* been a good man.

'No more...' Juan said, incoherent almost as he sobbed.

But there was more and tonight he let it out.

Graciela stood there and wiped Eduard's tears as

they glimpsed for the first time Juan's desolation and rage, and she swallowed a couple of tears of her own.

All Juan's roommates cried quietly along with him. Two had been there before, giving in to the grief and the fear in the still of the night, and Eduard soon would. There was no privacy in their worlds right now and all the men had heard the painful exchange between Juan and Martina.

All were with Juan as finally he gave in and wept.

No one was with him, though, when, eighteen months later, Juan woke up in a foreign country, feeling the desolation all over again.

CHAPTER FIVE

'HOW HAS YOUR week been?'

Cate stopped for a brief chat with her neighbour as both women headed for work. Bridgette and her husband James were both in the police. It was nice being neighbours with fellow shift workers and, over the summer, Bridgette and Cate had spent several afternoons lying in one or the other's garden and putting the world to rights.

'It's been good.' Cate smiled as she lied. It had been a long week spent trying not to think about Juan and trying not to worry about work. 'Have you had your interview?' Bridgette asked.

'Not yet, but I'm stepping in as Acting Manager on Monday.'

'So you're off the weekend?'

'No, I'm working it, but if I do get the job I'll have every weekend off.'

'No more shift work!' Bridgette exclaimed, and Cate gave a smile and a nod, then they chatted a bit about the unrelenting weather but soon enough Bridgette asked how Cate was doing since the break-up and if she'd met anyone else.

'Not really.'

'What does that mean?' Bridgette asked. She was far too perceptive sometimes!

'There is someone I like,' Cate admitted. 'Or rather there was. He's from overseas and he's heading off to New Zealand soon so, really, there's no point.'

'No point in what?'

'Starting anything.'

'What are you talking about?' Bridgette gave her a very queer look. 'He sounds perfect for having a bit of fun with after Paul! You're not looking for forever, are you?'

'No, but...'

'Let you hair down and live a little while you're single.' Bridgette held up her hand and flashed her wedding ring. 'While you still can...' She winked. 'I'll come around over the weekend and we'll have a proper chat.'

'Do,' Cate said. 'I'd like that.'

Cate drove to work and tried to ignore the small bubble of disquiet that kept making itself known.

It had been the same towards the end of her relationship with Paul—everything had been going well, they'd got on, she'd cared about him; but when Paul had suggested moving in, they had been together for two years after all, Cate hadn't wanted that. When he'd suggested that they look for somewhere together, Cate had really had to sit and examine her feelings.

Cate turned on the radio instead—she didn't want to examine them now.

The staff car park was busy and Cate had to park well away from Emergency, which usually wouldn't matter but the temperature had barely dropped overnight and Cate couldn't wait to be in the air-conditioned hospital. The sky was a curious pink, even though the weather warned of no change or storms. Then, a week to the day after they'd shared that sizzling kiss, Cate saw him.

Only a madman would go running in this heat, Cate thought. An incredibly fit madman, though.

Juan was at the entrance to the hospital when she got there, trying to catch his breath before heading inside. He was bent over, his hands on his thighs, as he dragged in the sultry air. He was dressed in grey shorts and a top and they were drenched, as could be expected, given the considerable distance to the hospital from his apartment and that he'd run with a backpack on.

'Don't you listen to the warnings on the news?' Cate's voice was dry, deliberately refusing to reveal any awkwardness about their kiss last week. 'During a heat wave you're supposed to avoid exertion.'

'That is for the young and elderly,' he said, somewhat breathlessly bringing himself to stand upright, which was a bit disappointing for Cate as she'd been enjoying the opportunity of shamelessly looking at his legs. Long and muscular, pale-limbed with black hair and with a weight around one ankle. Briefly she wondered why, but only briefly—because as he looked down and spoke to her there was another image now to add to the Juan file she had stored away in her head. Juan smiled and added, 'And I am neither young nor elderly.'

'I think it was a given that no one would be crazy enough to go running in weather like this,' Cate said, trying not to blush, because now he was standing upright he looked amazing—he wasn't just unshaven, he practically had a beard. Harry wasn't going to be pleased, though Cate didn't mind in the least. He looked like a huge sexy god, Cate thought, and then corrected herself, because that was probably a wrong thing to think. He looked like a huge sexy…man.

It would just have to do.

'If a bit of heat and humidity stopped us, then no one in Argentina would ever run,' Juan said as they started walking into the hospital.

'So you're working here today?'

'They caved again.' Juan grinned. 'I got a call late last night to ask if I could come in for the morning shift.'

'You've been coming here for nearly three months now,' Cate pointed out. 'If you'd just signed the contract in the first place—'

'I've liked working all over Melbourne,' Juan interrupted, still slightly breathless. 'I've met loads of great people. It has been good not being confined.'

'Confined?' Cate frowned. 'It's not a prison.'

'Restricted,' Juan said. 'I don't know the word I am looking for in English,' he admitted.

'Doesn't it drive you crazy, though?' Cate asked. 'Never knowing where you'll be from day to day.'

'I love it,' Juan answered. 'It's the best thing I could have done.'

Cate could think of nothing worse and she told him so. 'I worked for an agency when I was a student. I loathed not knowing where I'd end up, where they'd send me, who I'd be working with…' She gave a small shrug. 'Maybe I'm boring like that.'

'You're never boring.' He turned and gave her a smile, just enough of a smile to let her know that he was thinking about the other night. 'Are you going to Christine's leaving do?'

Cate nodded. 'Are you?'

'She invited me.'

He headed into the changing rooms and Cate went to the staff kitchen and filled a glass with ice from the machine and then poured a cup of black tea with sugar over it and took her drink into the staffroom, where it was lovely and cool.

'Morning…' Cate smiled at two familiar faces—Charlotte and Adam were sitting dressed in their pyjamas and watching television. 'Have you two had breakfast?'

'No, we haven't eaten anything.' Charlotte was the louder of the two. 'Daddy said he'd get us something from the canteen before he took us to childcare.'

'Do you want me to get you something now?' Cate offered, and when they both nodded Cate went back to the kitchen and made them some cereal and juice.

'Christine's not doing the jump any more,' Kelly said as Cate came back in and served up breakfast for the twins, 'so there's a space if you've changed your mind.'

'Not a chance,' Cate said. Some of the staff had come up with the idea of a skydive to raise some much-needed funds to refurbish the interview rooms—but even if the funds were needed, even if it was for a good cause, Cate could think of nothing worse than jumping out of a plane, let alone paying for it. She much preferred to keep her feet on solid ground.

In came Juan, with that potent post-shower scent that had Cate's toes curling in her shoes. He was wearing scrubs, yet he still had on his signature boots and he was simply like no other.

'We've got hospital razors, Juan,' Kelly teased. 'I can get you a couple if you can't afford them.'

'Ah, but then you'd have to suture me after,' Juan said. 'They are lethal.' He looked at the twins, who had paused in their breakfasts and were staring up at this very large, very commanding man. 'Hello,' he said and then made Adam laugh. 'Are you the new consultants that are starting?'

'No,' Cate said, 'the interviews only started this week. These are Harry's twins, Charlotte and Adam.'

'Daddy got called in,' Charlotte said. 'For a sick boy.'

'Well, that's no good,' Juan said, and then looked at Cate's glass. 'Did you make me one?'

'No.' For a moment she thought he was going to take a sip of her drink.

For a moment he thought about it!

'Hey, Juan.' Kelly wasn't going to miss an opportunity for a little extra Juan time. 'A space has opened up on the charity dive next Sunday. You like all that sort of stuff.'

'I do.' He went and read the notice. 'I'll still be here. I fly out on the Tuesday...'

'We'll all go out afterwards,' Kelly said. 'It could be your leaving do.'

'Another one,' Cate said, and he turned at the slightly tart note to her voice but just smiled.

'Are you doing the jump?' Juan asked her.

'Absolutely not.'

'You should.'

'Why?' Cate challenged, but Juan gave no answer and went to get a pen from his pocket but, as usual, he didn't have one and he asked Cate if he could borrow hers.

'No,' Cate said. 'You already owe me three.'

'Just to put my name down on the list. I'll give it straight back.'

She ended up relenting and handed him her pen.

'Where are you going to next, Juan?' Sheldon asked.

'New Zealand! The south island first.'

'How long will you stay?'

'I'm not sure—I'll see how it goes, but I've heard that the skiing is spectacular, so I might stay there for the winter.'

'Then home to Argentina?' Sheldon asked as Juan wrote down his name to do the skydiving jump.

'I'm not sure…' Juan said. 'I was thinking of Asia.'

How could he have no idea where he was going? Cate wondered. He was hardly a teenager. He must be in his mid-thirties and just drifting through life, if you could call jumping off bridges and rafting down ravines and biking through the hills drifting. Cate just could not wrap her head around Juan's way of living.

'Come on, guys.' Cate glanced at the clock and stood. 'We'd better get round there.'

'You're not the boss yet,' Kelly teased.

No, she wasn't the boss yet, Cate thought. She said goodbye to Charlotte and Adam and turned on some cartoons instead of the news, telling them that someone would be around to check on them soon—but she wondered how she could tell Harry that he couldn't bring in the twins or, rather, if he did that the nurses wouldn't be watching out for them.

As they walked through the obs ward on their way, Cate was just about to ask the nurse who was working there to keep an eye out for Harry's children. But, seeing that the supervisor was there checking the bed status, Cate decided otherwise.

'Last day in the madhouse!' She smiled at Christine, who had just arrived at work.

Her smile wasn't returned.

'Thank God!' Christine rolled her eyes. 'If you can watch the floor, Cate, I'm going to go make sure all the ordering is up to date. Given all the fire warnings in place, I think it might be a good idea to order some extra burn packs and IV solutions…'

'I already have,' Cate said, and saw Christine's jaw tense.

'Of course you would have,' Christine said, and flounced off.

Cate knew she had annoyed Christine but, then, everything seemed to annoy Christine lately. Cate didn't particularly want to go to the leaving do tonight, especially now she knew that Juan would be there, but it would look rude and petty not to go. Handover was about to start and as she went to make her way over to the huddle Cate searched in her pocket for her pen, but of course, yet again, Juan had failed to give it back.

'Here…' He walked past and grinned as he saw Cate going through her pockets and he gave her back her pen, or what was left of it.

'You've chewed it!' Cate moaned.

'So did you,' Juan said, and opened his mouth and curled his tongue just a fraction. 'I had to taste you.'

He could be so filthy.

'Juan!' Harry came over to where they were standing, Cate's cheeks still on fire. 'I didn't know that you were on this morning.'

'Neither did I till late last night.'

'Well, it's really good to see you. Renée called me in a couple of hours ago—I've got a five-year-old named Jason that I'm really concerned about and am thinking of transferring. It would be great if you could come in and take a look.'

'Sure!' Juan said, and walked with Harry over to Resus as Cate went over to the group.

'Wow! I think Harry just gave Juan a compliment. He said that he was pleased that he was here. That's a bit of a turnaround.'

'I'm actually very glad to see Juan here this morning,' Renée, the night nurse, said. 'The child Harry is concerned about has got Goldenhar syndrome. Have you heard of it?'

Cate shook her head. There were many, many different syndromes, some relatively common, some rare, as was the case with this admission.

'It mainly presents as facial abnormalities. In Jason's case he's got a very underdeveloped left ear and he was born with a cleft palate and other problems. I've looked it up on the computer if you want to read about it. The main problem today is that he has presented with severe asthma, for which he's had several ICU admissions. Usually he's seen at the children's hospital and, understandably, the parents tend to stay close but, given the heat, they thought a couple of days near the beach might be nice.'

'It should have been nice,' Cate said. 'Poor things.'

'Yes, Jason has a very tricky airway and is really difficult to intubate—he's had to have a tracheostomy in the past. I think that was why Harry was so pleased to see Juan. The on-call anaesthetist has already been down to check on him a couple of times.'

'How come Harry is here?' Cate checked. 'I thought that Dr Vermont was on call last night.'

'He was,' Renée said. 'He was here till one o'clock but then he was unwell and had to go home. Jason came in just before five. I tried to get the paediatricians down but they're busy with a sick baby and so really I had no choice but to call Harry in.' Renée grimaced. 'I didn't realise that he'd have to wake up the twins.'

'Well, it sounds like Jason needed someone senior on hand,' Cate said. 'So, what else could you do?'

'Do you want to go in and take over?' Renée suggested. 'From Monday you'll be spending a lot of time in the office.'

'No, I shan't be.' Cate didn't elaborate, it wouldn't be fair on Christine, but Cate had no desire to disappear for hours into the office, as Christine all too often did. Still, Cate knew that she wouldn't be able to get as involved with individual patients—like it or not, the more senior she had become, the more hands off her role had been, so it was nice to take the opportunity to look after Jason.

Cate took the handover from Mary, the night nurse, as Juan examined the young patient.

'The parents are incredibly tense.' Mary pulled Cate aside. 'I don't blame them a bit, it must be awful to be away from all the specialists they need, but I think they're really making Jason more upset. Harry was talking about transferring him to the children's hospital and getting them to send out their emergency transfer team, but Lisa, the mum, got really distressed. Apparently Jason is petrified of flying, especially given that he's had more than his fair share of emergency transfers.'

They went through the drugs Jason had been given so far, before a grateful Mary headed for home.

Juan had been speaking with the parents, and had only just started to examine Jason. The little boy was exhausted but, despite that, his eyes were still anxious.

'So, you're a regular on the ICU at the children's hospital, are you?' Juan asked, after listening to his chest, and Jason nodded. 'I was working there last week and I'll probably be there again soon. Do you know Paddy?'

'We know Paddy,' Jason's mum said.

'Ken...do you know Ken?' the little boy said. He could still talk but only just.

'Do you mean Kent?' Juan checked. 'The ICU nurse?' Jason nodded. 'He's good fun. I might just have to give Paddy a call and let him know that you're here.'

Cate knew Juan was just putting the boy at ease, letting Jason know that he knew the staff there, while letting the parents know he worked there too.

He must be as popular there as he is here, Cate thought, strangely jealous of the other worlds of Juan.

'I just want a look in your mouth, Jason. Can you open it, please?' Juan removed the mask that was delivering medication and shone a light in. He looked carefully and then replaced the nebuliser, which was nearly finished.

'Okay, Jason,' Juan said. 'Just rest now and let the medicine start to work.' Juan looked over at Harry. 'Continuous nebulisers now...' Juan said, which moved Jason from severe to critical; but Juan seemed calm and Cate was a little surprised how Harry was stepping back and letting Juan take over the case. She knew Juan was good and a trained anaesthetist, but as it turned out Cate didn't know just how good he really was.

'He does need to be transferred, Lisa.' Juan spoke now to the mother. 'But I'm happy to keep a close eye on him here at this stage. I think we can wait for the rush hour to pass and then we will go by road ambulance...'

'What if something happens in the meantime?' Lisa was clearly petrified of being stuck in the outer suburbs without all the specialist doctors. But it was then that Cate realised exactly why Harry had been so pleased to see Juan this morning, and why he was so readily stepping back. 'What if something happens in the ambulance?' Lisa said, her eyes filling with nervous tears.

'I have worked with a lot of children who have similar problems to Jason,' Juan said, and went on to explain that he had spent a year as an anaesthetist in America, working at a major craniofacial hospital, and was very used to performing the most difficult of intubations on children.

'You've seen children with Jason's problems before?' Lisa asked.

'I have.' Juan smiled at Jason but Lisa still wasn't quite convinced.

'Jason had to be put on a ventilator the last time he had an asthma attack,' she said. 'They couldn't wean him off and in the end they couldn't keep the tube in his throat for any longer and so he had to have a tracheostomy...'

'Let's just focus on today,' Juan said, and started checking all the equipment. Harry had already brought over the difficult intubation box and Juan commenced pulling up drugs and taping the vials to the syringes, as relaxed as if he were making a coffee rather than preparing for a difficult intubation, and chatting away to Jason as he did so.

In a child with severe asthma everything was assessed clinically, there were no blood gases taken as it would simply upset Jason further. The fact that he was petrified of flying was an important issue because it was important not to distress Jason, but if he became much worse, there would be no choice.

'What's the protocol for IV aminophylline here?' Juan asked, after having another listen to Jason's chest.

'We don't give it here,' Cate said, because it was a drug that required constant monitoring. 'It's only given on ICU.'

'This has just become ICU,' Juan said. 'I'm not leaving him.'

Cate looked over at Harry.

'Fine.' Harry nodded and rolled his eyes. 'In Juan we trust.' Which actually made Lisa laugh.

'How long are you on till?' Lisa asked Juan.

'All day,' Juan said. 'Don't worry, when Jason is transferred I will go with him.' He didn't need to ask Harry's permission. Yes, it left them a doctor down, which would have to be sorted, but that was simply how it must be and no one argued. You could feel some of the tension leave not just Jason's parents but Jason himself. Clearly black boots and long black hair and an unshaven doctor didn't worry Jason a bit.

'Well,' Harry said, 'I'll leave you in Juan's capable hands and I'll come back in soon and see how Jason is doing.' He looked at Cate. 'I'm just going to get the twins some breakfast and then take them over to childcare.'

'I've already given them breakfast,' Cate said, and Harry gave a grateful nod. 'They're just watching cartoons in the staffroom.'

'Thanks so much for coming in, Doctor.' Jason's father stood and shook Harry's hand. 'It meant a lot.'

'Not a problem,' Harry said.

It was, though, a huge problem, and Juan commented on it after they had set up the aminophylline infusion and were waiting for the paramedics to transfer Jason.

Juan had double-checked that he had everything and Cate had done the same until, happy they were well equipped, they moved to have a quick coffee at the nurses' station, watching Jason from a slight distance. They had no idea when they might get another chance to take a quick break because they would both go on the transfer with Jason and then rush back to work at Bayside—unless there were any emergencies on the journey.

'Harry got here at five a.m. to see Jason,' Juan commented.

'I know.'

'Did he bring the twins in with him then?'

Cate gave a small worried nod.

'And does he do that sort of thing a lot?'

'Harry's wife died last year,' Cate said, by way of explanation.

'I know that,' Juan said. 'I asked if he did this sort of thing a lot.'

'He hasn't for a while.' Cate sighed because it was clearly starting all over again and on Monday she'd be the one dealing with it.

'He needs to get a nanny or someone he can count on.'

'He had a nanny,' Cate said. 'She just left.' She glanced at Juan, but he didn't return her look as he was watching Jason. But she did see him smile when she revealed a little more. 'They tend to fall in love with him.' She watched as Juan's smile spread further as he responded.

'Then he needs to stop sleeping with them.'

'Stop it!' Cate blushed, but trust Juan to get to the heart of it. Harry was a widower and a very good-

looking, well-heeled one at that. There were plenty
of women only too happy to bring over a casserole as
Harry had once said with a wink and a tired roll of his
eyes—he'd thought they were just being nice at first.
No doubt he was having the same trouble with his bab-
ysitters. The thing was, it wasn't the Harry she knew.
'He adored Jill.'

'Of course he did,' Juan said. 'Sex and love are two
very different things. I hear he was wild in his student
days.'

'Please!' Cate said. She didn't even want to think
about Harry and his sex life, but then she confided in
Juan a little of what was troubling her. 'I've been told
that once I'm Nurse Unit Manger I'm to address him
bringing the twins in. Christine just ignores it, and Lillian says it's been going on for too long.'

'It needs to be addressed,' Juan said, and he glanced
over just long enough to see the flare of worry in her
eyes. That much he could do for her. 'I will speak with
him about it.'

'And say what?'

'Bro talk,' Juan teased. 'You are not allowed to
know.'

'But you barely know him.'

'Even better,' Juan said. 'Aside from everything, it's
not fair on the little ones to be dragged in here all time.'

Had she thought about it, she would have expected
him to take Harry's side, to say that it was no problem.
Juan really was the most curious mix—the last thing
she had expected was for him to actually be prepared
to address the issue with the boss.

She'd love to be a fly on *that* wall!

CHAPTER SIX

JUAN DRAINED HIS mug and as they headed back, the paramedics arrived.

'So we're not competent enough for you, Juan?' Louise, half of the team that would be transferring Jason, teased as she walked into Resus with the stretcher.

'Jason has a very special airway, don't you, Jason?' Juan said.

Jason had, in fact, picked up considerably but he was on strong drugs that meant he needed very careful monitoring. All joking aside, it was good to have Matthew and Louise as the paramedics—they were an excellent team and Juan went through all the history and the equipment with them and told Louise the medications Jason was on.

'I want to get there quickly,' Juan said, 'with as little upset to him as possible.'

'Do you want one of his parents to come?' Louise checked, but Juan shook his head.

'I've already told them no. We're going to play chase.'

'Sorry?' Louise frowned but Juan just smiled.

There really wasn't room for either of Jason's parents to come in the ambulance, especially as there was the potential for an emergency on the way. Even with the anti-emetic he had been given, Juan was worried that Jason might vomit and that could prove urgent in itself with his poor breathing and difficult airway.

Fortunately, though, Jason was so taken with Juan and so delighted to have escaped the helicopter that he didn't protest in the least and neither did his parents. They headed off as soon as the paramedics arrived in the hope of beating the ambulance to the hospital. There was a good chance they might, as Juan took his time making sure everything was ready for the transfer, and ensured that Jason was as stable as he could be.

'Come on, then,' Juan said a good twenty minutes after Louise and Matthew had arrived. 'We've given your parents a good start, shall we see if we can catch them up? We might have to put the sirens on if we're going to have a chance.'

He winked to Louise, who smiled because she understood the game.

It was so much better with him than without, Cate thought as they sped with sirens and lights blazing to the city, trying to *beat* Jason's parents! The stars really had aligned for Jason today and they pulled up at the children's hospital without incident. Just knowing that Juan could deal with whatever presented had made a difficult transfer so much more straightforward. Juan was more than highly skilled—clearly his career had, at one time, been his major focus and yet here he was drifting around the world.

Cate wanted to know why.

She wanted to know more.

But soon he'd be gone.

'We got here first!' Juan said as the ambulance doors

opened and there was no sign of his parents. An exhausted Jason even managed a quick high five.

Jason was a direct admission to ICU and a very pretty nurse looked up and turned purple before smiling when she saw Juan walking in. From the general reaction to his entrance, Cate knew he was just as popular here as he was at Bayside.

'Juan!' A huge bear of a man came over and shook Juan's hand. 'I thought you were in New Zealand by now.'

'Soon! How are you, Paddy?' Juan said, and proceeded to hand over the young patient as, just a little behind them, Jason's parents arrived.

'You beat us!' Lisa kissed her son. She was looking a lot more relaxed in more familiar surroundings with staff that she was more used to. 'How was the journey?'

'It went really well.' Cate smiled. 'Juan will come and speak with you soon, he's just handing everything over.'

'He's good, isn't he?' Lisa said to Cate, glancing over to where Juan was chatting with Paddy.

'Very good,' Cate said, as Juan made his way over to them.

'Okay, the journey was without incident,' Juan said to Lisa. 'I've spoken with Paddy about all that has been done for Jason and you are safely in the right place.'

'Thank you so much.'

'No problem,' Juan said. 'I am just glad he is here without any more drama for you.'

'Well, we won't be going far again,' Lisa said, but Juan shook his head.

'Did you have a good week?'

Lisa nodded.

'Would he have got the asthma anyway?'

Lisa was nearly in tears as she nodded again.

'So he is here, where he would have been anyway, but also he has had a week at the beach, and that is a *good* thing.'

He gave Lisa a cuddle, just a brief one, told her what an amazing mother she was, and Cate felt a sting of tears at the back of her eyes as Juan peeled another strip off her heart and nailed it to the Juan wall in her mind.

Don't go!

She stood there and looked at him, hating that very soon there would be no more Juan. She didn't even try to fathom her strong feelings towards a man she didn't really know, because everyone was crazy about him, everyone wanted more Juan in their life.

He shook Jason's father's hand and, oh, what the hell, Juan gave him a hug too and then went to say farewell to Jason. Cate was more confused than she had ever been, because she didn't want, ten days from now, to have Juan gone from her life and to have done not a single thing about it.

Then he spoiled it by going missing as they were about to head back to Bayside.

'I'll go and find him,' Cate offered.

She soon did!

Talking to Nurse Purple Face and making her laugh.

'You're quiet,' Juan said as they rode back in the back of the ambulance with Louise.

'I'm just tired,' Cate lied, not sure if she was jealous or just cross with herself. Or was it regret that she simply couldn't push aside her usual rules, wave her knickers over her head and give in to him?

'Well, that was worth the trip for me,' Juan said, 'I

have my shifts for next week all sorted I am working Friday through to Saturday on ICU there.'

Cate glanced up.

He only did one or two shifts a week, she knew that, preferably one long one, and he'd just been given that.

Today really could be the last time she saw him.

Apart from tonight.

CHAPTER SEVEN

CATE WAS SO distracted she didn't even hear Matthew talking on the radio until he called out to Cate and Juan. 'We've got an eighty-six-year-old in an independent living facility, she's waiting to be admitted for a chest infection but she's developed chest pain. Are you guys okay with us accepting?'

'Sure,' Juan said. 'So long as you go fast.'

On went the lights and sirens and Cate felt a flurry in her stomach as the ambulance sped off.

'You love this part, don't you?' Louise smiled.

'I do.'

'Are you still thinking about joining us?'

Cate shook her head. 'It's not for me. Sometimes I do still think about it, though.'

'You've thought of being a paramedic?' Juan's eyes widened in surprise.

'Cate came on a ride along with us,' Louise told him. 'About six months ago, wasn't it, Cate? I said to try a Saturday night in the city before she made up her mind.'

Cate could feel Juan's eyes on her.

'You didn't like it?' he asked.

'I loved it,' Cate said. 'It was an amazing experience but...' She gave a small shake of her head. 'It made me appreciate even more all the back-up that we have in Emergency, and I decided that it just wasn't for me.'

They were pulling into the independent living facility—the gate had been opened for them and a staff member directed them to the small unit where the patient was. Matthew and Louise took all the necessary equipment and then the four of them walked into a small house that was crammed full of furniture—huge old bookshelves and old-fashioned sofas—that looked a little out of place in the more modern surroundings.

'Her name's Elsie Delaney,' the on-call nurse explained. 'We had the doctor in to see Elsie last night for her cough and she was started on antibiotics for a chest infection. When I went to check on her this morning, she didn't look well and finally admitted she had chest pain. She's very independent and didn't want me to call you, of course.'

'Hi, Elsie!' Matthew walked in first and greeted the patient.

'What are all of you doing here?' came an irritated voice as the room started to fill up.

'You're getting the works today, Elsie,' Louise said. 'We had a doctor and nurse already with us, so that's why there are so many of us.'

The bedroom was as full of furniture as the rest of the house and, with Juan walking in front of Cate and his shoulders taking up most of the doorframe, it took a moment before Cate glimpsed Elsie.

She was tiny, sitting up in bed, her straggly white hair held back with a large, jewelled hair clip. She had a pink shawl around her shoulders and was wearing an elaborate necklace, and on her gnarled fingers were several rings.

She looked absolutely gorgeous, but she was wary and disgruntled and complained as Louise and Matthew did obs and attached her to a monitor while Juan slipped in an IV.

'I'm feeling much better,' she kept protesting.

Really, they weren't needed at all. Cate and Juan were completely supernumerary as Louise and Matthew had it all under control. They soon had a heart tracing and were giving Elsie some medication for pain and, despite having said she had little pain, as it took effect she lay back on the pillow. Elsie finally agreed that, yes, they could take her to hospital.

'Are there any family for us to inform?'

'She has a daughter, Maria, who lives nearby,' the nurse said, and spoke then to Elsie, 'I'll ring Maria and let her know what's happening.'

'She'll be very disappointed that I'm only sick and not dead,' Elsie said. 'It's the truth!' Elsie turned to Cate and winked, and Cate found herself smothering a smile. 'Does Maria even have to know that I'm going to hospital?' Elsie asked.

'Of course she does, Elsie!' the nurse answered. 'And you're wrong, Maria will be ever so worried.'

Elsie gave a huff to indicate that she doubted it. 'I'm not going out on a stretcher,' Elsie said.

'Fine.' Louise smiled. 'I'll go and get the chair.'

'Do you want to leave your jewellery here?' Cate suggested, knowing that one of the first things that would happen when they got to Emergency was that they would take it all off and lock it up in the safe. But Elsie wasn't going anywhere without her finery.

'And I want my photo album too...' She pointed to a shelf and Juan went over to fetch it.

'You might only be there a few hours,' the nurse pointed out.

'Then I'll have something to look at while I'm waiting,' Elsie retorted.

'Where's this, Elsie?' Juan asked, pointing to a picture in a frame where a younger Elsie was smiling into the camera against a stunning backdrop of houses and a glimpse of the ocean behind her.

'Menton,' Elsie said. The medication wasn't stopping her from talking! 'They call it the pearl of France. Have you been?'

'To France, yes,' Juan said. 'To Menton, no, but I want to now!' They chatted about it even as she was loaded into the ambulance and transferred from the chair to the stretcher. She was in a seated position for comfort and she and Juan chatted all the way to Bayside.

'I was there for six months,' Elsie said. 'Then I went back, oh, ten years ago now and it's still just as lovely.' She looked at Juan. 'Are you Spanish?'

'I'm from Argentina.'

'Well, I'll try not to hold it against you,' she said, and Juan laughed. Elsie peered at him for a while, slowly looking at his hair and then down to his boots before looking at Cate.

'He's a good-looking one, isn't he?' Elsie said.

'You just caught him at a good time,' Cate answered back.

'That's what I'm here for,' Juan responded, and Cate felt her cheeks burn a little, because a good time was *all* that he was here for—and she would do very well to remember that fact.

'So you don't live in Australia?' Elsie asked him.

'No,' Juan said. 'I am here for a working holiday.'

Elsie frowned for a while before speaking. 'You're a bit old for all that, aren't you?' And for the second time since meeting Elsie, Cate found herself suppressing a smile. Elsie was funny and wise and old enough to say what she liked and not care what others thought.

'Never too old, Elsie,' Juan said. 'Surely you know that?'

For the first time since their arrival it was Elsie smiling—at Juan. 'You're a charmer, aren't you?'

'Am I charming you, Elsie?' Juan smiled back.

Of course he was.

Christine didn't seem too impressed when they arrived back at the department. 'Finally, the wanderers return!' And she wasn't too pleased to have been forced out of her office during Cate's absence. 'I'm going to go and do some work now,' Christine said. 'There are incident forms to fill in. I don't want to leave them for you.'

'Sure,' Cate said, as Christine handed over the drug keys to her.

'She's a sour one!' Elsie muttered, as she was moved over onto a gurney.

Cate made no comment. 'I'm just going to go find you a gown,' she said to Elsie when she realised that there wasn't one. Now, that was one thing that *was* going to change when she was in charge. Cate really hated it when the cubicles were not properly tidied and stocked.

'Can't I just wear my nightdress?' Elsie grumbled, but Cate explained that she would need to take off her bra and necklace as the doctor would probably order a chest X-ray.

First, though, Cate did a routine set of obs and then headed off in search of the elusive gown. The linen trolley was void of them—the staff from the wards were always coming down and pinching linen from the emergency trolley and so Cate often hid a few pieces as soon as they were delivered. She went to her secret stash in the storeroom, where she kept a few gowns hidden behind the burn packs.

The phone was ringing as she made her way back and, with the ward clerk not around, Cate took the call—it was Maria, Elsie's daughter.

'She only just arrived in the department,' Cate explained. 'The doctor should be in with her soon.'

'She's talking?' Maria checked.

'Oh, yes!' Cate smiled, because Elsie hadn't stopped talking since she had laid eyes on her. 'Should I tell her that you're coming in?'

'No, no,' Maria said. 'I'll call back later this afternoon to see what's happening. It doesn't sound as if it is anything too serious. I don't know why they called an ambulance.'

'She developed chest pain,' Cate said. 'I'm quite sure it was more severe than even Elsie was letting on, though she's very comfortable now.'

'Still, I think an ambulance is taking things a bit far. We don't want any heroics.'

Cate blinked for a moment at the matter-of-fact way Maria addressed a rather sensitive issue. 'Is that something that has already been discussed?' Cate asked carefully. 'Does your mother have a DNR order?'

'No, but at her age surely we should just let nature take its course?'

Cate continued the difficult conversation, explaining that Elsie was lucid and comfortable and that it was something Elsie could discuss with the doctor if she saw fit. 'Is there any message that you'd like me to pass on to your mother?' Cate asked.

'Just tell her that I'll call back later,' Maria said, and then rang off.

Cate let out a breath, and when the phone rang again, on instinct she answered it, though she soon wished that she hadn't.

'Can I please speak with Dr Morales?'

'I'll see if he's available,' Cate said. 'May I ask who's calling?' As soon as the words were out she regretted them; she had made it clear that Juan was here but her mind had been so full of Elsie and her daughter that she had forgotten Juan's little lecture from last week.

'Tell him it is Martina.'

She found Juan in with Elsie, taking bloods.

'Sorry I took so long, Elsie,' Cate said. 'Your daughter just called...'

Elsie rolled her eyes and dismissed the information with a flick of her hand. 'You can ring her when I'm dead,' Elsie huffed. 'That will cheer her up.'

'She's going to call back later,' Cate said, making a mental note to speak to whichever doctor Elsie was referred to, so that Elsie's wishes could be discussed properly. 'Juan, you've got a call too—Martina is on the phone for you, I'm very sorry, I forgot and I—'

He interrupted her excuses. 'Tell her that I am with a patient,' Juan answered, labelling the vials of blood he had taken.

'Just to have her call back in ten minutes?' Cate checked, because Martina called fairly frequently. 'Why doesn't she ring your mobile?'

'Because I've blocked her.' He muttered something

under his breath in Spanish but then winked at Elsie. 'Excuse me, I need to take a phone call.'

'Be nice when you do,' Elsie warned, and Juan smiled and gave a small shake of his head.

'It gets you into more trouble sometimes.'

It did.

Juan had tried being nice, had tried being firm, had been downright rude a couple of times and the calls had stopped for a while. But as the date of what would have been their first wedding anniversary approached, Martina was more determined than ever to change history.

'Juan, I was hoping to speak to you.'

'I'm at work.'

'Then call me from home.'

'Martina—'

'You won't let me properly explain,' Martina interrupted. 'And I'm hearing from everyone the ridiculous things you are doing—that you are going to do a season of skiing. Why would you take such risks?'

'I'm not your concern, Martina. You made that very clear.'

'I would have come round. Juan, please, we need to speak.'

'Stop calling me at work,' Juan said, and hung up and sat for a moment, thinking of the man he had once been, compared with the man he was now.

Martina didn't know him at all.

She couldn't.

Not even *he* knew yet who the new Juan was.

'Poor Martina,' Elsie had said as Juan had left the cubicle to take the call and Cate had laughed. She loved old people, they knew about a thousand times more than the whole of the staff put together. It had taken

Elsie about two seconds to work out what a heartbreaker Juan was.

'I had one like that once,' Elsie said, nodding to the curtains Juan had just walked through, as Cate helped her undress and get into a gown.

'What, a six-foot-three Argentinian?' Cate quipped.

'No, a five-foot-eight Frenchman!' Cate wanted to put Elsie in her handbag and take her home. 'I was in my fifties and I'd been widowed for two years.'

'That's young to be a widow.'

'Don't waste any sympathy, I had a terrible marriage,' Elsie said. 'You can call me the merry widow if you must, but I was just sick of feeling like I was in my daughter's way and being told what to do. I took myself off to France—I'd always wanted to go and I was so glad I did. We had one week together and I had the best time of my whole life!' She pointed to a large silver bezel-set amethyst ring on her finger. 'No regrets from me,' Elsie said. 'We had completely different lives, it would never have worked long term but we kept in touch a little bit. He sent me a card now and then, and when he died ten years ago I went back and visited his grave and thanked him.'

She opened the album and showed Cate a picture of the love of her life, a love that had lasted just a few days.

'Have you ever been adored?' Elsie asked, and Cate frowned as she met Elsie's pale blue eyes.

'I don't think so,' Cate admitted, as the reason for her break-up was delivered to her, as the word she had needed was revealed.

'I highly recommend it,' Elsie said. 'Have you ever adored anyone?'

And Cate faltered. 'Adored?'

'It's a rare kind of love,' Elsie said, 'and I got to taste it.'

'Was it worth it, though, Elsie?' Cate asked. 'Lugging a broken heart around for the rest of your life.'

'My heart wasn't broken.' Elsie smiled. 'It soars every time I think of him.'

Cate's heart wasn't soaring, though, as Juan pulled her aside a while later and warned 'for the third time' that she had to have a word with the nursing staff and receptionist and remind them about privacy on the phone. They were not to reveal any of the staff rosters.

It was the closest she had come to seeing him angry or, rather, very disgruntled.

And so too was Cate, as she had a word with the staff as per Juan's instructions!

There she was, mopping up the chaos of his love life. It was a relief not to have slept with him.

Then she saw him laughing with Elsie, chatting with her as she was waiting to be moved to the ward, just standing by her gurney and putting a smile on the old lady's face. She was in a white hospital gown now, all the rings and jewellery off, but she had her pink shawl around her shoulders and was smiling as she showed him pictures.

No, it was no relief not to have slept with him.

It was simply self-preservation.

CHAPTER EIGHT

'CATE?'

Cate heard her name being called over her side gate as she hung out her uniform. She was in a rush, she'd just come out of the shower and, yet again, she was driving, so she really didn't have much time. But that never stopped Bridgette, who would chat happily as Cate got ready.

'Come over, Bridgette, but I can't chat for long.'

'Going out?'

Cate nodded. 'Yes, and I have no idea what to wear.'

They headed into the kitchen and Cate put on the kettle and did her usual thing with tea and ice—it was the only way to get through the long hot summer. Then they headed upstairs to decide what Cate should wear. 'I need a new wardrobe,' Cate sighed.

'So do I.'

'No, I really need one,' Cate said. 'Everything I've got I wore when I was going out with Paul. I've got my black dress, my going-out-for-dinner dress, the dress I wore when I met his family...' It was hard to explain.

'What about this?' Bridgette pointed out Cate's lilac skirt.

'It's the one new thing I have but I wore it last week.'

'Are you missing him?'

'No,' Cate said. 'And then I feel guilty that I don't.'

'So who's this other guy?'

Cate was about to shake her head but there was no chance of Bridgette meeting Juan and it would be so nice to get her advice—even if she had no intention of taking it! Bridgette was a lot more open-minded than Cate and always made her laugh.

'There's a casual doctor at work,' Cate said. 'He's from Argentina and is travelling for a year or two...'

'Nothing wrong with a younger man.'

'He's not younger, though,' Cate said, because, yes, most doctors were in their twenties when they travelled the world. 'He's in his mid-thirties, I think. It sounds like he had a really good job and then just took off...'

'He's a bit young to be having a mid-life crisis.'

'He's not in crisis!' Cate laughed. 'He's having a ball. He's stunning, everyone fancies him, he makes no bones that he's moving on soon and that he's not interested in anything serious, not that it stops anyone.' She paused for a moment. 'He works all over Melbourne and from what I saw today he's having just as much fun at the other hospitals as he is at Bayside, but...' Cate took a breath '...we get on, he likes me...'

'And you clearly like him.'

Cate nodded. 'He leaves the country soon so it's not going anywhere except bed...' She looked at Bridgette. 'And that's just not me.'

'Who knows where it could lead?'

'No.' Cate shook her head. 'That's the one thing I

can't let myself think. The whole point is, it *will* go no-where and I don't know if I can get my head around that.'

'You take things so seriously.'

'I know I do,' Cate said. 'I don't want to, but I do. I want to be carefree, I want to just let loose and have fun and live a little...'

'Then do.'

To Bridgette it was that simple.

Maybe, Cate thought, it could be.

She thought of Elsie and her one wild fling, thought of Juan, who was, quite simply, beautiful, and she felt as if she was standing on the edge of a diving board and peering down.

She wanted to have done it, wanted to be climbing out of the water, high from the thrill. It was just throwing herself over the edge that Cate was struggling to come to terms with.

'I've got a dress you can have,' Bridgette said. 'It's too big for me but it would look great on you. It's still got the tags on. Go and get ready and I'll fetch it.'

They borrowed and swapped things all the time. Bridgette was always buying and selling things on the internet. Cate did her make-up until Bridgette returned.

'Oh!' She stared at the dress. 'White?'

'First after Paul.' Bridgette winked. 'You need sexy undies.'

Cate opened her top drawer and let out a sigh. Juan was right, her relationship with Paul had gone on too long—two years in and they'd long since passed the sexy underwear stage.

'You are joking?' Bridgette said, as Cate pulled out

some rather plain white panties. 'You'd be better off not wearing any!'

Well, that wasn't going to happen—so she had to wear the sensible ones.

Cate never usually wore white, but when she put it on she found it suited her. The dress tied under the bust and scooped a little too low and certainly, when she looked in the mirror, the word virginal didn't spring to mind.

'It's too much! Or, rather, it's way too little,' she said, pulling the dress down over her bottom.

'Go for it,' Bridgette said. 'Take a taxi.'

'I'd rather drive,' Cate said. 'Anyway, I'm working tomorrow.'

She put on her new wedges and there was a flurry of nerves in her stomach as she looked in the mirror, and then there was the most terribly unfamiliar feeling as she filled her bag not just with lipstick and breath mints but with a few condoms too.

It was so not her.

Just so against her nature.

Cate picked up Kelly and Abby and kept having to force herself to keep up with the conversation, her mind was so full of Juan.

There was a flurry of hellos as they entered the garden to the restaurant where Christine's leaving do was being held.

They had chosen outside, not just because of the balmy heat but because thirty Emergency workers tended to be loud at the best of the times.

Cate slipped into a seat beside Louise and, although she did her best not to look over, the second she arrived she searched for him. She saw that Juan was already there. He was, of course, in the middle of the long table, sitting beside Christine and enthralling his adoring audience.

Maybe, Cate thought, all this indecision was for nothing, because he'd barely looked in her direction.

Maybe she'd said no one too many times.

'He could have his pick, couldn't he?' Louise said.

'Almost,' Cate sighed, they both knew who she was talking about.

'It's a shame he's leaving.'

'I just don't get the drifting-around-the-world thing,' Cate said. 'He wouldn't even commit to a three-month contract. I could understand it if he was in his twenties.'

'I don't need three months with him...' Louise nudged, and Cate pushed out a smile.

It was actually a very nice night—at first. The restaurant was set high on Olivers Hill and looked over Port Phillip Bay. The view was stunning and the drink was flowing a bit too freely because Christine's laughter was getting louder and louder, the stories at the table more outrageous. Cate laughed and joined in but her heart really wasn't in it. She just wanted to go home, not to be sitting waiting for a sliver of Juan's attention, not to be like Christine and hanging onto his every word.

And, yes, it hurt that he hadn't so much as spoken to her once.

It was still, at eleven p.m., unbearably warm and Cate blew up her fringe as she let out a long breath. 'Another sleepless night, tossing and turning...'

'Well, if you insist.' Juan's voice from behind her made Cate jump but she managed to answer in her usual dry fashion when she turned round. 'In your dreams, Juan!'

He lowered his head and gave her a brief kiss on the cheek, just as a few other colleagues had, but because it was Juan he took the tease one step further. 'Often.'

'You don't know when to stop, do you?' Cate really tried not to take his flirting seriously, for pity the woman who believed that any words that slipped from those velvet lips hadn't been used many times before.

'I brought you a drink…' Juan put a glass of champagne on the table.

'It's very nice of you, but I'm driving.'

'You can have one.'

'I don't want to have one.'

'I'll have it.' Louise smiled.

'Help yourself.'

He moved into an empty seat beside her—a few of the gathering had gone to dance and once she'd finished her drink Louise drifted off to join them.

'Are you looking forward to Monday?' Juan asked.

'I don't know that much will change,' Cate attempted.

'Of course it will.'

'It might only be temporary,' Cate pointed out. 'I might not get the job.'

'You know you will.' He saw the swallow in her throat. 'Is it what you want?'

'Of course it is.'

'Why?'

'Why wouldn't I?' She gave a small shake of her head. She wasn't about to discuss her career with a man who had turned his back on his.

'Have you thought about doing the sky jump?'

'The places are all taken.'

'You can have mine.' Juan grinned. 'I'd happily pay

to watch you jump out of a plane. I think it would be very freeing for you.'

'I don't need freeing.' Her eyes narrowed as she looked at him. 'I don't need a shot of adrenaline from jumping out of a plane to prove that I'm alive...' It annoyed her that he smiled. 'I don't.'

'I'm not arguing.' Still he smiled. 'I wish you good luck with your interview. If I come back in a couple of years, I expect you'll be carrying a clipboard and be the new director of nursing.'

'And what will you be doing in a couple of years?' Cate asked, because even though he was smiling she felt there was a challenge in his tone. 'Still roaming the globe, still doing casual shifts and not knowing where you're going to be each day?'

'I don't know,' he admitted. 'I try not to think that far ahead, but I am thinking ahead now—after you've dropped everyone off, come back to mine.'

'Pardon?'

'I would like to have some time to speak with you.'

'We're speaking now.'

'Okay, I would like to talk to you some more.' He would. Juan was more than aware that this might be the last time they were together and he cared enough about Cate to prolong the conversation. She clearly didn't want his career advice, so he switched track to something a little more palatable. 'I would like to be a bit more hot in my pursuit but I don't think you would appreciate it. You are senior, you don't need the Dr Juan walk of shame, so I'm inviting you to come over afterwards...'

'Why would I come back to yours?'

'Because, as I said when I brought your drink, I think about you often and think it is the same for you.

I believe if you want something you should at least try, and so I am.'

'I don't think—'

'Don't think, then.'

She couldn't really believe he could be so upfront about it.

'Juan…'

'I can't talk too long. Christine is being a pain and I don't want to upset her at her leaving do. We can talk some more back at mine.'

Cate excused herself and nipped out to the toilets. She wished for a guilty moment that she hadn't when she saw Christine in there in tears. Cate really didn't know what to say.

'It's hard, leaving,' Cate attempted, 'but you'll still keep in touch…'

'Do you really think I'm crying about that place?' Christine looked at her. 'I couldn't be happier to be getting away from it. It's Juan.'

'Oh.'

'I made a bit of a fool of myself,' Christine said. 'I asked if he wanted to come back after…' She cringed. 'I was very politely rebuffed. I told myself before I came out not to drink and Juan.' Cate gave a thin smile at Christine's pale joke—she knew exactly what she meant.

'Our livers will be thanking him,' Cate said, because she wasn't just being a martyr, driving everyone around—since she'd met Juan she'd been clutching water, terrified that a thimble of wine and all restraint would be gone.

'I should have known better.' Christine started the

repair job on her face. 'I knew it wasn't going anywhere, but it was so great being with him…'

Cate really didn't want to hear this; she didn't want to hear from Christine how good he was in bed. She was just about to excuse herself, skip to the loo, do anything to avoid that conversation. She had no idea what was coming next.

'It was all going great until you came back from leave.'

'What?'

'Oh, come on, Cate…'

'There's nothing going on between us.'

'I'm not blind.'

Cate just stood there; she knew this could get nasty and she certainly didn't have to explain one kiss to bloody Christine.

'What's going on between the two of you, then?' came Christine's slightly drunken demand.

'I don't know about you, Christine, but I left school years ago,' Cate said, and walked out.

She went to get her bag but she'd promised Kelly a lift.

Kelly could pay for a taxi for once, Cate decided. But there was no need to rush off. The drama was over—Juan had already gone.

Once the bill had been paid, even Kelly didn't want to head off to a club; so Cate drove her home and then dropped off Abby, which took her unbearably close to Juan's.

She couldn't just walk up the garden path for sex.

'Hi, Juan.' She could just picture it. 'I'm here.'

Cate was nothing like that, she did nothing like that. She had fewer regrets than Frank Sinatra.

Yet Cate didn't want to be sitting on a gurney in fifty years' time, speaking about this stunning six-foot-three Argentinian who had offered no strings, who had offered nothing but a night, maybe a couple of days...

'What did you do?' She could just see the young nurse asking her half a century from now.

'I went home.'

'Oh.'

'Nothing could have come of it,' Old Cate would rationalize. 'There was no point if it was going nowhere.'

Elsie would be disappointed

Bridgette too.

Even the imaginary nurse of the future would be disappointed in her tonight, Cate thought as she refused to give in to temptation.

She arrived home—there was a present on her doorstep and Cate opened the note with it as she stepped inside.

Hope you don't get this till morning and you can take this beauty out for a whirl tonight.
B xxx

Lilac velvet panties, still fresh in their pack, and they'd cost an absolute fortune, Cate knew, because Bridgette had been trying to sell them to her!

Wasted, she thought, crunching them into a ball in her fist and trying not to cry.

Lying in bed alone at two a.m., Cate was disappointed in herself too...at her wasted chance.

CHAPTER NINE

IN HIS NIGHTMARES he relived it.

Juan had waited for Cate until one and then given in and gone to bed, but he left the lights on outside and in the hall, just in case she changed her mind. He dozed off, trying to keep one ear open for her car, trying to fathom what it was about Cate that held his attention so, when he found himself back in his hospital bed.

'I felt that!' Juan said.

Manuel was washing his arm and Juan felt something, a vague sting, but at least he felt it.

His breathing came faster, scared to hope.

It was two a.m., the nurses were doing their rounds the night after his meltdown.

His roommates had all been wonderful.

'Love you, Juan,' André had called to him that morning as Juan had woken up. He was so ashamed for what he had put his roommates through, not knowing it was part of the process, not knowing two of them had done it too.

'Love you, Juan,' José had called, and Juan had closed his eyes.

'Does it make me gay if I say I love you?' young Eduard had called out, and Juan had smiled at the ceiling.

'No,' Juan finally answered. 'I love you guys, too,' he said. 'Thank you.'

It had been a day of conversation, a day of comradeship in the room as they'd stared up at the ceiling and joked and laughed. With the nurses' help they had even video-called each other that afternoon, finally face to face with each other. Eduard had told them about his amazing girlfriend, Felicia, who was currently flying back from a student exchange in France and would be coming in to see him tomorrow.

Juan had woken at two a.m., as he always did when the nurses approached.

'Not like this!' Juan's eyes snapped open as he heard Eduard shout. 'I don't want Felicia seeing me...'

Poor man.

Juan closed his eyes in agony as he heard Eduard screaming to Graciela, who was by his side. Poor man. Juan wept as Manuel wiped his tears and Eduard's deranged, grief-filled rant continued.

Oh, Eduard!

Juan wanted to go over and hold him. He wanted to fix him, to heal him, but all he could do was lie in respectful silence, grimacing over and over in agony as Eduard let out his fears in a room, in a ward, that understood.

Poor man.

Good man.

He looked up at Manuel, saw that his eyes were filling up too, but he gave a small smile of comfort to Juan.

'It's okay,' he said quietly. 'He will be okay.'

Juan's eyes snapped open and his heart was pounding as he came out of the memory. He moved his hands and it was luxury, checked that his legs still moved and then his hand moved to the heaven of an erection he could feel, even if was unsated, and he cried in the darkness, feeling the hell of that night again.

He sat up and gulped water and then reached for his laptop. He blew his nose as he made the call on his computer and waited for the comfort of a familiar face.

'Juan!' Eduard smiled as he came into focus.

'Does it make me gay if I call you in the middle of the night to tell you I love you?' Juan asked.

'Bad night?' Eduard asked, and Juan nodded as he wiped the tears from his face. Their friendship was worth more than gold, silver and platinum combined. It was Juan's most treasured possession. André struggled with Juan, jealous at his recovery, but they were trying to work through it. José was doing well and had movement in his arms and they kept in regular touch. But it was Eduard and Juan who were closest. The bond they had made back then was unbreakable and Juan smiled to see Eduard's cheeky grin. 'Bad luck for you if you are gay,' Eduard said. 'Felicia and I are getting married.'

'Eduard…' Juan was smiling and crying and then just smiling. Eduard was quadriplegic, with some small movement in his left hand and wrist. How he treasured that movement, how grateful he was for the exercises the nurses had performed over and over so that meant, with special equipment, he could type, could raise a beaker and drink from it. 'She is so beautiful,' Juan said. 'She is amazing…'

'I know.' Eduard was serious. 'Juan, will you be my best man?'

'We don't have best men in Argentina,' Juan teased lightly, but then he was serious. 'Except, for all that has happened, we do. I would be so proud to be your best man.'

'I don't want you to come home if you are not ready. I understand why you had to get away…'

'You tell me the date and I will be there. Nothing would keep me from being there to share in your day.'

'We are sorting the date out. Juan?' Eduard's tone changed to being tentative. 'There is something I wish to discuss with you. We're so grateful, but you don't have to keep paying for my pills.'

'Are the pills working?' Juan asked, and grinned as Eduard gave a shy smile back. This was no crude conversation, there was nothing they did not discuss, and Juan, loaded with survivor guilt, refused to leave anything out of bounds.

'Yes,' Eduard said. 'We have sex and it is getting better. She enjoys it, I think, and I love her pleasure.'

'Then that money is there,' Juan said. He knew the tablets were expensive and the young couple could not afford many, knew what must sometimes be on Eduard's mind, so he said, 'If I kill myself doing all this crazy stuff I have left money for you in my will. You will be pleasing your beautiful Felicia all your life, my friend.'

'Thank you.'

'No need,' Juan said, and he meant it.

'I tried what you said with my mouth,' Eduard said, 'and she was not faking!'

'I'll teach you more tricks another time,' Juan said. No, it was no crude conversation—younger, far less experienced, Eduard had cried and cried to Juan about losing his ability to make love to Felicia, had doubted that he might ever please her again. But even as Juan smiled, it faltered. His tears were coming again, and he felt guilty because he was the one walking and yet he was the one crying. 'Sorry, Eduard, you don't need this today...'

'Hey!' Eduard said. 'It's me.'

'I know.' Juan looked at his friend and nodded, because they had agreed it went both ways. For it to work, Eduard had to be there for him too. How different Juan was from how he had once been—how much his priorities had changed since that day.

'I was going to call you on Sunday,' Eduard said. 'I know it will be a difficult day.'

It would have been Juan's first wedding anniversary.

'It's not just the wedding anniversary,' Juan admitted. 'I like someone, Eduard. For the first time in what feels like for ever there is someone that I cannot get out of my mind and yet I cannot get her into bed.'

'You can.'

'I leave a week on Tuesday.'

'You have to leave?'

'Yes,' Juan said. 'My visa expires and anyway I don't want to get too involved.' He trusted so few now, had sworn never to let go of his heart—to just love them and leave them. 'She reminds me a bit of your Felicia, she is loyal, she is so serious...' He smiled as he spoke. 'She is so sensible and cautious but I am sure she is wild too...'

'You've got it bad,' Eduard said. 'Have you told her about the accident?'

'No.'

'Will you?'

Juan shook his head. 'No, I don't want her sympathy.' He shared it with no one apart from the people who already knew. 'I don't want to even try to explain what happened, what it was like.' Juan thought for a long moment and Eduard patiently sat through his silence. 'I don't want to get involved or anything. Really, I just want it to be a week on Tuesday and to be gone…I think.' Juan honestly didn't know how he felt. 'Perhaps it is just that she has said no. Perhaps that is the reason I can't forget her. If I could sleep with her, maybe I'd get her out of my mind.'

'Have you cooked for her?' Eduard said, and Juan grinned. 'Has she had the full Juan treatment?'

'No.'

'Go!' Eduard said. 'Sort it now.'

Juan laughed.

They chatted a little while longer then said goodbye and Juan found himself naked in the kitchen at three a.m. He lit the gas under the frying pan then he went and put a towel around his hips to save the precious bits from any oil splashes.

Hopefully he'd be needing them tomorrow night!

CHAPTER TEN

CATE WOKE TO the heat of summer and the scald of her own thoughts about Juan, insisting she should be proud of herself.

Imagine how much worse you'd be feeling if you'd slept with him, Cate tried to tell herself as she took her uniform off the line and quickly ironed it. *Imagine how much worse you would be feeling if you'd gone and got involved with him,* Cate told herself as she drove to work.

She had almost convinced herself she was proud for resisting, but it actually felt horrible, walking into the department and knowing she wouldn't see Juan.

That she probably wasn't ever going to see him again.

These last few weeks, when she should have been missing Paul, when she should have been trying to get over a two-year relationship, when she should have been sorting out what she wanted from her career, instead her thoughts and emotions had all been taken up with Juan.

Funny that a heart could be so raw and bruised by a man she barely knew when it was not damaged by the man she had spent two years with.

It surely just showed how right she had been to end things with Paul.

Cate looked at the roster, devoid of Juan's name, and thought of the sky jump next Sunday.

Her last chance to see him.

A farewell shag before he flew? Oh, God, she was actually thinking about it, Cate realised. *That* was how much she regretted saying no last night!

'How was Christine's leaving do?' Harry yawned. He had been working all night and was now about to go off duty until Monday.

'Good,' Cate said. 'Who looked after the twins last night?'

'Mum.' Harry sighed.

'Are you having any luck with getting a new nanny?'

'I've got a couple of people to see next week,' Harry said. 'But most of the people on the agency books want to live in the city, not a good hour away from it, and I've got the consultant interviews too.'

'Any luck?'

'Nope.' Harry shook his head. 'Same problem I'm having with the nannies—all the good ones want the bright lights of the city. Honestly, Cate, I need to sort something out as soon as I can. I can't keep just dropping everything and coming in because we don't have enough staff...' Harry shook his head. 'At least I don't have to think about it for a couple of days now. The department is Dr Vermont's problem this weekend. I'm going to spend some quality time with the twins.'

'You have a good one,' Cate said.

It was, thankfully, a busy morning, so there wasn't much time to dwell on Juan and the night that had never happened, but it was there in the back of her mind, just waiting for her thoughts to turn to it, and Cate was determined they would not.

She was heading off to lunch, having decided to spend the hour sorting out what would be her office come Monday. She did not want to sit in the staffroom and join in the post mortem about last night. There always was one after a department do. As the late staff trickled in, more and more would be revealed—who'd got off with who, who had said what, and people were already talking about Christine and the fool she'd made of herself last night.

Cate simply didn't want to hear it. She was just about to hand the keys to Kelly when she saw a well-dressed woman, looking a little lost, and Cate asked if she could help her.

'I've been told to come here to get my mother's valuables,' she said. 'I don't know who to ask for.'

'I can help you with that,' Cate said. 'Do you have the receipt?'

'Yes, it's in my bag.' She started to open it.

'It's okay,' Cate said, 'you can give it to me when you need to sign.'

Cate walked with her towards Reception, where the valuables safe was located. 'What ward is your mum on?' Cate asked, really just making polite conversation.

'She was on the emergency medical unit, but she passed away last night…'

'Oh.' Cate turned in surprise. She was used to upset relatives coming down to collect their loved one's valuables but this lady didn't seem upset in the least. Cate had assumed she was just collecting a relative's things to take home. 'I'm sorry to hear that,' Cate offered.

'It's a blessing really,' the lady said as she handed her the receipt and Cate looked down and saw Elsie's scrawling signature on the piece of paper. 'She just sat in her bed or her chair all the time, staring at photos. She couldn't really get out—it's no life!'

Cate didn't really understand the blessing. It might have been considered a blessing if Elsie had suffered a serious stroke or had been struggling with dementia, or had been in chronic pain. But, no, as she filled out the paperwork and Maria chatted on, it became apparent that Elsie had passed peacefully in her sleep—the nurse had gone to check on her at two a.m. and had found Elsie deceased.

Yes, perhaps it was a blessing to slip away like that, but as Cate handed over the envelope that contained the necklace and rings, tears were stinging at the back of her eyes. She wondered if the daughter had just sat down and spoken to her mother—if she had found out all the wonderful things her mother had done, all the stories Elsie had still been able to tell—would it have seemed such a blessing then?

Cate headed to the office and surprised herself when she started to cry, and it wasn't just over Juan, and that he was gone, her tears really were for Elsie. Death was commonplace here and so, of course, there were tears at times, although not usually for an elderly lady who had died of natural causes. Elsie had been so lovely and Cate had been so glad to know her even for a little while. She blew her nose into a tissue and when the phone rang in her new office, Cate picked it up with a sniff and gave her name.

'Are you crying because you regret not coming back to mine last night?' She heard his deep voice and smiled into the phone.

'Of course I am.' Cate attempted sarcasm, although she was speaking a bit of the truth.

'Or are you crying because you miss me?'

'It's just not the same here without you, Juan,' Cate teased, and then told him the real reason for her tears. 'Actually, I just found out that Elsie died in the night. I know she was old and everything...'

'She was a complete delight,' Juan said. 'She had a wild side to her, you know...'

'I heard about it!' Cate smiled. 'So, what can I do for you?'

'Well, this morning I went on a culinary trip of the Mornington Peninsula. We caught our own fish and then when we got back we cleaned and prepared them and were taught how to cook them...'

'That's very tame for you.'

'I can be tamed at times...' He said it in a way that had Cate blushing. 'So, I have some beautiful fish steaks that tonight I'm going to prepare with a *chimichurri* sauce, which I will serve with cucumber salad. I don't have a deep fat fryer so I cannot do *papas fritas*...'

'Sorry.' Cate frowned, not just because she didn't understand some of the words, more that she did not understand why he was reeling off a menu.

'French fries,' Juan translated.

'Haven't you heard of frozen chips?'

'I don't believe in them.' Juan tutted and Cate found herself both frowning and smiling at his strange response.

'So,' Juan said. 'Do we get to say goodbye, just the two of us? Will you join me tonight for dinner?'

Cate thought of Bridgette and the nurse of the future. She thought of Elsie and her Frenchman and then thought of a life with too many regrets, and even though she had been teasing him before, yes, Cate would miss Juan when he had gone.

It might as well be for a reason.

'Fish and salad sounds lovely.'

'Good.'

'What time do you want me to get there?'

'Whatever time suits you,' Juan said. 'I'll see you when I'm looking at you.'

Cate put down the phone. She couldn't wait until he was looking at her!

'No regrets, Elsie,' Cate said to the room.

She didn't feel quite so brave at six p.m.

What to wear when you knew it would be coming off?

Yes, she could eat her fish, have a lovely conversation and then go home—he wasn't going to be tying her to the bed, or maybe he was?

Strange that Cate shivered just at the thought, when she had never thought of such things before. But what she had meant was that Juan wasn't going to be forcing her.

She was consenting to be bad.

For the first time in her life.

Cate put on the lilac skirt and it would have to be the black halterneck again, though she loathed the strapless bra that squashed into her breasts and made her look like she had four. Then she remembered, with a thrill low in her belly, how easily he had removed it and the exploration of his hands during their one kiss.

Cate left it off.

Hardly daring, as she didn't have the biggest bust, but for sensible Cate it felt reckless.

And it felt even more reckless when she took off her skirt and shaved in a place she rarely did, her fingers lingering on her mound as she thought of Juan and what was to come.

'Me,' Cate said with a shocked giggle, and then dried herself and put the lilac velvet panties on.

She stopped for some wine on the way to Juan's, asking for help to choose one that went well with fish. She took the suggestion of a nice refreshing white but, as she approached his house, Cate worried about bringing wine—if she did, would he assume she was staying?

Was she staying?

Of course!

Cate had no idea what she was doing, even if Juan might think it easy for her. The thought of getting through the meal, knowing there was this big sexy slab of Argentinian for dessert, made her glow like the bush fires that were still raging.

When she got to the bottom of the hill, she was just about to turn the car round and go home, but the thought that he might see her doing that forced her to push on. She was determined not to appear nervous, absolutely determined to enjoy her one wild night, and, taking a deep breath as she approached his home, Cate parked and climbed out.

Juan opened the door before she knocked, took the wine and grinned, and she was relieved when he didn't welcome her with a kiss, for she was almost petrified of touching him.

'Did you go to the store on the corner of Beach Road?' Juan asked.

'Yes, why?'

'He suggested this one to me, too. I am still not up on

Australian wine.' Juan led her through. He was wearing black jeans and a silver-grey shirt and there was his bottle already open. He was chopping up cucumbers, it would seem, and sexy music was on.

'We put this one in the fridge...' Juan said, and took it. He went to get a glass, but first he seemed to remember what he had forgotten to do at the door. He gave her a brief kiss on the cheek, a sort of European greeting kiss, which was very nice and very friendly and very tame...

She glanced down to see that he was barefoot. Cate had never found feet sexy, but his were: he had very long toes, which made her aware that her own toes were curling. His eyes were looking not at her but at her oiled and scented body and at two thick nipples that were poking out like two mini-erections. There was a throb between her legs and, for safety's sake, she should have worn a bra, Cate thought.

'You're shorter without your high heels on.' Cate said and, as she spoke, even Cate didn't recognize her own voice—it was thick and loaded with lust—and it was then she found out how nice the wine she'd bought was, because she got a taste, and not from the glass.

He wedged her to the kitchen bench and she was kissing him back. Frantic, hungry, pre-dinner kisses. She wondered what on earth she'd been worrying about, wondered why on earth she hadn't spent the last few weeks being slammed up against his kitchen bench or taken on the floor.

'Sorry,' he breathed, prising his face from hers. 'That's why I didn't kiss you at the door...'

'It's okay.' Cate understood, she understood completely.

'I'll get you a drink,' he said, 'and then...'

Oh, what was the point? She was hauling him back now, because they *had* to have sex, they absolutely had to. Cate had never *had* to have sex before—it had never been an absolute command. Juan was kissing her again, lifting her up onto the kitchen bench and undoing the tie on her top.

'God, I've been wanting you for weeks,' Juan said.

She was naked from the waist up on the kitchen bench; she'd never been devoured like this before.

Not once.

Not once had she known the bliss of absolute unbridled lust. His tongue was at her nipples, licking, nibbling, sucking. He uttered breathless words that he would get to them later, that now, just now... 'I have to be inside you.'

Cate's hands were just as busy as she almost ripped off his shirt, because she wanted to, *had* to, see the bits of him she hadn't seen before. She wanted to prove to herself, as if she needed to, just how delicious he was. Cate pulled his shirt down over his shoulders but it was difficult to get the last bit over his arms as he was face down and buried in her breasts, but the second his hands were free Juan was lifting up her skirt. It was as if she'd known him for ever, as if it was completely normal to be heading for the zipper she was sliding down. Her only regret as she ran her hands over his delicious length was that, when she'd got ready for tonight, she had even bothered with panties.

Time really was of the essence but it didn't deter Juan; his fingers parted her and he was stroking her, his mouth a hot, wet demand on the senses in her neck.

'I want to see you,' Cate said, as she just about

pushed him off. She looked down at the sight of him huge and erect in her hands and moaned with want.

'We have to go to the bedroom,' Juan breathed. He went to lift her but she resisted, frantically patting the bench for her bag. Yes, she was taking a chance tonight, but not a chance like that—and the groan of relief from him as she pulled out some condoms was her delicious reward for being sensible.

'Good girl…' Juan said, grabbing the foil.

He had it on in an instant, and she should be ashamed of herself, Cate thought, except she wasn't.

She didn't even get to take off her panties. He merely pushed them aside and, huge and precise, he was inside.

'Oh…' He said something in Spanish, something that sounded crude, that matched their mood. He switched to English. 'I want to see you too,' Juan said. 'I *have* to see you.'

He took the knife he had been chopping the cucumbers with. She was trying not to come, trying to stay still as he cut off her knickers, and she felt the twitch of him inside her as he tried to hold back too, his eyes devouring her, freshly shaved and just for him.

They watched for a moment, just for two decadent thrusts, before her legs were tight around him and there was no need to look any more.

No, need for 'Is that nice?' she thought as he bucked inside her. No, 'Like that?' or 'Is that better?'

There was absolutely no need for Juan to question her enjoyment or pleasure, for Cate was sobbing it to the room. Her nails were digging in his back as he came deep inside her, as nearly three months of foreplay exploded inside Cate and she pulsed around him in turn.

'Dirty girl,' he said, as she swore for the first time.

'Beautiful girl,' he said, as he shot inside her again, as her deep pulses milked him dry. Then as she tried to get her breath back while resting her head on his shoulder, as she looked down at the chaos of their clothes, they started laughing.

Juan still inside her.

'I needed that bad.' Juan kissed her, kissed her and chased away the embarrassment that was starting to come.

'So did I.'

'Now,' he said, sliding out, remarkably practical as Cate sat there feeling dizzy, 'you sit over there on a stool and I can get you that drink, and then I can concentrate properly on making dinner.'

'Did you just say what I thought you said?'

Had they just had sex?

'Yes,' Juan said. 'You are a bad distraction in my kitchen.'

CHAPTER ELEVEN

JUAN KEPT A very neat kitchen. All evidence was removed—he even tied up her halterneck for her—and
then he parked Cate on a bar stool and threw her expensive knickers in the bin. He handed a glass of wine
to her.

'Better?' Juan said.

'Better.'

She couldn't believe it. Five minutes in his house
and she'd had the best orgasm she had ever had. She
felt a little stunned, a little breathless but enjoying the
view. She was sipping her wine as if it was normal to
watch him cook and see the scratches on his back that
had come from her.

'Can I help?' Cate offered, because wasn't that what
you were supposed to say?

'Relax,' was Juan's response.

It was bizarre that, for the first time around him, she
could relax properly.

Juan picked up the knife that had sliced her panties
and with a smile that was returned he carried on chopping the salad.

He could chop too.

Fast, tiny, thin slices.

'You've done that before.'

'I helped in the family business,' Juan said. 'After school and during medical school. My family have a…' he hesitated for a moment, perhaps choosing the right word '…café.' He moved and took the fish steaks out of the fridge and she heard the sizzle as they were added to the pan.

'They smell fantastic,' Cate said. 'What was the marinade?'

'Chimichurri,' Juan said. 'It is Argentinian. There are many variations but this is my mother's recipe that I make for you tonight.'

It was soon ready and they took the food outside to the table that had been laid. There was even a candle and, as she took the seat looking out to the ocean, Cate blinked a little when he put a plate in front of her. It looked amazing.

'You can cook too!'

'You haven't tasted it yet.'

'Ah, but it's all in the presentation.'

'No.' Juan smiled as he sat opposite her. 'It is no good to look beautiful and taste of nothing, or, worse, when you do bite into it, to find out it is off.'

'Well, it's a treat to have someone cook for me,' Cate said. 'It's beans on toast more often than not at mine.'

Cate loaded her fork. Of course she was going to say it was lovely, of course she would be polite, she meant what she had said, it was nice to be cooked for, but, more than that, it could taste like cardboard and the night would still be divine.

'Oh!' She forgot her manners completely, spoke with her mouth still full as she took her first taste. 'It's amazing.'

It was. The fish was mild and so fresh it might just

as well have jumped out of the ocean and landed on her plate, yet the marinade… Cate was not particularly into food unless it was called ice cream, but there was a riot happening on her tongue.

'It is very fresh…' Juan took a bite '…and my mother's *chimichurri* is the best.'

'I think I'm having another orgasm,' Cate said.

'Oh, you will later,' Juan said. 'And you won't think, you'll know.'

But there was only so much you could say about fish and, with sex out of the way, conversation turned a touch awkward at first. They knew little about each other, and it was supposed to be that way, Cate told herself, but she couldn't help asking about his homeland when he spoke briefly about it.

'Do you miss it?'

'No,' Juan admitted. 'I speak to my family a lot and to my friends, of course.'

'What made you decide to travel?'

'The woman who rings…' There was a tight swallow in Cate's throat as she found out a little about the man. 'Martina. We were engaged but it didn't work out. I think when any relationship ends you start to question things,' Juan said. 'Don't you?'

'I guess.' Cate took a swallow of her wine.

'Did you?' Juan pushed, when normally he didn't. Normally he didn't want to know more, but with Cate he did.

'A bit.' Cate gave a slightly nervous lick of her lips and put down her knife and fork. 'That really was delicious.' She tried to change the subject, but Juan pushed on.

'Really, my parents were never pushy with my education. They thought I would join them in the family business but I wanted to do medicine, so I spent a lot of time studying as well as working part time for them. I never really took some time to do other things I wanted.' He gave a small shrug. 'Now seemed like a good idea. I think it is good to step back. It is very easy to get caught up in the rat race...'

Cate shook her head. 'I don't see it as a rat race. I have no desire to step off.'

'None?'

Cate took a deep breath, felt the bubble of disquiet she regularly quashed rise to the surface. 'I'm not sure that I'm happy at work.' She looked at his grey unblinking eyes. 'I'm not unhappy, but sometimes...' Her voice trailed off and Juan filled the silence.

'Is that why you considered being a paramedic?'

Cate nodded. 'But it's not for me.'

'What is for you?'

'I'm working that out,' Cate admitted. 'Don't you miss anaesthesia?'

'No,' Juan admitted. 'I expected that I would and I admit I enjoyed looking after Jason the other day, but I don't miss it as much as I thought I might. I had a lot of ego,' Juan said, then halted, not wanting to go there. 'I like Emergency, that was where I started, then I did anaesthesia and was invited to a senior role. I enjoyed it, but being back in Emergency I realise how I enjoy that too.'

'And your fiancée?'

'Ex.'

'Who still calls regularly.'

Juan grinned. 'She misses me, can you blame her?'

'Did it end suddenly?' Cate knew she was teetering

outside the strange rules of a non-relationship—it was just that she wanted to know more about him.

'Yes.'

'Were you…?' Cate's voice trailed off.

'I can't answer a question if you don't ask it.'

'Were you cheating?'

'No,' Juan said. 'I took our engagement seriously. It was ended by mutual agreement—now it would seem that she has some regrets.'

Cate looked at him, looked at that full mouth, slightly taut now, saw a flicker of pain in his eyes. He wasn't over her, Cate knew it.

And Martina wasn't over him, Cate could guarantee that. Imagine having that heart and losing it?

'All I've learnt is that nothing lasts for ever,' Juan said. 'So enjoy what you have now, live in the moment…'

'Well, that's where we're different,' Cate said, hoping that he'd leave things there, but Juan did not. His hand reached across the table and took her tense one.

'Why so cautious?'

She looked up, looked at him, and he saw the tiny creases form beside her eyes.

'We're just talking,' Juan said lightly, but he wanted to know more.

'Having three brothers makes you so…' She attempted to sound dismissive but it was an impossible task. 'All my brothers were quite wild, but my middle brother decided to steal a car with his girlfriend when he was eighteen,' Cate said. 'I was nine. He nearly killed his girlfriend—I just remember the chaos, the hospital, the court cases, what it did to Mum and Dad… "Thank God for Cate," Mum and Dad always said. I never caused them a moment's worry, I guess it became who I thought I was...' She looked back up. 'Now I'm trying to find out who I am. So, yes...' She gave a tight smile. 'I guess the end of a relationship makes you examine things.'

She was trying not to examine things a little later as they headed to his bedroom and she saw that huge white bed. She was trying to live in the now—except she knew she would remember and miss him for ever.

He undressed her and she was more nervous than when she'd arrived at his door as he took off his boots, as he kicked them to the floor, because a night in his arms was simply not enough.

He pulled her to the bed.

'You're shaking?'

'I...' She didn't know what to say. In Juan's world the bedroom wasn't the place to tell him you had the terrifying feeling that you loved him. 'The air-conditioning,' Cate said, and she lay there as he went to turn it down, lay in his bed and replayed his words, told herself she could just enjoy what they had now.

As he climbed into bed and started to kiss her, at first her response was tentative. It was too late to be chaste, Cate told herself, and, yes, there was the heaven of his touch.

She felt the skin of his back beneath her fingers, felt the strength of his arms pulling her closer, and she was a mire of contrary feelings, because she wanted this and yet she was scared to give in. His tongue was as necessary as water to her mouth, his scent embedded in her head for ever and his touch almost more than her heart could handle. Her hands moved over his shoulder, to his neck and then her fingers paused, felt the ridge at the back of his neck. Then Juan's hands were there, moving hers away.

Again.

Her eyes opened to him and they stared for a moment, still kissing, but a part of him was out of bounds and he felt her withdraw, knew that tonight was about to end, and he didn't want it to, so Juan moved to save it.

Cate felt the shift in him. It was more than physical—he dragged her back to him, not with passion but with self; he just brought her back to him with his mouth.

He kissed down her neck and to her breasts and Juan lost himself for a moment, just lingered. He wanted her hot beneath him, he wanted them both sated, or he usually did, but tonight he let himself pause. He tasted her skin and licked and caressed with his mouth and then moved down.

She could feel the scratch of his unshaven jaw, such a contrast to the warm wetness of his mouth.

'I'll be sitting on ice tomorrow.'

It was her last feeble attempt at a joke, because she felt like crying from the bliss. His mouth, his touch, was slow but not measured. There was no blueprint—he followed her gasps and breaths, guided by them. It was more than sex. Her hands went to his head to halt him, scared to hand herself over, and then she felt his tongue's soft probe and heard the moans from him—and she gave in to being adored.

Juan hadn't done this in a long time; he hadn't been so enchanted ever. He buried his tongue in warm folds and she gave in to his intimate caress. Cate wanted him to stop, because she could feel herself building, in a way she never had. She wanted the trip of orgasm, a textbook pleasing, not the new feeling of delayed urgency he stoked.

'Stay still.' He wasn't subtle, he held her legs wider open and she looked down at him. Every stroke of his tongue was dictated by her response and when she sobbed he went in more firmly; when she arched, his mouth held her down. He tasted her, he ravished her.

He adored her.

Why, she was almost begging as his mouth took her more fervently. Why did he have to take all of her? Why did he have to show her how good things could be? She was coming and fighting it; she was loving it and scared of it, scared of loving him.

Juan held her in his mouth and he just about came himself as he felt her throb and finally still.

'Cate.' He said her name as he slid up her body. He did not allow her time to calm; he had taken her rapidly once and she sobbed now as he took her slowly. It was torture to be locked with him, to be consumed by him, to gather speed together with each building thrust.

Cate arched into him, her orgasm a race down her spine and along her thighs. The powerful thrusts of him had her dizzy, the feel of his final swell that beckoned his end was like a tattoo being etched in her mind. And then he collapsed on top of her; incoherent thoughts were voiced. It was a moment she would never forget.

'We could have had three months!' Breathless, Juan berated the time lost to them.

Breathless, Cate thanked God she had waited, because she couldn't have given him months of this with the end looming.

She was beyond confused; his bed was no place to

examine her true feelings, because she was only here for one night, except both knew they had just gone too far.

They both lay, pretending to be asleep, until finally they were—but it was an uneasy sleep, a difficult sleep. Cate didn't want to get too close to the man who lay beside her and Juan, with a mind that raced through the dark hours, chose not to hold onto her throughout the night.

Juan woke at two.

He always did.

He moved his legs, just a little, he moved his hands and then remembered Cate's hands on his neck and the look they had shared. He wondered if she might guess.

Asleep, she rolled into him and after a moment he put his arm around her; the luxury of that she could not know. He allowed himself the bliss of contact as he faced tomorrow—the anniversary of the wedding that hadn't happened was the day he had dreaded the most.

He dreaded another day now, one week on Tuesday when he left Australia. It was already drawing eerily close.

CHAPTER TWELVE

'*HOLA, MAMÁ!*'

Cate lay in bed, awaiting the promised coffee, but since Juan had got up his phone had rung three times and she had listened to him chatting away in the kitchen in Spanish, sounding incredibly upbeat.

Cate felt anything but.

Last night had been amazing, possibly the best night she had ever had, except she had got too close, had given away too much. Not just with words; last night had been way more intimate than she had intended.

Perhaps more intimate than Juan had intended too, for he didn't quite meet her eyes when he walked into the bedroom and waited while she sat up in bed and then handed her a mug. 'Sorry that the coffee took so long.'

'Is it your birthday?'

'No,' Juan answered. 'Why?'

'All the calls?'

'Just family.'

He wasn't so upbeat now; if anything, things between them were back to being a touch awkward.

'What time are you working?' Juan asked.

'Twelve,' Cate said, glancing at the clock. 'What about you?'

'I have the rest of the week off till Friday. I have to move out of here on Tuesday.'

'Where will you go?'

'I am staying with a couple of nurses I met, travelling, who work at the Children's Hospital.'

Nurse Purple Face, Cate thought. This was big-girl's-pants time: it was time to hide the truth and lie; it was time to smile and pretend it had been good while it lasted.

Good didn't even come close.

Cate gulped down her coffee and then climbed out of bed. 'Well, I'm going to head home.' She started to pull on her clothes.

'Have a shower,' Juan offered. 'I'll find a towel...'

'I'll get one at home.' She didn't want a beach towel or a Juan towel wrestled from a backpack. She wanted a cupboard with towels in it and a home that wasn't about to be abandoned without a backward glance a couple of days from now.

Even if the views were to die for.

Even if it had been fun.

'I'll see you.' He gave her a kiss and she returned it briefly, because it was very hard to not ask when, not to know if this was the last time.

'Cate...' He walked her to her car. 'I'll call you.'

'Sure.'

His phone was ringing again and she gave a cheery wave and drove off, her hands so tight around the steering-wheel that she turned the wipers on instead of the indicators as she turned into her street. She ignored the horn and the abuse from a driver behind.

She waved to Bridgette as she climbed out of her car.

'What time do you call this?' Bridgette joked, and

Cate gave another wave and bright smile but it died the moment the door closed.

Pull yourself together, Cate, she told herself.

She'd done it.

Slept with him.

Succumbed to him.

Now she just had to work out how to put together the pieces of her heart…

'Are you even listening?' Kelly asked as they sat in the staffroom, waiting for their shift to commence.

'Sorry?' Cate said. 'I was miles away.'

'It must be hell for those firefighters,' Kelly said, pointing to the news. 'Imagine having to wear all that gear in this heat and be near the fires.'

Cate couldn't imagine it. The fires were inching closer. It took up half the news at night and everyone was just holding their breath for a change to cooler weather to arrive, but there was still no sign of it.

They headed around to work and, though it would be tempting to hide in the office she still hadn't got around to sorting out, there were, of course, a whole heap of problems to be dealt with.

'I'm not happy to send him home, Cate,' Sheldon said.

There was a child, Timothy, who Sheldon had referred to the paediatricians. They had discharged the boy but Sheldon wasn't happy and wanted a second opinion.

Cate agreed with him, except Dr Vermont had called in sick.

Again.

Which meant there was no senior doctor to call in.

'What about Harry?' Sheldon said, but Cate shook her head.

'Harry needs this weekend,' Cate said. 'Unless there's a serious emergency, we should try not to call him. I've let him know that Dr Vermont is sick but...'

'What about Juan?' Sheldon suggested. 'He's senior.'

She could *not* face calling him, so instead she asked Frances on Reception to ring and ask if he could come in.

'He's not available today.' Frances came off the phone and then smiled as Jane, a new ward clerk, came over. 'I've got a job for you,' Frances said. 'Start from here and work your way down and see if you can get any of these doctors to cover from now until ten p.m. I've already tried the names that are ticked.'

Cate stood there as Timothy's screams filled the department and his anxious mum came racing out.

'Do you really think he should be going home?' she demanded.

'We're just waiting for someone to come and take another look at Timothy,' Cate said. 'Kelly, can you go and run another set of observations on him...' Cate let out a breath then turned to Sheldon. 'I'll ring Harry.'

Harry sighed into the phone when Cate called him and they briefly discussed Dr Vermont. 'He's never taken a day off until recently for as long as I've known him,' Harry said. 'Did he say what was wrong?'

'No,' Cate admitted. 'And I didn't really feel that it was my place to ask. I just said I hoped he got well soon and I would arrange cover.' She gave a wry laugh. 'Which is proving easier said than done on a Sunday afternoon. Sheldon is concerned about a two-year-old who's really not right. They've diagnosed an irritable hip and the paediatricians have discharged him...'

'Do you want me to come and have a look at him?'

'I want you to finally have a weekend off, without being called in.'

'Well, that's not going to happen for a while.' Harry let out another long sigh. 'Have you tried Juan?'

It was a compliment indeed that Harry was thinking of asking Juan to cover for the rest of the weekend because, despite his impressive qualifications, Juan only covered as a locum resident.

'We tried,' Cate said. 'He can't.'

'Okay, I'll be there in ten minutes but I'll have to bring in the children.'

'That's fine,' Cate said. 'I've got Tanya sitting in the obs ward, watching one elderly patient, I'm sure she won't mind.'

Juan ended the call with Frances.

He had thought for a moment about accepting the shift at Bayside but he knew that he might not be the best company today.

Martina would be ringing him soon, pleading with him to give them another go. She would say that she had just panicked, that in time, of course, she would have come around to his injuries.

Juan turned off his phone, not trusting Martina not to use a different number just so that he wouldn't recognise it and pick up.

He would go for a drive, Juan decided. For the most part, while in Australia, he had enjoyed not driving, but now and then he hired a car. It was just so that he could explore, but today he wanted to do something different.

Juan hired a motorbike—it was his main mode of transport back home.

Or once had been.

Juan felt the machine between his legs and guided it up the hills, felt the warm breeze whipping his face and arms, and he relished it.

The view was amazing; to the left was the bay, and ahead he could see the smoke plumes far in the distance where bush fires were still raging, swallowing hectares of land but thankfully no homes.

He had enjoyed travelling around Australia—it was an amazing and diverse country and it had been everything he needed. It had been the last few weeks that had made him feel unsettled, wondering if it was time to think of returning home.

He swallowed down a mouthful of sparkling water, thought about New Zealand and Asia, and was suddenly weary at the thought of new adventure. He just couldn't get excited at the prospect of starting over again, and finally he knew he had to acknowledge the day.

His family had been ringing all morning, trying to see how he was coping, whether or not he was feeling okay.

Juan really didn't know how he was feeling.

He sat there, staring into the distance, trying to picture how his life might have been had the accident not happened. He and Martina would have been married for a year now—perhaps there would have been a baby on the way by now.

Juan asked himself if he would have been happy.

Yes.

Then he asked himself if he was happy now.

There was no neat answer.

Juan dragged his hands through his hair and his fingers moved to the back of his neck. For a moment he felt the thick scar and recalled pulling Cate's hand away from it.

He hated anyone knowing.

Not just about the accident but about what had happened afterwards.

Still, eighteen months on, he could not quite get his head around the moment when everything had fallen apart—and it hadn't been the moment of impact.

Juan closed his eyes, remembered when he had looked up into the eyes of the woman he was due, in six months' time, to marry. He had realised then that it was not a limitless love.

Juan didn't want to dwell on it, he hated the pensiveness that swirled like a murky haze, that billowed in his gut like the plumes of smoke in the distance.

He should be enjoying himself, Juan told himself, heading back to his bike. He should be getting on with life, living as he had promised to on those dark, lonely nights when his future had been so uncertain. He should not be thinking about some imagined past that had never happened, a marriage that hadn't taken place. He should be embracing the future, living for this very minute, not dwelling on a wedding that had been cancelled and a future that had never existed.

He was happy being free, Juan told himself, and he intended to remain that way. He climbed back on his bike and started the engine, ready to move on with his life—as he had said to Cate last night, nothing lasted for ever. It was about enjoying what you had now—and Juan was determined to do that.

He *was* happy.

Juan rode the bike up the hill, along the curved roads, hugging the bends and telling himself he loved the freedom, loved the thought of a world that was waiting for him to explore it.

A small animal burst out of the bushes and his mind told him not to swerve, but instinct won.

The bike skidded and he tried to right it but failed. But he was skilled on a motorcycle and he was not going fast, so he controlled the landing. He felt the bitumen burn along his shoulder as he and the bike skidded into the bush, regretting that he had ridden without leathers.

Great.

He lay there a moment, getting his breath back, winded, a bit sore. His ego was a touch bruised, especially when Juan heard a voice and the sound of someone running towards him.

'Stay still!' He heard the urgent command. 'It's very important that you stay still.'

'I'm fine,' Juan called back, and moved to sit up, to get the bike off that was pinning him down.

'You *have* to stay still.' A man was looking down at him. 'I'm a first-aider.'

Brilliant.

'My wife's calling an ambulance.'

Better still!

'I'm fine, really,' Juan said through gritted teeth. 'If you could just help me move the bike.'

'Just lie still.'

'I know what I'm saying—I'm an anaesthetist,' Juan said. 'I work in Emergency...'

'They say that doctors make the worst patients.' Still he smiled down. 'I'm Ken.'

Trust his luck to get an over-eager Boy Scout come

across him. Juan lay there as Ken's wife came over, telling them that the ambulance was on the way.

'Hold his head, darling,' Ken said. 'I'll lift the bike.'

'What about the helmet?' She looked down at Juan. 'I'm Olive, by the way.'

'Don't try and remove it,' Ken warned. 'Leave that for the paramedics.'

His day could not get any better, Juan thought, lying there. Of course he could shrug them off, get up and stand, but they were just trying to help. He *should* be grateful, Juan told himself. Technically they were doing everything right, except, apart from a grazed shoulder, there was not a thing wrong with him.

He *was* grateful.

Juan looked up at Olive and remembered the last time he'd had an accident. He had been lying on his side, begging bystanders not to touch him, not to roll him, not to move him.

It's *not* like last time.

Over and over he told that to himself and held onto the scream that was building.

He'd explain things to the paramedics, Juan decided, closing his eyes and hearing the faint wail of a siren far in the distance. He tried to calm himself, but there was an unease building as he thought of the paramedics' response when he told them about his previous injuries. An appalling thought occurred when he tried to work out his location and the nearest hospital.

He did not want Cate to know.

Juan did not want his past impinging on the little time they'd had, yet he could hear the paramedics making their way over to him and knew that it was about to.

'Juan!' Louise smiled down at him, shone a torch in his eyes as she spoke to him. 'What happened to you?'

He told her. 'It was a simple accident. I have only grazed my shoulder. I'm not going to hospital.'

'Let's just take a look at you, Juan.' Louise was calm. 'Were you knocked out?'

'No.'

'How did you land?'

'On my shoulder.'

Her hands were feeling around his neck. 'Do you have any pain in your neck?'

'None.' He felt her fingers still on the scar and then gently explore it.

'Is there any past history that we need to know about, Juan?'

He stared up at the sky at the tops of the trees and he absolutely did not want to reveal anything, except only a fool would lie now.

'I had a spinal injury.'

'Okay.' Louise waited for more information.

'Eighteen months ago.'

He just stared up at the trees as the routine accident suddenly turned serious. 'I'm fine, Louise.' He went to sit up but hands were holding his head.

'Just stay still, Juan.'

'My neck is stable, better than before…'

'What injury did you have?'

'I had an incomplete fracture to C5 and C6.'

He lay there as they carefully removed the helmet and he was placed in a hard collar, and the spinal board was brought from the ambulance.

'I don't want to go to Bayside,' Juan said as they lifted him in.

'I'm sorry, Juan. We need to take you to the near-est Emergency.'

'Nothing is wrong.'

'We have to take all precautions. You know that.' Louise cared only for the health of her patients and pulled out the words that were needed. 'I'm following protocol.'

He couldn't argue with that.

The best that he could hope for was that Cate might be on her break, that he could somehow slip in and out of the department unnoticed by her. She might even be holed up in her office.

Except she wasn't Christine.

She wasn't like anyone.

Cate was like no one he had ever met.

Juan stared up at the ceiling of another ambulance and said it over and over again to himself.

It's not like last time.

CHAPTER THIRTEEN

CATE REGRETTED THAT she'd had to ask Harry, she truly did, but she had never been more grateful about how approachable Harry was than when he came in to examine young Timothy.

The boy was, in fairness to the paediatricians, markedly more distressed by the time Harry arrived. Harry took some bloods, called the lab and asked for the tests to be put through urgently. Then he called the orthopaedic surgeons as it began to look more and more as though the child might have septic arthritis, which was a surgical emergency and needed to be dealt with as quickly as possible.

'They're going to take him up for aspiration of the hip under sedation,' Harry explained to Cate a short while later, 'and they're getting started immediately on antibiotics.' He was just writing up his admission notes when Lillian, the director of nursing, came and asked Cate if she could have a word.

'Over here.'

Lillian gestured to a place away from the nurses' station and as they walked up to the drug fridge and out of Harry's earshot, Cate took a deep breath, because she knew what was coming next. 'Why,' Lillian asked, 'is the student nurse sitting in the observation ward, drawing pictures with Harry's children?'

'Because Dr Vermont, who was supposed to be the on-call consultant this weekend, has rung in sick. Sheldon was worried about a patient the paediatricians have discharged and luckily for us Harry came in. As it turns out, it would seem that the child has septic arthritis.'

'Then why,' Lillian persisted, 'is a student nurse, who should be getting clinical experience, acting as a childminder, instead of being out on the floor?'

'Because she was already rostered on the observation ward...' Cate was saved from having to explain herself further when she looked up and saw that Louise was signalling her to come over so that she could have a word.

'Excuse me,' Cate said. 'I'm needed.'

'We'll discuss this later.' Lillian said. 'This really can't continue.'

Cate knew it wasn't over yet, but for now she was happy to escape a lecture and walked over to Louise.

'What you got for us?' Cate asked.

'A very reluctant patient,' Louise said.

'So, what's new?'

'It's Juan,' Louise said, and Cate felt the colour drain from her face. 'He didn't want to come here but I've stuck to protocol and brought him to the closest Emergency. He seems okay...' Louise frowned at Cate's pale lips. 'He came off a motorcycle. He's got a few cuts and a nasty abrasion to his shoulder, but he's had a previous spinal injury.' Cate stood for a moment as she heard that it wasn't whiplash they were talking about, that, in fact, Juan had broken his neck and had been paralysed for a period. She could almost hear her brain clicking as things fell into place.

'Incomplete C5 and C6…' Louise said, and Cate remembered her hands being removed from his neck.

'There's a slight weakness in his left leg,' Louise continued, 'but he insists that since the accident there always has been.'

Cate recalled noticing the weight on his leg as he'd run and thought she might be sick. She really knew nothing about him, yet he had insisted on finding out about her.

'We've taken all precautions,' Louise continued. 'I said I'd come in and try to do this as discreetly as possible.'

'Okay.' Cate nodded. 'Bring him in.'

If she had thought it might be hard facing Juan after last night, it was going to be close to impossible now.

'It had to be you.' Juan gave a tight smile as she came over. He was staring up at the ceiling and only glanced at her briefly. There were a few scratches on his face and his shirt was torn and she could see that his teeth were gritted and that he was struggling.

'Well, they came and got the most senior nurse on.' Cate tried for practical, tried to hold onto a strange anger that was building inside her. She was about to add that if he'd asked to be dealt with by someone he hadn't slept with then he'd be lying on that stretcher for quite a while.

She tried to hold onto the shout that was building.

'I don't need to be here,' Juan said.

'Then you shan't be for long,' came her pale-lipped response.

They slid him over on a board and Cate held onto

the top of his head and then covered him with a sheet to undress him, but as she went to unbutton his shirt he asked that she not.

'I'll just do some obs, then.' Cate said, knowing how embarrassed she'd be if the roles were reversed. Not that she'd have been riding a motorbike through the hills with a previously broken neck.

Neither would she have been white-water rafting.

Or considering hitting the ski season in New Zealand or, next Sunday, diving out of a plane.

Her hands were actually shaking as she did his routine obs and then a set of neurological.

Juan answered her questions. Yes, he knew where he was and what day it was.

As if he could ever forget.

Yes, he could squeeze both of her hands tightly.

'Just get the doctor in to see me,' Juan said as she lifted the sheet to see two black boots.

'Lift your leg against my hand.' He did with the right.

'And the left.'

There was perhaps a slight weakness. Cate wasn't sure she would even have noticed had Louise not pointed it out.

'That leg has some residual weakness from my previous accident,' Juan said.

'I'll just take your boots off.'

'Please, don't.'

'It's fine.' Harry swept in and picked up on the tension. 'Juan, how are you?'

'I've been worse,' came Juan's wry response.

'So I hear.'

'I thought Dr Vermont was on this weekend,' Juan said to Harry.

'So did I, but I'm afraid you're just going to have to make do with me.' Harry was brisk and efficient as he started his examination. 'Okay, Juan, you know the drill.'

He went through today's accident with him, which Juan could remember clearly. 'A small animal came out of the bushes, I swerved...'

'And your past medical history?'

'Can we just...?' Juan closed his eyes in impatience. Cate thought he was about to ask for the collar to come off, or to say that it was all unnecessary again; instead she raised her eyes slightly at what he said next. 'Can you leave, please, Cate?'

Two spots of colour burnt on her cheeks as Harry turned round and smiled. 'We'll manage, Cate.'

Had it been a door and not a curtain, Cate might have slammed it as she walked out. She simply didn't know why—she was not upset, she was angry.

Harry went round with him for the CT and Cate tried not to let his dismissal of her sting.

She tried her best to not give a sarcastic response when Harry came to speak with her some time later. 'All the tests look good and Juan's neck's fine. I've had the orthopods take a look at the images. He's got a lot of titanium in there! He needs a dressing to his shoulder—'

'I'll get someone to do it.'

'Cate...' Harry sighed. They had worked together for a long time and he knew her well, though he hadn't guessed until now that there was anything going on between them—Juan was for too depraved for Cate, or so Harry had thought! 'Juan didn't ask you to leave because he didn't want you looking after him.' He shook his head and tried to explain. 'He's a proud guy,

Cate. He's been through a lot...' Harry let out a breath through his teeth. 'I told Juan that you'd be in to do his shoulder and he's fine with that. I want him in the obs ward for a few hours, he's a little bit tender over his left kidney but it all looks fine. I want his urine tested and to be sure he's okay before I discharge him, because there's no one at home. Hourly obs, and I'll come in this evening again to see him.'

'Thanks Harry.' Cate attempted to snap back to normal. 'I really am sorry to rot up your weekend.'

'It's not a problem,' Harry said. 'It just makes me more determined that we hire the right staff. This place is running on empty...'

Harry headed off with the twins and Cate buzzed Tanya to tell her that they would have a new admission in the observation ward soon; then she prepared a trolley to sort out Juan's shoulder. She could feel tears pricking at the back of her eyes as she set up but she swallowed them down before making her way in.

Someone, perhaps Harry, had helped him into a gown and his clothes and boots lay in a heap beneath the trolley next to his crash helmet. His cervical collar had been taken off.

'Harry wants your shoulder cleaned and dressed and I need to look at the scratches on your face. Would you like someone else to come in and do that?' Cate checked.

'Why would I want someone else?' Juan asked, although Cate could tell he was just as tense with the situation as she was.

'I just thought you might.'

'Just do what you have to.'

Cate sorted out his face first, cleaning a few superficial abrasions and cuts and closing them up with couple of paper strips. They didn't speak much; Juan was more than used to staring up at a hospital ceiling in silence.

'I need you to roll on your side,' Cate said when she had finished sorting out his face.

'For what?'

'So that I can pick the road out of your shoulder.'

The gown was far too small for him and hadn't been tied up at the back. The abrasion was large and it would take a while to clean it up. Cate moved his hair out of the way and could clearly see the thick scar that ran the length of his neck and the clips scars either side—the reason why he had always halted her hands.

'This might sting a bit,' Cate said as she squirted a generous amount of local anaesthetic onto Juan's shoulder. She knew it must sting but he didn't wince. While she waited for it to take effect, Cate took a moment to get some more equipment for her trolley so that she wouldn't need to keep going in and out—they both wanted this over and done with.

Silence dragged on as Cate cleaned his shoulder. Thankfully he was on his side, facing away from her. It was already hard enough without looking at each other—it was going to take a long time to do it properly, and Cate would have loved to take the opportunity to hide in an office.

She knew the severity of his previous injury and she could not believe that someone who'd been given another chance at life could take it so lightly.

It was Juan who broke the silence. 'Cate, could I just explain—?'

'The same as you, Juan,' Cate said through tight lips, 'I really don't want to talk about it.'

'Cate, the reason I didn't mention it is that I don't want to be reminded every five minutes about it. I don't like talking about it.'

'That's fine.'

'Am I supposed to have given you a full medical history before I asked you to dinner?'

Cate was saved from answering when Kelly came in behind the curtain. 'We've got someone on the phone enquiring after you, Juan.'

'We've been through this,' Juan said. 'Just say that you're not sure if I'm on duty and take a message.'

'The call actually got put through to Reception.' Kelly grimaced, not that Juan could see it. 'Jane's new, she's the receptionist on duty and she didn't realise that you worked here. She thought it was your girlfriend enquiring as to how you were after the accident. It's Martina...'

'What did she say to her?' There was an ominous note to Juan's voice.

'That you were in X-Ray and she told her to call back in half an hour or so. She has just—'

The expletive that came from Juan's lips was in Spanish and possibly merited.

'She's a bit upset,' Kelly elaborated. 'I've tried to reassure her but she isn't listening to me, so I brought the phone down. I thought if you perhaps could speak to her, she would realise that you really are okay.' Kelly handed him the phone and, still on his side, Juan took it.

'I'll leave you to speak to her in private,' Cate said, as it was already more than awkward. 'I'll come and finish doing your shoulder afterwards.'

Cate turned to go but as she reached the curtain Juan

called out to her. 'Cate, would you mind speaking with her, please.'

'Juan…' She could not stand to speak Martina, given she had been in Juan's bed last night—except that wasn't relevant here. Juan was a patient.

'She is my ex-fiancée,' Juan said. 'Someone I specifically asked your staff not to give any information to.' And then he lost the warning note from his voice. 'Cate, I really don't need this today, of all days.'

'Sure.' Cate took the phone, doing her best to simply treat him as a patient. 'What would you like me to say to her?'

'Just say as little as possible. Tell her that it was a minor accident and that I'm fine.'

Cate took the phone and introduced herself.

'I would like to speak with Juan Morales.'

'I'm afraid that's not possible. Can I help you with anything?'

'I want to know what is happening. I'm in Argentina. Have you any idea how stressful this is to not be able to speak with him?'

'Juan had a small accident this afternoon. He's got some abrasions, which are being dressed at the moment. Apart from that, he's fine and will be going home later today.'

'How did it happen?'

'I'm sorry,' Cate answered. 'I can't give out that sort of information without Juan's permission.'

'He does this!' She could hear Martina's mounting exasperation. 'He wants to pretend he has not had an accident. He's going to kill himself one of these days; he just pushes everyone who loves him away. I don't know what he is trying to prove. Today would have been our first wedding anniversary and instead he's lying in hospital…'

'Give me the phone.' She didn't know if Juan had heard what Martina had said but she handed him the phone and Juan spoke in short, terse sentences, before ringing off.

The silence was deafening as Cate resumed cleaning his shoulder.

'She seems to think that because we were once engaged—'

'Juan.' Cate was struggling to keep her voice even, could scarcely believe the information she had just heard, understood now why his family had all been ringing him. 'You don't owe me any explanation. I don't blame Martina for being concerned. If I cared about you, I'd be concerned too.'

'Ouch,' Juan said as her tweezers picked out a particularly deeply imbedded stone, and Cate even managed a wry smile—she had no idea if he was referring to her words or the sudden pain in his shoulder.

She had no idea about Juan at all.

But wasn't that the whole point of a one-night stand or a brief fling? It was why she simply wasn't any good at them.

She carried on pulling out some of the deepest stones. He tensed a few times but said nothing and Cate got on with her work, trying not to look at the scratches on his back.

The ones that were courtesy of her.

Kelly noticed them, though.

She came in to get the phone and to ask Cate to cast her eyes over an IV flask—a simple procedure, but because the solution contained potassium it needed to be checked by two nurses. Cate nodded that all was fine.

'Your poor back, Juan,' Kelly said, eyeing the scratches and giving Cate a wink as she walked out.

'It shouldn't be too much longer,' Cate said. 'And then we'll get you round to the observation ward.'

'I don't need to be observed.'

'Harry thinks you do. If you choose not to follow instructions I'll get the necessary paperwork...'

'I'm not stupid enough to discharge myself.' He turned, just a little but enough to nearly send the sterile paper sheet flying. 'Cate, I didn't tell you because I don't need your sympathy.'

'Oh, believe me, there's no sympathy coming from behind you, Juan.'

'You're upset.'

'No. I'm not upset.'

'I can hear your voice shaking.'

'I am so not upset, Juan.' She shook her head. This wasn't the place but, what the hell, she told him her truth. 'I'm angry.'

'Angry?' This time he turned enough to knock off the sheet completely and looked into her eyes and, yes, she was angry all right. 'Angry, about what?

'It doesn't matter. I'm going to get Kelly to come in and finish off your shoulder.'

'Why?'

'Because you're a patient and it doesn't look good for a nurse to be shouting.'

'Don't worry about that—I'm fine with the conversation.'

'Well, I've got work to do.'

'I don't understand what you're angry about.'

'Your carelessness,' Cate answered. 'Your lack of limits...'

'You know what, Cate?' Juan was surly and in no mood to sweeten things. It had been one hell of a day after all. 'I don't think you're actually angry at me. I think you're more cross at your own...' He couldn't think of the word he wanted so hers would have to do. 'Limits.'

'I'm going to get Kelly.'

'Fine,' Juan said. 'Go and count your stock.'

It was lucky for Juan she had already put the tweezers down!

She asked Kelly to come in and take over and then walked to what would soon be her office. She took a long, calming breath and tried to remember what she'd been doing before she'd been called away for the problems with Dr Vermont.

Stock orders.

Cate drew in a less than cleansing breath.

And there were outstanding complaints and incident reports to be dealt with too. Despite promising to complete them, Christine had left them unfinished.

Damn you, Juan, Cate thought.

At least she knew where she was going; at least she knew what was happening from week to week—at least she wasn't ricocheting around the world with a handful of titanium in her neck.

She *was* hiding in her office, though.

But at seven p.m., when Tanya hadn't had her break, Cate had to go in and relieve her. Thankfully, Juan was asleep.

'His observations are all stable,' Tanya said. 'Harry

just stopped by and is happy for him to be discharged in an hour or so. Or, if Juan prefers, he can stay overnight.'

'I'm sure he won't want to.'

Tanya also told her about the elderly lady. 'She's waiting for a bed on the geriatric unit and one might be coming up soon. I've just done observations and they're all fine. She's very deaf and she refuses to wear her hearing aid but she knows exactly where she is and what is happening.'

'Thanks.' Cate smiled. 'Go and have a break and I'll keep an eye on them both.'

Cate was glad that Juan was asleep as she took a seat and saw that his obs had only just been done. Determinedly, she didn't read his notes. She didn't want to know about his past and she really wasn't in the mood for conversation. The director of nursing was, though.

'Where's Harry?' Lillian asked as she walked through the observation ward.

'He's at home.'

'He's still on call, though?'

'Yes.'

'Cate, something has to be done,' Lillian said. 'What if he gets called in tonight?'

'I believe he's making arrangements, although the consultants' childcare plans are not a nursing concern.' Cate did her best to terminate the conversation but Lillian was having none of it.

'It becomes a nursing concern when it's the nurses who end up watching the said consultant's children. Cate, you're the acting nurse unit manager.'

'As of tomorrow.'

Juan's eyes snapped open as he heard Cate's tart response. He hadn't been asleep for a moment, but since his time on the spinal unit he was exceptionally good at pretending that he was.

'Well, as of tomorrow, Cate, it will be up to you to ensure it doesn't happen.'

'That what doesn't happen, Lillian? That we don't ask Harry to come in when we're without a consultant or concerned about a patient? Is that what you want?' Cate looked her boss in the eye. 'I happen to be very grateful that the nursing staff have a consultant who, despite personal problems, is prepared to come in at short notice when he's not even rostered on. I'm very grateful to have a consultant who will accept a worried phone call from a member of the nursing staff and get in his car and come straight in.'

'It can't continue.'

'I'm sure Harry is more than aware that the situation is far from ideal.'

Juan lay there and listened as the director of nursing pointed out some health and safety issues. He listened as the nurse who had admitted she liked working in Emergency because of the back-up she received from her colleagues backed up a member of her own team one hundred per cent.

'What if one of the nurses can't get a babysitter?' Lillian challenged. 'We can't run a crèche in the staffroom!'

'I'll cross that bridge when I come to it.'

'Not good enough, Cate.'

'No, it's not,' Cate responded. 'And it's a poor comparison. If a nurse can't come in I can ring the hospital bank to have them cover a shift or I can ask for a nurse to be sent from the wards. We have ten nurses on duty at any one time, but there aren't very many emergency consultants to call on at short notice.'

He heard the director of nursing walk off and he heard a few choice words being muttered under Cate's breath and he couldn't help but smile, but it faded as Cate took a phone call and then came over.

'Are you awake?'

Juan turned over and looked at her. 'I am now.'

'How are you feeling?'

He gave a wry laugh.

'I just took a phone call from a Ken Davidson,' Cate told him. 'Apparently he helped you today. He said he waited until your bike was picked up.'

'Did you get his number?' Juan asked, relieved that the call hadn't been from Martina. 'I need to thank him.'

'I did,' Cate said. 'He's also got your wallet.'

'Thanks.' Juan said. 'And I'm sorry for what I said before about you getting back to your stock. You do a great job—I guess I was just spreading the misery.'

Cate gave a small nod of acceptance. 'Harry's happy for you to go when you're ready or you can stay the night.'

'I'll go home, thanks.'

'Do you want a lift when I finish?'

'Do you always offer patients a lift home?' Juan asked.

'I would offer any colleague a lift home in the circumstances.'

'Then that'd be great.'

It was either that or ask to borrow fifty dollars for a taxi.

For Juan, it was Indignity City today.

Juan borrowed a pair of scrubs and she watched him try not to wince as he bent down to pull on his boots.

He carried a bag containing his clothes and crash helmet and they walked, pretty much in silence, to her car.

It wasn't how it was supposed to have been, Juan thought. He loathed all his secrets being out, but now they were and, as he had expected, she was acting differently with him.

'Watch the speed bumps,' Juan said as she drove him home slowly. 'I might jolt my neck and suddenly have no feeling from the chest down.'

'You don't need to be sarcastic.'

'You're driving as if you have a Ming vase rolling around on the back seat,' he pointed out.

'I'm a careful driver,' Cate said, about to add, *unlike some of us*, but Juan turned and saw Cate press her lips firmly closed.

'I should have just run it over,' Juan said. 'I should have killed the baby koala bear.'

'It wasn't a koala,' Cate said, and she almost smiled. *Almost*. But Juan knew she thought he shouldn't have been out motorcycling in the first place.

'So, I am supposed to walk slowly, not run, not climb, not surf or ski…' He looked over at her. 'Athletes go back and compete after the injury I sustained. I am not doing anything my doctor does not know about. I walk everywhere, I run most days. I take my health seriously.'

'I get it.' Cate gripped the wheel.

'I don't think you do.'

'I get it, okay?' There were tears in her eyes as she realised he was right, and yet her fear had been real. 'I just got a fright when I heard how seriously injured you had been.'

He looked at her tense profile.

'Fair enough,' Juan conceded. 'Do you know how my

accident happened?' Cate said nothing. 'I was going to get a haircut...' He gave a wry laugh as Cate drove on. 'It was embarrassing really on the spinal unit. There were guys who had been diving, playing sport, car accidents—I had been walking to get a haircut. A car driven by an elderly woman mounted the kerb and really only clipped me, but the way I fell...' He let out a long, exasperated sigh. 'It was bad luck, chance, whatever you want to call it.'

'So now you take risks?'

'Yes, because I never did before and look where it got me, lying on my back paralysed from the neck down. Now I live, now I do as I please...'

'It's all just a game to you, isn't it?'

'It's no game,' Juan said. 'I have ridden a bike for years, it is how I get around back home. I'm not on some daredevil mission. I'm living my life, that's all.'

'Well, your fiancée is beside herself.'

'Ex.'

'Because you're too bloody proud and have too much to prove.'

'You don't know me.' His grey eyes flashed back; it was the closest Juan had come to a row in a very long time. It was the closest he had come to anyone in a long time and that was what he had been trying to avoid, Juan reminded himself as they pulled up at his apartment and he climbed out.

'I know that today would have been your first wedding anniversary,' Cate called to his departing back, and watched as he turned slowly.

'It would have been, except Martina decided she didn't want to marry a man in a wheelchair.'

Cate sat there, her knuckles white as she clutched

the wheel. Of all the things he might have told her, that was the last she had been expecting.

'Juan!'

She went to step out of the car.

'Please, don't.' Juan put his hand up. 'Thank you for the lift.'

'Juan,' Cate said. 'I didn't know.'

'Because I didn't want you to know.'

'I don't want to just leave you—'

'Why?' His eyes flashed. 'I want to be on my own. I don't want a heart to heart, I don't want to sit and talk, I don't want company.'

Cate bit her lip as he threw out his final line.

'I never wanted you to know. I never wanted any more than what we had.'

She watched his departing back and, yes, she should leave it there, except she couldn't. If Juan didn't want kid gloves because of his injury, or because of the phantom anniversary, then he wouldn't get them from her, she decided as she opened the car window.

'Why didn't you just leave it at sex, then?' She watched his back stiffen but he didn't turn round. 'It was supposed to be sex and dinner, Juan, but, oh, no, you had to delve deeper. You had to take it that step further and ask about me and my past and future. So much for living in the now!'

She didn't wait for his response. She knew she wasn't going to get one; instead, she drove off as Juan let himself into his home.

His temporary home.

What had they had? Cate asked herself.

A whirlwind romance?

Holiday fling?

A rebound after Paul?

Not one of them fitted.

They didn't fit for Juan either. He turned on his phone and saw the many missed calls. He looked around the empty apartment and told himself it was time to move on. The day he had dreaded was almost over, yet, instead of dwelling on the woman he should have married a year ago today, it was Cate who consumed his thoughts.

She was right—it had been more.

CHAPTER FOURTEEN

CATE HAD MORE than enough to keep her occupied.

Or she should have had.

Yet, despite working as Acting Nurse Unit Manager, despite telling herself over and over that Juan was not her concern, she could not stop thinking about him.

Through the week she attended meeting upon meeting, caught up with the backlog Christine had left and sorted out her new office. She was determined to make a stand and, even though there were so many other things that she should be doing, she put in mandatory appearances on the floor, though sometimes she wished that she hadn't. It felt different without Juan—even the knowledge that he might possibly be called into work, that she might see him again, had meant more than Cate had, until now, understood.

That was why she didn't do one-night stands, Cate told herself as she walked back from yet another meeting.

Then she felt her heart squeeze when she glimpsed him entering the department.

He had to save the best until last.

He was wearing black jeans and his boots but the silver buckle on his belt was larger than usual and the white, low-necked T-shirt he was wearing was too tight and showed his magnificent physique along with a generous flash of chest hair as well as his nipples. He hadn't shaved since she'd last seen him. He looked like a bandit, or an outlawed cowboy, Cate thought, waiting until he went into the department and then walking along behind him, almost willing him not to turn round.

'Juan!' Of course he was pounced on and Cate walked on quickly, rather hoping he had not seen her—his final words to her were still ringing in her ears and she wasn't quite sure she could pull off a farewell without tears invading.

Cate headed to her office and as she closed the door she let out a sigh. She'd left it neat but already her inbox was full again and there was a list of messages to attend to. Gritting her teeth, she went to take off her jacket but was interrupted by a knock on the door—she knew it was him.

'Nice jacket,' Juan said.

Cate loathed it.

She was to wear it to meetings, she'd been told, and it was an authoritative touch, apparently, if she was called on to attend to upset patients or relatives.

'How's it going?'

'I'll tell you when I find out.' Cate gave a terse smile. 'So far all I seem to do is sit in meetings.'

'Is that where you've just been?'

Cate nodded. 'I've just been to the nurse unit managers' meeting and after lunch it's the acute nurse unit managers' meeting!' She rolled her eyes. 'I didn't know that you were working.'

'I'm not,' Juan said. 'I had to come in and sort out the health insurance forms from my accident. It was easier to do it in person.'

There was a knock at the door, which was already half-open, and Harry popped his head in. 'Cate, I was just wondering if you could...' Harry's voice trailed off. 'Juan, I didn't know that you were on.'

'I'm not,' Juan said. 'I wanted to come in and say goodbye and I also wanted to apologise if I was a bit difficult on Sunday. I do appreciate all the care that was taken.'

'We do tend to panic a little bit when it comes to spinal injuries.'

'With reason,' Juan said. 'I was very lucky to recover so well—I know that is often not the case. I was also hoping to have a word with you before I go.'

'Of course,' Harry said. 'But you'll have to make it quick, I've got an interview in fifteen minutes.' He looked at Cate. 'I'm interviewing right through till six. If I run over, is there any chance that you could pick up the twins and watch them for five minutes?'

'I finish at five, Harry,' Cate said, and Juan watched her cheeks glow red as she attempted to say no to Harry and then gave in. 'Though I doubt I'll get away on time...' Cate gave a small flustered nod. 'Sure, don't worry about it. I'll collect the twins if you're running behind.'

Harry gave a grateful smile and, as he left, Juan told him that he would be there in a moment.

'So, this is the new assertive Cate?' Juan smiled.

'I can be assertive when it's required.'

'I know that,' Juan said, recalling how Cate had stood up to the director of nursing on Harry's behalf.

'I could make a stand today and tell him that I won't pick up the twins,' Cate said, 'but the fact is this place needs new consultants more than it needs me to get away on time, and if watching Harry's children for fifteen minutes facilitates that…'

'I lied,' Juan interrupted Cate, to tell her the real reason that he was there. 'It would have been just as easy to deal with the health insurance forms online.' He looked into her serious eyes and loathed having hurt her. 'I hated how we ended things the other day,' Juan admitted. 'It was supposed to be fun, it was supposed to be…' He didn't know how best to explain it. 'It wasn't supposed to end like that.'

She gave a watery smile. 'I know Sunday was a difficult day for you.'

'That was the reason I chose to take myself far away,' Juan explained. 'The last place I thought I'd be was in Emergency, being looked after by you. I overreacted.'

'I can understand why.' Cate gave a smile. 'How's the house-sharing?'

Juan rolled his eyes. 'Awful,' he admitted. 'I think I am maybe too old to share, they are getting on my nerves.' He didn't tell her Nurse Purple Face was sulking from his lack of advances, or how he had stayed in for two nights in a row for the first time since his arrival in Australia. Neither did he tell her just how much he wanted to see her again, so they could end things better.

'Are you going to watch the skydive on Sunday?' Juan asked.

Cate shook her head and then shrugged. 'I don't know,' she admitted. 'Kelly wanted me to go along for moral support but…' She was blinking back threatening tears, could not stand the thought of saying goodbye to him in a crowd, on another wild night out. It was perhaps better here, in her office, alone with him.

'Do you want to keep in touch?' Juan offered. 'I tried to look you up on the internet...'

'I changed my privacy settings,' Cate admitted. She could not stand the thought of keeping in touch with him, of watching his life from a distance. She could not imagine keeping up the pretence of being mere friends who'd had a thing going once, however briefly. 'I think we should just leave it as it is. It was fun.'

There was nothing fun about how she was feeling but she tried to keep things light.

'I brought you a present,' Juan said.

'Bought.' Cate smiled.

'No, brought,' Juan said, and went into his bag. It was perhaps the strangest present she had ever received and one only he could give. 'I made it for you before I left the apartment. I was cleaning out the fridge...' It was a huge jar of *chimichurri* and Cate had this vision of her dividing it up into freezer bags, sustaining the memory of Juan with one tiny taste each Sunday.

'Thank you.'

'I have to go. I need to speak to Harry. I never did get around to it.'

'You're not going to discuss the children?'

'Of course I am,' Juan said. 'I told you that I would.'

'But you can't...'

'I have dealt with colleagues,' he said. 'In another life, I was quite a demanding boss.'

'I can't imagine it.'

'I know,' Juan said. 'So...' He gave her a smile and pulled her into his arms, a sort of big-brother hug that lasted about a third of a second because she just melted against him. His touch was so fierce that she was at risk

of breaking down and breaking the rules and admitting
the heartbreak he was going to cause her.

'Please, don't say, "This could be it,"' Cate said.

'I won't,' Juan said, 'because it is.'

'You could come for dinner…' She could not stand
to say goodbye like this, didn't want it to be a quick hi
and bye in her office. They may not have counted for
much but surely they counted for more than that. 'No
big deal…' She pulled back, forced a smile. 'My neighbours will probably be there, it would just be nice to
say goodbye properly.'

'It would,' Juan said, and his smile was slightly
wicked. 'You know, though, that it will end in bed?'

'I would hope so if I have to cook.'

A two-night stand was surely better than one?

She gave him her address, signed over her heart to
the certainty of more misery for the sake of tonight, but
it would be worth it one day, Cate hoped. And, despite
saying it was no big deal now, Cate, who never planned
her meals, had to suddenly plan dinner!

'Bridgette?' Cate winced a bit as she called in a favour from her neighbour and friend, because it involved
shopping and lighting a barbeque and putting dinner on.
Oh, and could she also get wine and beer…?

'Anything else?' She could tell Bridgette was smiling.

'I can't ask.'

'You want me to make your bed, don't you?'

'And maybe a little tidy?' Cate cringed.

'So long as I get to meet the man I'm cooking and
cleaning for!'

Cate hung up the phone, smiling. It was nice to have
friends you could lean on, nice to have people who you

had enough history with that you could call on at times like this—she wondered how Juan managed without them. She wondered how he functioned in a world without that team, people who stepped in for the big and the little without question. She headed out of her office and passed Harry's office, where a couple of people sat waiting outside to be interviewed. As she did so, she silently thanked Juan for the forced introspection.

Cate knew what she wanted now—to be a part of a team, to be a part of the back-up, not to be finding solutions to a problem that she didn't think was one.

Cate walked up to Admin and knocked on Lillian's office.

'Cate!' Lillian looked up. 'I was just about to email you. We've sorted out the interview times.'

'Actually, that's what I wanted to discuss.' Cate took a deep breath. 'I'm withdrawing my application.'

'Cate?'

'I'll stay on till you find someone suitable, of course. I'm going to have a think, but I might resign as Associate. I want to get back to nursing.'

'You're a good manager, Cate.'

'Maybe,' Cate said, 'but I think I'm a better nurse.' She shook her head. 'It's just not for me.'

CHAPTER FIFTEEN

PERHAPS THE BIKE accident combined with the anniversary had unsettled him more than he'd realised, Juan thought as he stepped off the train that evening and walked in the direction of Cate's house. Saying goodbye had always been easy until now—it had always been about having fun, living life and then moving on.

And he would move on, Juan told himself. So too would Cate, he thought with a wry smile as he knocked at her front door and there was no answer.

She wasn't even home.

Juan had never been stood up and wondered if maybe she had just changed her mind or, more logically, she had been caught up at work, minding Harry's kids—then he heard the sound of laughter coming from the back of the house.

'Cate?' Juan peered over the gate. She was sitting at an outdoor table, dressed in shorts and that black halterneck and looking completely relaxed, smiling and laughing with a friend as she turned to him.

'Juan?' Cate gave a wide smile. 'Were you knocking? I should have said—if I'm outside, just come through the gate.' Cate walked over and unlatched it. 'Sorry, I never thought. Everyone knows...'

Everyone who was in her life, Juan thought, handing her a bottle of wine and taking in the gorgeous fragrance of meat cooking on the barbeque.

'This is Bridgette, my neighbour,' Cate introduced them. 'She came over to borrow an egg!'

'An hour ago,' Bridgette said, unashamedly looking Juan up and down.

Juan smiled and saw the nuts and the bottle of champagne on the table and, no, Cate hadn't been nervously awaiting his arrival—her world would carry on just fine without him.

'I'll leave you to it.' Bridgette went to stand.

'Don't go on my account,' Juan said.

Bridgette didn't need to be asked twice; she sat down again as Cate went to offer Juan a drink and then realised she needed a glass.

'I can get it,' Juan said, and held up his bottle of wine. 'Shall I put this in the fridge?'

'Please.'

As he walked through to the kitchen, Bridgette's eyes widened and her mouth gaped as she looked at Cate. 'Oh, my word!' she mouthed.

'Told you.'

'I've never considered a foursome till now.' Bridgette winked, making Cate laugh out loud.

Juan could hear the laughter coming from the garden. It was the strangest feeling, stepping into Cate's home—it was just that, a home. To the right were two sofas piled high with cushions and in the centre a coffee table brimmed with magazines. There were bookshelves, which was something he hadn't seen in a while, and he would have loved to browse but he saved that for the fridge! Smiling, he opened it and saw the contents were those of a busy single woman who didn't have much time to cook.

Yes, it was a home but more than that it was *her* home.

It was almost as if Juan recognised it.

It was a lovely evening. James, Bridgette's husband, came home from work and must have heard the laughter and known about the gate too, because he came straight from the car to Cate's garden.

Juan wanted time alone with Cate, yet he wanted this as well. For, somehow, this way he knew her more.

It was nice to pause, to enjoy the end of summer.

'There's a cool change coming tonight.' Bridgette fanned herself as Cate went over and lifted the lid on the barbeque and checked dinner.

'Your skydive might be rained off.' Cate smiled at Juan.

'No, it is forecast to be fine again for the weekend,' Juan said. 'Are you sure you won't change your mind?'

'Cate, skydiving?' Bridgette laughed. 'James had to come and change the light bulb on her staircase a few weeks ago!' Bridgette drained her drink and went to stand. 'Now we really do have to go.'

'Stay,' Cate offered, as Juan took up the knife and started to carve. Her offer was more out of habit than politeness. 'There's plenty.'

'I'll leave you two…'

'It's not a romantic dinner for two.' Cate grinned, trying to keep up the pretence for just a little while longer, trying to keep things casual for just one more night.

'James has to ring his mum,' Bridgette said as James frowned. 'It's her birthday.'

'Oh, God, so it is!' James suddenly stood.

'Take some lamb if you want, save you cooking,' Cate offered.

Juan had sliced the lamb in a way Cate would never have—thin slivers instead of her usual rather messy effort, and it looked somehow elegant. Bridgette licked her lips.

'Yes, please.'

She gave them some jacket potatoes too and a plate with the mango salad Bridgette had prepared.

'It's normally Bridgette and James feeding me,' Cate explained as she loaded the plates.

'Yes, you're not exactly known for your cooking skills.' Bridgette said. And then there was the most terribly awkward bit. 'It was lovely meeting you, Juan. Next time…' And Bridgette hesitated. 'Well, it was lovely meeting you.'

'Same here,' Juan said, and gave her a kiss then shook James's hand.

'They seem really nice,' Juan said when it was just the two of them.

'They are.' Cate nodded. 'Bridgette knows when I need tissues and when I need champagne bubbles!' She met his eyes. 'I just withdrew my application for the nurse unit manager's job.'

Juan gave a wry smile. For a moment there, he had thought the tissues or bubbles had been about him. 'How come?' he asked.

'I don't want to talk about it.'

'Why?'

'Because…' She blew a breath upwards that made a strand of hair lift on her forehead. 'Because I just spent nearly an hour going over it with Bridgette and…'

'She'll still be here next week?' Juan finished for her.

Cate nodded.

'You know...' Juan smiled. 'I've got addicted to day-time soaps while I've been here. If I miss a couple of episodes I can soon catch up. I love watching it when I wake up from a night shift. I can't believe I'm not going to find out what happened to the baby...'

Cate laughed.

'And I can't believe I'm not going to know what happens with you.'

It was the closest either of them had come to admitting how hard this was.

'Well, you're not going to find me with a clipboard as the director of nursing in a couple of years,' Cate said. 'I've just shot my career in the foot.'

'If it changes anything, I did speak to Harry,' Juan said. 'Things should improve there.'

'It's not just Harry. I haven't been as happy as I should be at work for quite some time now. That's why I was thinking about being a paramedic. I've been trying to sort out what I wanted, what was wrong, and when I actually sat down and really thought about it I realised I've only been unsettled since I started climbing the ranks. I know what I love, being a nurse in Emergency, and so that's what I'm going to do.'

'Good for you.'

'I might regret that choice when I get my pay cheque,' Cate sighed. 'And I might regret it again when the new manager starts. I think they're going to be pretty rigorous about who they choose.' She gave a shrug. 'Not my problem any more.'

It was such a bitter-sweet night.

Never had she laughed so much as he tried to teach her to tango and never had he relished more the sensual movement, the feel of a woman in his arms, the touch of another person and the ability to simply move.

To climb the stairs and see for the first time her bedroom. To have fingers that moved and could untie the knot of her halterneck—he took not a second of it for granted.

'I am going to leave you money by the bed.' Juan smiled as he undressed her. 'Not for the sex but for a new top…'

He made her laugh. 'It's my Juan top, the rest are…' Paul's name did not belong in this room any more, the only name that would be uttered here was Juan's.

She felt his mouth on her shoulder.

'You are over him?' Juan checked, and then made slow love to her.

Yes, she was over Paul, so much more than he knew.

Now she just had to get over Juan.

'The reason I didn't just leave it at sex…' Juan spoke to the darkness as they both tried to sleep later, answering the bitter questions she had hurled that night '…is because I care about you and what happens. If things were—'

'Please, don't,' Cate interrupted. 'I don't want to hear that if things were different we might have made it. I don't want to think how it might have been if we'd had more time, because…' It was as simple as that—his visa ran out next week. 'We don't.'

CHAPTER SIXTEEN

JUAN WOKE AT TWO.

He was on his back, Cate curled up in a ball by his side. He could hear the rumble of thunder in the distance and, as always, he moved his hands and then his feet...

Just to check.

He wondered if it would disturb Cate if he went downstairs and made a drink, perhaps put on the television. He didn't even have a book with him to read.

'What was it like?'

Her question filled the darkness; he was glad she did not turn. The psychologist on the spinal unit had asked on many occasions and the nurses had been amazing, but he'd answered them all correctly and just kept it all in.

By day.

Martina certainly hadn't wanted to know and his parents and family he had not wanted to burden.

Cate didn't see it like that.

'You really want to know?' he said to the darkness. 'I do.'

'Stay there,' he said, and Cate screwed her eyes closed and did not turn to him.

'It was very busy,' Juan said. 'For the first few days

there are tests and Theatre and endless examinations and equipment and you keep waiting for things to change. Everyone is waiting for news, for updates and progress and it really has not sunk in. I had my fracture stabilised and it was wait and see. I had severe spinal swelling so they were unsure of the extent of the damage. I tried to stay positive for Martina and my family but I wasn't feeling positive at all,' Juan explained. 'I knew, almost as soon as I hit the pavement, that I had broken my neck.' He closed his eyes for a moment before carrying on. 'I did not believe that anything the surgeon could do would help.'

'You thought that was it.'

'Completely,' Juan said. 'All the tests, the tentative diagnosis, my family trying to keep positive, I went along with it for them, but in my heart I was sure it was permanent.'

'Were you scared?'

'You are too busy to be scared,' Juan said. 'The day is full. You start at six with obs and a drink, then breakfast, then wash, then doctors' rounds, then physio, visitors, more physio, exercises every hour...' He listed the day. 'Then at about ten you are settled and perhaps watch a movie. I used to sleep with the television on, but someone would turn it off and I used to wake...' He hesitated. 'You really want to hear this?'

'Yes.'

He told her about the nights.

Finally, he told somebody about the nights. How it felt to be trapped in only your head, how every missed opportunity, every wasted moment taunted, how the simplest things mattered in a way that they never had before.

'Every hour the nurses come around, day and night, and you have passive exercise. They move your limbs, your ankles, your hands. One of the nurses was trying to chat to Martina, trying to show her how she could move my fingers and wrists.' He lifted his index finger and thumb and, unseen by Cate, started pulling them together and then apart. '"That might mean he can hold a cup," the nurse told Martina, "or do up a shirt." And then she showed Martina how to turn my wrist in the hope I could one day have a drink by myself, and I saw her face…'

'Was she overwhelmed?'

'She couldn't do it,' Juan said. 'I saw her expression and when the nurse had gone she broke down.'

Then he told Cate about the night only three others knew about.

Because they had lain there in silence as they'd heard it.

'"I can't do this, Juan…" Martina couldn't even look me in the eye to tell me; instead she sat down by the bed.

'"It will be okay," I said.

'"When?"

'I just lay there. I'd have loved to know that answer too.

'"It's not what I envisaged, Juan. When you asked me to marry you, when I said yes, this was not how I planned things to be."' He'd hated how she'd attempted a joke. '"You always said that I would be a terrible nurse."

'"I don't want you to be my nurse."'

Cate listened as he told her some more of Martina's words, how worried she was about what others might think about her leaving him while he faced a future in a wheelchair.

'I told her that I would always say it was by mutual agreement and I would have stuck to that, except she calls me now. Martina has a different recollection of our conversation. She says she was in shock, that she just needed some time to adjust...'

Cate swallowed, wondered if it was pride holding him back from returning to Martina, but Juan shook his head when she asked him.

'I know, had I not got better, that I would never have seen Martina again.'

He told her how slowly, so slowly, sensations had started to come back. How it had hurt when they did, first his arms and then later his wrists. Then his thighs and slowly his calves and feet. 'I did the rehab, I dragged myself to physio, I learnt to walk, and then she started to visit. Martina had decided that maybe we could work through it, that maybe I did need her help after all. I needed her long before that,' Juan said. 'I certainly don't need her now. I flew to Australia. We were going to come here for our honeymoon but I came by myself. I was very thin and weak when I got here, but I spent months building my body up.'

Cate knew she had been right.

She had known so little about him.

'Martina wants it to go back to the way it was.'

'It can't?'

'No,' Juan said, 'because something like that is life-altering. You don't go back to how you were. When something that big happens, you find out who you really are...'

'And you are?'

'I'm still finding out,' Juan said. 'But I'm not the person I once was.'

She understood that.

Cate lay in the silence, listening to his breathing, and, even though it was nowhere near as severe as what had happened to him, Cate felt she had been through something life-changing. Juan had changed her. She couldn't go back to how she had been.

'I'm a different person now,' Juan said.

So too was she.

So different.

Cate woke to a sound that was unfamiliar—rain was beating against the window, heavy rain that was so needed. She thought of the firefighters and how thankful they would be for the reprieve, and the homeowners who had lived under the shadow of imminent danger for weeks now.

The threat had passed.

Just as Juan would soon move on.

All the attempts to safeguard her heart had been in vain and in a little while she would be doing what she most dreaded and saying goodbye to him.

She turned and looked over to the sight of Juan sleeping and smiled because she'd never thought she'd find the spill of long black hair on her pillow sexy, or that her toes might curl at what was now more than a few days' growth—he officially had a beard!

And she'd never thought she'd be so bold as to move over and start to kiss his flat nipples.

More than that she'd never felt so *inclined*, or had wanted another so much.

He felt her lips on his chest and he lay there; he

felt her mouth over his nipples and her tongue and he closed his eyes.

Juan loved sex, preferably quick. Hot, passionate sex was how things had had to be, not lying there with a mouth exploring, working its way down his stomach. He felt her hands move along his thighs, sensations returning, flooding his body, the slow burn of making love and being made love to.

He felt her hand grip his shaft, felt lips start to explore him, and for a second he wanted to stop her for, as it had in the hospital, sometimes feelings hurt as they returned.

Her mouth was hot and intimate and he moaned in pleasure and gave in to her.

Cate felt his hands in her hair, the gentle guidance of his palm. So many things had changed since Juan had come into her life—she could explore without shame and taste without guilt, just let herself live in the moment, for this moment at least.

He tasted of both him and of her, and she heard his ragged moan as she kissed him deeper, taking him further, and Juan gave in then.

The shout was primal and it came from somewhere he had never been.

She felt the jerk and the rush at the back of her throat and she was coming just from feeling him, from tasting him.

From adoring him.

CHAPTER SEVENTEEN

'STAY THERE,' JUAN said as the alarm blared like a siren. 'I'll bring us coffee.'

It was stupid to lie there and listen to him in her kitchen for the first time and to think she could miss something that had only happened once.

She was very close to crying and absolutely determined not to.

He brought her coffee and they drank it in strained silence. Juan headed off to the shower and then came out and dressed. He sat on the bed and she watched him pulling on his boots for the first and last time.

He made every moment matter.

'It's good to hear the rain.'

'It is,' Cate said. 'I'll be told off now for ordering too many burn packs.'

'Better too many than not enough,' Juan said. 'I think you made the right choice about work.'

Cate nodded, she didn't trust herself to speak.

'I'd better go,' Juan said, when it was clear she was struggling. 'I start at eight...'

'Sure.'

'Thank you for last night, for all our times...'

'Go,' Cate said, 'or I'm going to fail...'

'Fail what?'

'Living in the moment, not getting too involved.'

'Will you be okay?'

'Of course, as long as I avoid any tall Argentinian doctors that happen to be passing through…'

'No regrets?'

'No.' Cate shook her head. 'I don't think so anyway. You?'

'Potentially,' Juan said. 'Will you be there on Sunday?'

'No…' Cate shook her head, she couldn't put herself through this again, but a part of her couldn't stand never to see him again. 'I don't know.'

He kissed her again but it didn't quite work out and he stood. 'I'm going to go.' She went to get up, to see him out.

'Stay there,' Juan said.

So she did.

Hearing the door close hurt a million times more than it ever had.

Cate did get up. She stood back from the window, watched him walk in the direction of the train station.

She knew then what she'd been scared of right from the very start—not the one night with him, not the casual aspect. It was this part she'd been dreading, and the next part and the next.

Juan did not look back.

He felt the rain on his face and he loved it, loved living, loved the freedom. It was time to move on, he told himself.

He took the train to the city and watched as a young woman in a wheelchair boarded and gave him a dark look as she caught him staring.

'Excuse me,' Juan said. He did not look away and

maybe their souls recognised each other because they got talking, so much so that Juan was going to be late for his final shift in Australia. He was sitting at a train station, having a coffee, when his new friend told him a truth.

'Maybe it's time to go home, Juan, and face things,' she suggested. 'Maybe it's time to stop running away.'

'I think it is.'

He was only ten minutes late for work and no one seemed to notice. He walked around the unit with Paddy taking the handover then told him he hoped that he had a good weekend.

'Jason!' Juan looked down at his very drowsy patient. 'Do you remember me?'

'Of course he does,' Lisa said. 'Jason, it's Juan, the doctor who brought you here.'

He saw Jason's eyes flicker open.

'You've had a rough time, haven't you, my friend?' Jason had gone downhill a few days after his admission and had been intubated two days ago. They were trying now to extubate him.

Juan looked over at Jason's mother and saw Lisa's eyes brimming with tears. 'We're hoping he finally gets the tube out today.'

'It will happen when it's ready,' Juan said. 'You will have heard the saying—difficult intubations mean difficult extubations. We expect this…'

Lisa nodded.

'We just want him home.'

There was that word again.

'He will be,' Juan assured her. 'It makes it no easier on you but this is, for Jason, normal.' Juan sat on the bed with his young friend. 'We're going to let the sedation wear off this morning and see how his breathing goes, and if he's keeping his saturations then we'll think about removing the tube later today.'

'Will you be here?'

'I'm on till tomorrow evening,' Juan said. 'We'll get through this.'

'Then you're off. To New Zealand, isn't it? Or so I've heard,' Lisa said.

'I'm not sure...' Juan looked up as Kent came over.

'You're popular this morning,' Kent said. 'I've just taken a couple of calls for you. I said I didn't know if you were working today but that I'd find out and pass the message on if you were.'

They were so much more efficient here than at Bay-side!

'Thanks,' Juan said to Kent, and then looked at the note. He grimaced when he read it and then put it in his pocket.

'So, you're not sure about New Zealand?' Lisa re-sumed the conversation.

'Nope,' Juan said. 'I think it might be time for home.'

He gave Jason's shoulder a squeeze and told him he'd be back to check in on him in a little while. He went out to the on-call room to make a couple of calls that he'd been putting off for way too long now.

'Martina.' He was kind, he was firm and there was no arguing with someone who had made up their mind. 'You need to stop calling me.'

They spoke for a little while and as Juan went to end the call she asked him a question.

'Can we at least be friends?'

Juan was about to say no, because he didn't need the

constant reminders, but perhaps that did not matter any more—maybe they could be.

'Some day perhaps,' Juan answered.

He rang off, but sat there for a very long time with the phone still in his hand. He understood fully why Cate couldn't stand to catch up with him on social media, how it would hurt to watch someone's life from a distance.

Martina didn't hurt any more.

He wasn't just letting go of a love that had once been, he was letting go too of the man that he'd once been. All the dreams and aspirations, even thoughts, that had existed were alien to Juan now.

The old Juan was gone and it almost hurt to finally let go, but there was a sense of relief when he did.

He *was* a different person.

A wiser person.

A happy person.

A good man.

The second phone call Juan had expected to be the tough one—but it turned out to be the most straightforward decision in his life.

He wanted to go home.

CHAPTER EIGHTEEN

SOON SHE WOULD have no regrets, Cate told herself.

In a few weeks from now, surely it wouldn't hurt so much?

Cate fervently wished that she could do the casual relationship thing, wished that she hadn't had to go and fall quite so hard. Walking to the shops on Saturday morning, Cate looked up at the rainbow that had come out, telling herself it meant something. She was determined to buy a delicious top with the money she'd found on the hall table after he'd gone.

No, it hadn't offended; instead, it had made her smile.

Cate wasn't smiling now.

Tears were precariously close and she could see Kelly coming out of the boutique. The last thing Cate wanted now was conversation and she turned to look into a shop window, hoping that Kelly wouldn't notice her.

It was an antique shop and Cate looked at the rings, her eyes catching sight of a bevelled silver one with an amethyst and she walked inside.

'Can I look at a ring in the window?' Cate pointed it out and the assistant chatted as she headed over to fetch it.

'It just went in the window this morning.' The assistant smiled as she handed it over and as Cate looked, there inside she saw the words she really needed to see, and she thanked Elsie and her lover for them.

Je t'adore.

Cate thanked the wonderful old woman who had given her that push to live a little more, as she wanted, rather than how she felt she should. She thanked too the man who had made her feel more adored than she ever had.

It wasn't an impulse buy, it was an essential buy, and as she handed over the money he had left, yes, it came from Juan.

'Cate!' Kelly saw her coming out of the antique store. 'What are you up to?'

'Shopping.' Cate was getting good at forcing that smile. 'Ready for your jump tomorrow?'

'I can't wait,' Kelly smiled. 'You should come.'

'I might come along and watch.' Cate wondered if it would just make things worse, but the chance of seeing him again, even the sight of him hurtling out of a plane, was surely better than not seeing him at all.

'I meant you should come and jump.'

'It's too late now, the bookings are all done.'

Kelly shook her head. 'There's a spot that's opened up. It's all paid for—it was too late for a refund.'

Cate twisted the ring on her finger and made the second most foolish choice of her life.

'I'll jump,' Cate said, terrified not just at the prospect of leaping out of a plane but at the thought of seeing Juan again and having to say goodbye—again. 'But I can't just take someone's place without paying. Who do I owe?'

'Juan.' Kelly said, and Cate simply stood as Juan

moved out of her life for ever, just as she had always known that he would one day. 'He said he'd been looking forward to it but had somewhere he needed to be. I think he's already gone.'

Cate made it home without crying and when there was a knock at the door she forced that smile and saw that it was Bridgette.

'Thanks so much for your help the other day,' Cate said.

'It was no big deal. I brought back your plates.' She handed them to Cate. 'The lamb was delicious.'

'Thanks to you.'

'So was Juan!'

'I know,' Cate said. 'He's gone to New Zealand…' She tried to sound upbeat. 'I knew all along he would, it was just…' She couldn't finish, couldn't pretend that it wasn't agony for even a second longer.

'Do you want…?' Bridgette stood there. By now Cate usually would have opened the door and invited her in. 'Do you want company?'

'No, thanks.' Cate shook her head.

'If you do?'

'I know,' Cate said, closing the door, her eyes so full of tears that as she walked into the kitchen she faltered and tripped and the plates crashed to the floor.

Yes, she could have broken her neck.

As easily as that.

She stared at the mess and then the tears fell.

It hadn't been a fling or a holiday romance, neither had it even been a rebound.

It was love and she'd lost it.

CHAPTER NINETEEN

CATE FELT MORE than a pang of guilt for the lecture she'd delivered to Juan about being reckless to even consider the skydive. There was a disabled group jumping before the emergency team and Cate knew that she should have got her facts straight before accusing him of being careless.

But, then, she hadn't been thinking very straight at the time and, really—a motorbike?

Then she thought of Juan riding through the hills, the elation he must have felt, and still felt each day over and over again, as he chose to live his life the way he wanted to, and she smiled for him instead.

'You need to take that ring off,' the instructor told her, and Cate pulled it off and pocketed it, having visions of it knotting in the strings as she jumped into the sky.

'Are you okay?' Kelly asked through chattering teeth.

'I've never been more scared in my life,' Cate admitted. 'Tell me, why am I doing this again?'

'For a good cause?' Kelly offered as, instructions over, they walked towards the plane. Kelly wasn't looking quite so confident now.

'I'm sorry I pushed you into this, Cate,' Kelly said. 'I'm petrified.'

It came as little comfort to know she wasn't the only one as she sat with her fellow suicide and the plane rose into the sky.

Kelly went first. She left the plane screaming. Abby went second and one by one the rest followed.

Cate was last, which was so much worse in so many ways—there were no friends to bolster her, no one to watch her shame as she said, no, she couldn't do it.

'I can't,' she said, as she was strapped to her sky-diver. 'I've changed my mind.'

'All you have to remember is to lift your legs as we land.'

'I can't.'

'Cate…' The instructor was more than used to this, but when over and over Cate insisted that, no, this really wasn't what she wanted, he was about to relent and unstrap her.

'You'll regret it if you don't,' he warned her.

Cate had heard something like that somewhere before.

'I'll do it.'

The instructor took the small window but, even if he hadn't, now Cate's mind was made up there would be no changing it.

That much she knew about herself.

There was no feeling like it.

Even with her eyes closed, even pretending she wasn't really doing it, there was nothing, Cate quickly found out, like it in the world.

She screamed and screamed as she opened her eyes to a world that was amazing. The sky and the bay were dressed in vivid blues as far as the eye could see. Then she saw the white chop of the waves on the back beaches and the calm stillness of the bay, felt the pressure of the air, and Cate knew why she was doing this now.

I'm doing this for me.

She was doing it for the exhilaration of jumping out of a plane and feeling the pressure and the surprisingly strong cushion of thin air, for the fear and the fun and the uncertainty that all too often she had refused to embrace.

But finally she had.

Cate felt the chute jerk and the freefall break, and she thought about Juan, understood his need to embrace things, to experience and to fully sample the world. Floating above the tea trees, it happened then, just as Elsie had said it would—her heart soared for him.

'Juan!' Kelly turned. Still giddy from jumping, she smiled when she saw who it was. 'I didn't recognise you.'

'I figured it was time for a haircut,' Juan said. 'I wanted to come and watch the jumping but I am later getting here than I thought I would be.' His eyes scanned the gathering, hoping to get a glimpse of Cate; he had been to her home but she wasn't there and he had hoped she might have come along to give her colleagues moral support, but there was no sign of her.

'We're going out for dinner afterwards,' Kelly said.

Juan gave a noncommittal nod. 'How was your jump?' he asked her.

'It was the scariest moment of my life,' Kelly admitted. 'I feel terrible for pushing Cate into it, though

I don't think she'll jump. She was pea green the last time I saw her.'

'Cate's jumping?'

'There she is!' Kelly shouted, and Juan looked up, watched the two figures jumping out of a plane, and he grinned, for he'd known there was a wild side to her.

'Who'd have thought?' Kelly said as Cate's screams and laughter came into earshot.

Me, Juan said silently, because he'd seen a different side to her, the untapped spirit that lay inside and the quiet strength too. He could only smile that she wasn't crying or miserable, though his ego would have liked a slightly more subdued Cate after he had seemingly left.

No, he wouldn't, Juan decided as he watched her land, heard her laughing as she untangled herself and then, dusting down her legs, she walked to the group.

'That was amazing!' Cate shouted. 'I can't believe I'm saying this but I want to do it….' Then her voice halted as she looked at the group of colleagues and friends and saw that Juan was amongst them.

A different Juan because that long shock of black hair had been cut. She'd loved his hair, yet he looked incredible with it shorter too. And what was with the clean-shaven jaw?

'I thought you were in New Zealand!' She tried to hide her exhilaration; she didn't want her colleagues knowing what had gone on between them, but the unexpected sight of him was more breathtaking than jumping out of a plane.

'So did everyone.' Juan grinned.

'You've had a haircut!'

He nodded.

'How was it?'

Juan pulled her aside. She knew him, knew the big deal it must have been, and he told her the truth. 'Can you believe I broke into a sweat as I walked in?'

'Yes.'

'The girl must have been all of eighteen and could not have been more bored as she cut my hair. "What did you do to your neck?" she asked when she saw the scar.'

'What did you say?' Cate smiled at grey eyes she had thought she might never see again.

'That I went to get a haircut.' Juan grinned. 'She did not get the joke, of course. I think she thought my English was no good.'

'So how come you finally got it cut?'

'My gap year is over,' Juan said. 'It is time to get to work.' He saw her frown. 'Harry rang me at the children's hospital on Friday and said that he had found only one applicant suitable and that they really needed two. He said that he wanted me to work at Bayside. The applications have to be in Personnel by Monday and, given I was working till last night, this morning was our only chance for a formal interview.'

'For a three-month contract?'

'No.' They started walking towards the crowd, who were calling to them to get a move on. 'For a permanent role.'

Cate blinked, because seeing Juan every day was going to be hard. Yes, she knew they had something, should be pleased they didn't have a clock hanging over them now, but to get closer to him, to have to work alongside him...

'I might have to go to New Zealand while the applications are sorted. Harry is going to try and help to sort things with Immigration but we will have to see what happens.' Then he stopped walking and caught her hand and turned her to face him. 'Marry me?' He said it just like that, walking towards the shed where all their colleagues were. 'I was going to ask that we take things more seriously, that we see how things work out, but I already know what I want.'

'Marriage?' She looked at him. 'For a visa?'

'Cate.' He held her eyes. 'Ask yourself that question again. Why do you think I want this job, why do you think I want to be here?'

'Me?'

'You,' Juan said. 'We can live here or in Argentina, or...' He looked at her. 'I don't care. I just don't want to be apart from you. I take marriage seriously, and today I watched you jump out of that plane and, yes, like anyone, I had some concerns. If something terrible had happened, I would have been there. I knew it as truth as I watched you fall. I knew too that if something happened, you would be the first to say we have only been with each other a little while, it is not serious, that I don't have to hang around...'

She could feel tears stinging the back of her throat as he continued.

'I want the good and bad, in sickness and in health, and I want them with you.'

It wasn't a game.

The feelings she had been fighting, glimpsing, scorning herself for feeling had been real after all.

'Do I have to ask twice?' Juan said, and she shook her head.

'That's a yes,' Cate said, and it was hardly even a decision because it needed no thought when her heart knew the answer.

'I should warn you,' Juan said. 'I'm guaranteed to have a limp when I'm older.'

'I'll buy you a cane.' Cate smiled, and her heart swelled as she glimpsed the truth. They had a future, one where his black hair would go silver and he wasn't temporary but was there with her, for all of it. It was overwhelming, more overwhelming than jumping out of a plane, more exhilarating than freefalling.

'We're going shopping,' Juan said.

'Shopping?'

'For a ring.'

She caught his hand. 'I've already bought the ring, or rather you have.'

'What?' He half smiled and frowned as she took a silver ring out of her pocket and handed it to him. He turned it over and over in vague recognition.

'I used the money you left for me to get a top on this instead. It was Elsie's,' Cate explained. 'I found it in an antique shop in the village.'

He looked at the silver ring in his hand and read the inscription and then he looked at her, a woman who didn't want diamonds, who wanted only his love.

'*Je t'adore*,' Juan said, and took her right hand. 'We don't have separate engagement rings in Argentina, so this is your wedding band,' he told her. 'It is worn on the right hand till our wedding day,' he explained, slipping the ring on her finger, and it fitted perfectly. It was absolutely meant to be.

She could hear the screams and shouts from Kelly and Abby as Juan bent over and kissed her in full view of everyone. Readily, Cate kissed him back.

'They'll want us to go out and celebrate when we tell them,' Cate warned, as they started running over.

'No,' Juan said, and he thought about the friend he had made on the train, about the conversation that, since he had met Cate, had been running through his mind. He recalled the feeling of stepping into her house and hearing the sound of her laughter from the garden. 'We are going back to yours. It's time for me to stop running away.'

Juan took her hand in his. 'We're going home.'

CHAPTER TWENTY

'I AM SO glad to be out of that place for four weeks.'

They were high above the clouds, on their way to Argentina to get married. Cate's family was coming out next week, but for now Cate and Juan were sitting sipping champagne. Cate felt guilty that Juan had got business-class tickets and it was nice to be grumbling about work but, in truth, to be happy at work, too. The new nurse unit manager had started and was making very sure that Cate knew who was boss. 'Marnie's awful.' Cate sighed. 'I don't think she understands that I resigned rather than that I was demoted and that I have absolutely no desire to do her job.'

'I like her,' Juan said.

'You like Marnie?'

'I do.' Juan shrugged. 'The place is running well. She's very strict and she takes no nonsense and Marnie's certainly stopped all the carry-on with Harry and his children.'

'Leave Harry alone,' Cate said.

'No. If something happened to you, would you want me dragging our baby in at four a.m.?'

'No,' Cate admitted. 'But we don't have a baby and—'

'We could,' Juan interrupted.

'Isn't it too soon?'

'Not for me,' Juan said. He'd seen the look in her eyes last night when Bridgette had told them she and James were expecting a baby.

Cate looked at him. Sometimes she had to pinch herself, sometimes she actually jumped when she walked into the house and he was still there.

'You were supposed to be a one-night stand,' Cate said. 'My wild fling. And now, here we are, talking about babies.'

'You don't do wild flings,' Juan said.

'I know.'

He sat as she contemplated the future. Cate was the least impulsive person he knew, but when she made her mind up, she made it up—he'd realised that.

'Next year,' Cate said. 'I want a year of just us and getting to know each other and being as happy as we are. Anyway,' Cate said, 'we need to save for it. I've just had my first full pay since I demoted myself.' She gave a small wince. 'And you've blown your savings flying my family out for the wedding and you've only just started back at work full time.'

'Whenever you're ready,' Juan said and he looked over. There was so much to learn, so much to know and so much that hadn't mattered to Cate that had mattered to so many others.

As they approached Buenos Aires some time later, Cate woke up and saw a pensive Juan looking out of the window, staring down at his home town. He only stopped when the flight attendant told him to close the shutter for landing.

'Nervous?' Cate asked.

'Not for myself,' Juan admitted. 'I never thought I

would be so ready to go back. I just wonder how they are going to react to me.' He gave her a smile. 'To the new Juan.'

They loved him.

All his family were there at the airport—as unconventional and as glamorous and as exotic as Juan. They welcomed Cate with open arms and it wasn't just blood family who were there to greet him on his return.

'This is Eduard,' Juan introduced them, and Cate hugged him as fiercely as Juan had. 'And this is Felicia…'

'We are so excited,' Felicia said. 'My English is crap.'

'I taught her,' Juan said.

'Of course you did.'

'We are so excited,' Ramona, his mother, told her as they drove towards their home. 'Pardon my crap English.'

Cate started to laugh. 'You have to tell them what they're saying,' she said to Juan.

'But I love it too much to spoil it,' Juan said.

They chatted about the plans for the wedding and the menu. Their English was littered with the swear words Juan had told them were the words Cate would want to hear.

'It sounds wonderful,' Cate said to the blue air, even though she had no idea what the dishes that were being talked about were.

'Wow!' Cate looked out of the window the whole ride from the airport and she had said it often. Buenos Aires was such a busy, vibrant city, a lot like the man it had produced, yet there was incredible elegance too.

'I was expecting fields and horses.'

'This is Recoleta,' Juan explained. 'We are nearly at

my parents'.' Cate swallowed as they drove down the very affluent streets. The houses were amazing, the streets lined with trees and golden streetlights. 'There is Medicina,' Juan explained, 'where I studied medicine…and over there is the best dance school. You have to learn the tango before the wedding.'

'Please!'

'You do. I have booked you for lessons, and over there…' her head turned to where he was pointing '…is where we will be having our celebration.'

He watched as Cate's jaw gaped. It was the most beautiful restaurant and she cringed when she thought of the cost, worried as her parents had offered to help pay for the wedding of their only daughter.

She doubted they were expecting something so grand.

'Don't worry.' Juan winked as he watched her lick dry lips. 'We're getting a good discount, given that it's the owners' son's wedding.'

'That's your parents' restaurant?' It was beyond amazing, a huge Parisian-style building, nothing like the corner café she'd been expecting.

'When you said you worked in the café after school…' She'd had visions of young Juan wrapping up kebabs and mopping floors.

'Oh, I meant restaurant,' Juan said, and she remembered then how carefully he had chosen that word.

'Liar!' Cate laughed.

'I was then.' Juan smiled. 'I told no one anything of my past. It is one of the best restaurants in Buenos Aires, perhaps the best. My parents are world-renowned chefs—they hoped I would follow in their footsteps and I thought about it for a while.'

'Oh.' Cate swallowed. 'So that fish that tasted more amazing than I could begin to describe, that marinade…'

'Is my mother's recipe,' Juan explained. 'I didn't go fishing that morning—but I knew I could seduce you with food…' He gave her a nudge. 'As it turned out, I didn't need it.'

'Stop!' Cate blushed at the memory of them in the kitchen.

'Juan is a beautiful cook,' Ramona sighed. 'A waste of your talent…'

They were all mad, all gorgeous and all about to become her family, and then Cate remembered. 'Oh, God! All those meals I've cooked you…'

'What meals?' Juan checked. 'You mean cheese on toast, egg on toast, beans on toast…?' How he teased. 'You do make a nice roast lamb, if a little dry.' He put his arm around her. 'I'm a good catch.'

He looked at her serious hazel eyes and he was certain.

More certain in love than he had ever been.

'And I am so glad that I caught you,' he said.

EPILOGUE

IN CATE'S DREAMS she relived it.

'You look wonderful,' Juan said as he kissed her at the entrance to the church.

Cate had never seen Juan in a suit, and he looked exquisite. He had on a slate-grey tie that matched his eyes and she knew he would have been so grateful for the fingers able to knot it, so grateful for each button on his shirt that he was able to do up. The dawning smile on Juan's face when he saw her wedding dress made her blush. It was a very pale lilac, like the skirt she had worn when he'd first kissed her, and it had a halterneck top—together they smiled at the memories they had already created, in the knowledge there was so much more to come.

'We do this walk together,' Juan's rich voice told her as, with Juan's father and Cate's mother and Eduard behind them, hand in hand they walked down the aisle. And then they faced each other and offered their vows, and Cate needed no translation.

Every word was heartfelt in whatever language it was spoken.

Their future was together, come what may, Cate had

known as a very special ring was moved from her right hand to her left.

Caught between waking and sleeping on her first morning as Juan's wife, she remembered the reception, surrounded by family and new friends. Dancing a terrible tango and drinking *fernet* and cola, then coming back to the hotel.

Cate moaned in her sleep as she recalled their love-making, because if ever there was a bride more inappropriately named it was Mrs Morales!

'Cate?'

She heard her name being called but she didn't want to wake up, didn't want to move away from the bliss of being kissed by him. His tongue mingled with hers and she relished the scent of him, the feel of his hands roaming her body.

Juan checked her finger and the ring was there. He ran a hand along her legs and kissed her until they moved and wrapped tightly around him.

'Cate?'

She heard her name again and moaned as he slid inside her, wanted to be woken like this each and every morning. Her hands slipped up his shoulders and to his neck and he didn't halt her this time. Nothing was out of bounds now. Instead, she opened her eyes to him as together they lived the dream.

* * * * *

IT HAPPENED
ONE NIGHT SHIFT

AMY ANDREWS

I dedicate this book to all my lovely nursing friends from the former Royal Children's Hospital. Twenty one years is a long time to be in any one place and I have enjoyed every moment – even the harrowing ones. I will miss you all.

CHAPTER ONE

GARETH STAPLETON DROPPED his head from side to side, stretching out his traps as he kept his eyes on the road.

He was getting too old for this crap.

It had been a long, crazy shift in the emergency room and he needed a beer, a shower and his bed.

Saturday nights in a busy Brisbane ER were chaotic at the best of times but the full moon had added an extra shot of the bizarre to the mix. From now on he was consulting astrological charts when requesting his roster.

He yawned and looked at the dash clock—almost midnight—and was grateful for his shift ending when it had. The waiting room had still been full as he'd clocked off and he didn't envy the night shift having to deal with it all.

Suddenly, the car in front of him—a taxi—swerved slightly into the opposite lane and Gareth's pulse spiked.

What the hell?

Despite only going at the speed limit, he eased back on the accelerator as the taxi corrected itself. Gareth peered into the back windscreen of the car, trying to see what the guy was doing. What was distracting him? Was he texting? Or talking on the phone?

He couldn't tell *what* the driver was doing but at least the taxi appeared to be empty of passengers.

Gareth eased back some more. He may only be driving a twenty-year-old rust box but he had no desire to be collateral damage due to this clown's inattention. Luckily they were on a long, straight section of road linking two outer suburbs so there were no houses, no cars parked on either side, just trees and bushland.

The taxi wobbled all over the lane again and Gareth's stomach tightened as a set of oncoming headlights suddenly winked in the distance. His fingers gripped the steering-wheel a little firmer as a sense of foreboding settled over him.

Gareth's sense of foreboding had served him well over the years—particularly in the Middle East—and it wasn't going to be disappointed tonight.

He watched in horror as the taxi swerved suddenly again into the path of the oncoming car. Gareth hit his horn but it was futile, the crash playing out in front of him in slow motion.

The driver of the other car slammed on the brakes, swerving to avoid what Gareth could have sworn was certain collision. He waited for the crash and the sound of crunching metal but, thankfully, it never came. The taxi narrowly missed the other car, careening off the road and smashing into a tree.

But now the oncoming car was in his lane and Gareth had to apply his brakes to prevent them crashing. Luckily the other driver had the good sense to swerve back into his own lane and they both came to a halt almost level with each other on their own sides of the road.

Gareth, his heart pistoning like a jackhammer, automatically reached for his glove box and pulled out a bunch of gloves from a box he always kept there. He ripped his seat belt off and pushed open his door.

'Are you okay, mate?' he asked as he leapt out, his fingers already reaching for the mobile phone in his pocket as he mentally triaged the scene.

He wrenched open the door of the other car, noticing absently it was a sleek-looking two-seater, to find a pair of huge brown eyes, heavily kohled and fringed with sooty eyelashes, blinking back at him. A scarlet mouth formed a surprised-looking O.

A woman.

'I'm…I'm fine.' She nodded, looking dazed.

Gareth wasn't entirely sure. She appeared uninjured but she looked like she might be in shock. 'Can you move? How's your neck?' he asked.

She nodded again, undoing her seat belt. 'It's fine. I'm fine.' She swung her legs out of the car.

'Don't move,' he ordered. 'Stay there.' The last thing he needed was a casualty wandering around the scene. 'I'm Gareth, what's your name?'

'Billie.'

Gareth acknowledged the unusual name on a superficial level only. 'I'm going to check out the taxi driver. You stay here, okay, Billie?'

She blinked up at him and nodded. 'Okay.'

Satisfied he'd secured her co-operation, Gareth, already dialling triple zero, headed for the smashed-up taxi.

It took a minute for Billie to come out of the fog of the moment and get her bearings. She'd told Gareth—at least that was what she thought he'd said his name was—she was okay. Everything had happened so fast. But a quick mental check of her body confirmed it.

She was shaking like a leaf but she wasn't injured.

And she was a doctor. She shouldn't be sitting in her car like an invalid—she should be helping.

What on earth had caused the taxi to veer right into her path? Was the driver drunk? Or was it something medical? A hypo? A seizure?

She reached across to her glove box and pulled out a pair of gloves from the box she always kept there, her heart beating furiously, mentally preparing herself for potential gore. Being squeamish was not something that boded well for a doctor but it was something she'd never been able to conquer.

She'd learned to control it—just.

She exited her car, yanking the boot lever on the way out, rounding the vehicle and pulling out a briefcase that contained a well-stocked first-aid kit. Then she took a deep breath and in her ridiculous heels and three-quarter-length cocktail dress she made her way over to the crashed car and Gareth.

Gareth looked up from his ministrations as Billie approached. 'I thought I'd told you to stay put,' he said, whipping off his fleecy hoody, not even feeling the cool air. His only priority was getting the driver, who wasn't breathing and had no pulse, out of the car.

'I'm fine. And I'm a doctor so I figured I could help.'

Gareth was momentarily thrown by the information but he didn't have time to question her credentials. She was already wearing a pair of hospital-issue gloves that *he* hadn't given her, so she was at least prepared.

And the driver's lips were turning from dusky to blue.

He needed oxygen and a defib. Neither of which they had.

All the driver had was them, until the ambulance got there.

'I'm an ER nurse,' Gareth said, rolling his hoody into a tube shape then carefully wrapping it around the man's neck, fashioning a crude soft collar to give him some C-spine protection when they pulled him out.

'Ambulance is ten minutes away. He's in cardiac arrest. Thankfully he's not trapped. Help me get him out and we'll start CPR. I'll grab his top half,' Gareth said.

Aided by the light from the full moon blasting down on them, they had the driver lying on the dew-damp grass in less than thirty seconds. 'You maintain the airway,' Gareth said, falling back on protocols ingrained in him during twenty years in the field. 'I'll start compressions.'

Billie nodded, swallowing hard as the metallic smell from the blood running down the driver's face from a deep laceration on his forehead assaulted her senses. It had already congealed in places and her belly turned at the sight, threatening to eject the three-course meal she'd indulged in earlier.

She turned away briskly, sucking air slowly into her lungs. In through her nose, out through her mouth, concentrating on the cold damp ground already seeping through the gauzy fabric of her dress to her knees rather than the blood. She was about to start her ER rotation—she had to get used to this.

She opened the briefcase and pulled out her pocket mask.

Gareth kicked up an eyebrow as she positioned herself, a knee either side of the guy's head, and held the mask efficiently in place over the driver's mouth and nose.

'Very handy,' he said, noting her perfect jaw grasp and hand placement. 'Don't suppose you have a defib in there by any chance?'

Billie gave a half-laugh. 'Sadly, no.' Because they both knew that's what this man needed.

She leaned down to blow several times into the mouthpiece. Her artfully curled hair fell forward and she quickly pushed them behind her ears as the mask threatened to slip. The mix of sweat and blood on the driver's face worked against her and Billie had to fight back a gag as the smell invaded her nostrils.

If she just shut her eyes and concentrated on the flow of air, the rhythm of her delivery, mentally counted the breaths, she might just get through this without disgracing herself.

'What do you reckon, heart attack?' Gareth asked after he'd checked for a pulse two minutes in.

Billie, concentrating deeply, opened her eyes at the sudden intrusion. Rivulets of dried blood stared back at her and she quickly shut them again. 'Probably,' she said between breaths. 'Something caused him to veer off the road like that and he feels pretty clammy. Only he looks young, though. Fit too.'

Gareth agreed, his arms already feeling the effort of prolonged compressions. The man didn't look much older than himself. ''Bout forty, I reckon.'

Billie nodded. 'Too young to die.'

He grunted and Billie wondered if he was thinking the same thing she was. The taxi driver probably *was* going to die. The statistics for out-of-hospital cardiac arrests were grim. Even for young, fit people. This man needed so much more than they could give him here on the roadside.

They fell silent again as they continued to give a complete stranger, who had nearly wiped both of them out tonight, a chance at life.

'Come on, mate,' Gareth said, as he checked the pulse for the third time and went back to compressions. 'Cut us some slack here.'

A minute later, the silence was pierced by the first low wails of a siren. 'Yes,' Gareth muttered. 'Hold on, mate. The cavalry's nearly here.'

In another minute two ambulances—one with an intensive care paramedic—pulled up, followed closely by a police car. A minute after that a fire engine joined the fray. Reinforcements surrounded them, artificial light suddenly flooding the scene, Billie and Gareth continued their CPR as Gareth gave an impressive rapid-fire handover.

'Keep managing the airway,' the female intensive care paramedic instructed Billie, after Gareth had informed her of their medical credentials. She handed Billie a proper resus set—complete with peep valve and oxygen supply. 'You okay to intubate?'

Billie nodded. She could. As a second-year resident she'd done it before but not a lot. And then there was the blood.

She took another deep, steadying breath.

Gareth continued compressions as one of the advanced care paramedics slapped on some defib pads and the other tried to establish IV access.

In the background several firemen dealt with the car, some set up a road block with the police while others directed a newly arrived tow truck to one side.

The automatic defibrillator warned everyone to move away from the patient as it advised a shock.

'Stand clear,' the paramedic called, and everyone dropped what they were doing and moved well back.

A series of shocks was delivered, to no avail, and everyone resumed their positions. IV access was gained and emergency drugs were delivered. Billie successfully intubated as Gareth continued with cardiac massage. Two minutes later the defibrillator recommended another shock and everyone moved away again.

The driver's chest arched. 'We've got a rhythm,' the paramedic announced.

Gareth reached over and felt for the carotid. 'Yep,' he agreed. 'I have a pulse.'

'Okay, let's get him loaded and go.'

Billie reached for the bag to resume respiratory support on the still unconscious patient but the intensive care paramedic crouched beside Billie said, 'Would you like me to take over?'

Billie looked at her, startled. She'd been concentrating so hard on not losing her stomach contents she'd shut everything out other than the whoosh of her own breath. But the airway was secure and they had a pulse. She could easily hand over to a professional who had way more experience dealing with these situations.

Not to mention the fact that now the emergency was under control her hands were shaking, her teeth were chattering and she was shivering with the cold.

And her knees were killing her.

She looked down at her gloves. They were streaked with blood and another wave of nausea welled inside her.

Billie handed the bag over and then suddenly warm hands were lifting her up onto her shaking legs, supporting her as her numb knees threatened to buckle. A blanket was thrown around her shoulders and she huddled into its warmth as she was shepherded in the direction of her car.

'Are you okay?'

Billie glanced towards the deep voice, surprised to find herself looking at Gareth. He was tall and broad and looked warm and inviting and she felt so cold. She had the strangest urge to walk into his arms.

'I'm fine,' she said, gripping the blanket tighter around her shoulders, looking down at where her gloved hands held the edges of the blanket together.

Dried blood stared back at her. The nausea she'd been valiantly trying to keep at bay hit her in a rush.

And right there, dressed to the nines in front of Gareth and a dozen emergency personnel, she bent over and threw up her fancy, two-hundred-dollar, three-course meal on the side of the road.

CHAPTER TWO

BILLIE WAS THANKFUL as she talked to the police a few minutes later she'd never have to see anyone here ever again. She doubted if any of these seasoned veterans blinked an eye at someone barfing at the scene of an accident and they'd all been very understanding but she was *the doctor,* for crying out loud.

People looked to her to be the calm, in-control one. To take bloodied accident victims in her stride. She was *supposed* to be able to hold herself together.

Not throw up at the sight of blood and gore.

Billie wondered anew how she was going to cope in the emergency room for the next six months. For the rest of her life, for that matter, given that emergency medicine was her chosen career path.

Mostly because it was high-flying enough to assuage parental and family expectations without being surgical. The Ashworth-Keyes of the world were *all* surgeons. Choosing a non-surgical specialty was *not* an option.

Unless it carried the same kind of kudos. As emergency medicine, apparently, did.

And at least this way Billie knew she'd still be able to treat the things that interested her most. Raw and messy were not her cup of tea but infections and diseases, the run-of-the-mill medical problems that were seen in GP practices across the country every day were.

But Ashworth-Keyes' were *not* GPs.

And Billie was carrying a double load of expectation.

She glanced across at Gareth, who was looking relaxed and assured amidst a tableau of clashing lights. The milky phosphorescence of the moon, the glow of fluorescent safety striping on multiple uniforms and the garish strobing of red, blue and amber. He didn't seem to be affected by any of it, his deep, steady voice carrying towards her on the cool night air as he relayed the details of the accident to a police officer.

Billie cringed as she recalled how he'd held her hair back and rubbed between her shoulders blades as she'd hurled up everything in her stomach. Then had sourced some water for her to rinse her mouth out and offered her a mint.

It seemed like he'd done it before. But, then, she supposed, an ER nurse probably *had* done it a thousand times.

Still…why did she have to go and disgrace herself in front of possibly the most good-looking man she'd seen in a very long time?

She'd noticed it subliminally while they'd been performing CPR but she'd had too much else going on, what with holding someone's life in the balance and trying not to vomit, to give her thoughts free rein.

But she didn't now.

And she let them run wild as she too answered a policeman's questions.

Billie supposed a lot of her friends wouldn't classify Gareth as good looking purely because of his age. The grey whiskers putting some salt into the sexy growth of stubble at his jaw and the small lines around his eyes that crinkled a little as he smiled told her he had to be in his late thirties, early forties.

But, then, she'd always preferred older men.

She found maturity sexy. She liked the way, by and large, older men were content in their skins and didn't feel the need to hem a woman in to validate themselves. The easy way they spoke and the way they carried their bodies and wore their experience on their faces and were comfortable with that. She liked the way so many of them didn't seem like they had anything to prove.

She liked how Gareth embodied that. Even standing in the middle of an accident scene he looked at ease.

Gareth laughed at something the policeman said and she watched as he raked a piece of hair back that had flopped forward. She liked his hair. It was wavy and a little long at the back, brushing his collar, and he wore it swept back where it fell in neat rippled rows.

She'd noticed, as they'd tried to save the driver's life, it was dark with some streaks of grey, like his whiskers.

And she liked that too.

His arm dropped back down by his side and her gaze drifted to his biceps. She'd noticed those biceps as well while they'd been working on their man. How could she not have? Every time she'd opened her eyes there they'd been, contracting and releasing with each downward compression.

Firm and taut. Barely covered—*barely constrained*—by his T-shirt.

Billie shivered. She wasn't sure if it was from the power of his biceps alone or the fact he was wandering around on a winter's night with just a T-shirt covering his chest.

Why hadn't someone given him a blanket?

Although, to be fair, he did look a lot more appropriately dressed for a roadside emergency than she did. His jeans looked snug and warm, encasing long, lean legs, and he *had* been wearing a fleecy hoody.

It sure beat a nine-hundred-dollar dress and a pair of strappy designer shoes.

He looked up then, pointing in the direction she'd been driving, and their gazes met. He nodded at her briefly, before returning his attention to the police officer, and she found herself nodding back.

Yep, Billie acknowledged—Gareth was one helluva good-looking man. In fact, he ticked all her boxes. And if she was up for a fling or available for dating in the hectic morass of a resident's life then he'd be exactly her type. But there was absolutely no hope for them now.

The man had held her hair back while she'd vomited.

She cringed again. If she ever saw him again it would be too soon.

Gareth was acutely aware of Billie's gaze as he answered the police officer's questions. It seemed to beam through the cold air like an invisible laser, hot and direct, hitting him fair in the chest, diffusing heat and awareness to every millimetre of his body.

It made her hard to ignore.

Of course, the fact she was sparkling like one of those movie vampires also made her hard to ignore.

The gauzy skirt of her black dress shimmered with hundreds of what looked like crystal beads. Who knew, maybe they were diamonds? The dress certainly didn't look cheap. But they caught the multitude of lights strobing across the scene, refracting them like individual disco balls.

As if the dress and the petite figure beneath needed to draw any more attention to itself. Every man here, from the fireman to the paramedics, the police to the tow-truck driver, was sure as hell taking a moment to appreciate it.

Their attention irritated him. And the fact that it did irritated him even more. She was a stranger and they were at an accident scene, for crying out loud!

But it didn't stop him from going over to her when the police officer was done. He told himself it was to check she was feeling okay now but the dress was weirdly mesmerising and he would have gone to her even if she'd not conveniently vomited twenty minutes ago.

She had her back to him but, as if she'd sensed him approaching, she turned as he neared. Her loose reddish-brown hair flowed silkily around her shoulders, her hair curling in long ringlets around her face. Huge gold hoop earrings he'd noticed earlier as she'd administered the kiss of life swung in her lobes, giving her a little bit of gypsy.

He smiled as he drew closer. She seemed to hesitate for a moment then reciprocated, her scarlet lipstick having worn off from her earlier ministrations.

'You sure know how to dress for a little unscheduled roadside assistance,' he said, as he drew to a halt in front of her.

Billie blinked, surprised by his opening line for a moment, and then she looked down at herself and laughed. 'Oh, yes, sorry,' she said, although she had absolutely no idea why she was apologising for her attire. 'I've just come from a gala reception.'

This close his biceps were even more impressive and Billie had to grip the blanket hard to stop from reaching her hands out and running her palms over them. She wondered if they'd feel as firm and warm as they looked.

'Aren't you cold?' she asked, engaging her mouth before her brain as she dragged her gaze back to his face.

He did a smile-shrug combo and Billie's stomach did a little flip-flop combo in response. 'I'm fine,' he dismissed.

Billie grimaced. Where had she heard that already tonight? 'I really am very sorry about earlier.'

'Yeah.' He grinned. His whole face crinkled and Billie lost her breath as his sexiness increased tenfold. 'You've already said so. Three times.'

She blushed. 'I know but…I think I may have splashed your shoes.'

Gareth looked down at his shoes. 'They've seen far worse, trust me.'

'Not exactly the impression I like to give people I've just met.'

Gareth shrugged. She needn't have been worried about her impression on him—he doubted he was going to forget her in a long time, and it had nothing to do with his shoes and everything to do with how good she looked in those gold hoops and sparkly dress.

And if he'd been up for some flirting and some let's-see-where-this-goes fun he might just have assured her out loud. He might just have suggested they try for a second impression. But *hooking up* really wasn't his thing.

Hooking up at an accident scene even less so.

'We haven't exactly met properly, have we? I mean, not formally.' He held out his hand. 'I'm Gareth Stapleton. Very pleased to make your acquaintance—despite the circumstances.'

Billie slipped her hand into his and even though she'd expected to feel something, the rush of warmth up her arm took her by surprise. She shook his hand absently, staring at their clasped fingers, pleased for the blanket around her torso as the warmth rushed all the way to her nipples, prickling them to attention.

Gareth smiled as Billie's gaze snagged on their joined hands. Not that he could blame her. If she felt the connection as strongly as he did then they were both in trouble.

Just as well they wouldn't be seeing each other again after tonight. Resisting her in this situation was sensible and right. But if there was repeated exposure? That could wear a man down.

Sensible and right could be easily eroded.

'And you're Billie?' he prompted, withdrawing his hand. 'Billie…?'

Billie dragged her gaze away from their broken grip, up his broad chest and deliciously whiskery neck and onto his face, his spare cheekbones glowing alternately red and blue from the lights behind him.

What were they talking about? Oh, yes, formal introductions. 'Ashworth-Keyes,' she said automatically. 'Although if you want *formal* formal then it's *Willamina* Ashworth-Keyes.'

Gareth quirked an eyebrow as a little itch started at the back of his brain. 'Your first name is *Willamina*?'

Billie rolled her eyes. 'Yes,' she said, placing her hand on her hip. 'What about it?'

Gareth held up his hands in surrender. 'Nothing. Just kind of sounds like somebody's...spinster great-aunt.'

Billie frowned, unfortunately agreeing. Which was why she'd carried over her childhood pet name into adulthood.

'Not that there's anything *remotely* spinsterish or great-auntish about you,' he hastened to add. The last thing he wanted to do was insult her. The *very* last thing. 'Or,' he added as her frowned deepened, 'that there's anything wrong with that anyway.'

This woman made him tongue-tied.

How long had it been since he'd felt this gauche? Like some horny fifteen-year-old who couldn't even speak to the cool, pretty girl because he had a hard-on the size of a house.

Not that he had a hard-on. Not right now anyway. Or probably ever again if this excruciatingly awkward scene replayed in his head as often as he figured it would.

Billie's breath caught at Gareth's sudden lack of finesse. It made her feel as if she wasn't the only one thrown by this rather bizarre thing that had flared between them.

And she'd liked his emphasis on *remotely*.

She laughed to ease the strange tension that had spiked between them. 'Only my parents call me Willamina,' she said. 'And generally only if I'm in trouble.'

'And are you often in trouble?'

Gareth realised the words might have come across as flirty, so he kept his face serious.

Billie felt absurdly like laughing at such a preposterous notion. Her? In trouble? 'No. Not me. *Never me.*' That had been her sister's job. 'No, I'm the peacekeeper in the family.'

Gareth frowned at the sudden gloom in her eyes. The conversation had swung from light to awkward to serious. It seemed she wasn't too keen on the mantle of family good girl and suddenly a seductive voice was whispering they could find some trouble together.

Thankfully the little itch at the back of his brain finally came into sharp focus, obliterating the voice completely.

'Wait…' He narrowed his eyes. 'Ashworth-Keyes? As in Charles and Alisha Ashworth-Keyes, eminent cardiothoracic surgeons?'

Billie nodded. *Sprung.* 'The very same.'

'Your parents?' She nodded and he whistled. Everyone who was anyone in the medical profession in Brisbane knew of the Ashworth-Keyes surgical dynasty. 'That's some pedigree you've got going on there.'

'Yes. Lucky me,' she said derisively.

'You…don't get on?'

Billie sighed. 'No, it's not that. I'm just…not really like them, you know?'

He quirked an eyebrow. 'How so?'

'Well, I'm no surgeon, that's for sure. I'm a little too squeamish for that.'

Gareth surprised himself by laughing at the understatement but he couldn't help himself. 'Really?' he asked, looking down at his shoes. 'You hide it well.'

Billie shot him a cross look but soon joined him in his laughter.

'And?' he asked. 'What else?'

What else? Being a surgeon was all that mattered in the Ashworth-Keyes household. 'It's…complicated.'

Gareth nodded. Fair enough. Complicated he understood. It really wasn't any of his business anyway. 'So what field is the next Ashworth-Keyes going to specialise in? Clearly something…anything that doesn't involve the letting of blood? Dermatology? Radiology? Maybe…pathology?'

Billie shook her head. 'Emergency medicine,' she said. Even saying it depressed the hell out of her.

Gareth blinked. 'Really?' Surely Billie understood the squeamish factor could get pretty high in an ER?

'Yep,' she confirmed, sounding about as enthusiastic as he usually did just prior to starting a night shift. 'I'm starting my six-month emergency rotation at St Luke's ER next week in fact.'

Gareth held his breath. 'St Luke's?'

'Yes.

Crap. 'Ah.'

She frowned at him in that way he'd already grown way too fond of. 'What?'

'That's where I work.'

'You…work at St Luke's?'

He nodded. 'In the ER.'

'So we'll be…working together,' she murmured.

'Yup.'

And he hoped like hell she didn't look as good in a pair of scrubs as she did in a black sparkly dress or *sensible* and *right* were going to be toast.

CHAPTER THREE

BILLIE'S FIRST DAY at St Luke's wasn't as bad as she'd thought. Gareth wasn't there and she was able to slip into the groove of the department during daytime hours when there were a lot of senior staff around to have her back and take on the more raw and challenging cases.

She was content to take the nuisance admissions that everybody grumbled about. The patients that should be at their GPs' but had decided to save their hip pockets and clutter up the public waiting room instead.

Billie really didn't mind. It was satisfying work and she took to it like a duck to water. Her previous six months had been her medical rotation and she'd thrived there as well, treating a variety of cases from the humdrum to the interesting.

It was Thursday she wasn't looking forward to. Thursday was the start of three night shifts and from nine until eight the next morning there were just three residents—her and two others—and a registrar, dealing with whatever came through the doors.

Actually, Thursday night probably wasn't going to be so bad. It was Friday and Saturday night that had her really worried. The city bars would be open and the thought of having to deal with the product of too much booze and testosterone wasn't a welcome one.

There would be blood.

Of that she was sure.

Nine o'clock Thursday night rocked around quicker than Billie liked and she walked into St Luke's ER with a sense of foreboding.

Her hands shook as she changed into a set of scrubs in the female change room. '*St. Luke's ER*' was embroidered on the pocket in case Billie needed any further reminders that she was exactly where she didn't want to be. Jen, the other resident who had also started her rotation on the same day, chatted away excitedly and Billie let her run on, nodding and making appropriate one-word comments in the right places.

At least it was a distraction.

Thankfully, though, by the time the night team had taken handover at the central work station from the day team, Billie was feeling a little more relaxed.

Things were reasonably quiet. The resus bays were empty and only a handful of patients were in varying stages of being assessed, most of them with medical complaints that didn't involve any level of gore.

Billie knew she could handle that with one hand tied behind her back. In fact, she was looking forward to it.

A nurse cruised by and Helen, the registrar, introduced the three new residents. 'Who's on the night shift, Chrissy, do you know?'

'Gareth,' she said.

Billie's pulse leapt at his name. Helen smiled. 'Excellent.'

Chrissy rolled her eyes. 'Yeah, yeah,' she joked. 'Everyone loves Gareth.'

Helen laughed. 'He's highly experienced,' she said, feigning affront.

'Sure,' Chrissy teased. 'And those blue eyes have nothing at all to do with it.'

'Blue eyes? I hadn't noticed.' Helen shrugged nonchalantly.

'Who's Gareth?' Barry, the other new resident, asked as Chrissy left to attend to a buzzer.

'Brilliant nurse. Ex-military. Used to be in charge around here. Not sure why he was demoted…think there was some kind of incident. But, anyway, he's very experienced.'

'Ex-military?' Billie's voice sounded an octave or two higher than she would have liked but no one seemed to notice. No wonder Gareth had taken charge of the scene so expertly on Saturday night.

'Apparently,' Helen said. 'Served in MASH units all over. The Middle East most recently, I think. Exceptionally cool and efficient in an emergency.'

Billie nodded. She knew all about that coolness and efficiency.

'Also…' Helen smiled '…kind of easy on the eyes.'

She nodded again. Oh, yes. Billie definitely knew how easy he was on the eyes.

'Right,' Helen said. 'Let's get to it. Let's see if we can't whittle these patients down and have us a quiet night.'

A quiet night sounded just fine to Billie as she picked up a chart and tried not to think about seeing Gareth again in less than two hours.

Gareth came upon Billie just after midnight. He'd known, since he'd checked out the residents' roster, they'd be working together for these next three nights.

And had thought about little else since.

She had her stethoscope in her ears and was listening to the chest of an elderly woman in cubicle three when he peeled the curtain back. She didn't hear him and he stood by the curtain opening, waiting for her to finish, more than content to observe and wait patiently.

She looked *very* different tonight from the last time he'd seen her. Her hair was swept back in a no-nonsense ponytail. The long curling spirals were not falling artfully around her face as they had on Saturday night but were ruthlessly hauled back into the ponytail, giving her hair a sleek, smooth finish. Her earlobes were unadorned, her face free of make-up.

And…*yup*. He'd known it. Even from a side view she rocked a pair of scrubs.

'Well, you've certainly got a rattle on there, Mrs Gordon,' Billie said, as she pulled the stethoscope out of her ears and slung it around her neck.

'Oh, yes, dear,' the elderly patient agreed. Billie was concerned about her flushed face and poor skin turgor. 'I do feel quite poorly.'

'I don't doubt it,' Billie clucked. 'Your X-ray is quite impressive. I think we need to get you admitted and pop in a drip. We can get you rehydrated and give you some antibiotics for that lung infection.'

'Oh, I don't want you to trouble yourself,' Mrs Gordon said.

Billie smiled at her patient. The seventy-three-year-old, whose granddaughter had insisted was usually the life of the party, looked quite frail. She slipped her hand on top of the older, wrinkled one and gave it a squeeze. It felt hot and dry too.

'It's no trouble Mrs Gordon. That's what I'm here for.'

Mrs Gordon smiled back, patting Billie's hand. 'Well, that's lovely of you,' she murmured. 'But I think that young man wants to talk to you, my dear.'

Billie looked over her shoulder to find Gareth standing in a break in the curtain. He did that smile-shrug combo again and her belly flip-flopped once more. 'Hi,' she said.

'Hey,' Gareth murmured, noticing absently the cute sprinkle of freckles across the bridge of her nose and the clear gloss on her lips. Her mouth wasn't the lush scarlet temptation it had been on the weekend but its honeyed glaze drew his eyes anyway.

'Thought I'd pop in and see how you were getting on.'

'Oh…I'm fine…good…thank you.' She sounded breathy and disjointed and mentally pulled herself together. 'Just going to place an IV here and get Mrs Gordon…' she looked down at her patient and smiled '…admitted.'

Gareth nodded. She looked cool and confident in her scrubs, a far cry from the woman who'd admitted to being squeamish after losing her dinner in front of him on Saturday night. He had to give her marks for bravado.

'Do you want me to insert it?'

Billie frowned, perplexed for a moment before realising what he meant. He thought she'd baulk at inserting a cannula? Resident bread and butter?

God, just how flaky had she come across at the accident?

Another thought crossed her mind. He hadn't told anyone in the department about what had happened the other night, had he? About how she'd reacted afterwards?

He wouldn't have, surely?

She looked across at him and Helen was right, his blue scrubs set off the blue of his eyes to absolute perfection. The temptation to get lost in them was startlingly strong but she needed him to realise they weren't on the roadside any more. This was her job and she *could* do it.

She'd been dealing with her *delicate constitution,* as her father had so disparagingly called it, for a lot of years. Yes, it presented its challenges in this environment but she didn't need him to hold her hand.

'Do you think we could talk?' she asked him, before turning and patting her patient's hand. 'I'll be right back, Mrs Gordon. I just need to get some equipment.'

Gareth figured he'd overstepped the mark as he followed the business like swing of her ponytail. But he *had* seen her visibly pale at the sight of the blood running down the taxi driver's face on Saturday night. Had held her hair back while she'd vomited then listened to her squeamishness confession.

Was it wrong to feel protective of her? To want to alleviate the potential for more incidents when he was free and more than capable of doing the procedure himself?

Her back was ramrod straight and her stride brisk as she

yanked open the staffroom door. He followed her inside and Billie turned on him as soon as the door shut behind them.

'What are you doing?' she asked.

Gareth quirked an eyebrow at her. 'Trying to help? I wasn't sure if putting in IVs made you feel faint or nauseated and…' he shrugged '…I was free.'

She shoved her hands on her hips and Gareth noticed for the first time how short she was in her sensible work flats. He seemed to have a good foot on her. Just how high *had* those heels been the other night?

'Would you have offered to do anyone else's?' she demanded.

Gareth folded his arms. 'If I knew it made them squeamish, of course,' he said.

'Putting in an IV *does not* make me squeamish,' she snapped.

'Well, excuse me for trying to be nice,' he snapped back. 'You looked like you had a major issue with blood on Saturday night.'

Billie blinked at his testy comeback. She looked down at her hands. They were clenched hard at her sides and the unreasonable urge to pummel them against his chest beat like insects wings inside her head.

She shook her head. What was she doing? She was acting like a shrew. She took a deep breath and slowly unclenched her hands.

'I can put in an IV,' she sighed. 'I can draw blood, watch it flow into a tube, no problems. It's not *blood* that makes me squeamish, it's blood pouring out where it shouldn't be. It's the gore. The messy rawness. The missing bits and the… jagged edges. The…gaping wounds. That's what I find hard to handle. That's when it gets to me.'

Gareth nodded, pleased for the clarification. The ER was going to be a rough rotation for her. He took a couple of paces towards her, stopping an arm's length away.

'There's a lot of messy rawness here,' he said gently.

'I know,' Billie said. *Boy, did she know.* 'But that's the way it is and I don't want you protecting me from all of it, Gareth. I'm training to be an emergency physician. I'm just going to have to get used to it.'

She watched as his brow crinkled and the lines around his eyes followed suit. 'Why?' he asked. 'Surely this isn't the right speciality for you?'

Billie gave a half snort, half laugh. That *was* the million-dollar question. But despite feeling remarkably at ease with him, there were some things she wasn't prepared to admit to *anybody*.

'Well, yes…and there's a very long, very complicated answer to that question, which I do not have time to tell you right now.' *Or ever.* 'Not with Mrs Gordon waiting.'

Gareth nodded. He knew when he was being fobbed off but, given that she barely knew him, she certainly didn't owe him any explanations. And probably the less involved he was in her stuff the better.

He was a forty-year-old man who didn't need any more *complicated* in his life.

No matter what package it came wrapped in.

He'd had enough of it to last a lifetime.

'Okay, then,' he said, turning to go. 'Just yell if I can help you with anything.'

He had his hand on the doorknob when her tentative enquiry stopped him dead in his tracks.

'You didn't…you haven't told anyone about the other night, about what I…?' He caught her nervous swallow as he faced her. 'About how I reacted? Please…don't…'

Gareth regarded her seriously. If she'd known him better he would have given her a *what-do-you-think?* look. But she didn't, he reminded himself. It just *felt* like they'd known each other longer because of the connection they'd made less than a week ago.

It was hard to think of her as a stranger even though the reality was they barely knew each other.

He shook his head. 'I don't tell tales out of school, Billie,' he said.

He didn't kiss and tell either.

The sudden unwarranted thought slapped him in the face, resulting in temporary brain malfunction.

What the hell?

Pull it together, man. Totally inappropriate. Totally not cool.

But the truth was, as he busied himself with opening the door and getting as far away from her as possible, he'd thought about kissing Billie *a lot* these last few days.

And it had been a very long time since he'd *wanted* to kiss anyone.

CHAPTER FOUR

FIVE HOURS LATER, Gareth knew he was going to have to put Billie's I-don't-want-you-protecting-me convictions to the test. He had a head laceration that needed suturing and everyone else was busy. He could leave it until Barry was free but, with the Royal Brisbane going on diversion, a lot of their cases were coming to St Luke's and things had suddenly gone a little crazy.

They needed the bed asap.

If he'd still been in the army he would have just done the stupid thing himself. But civilian nursing placed certain restrictions on his practice.

Earlier Billie had demanded to know if he'd have given another doctor the kid-glove treatment he'd afforded her over the IV and had insisted that he not do the same to her.

Would he given any other doctor a pass on the head lac?

No. He would not.

Gareth took a deep breath and twitched the curtains to cubicle eight open. Billie looked up from the patient she was talking to. 'I need a head lac sutured in cubicle two,' he said, his tone brisk and businesslike. 'You just about done here?'

She looked startled at his announcement but he admired her quick affirmative response. 'Five minutes?' she said, only the bob of her throat betraying her nervousness.

He nodded. 'I'll set up.'

But then Brett, the triage admin officer, distracted him

with a charting issue and it was ten minutes before he headed back to the drunk teenager with the banged-up forehead. He noticed Billie disappearing behind the curtain and cursed under his breath, hurrying to catch her up.

He hadn't cleaned the wound yet and the patient looked pretty gruesome.

When he joined her behind the curtain seconds later, Billie was staring down at the matted mess of clotted blood and hair that he'd left covered temporarily with a green surgical towel. 'I'm sorry,' he apologised. 'I haven't had a chance to clean it up yet.'

She dragged her eyes away from the messy laceration and looked at him, her freckles suddenly emphasised by her pallor, her nostrils flaring as she sucked in air. 'I'll be…right back,' she said.

She brushed past him on her way out and Gareth shut his eyes briefly. *Great*. He glanced at the sleeping patient, snoring drunkenly and oblivious to the turmoil his stupid split head had just caused.

Gareth followed her, taking a guess that she'd headed for the staffroom again. The door was shut when he reached it. He turned the handle but it was locked. 'Billie,' he said, keeping his voice low, 'it's me, open up.'

The lock turned and the door opened a crack and Gareth slipped into the room. She was just on the other side and her back pushed the door shut again as she leaned against it.

Billie looked up at him, the swimmy sensation in her head and the nausea clearing. 'I'm fine,' she dismissed, taking deep, even steady breaths.

'I'm sorry. I had every intention of cleaning it up…so it looked better.'

Billie nodded. 'It's okay. I'm fine,' she repeated. 'I just need a moment.'

Gareth nodded as he watched her suck air in and out through pursed lips. She lifted her hand to smooth her hair and he couldn't help but notice how alarmingly it shook.

She didn't look okay to him.

'You look kind of freaked out,' he said. 'Do you need a paper bag to blow into? Are your fingers tingly?'

She glared at him. 'I'm not having a panic attack. I just wasn't expecting…that. I'm better if I'm mentally prepared. But I'll be fine.' She turned those big brown eyes on him. 'Just give me a moment, okay?'

'Okay.'

She nodded again and he noticed tears swim in her eyes. Clearly she was disappointed in herself, in not being able to master her affliction.

Gareth shoved a hand through his hair, feeling helpless as she struggled for control. 'Try not to think about it like it is,' he said. 'Next time you go out there it'll be all cleaned up. No blood. No gore.'

She nodded. 'Okay.'

But her wide eyes told him she was still picturing it. 'You're still thinking about it,' he said.

'I'm not,' she denied, chewing on her bottom lip.

Gareth took a step closer to her, wanting to reach for her but clenching his hands at his sides. 'Yes, you are.'

She gnawed on her lip some more and he noticed she'd chewed all her gloss off.

'Look. I'm trying, okay?' she said, placing her palm flat against his chest. 'Just back off for a moment.'

Her hand felt warm against his chest and he waited for her to push against him but her fingers curled into the fabric of his scrub top instead and Gareth felt a jolt much further south. As if she'd put her hand down his scrubs bottoms.

Oh, hell. Just hell.

Now he was thinking very bad things. Very bad ways to calm her down, to take her mind off it.

For crying out loud, she was a freaked-out second-year resident who needed to get back to the lac and get the stupid thing sutured so he could free up a bed. Gareth had dealt with a lot of freaked-out people in his life—the wounded, the addled, the grieving.

He was good with the freaked out.

But not like this. Not the way he was thinking.

Hell.

And that's exactly where he was going—*do not pass 'Go', do not collect any money*—because all he could think about now was her mouth.

Kissing it. Giving her a way to *really* forget what was beyond the door.

It was wildly inappropriate.

They were *at work,* for crying out loud. But her husky 'Gareth?' reflected the confusion and turmoil stirring unrest inside him.

The look changed on her face as her gaze fixed on his mouth. Her fingers in his shirt seemed to pull him nearer and those freckles were so damn irresistible.

'Oh, screw it,' he muttered, caution falling away like confetti around him as he stepped forward, crowding her back against the door, his body aligning with hers, his palms sliding onto her cheeks as he dropped his head.

Billie whimpered as Gareth's lips made contact with hers. She couldn't have stopped it had her life depended on it. Her pulse fluttered madly at the base of her throat and at her temples. Everything was forgotten in those lingering moments as his mouth opened and his tongue brushed along her bottom lip.

Back and forth. Back and forth. Again and again.

Maddening. Hypnotic. Perfect.

The kiss sucking away her breath and her thoughts and her sense. Transporting her to a place where only he and his lips and his heat existed. The press of his thighs against hers was heady, her breasts ached to be touched and her belly twisted hard, tensing in anticipation.

She didn't think she'd *ever* been kissed like this. And she never wanted it to stop.

She slid her hands onto his waist, anchoring them against his hips bones, feeling the broad bony crests in her palms, using them to pull him in closer, revel in the power of his thighs hard against her, fitting their bodies together more intimately.

A groan escaped his mouth, deep and tortured, as if it was torn from his throat and then Gareth pulled away, breathing hard as he placed his forehead against hers, staying close, keeping their intimate connection, not saying anything, just catching his breath as she caught hers.

'You okay now?' he asked after a moment, looking down into her face.

Billie blinked as she struggled to recall what had happened before the kiss. To recall if there had been anything at all—*ever*—in her life before this kiss.

He groaned again, his thumb stroking over her bottom lip, and it sounded as needy and hungry as the desire burning in her belly. 'We can't…do this here,' he muttered. 'We have to get back.'

She nodded. She knew. On some level she knew that. But her head was still spinning from the kiss—it was hard to think about anything else. And if that had been his plan, she couldn't fault it.

But it was hardly a good long-term strategy.

He took a step back, clearing his throat. 'You all right to do the lac now?' he asked.

The laceration. Right. That's what had happened before the kiss. She tried to picture it but her brain was still stuck back in the delicious quagmire of the kiss.

'Give me five minutes and then come to the cubicle. I promise it'll be a different sight altogether.'

Billie nodded. 'Okay.' She shifted off the door so he could open it.

And then he was gone and she was alone in the staff-room, her back against the door, pressing her fingers to her tingling mouth.

* * *

Billie took a few minutes to review the chart of her head lac patient. His blood alcohol was way over the limit. He'd gone through a glass window. The X-ray report was clear— no fractures, no retained glass—but she pulled it up on the computer to satisfy herself nonetheless.

The laceration wasn't deep but it was too large for glue.

Ten minutes later she pulled back the curtains of the cubicle. Gareth faltered for a moment as he looked at her and she didn't have to be a mind-reader to know what he was thinking.

The way his eyes dipped to her mouth said it all.

'All ready,' he said briskly, as he indicated the suture kit laid out and the dramatically changed wound. The blood was gone, leaving an uneven laceration, its edges stark white. It followed the still-sleeping patient's hairline before cutting across his forehead.

Billie swallowed as she took in the extent of it. It wasn't going to be some quick five-stitch job.

'Size six gloves?'

She nodded as she dragged her gaze back to Gareth, thankful for his brisk professionalism.

'Go and scrub,' he said. 'I'll open a pair up.'

Billie stepped outside the curtain and performed a basic scrub at the nearby basin. When she was done she waited for the water to finish dripping off her elbows before entering the cubicle again. She reached for the surgical towel already laid out and dried her hands and arms then slipped into her gloves, hyper-aware of Gareth watching her.

She took a deep breath as she arranged the instruments on her tray to her liking and applied the needle to the syringe filled with local anaesthetic.

She could do this.

She glanced at Gareth as she turned to her sleeping pa-tient. His strategy had worked—she wasn't thinking about the gruesome chore ahead, all she could think about was the kiss.

'Good grief,' she said, screwing up her nose as a blast of alcoholic fumes wafted her way. 'Think I should have put a mask on.'

'Aromatic, isn't he?'

'It's Martin, right?' she enquired of Gareth as if they'd been professional acquaintances for twenty years. As if he hadn't just kissed her and rocked her world.

Gareth nodded. 'Although he prefers M-Dog apparently.'

Billie blinked. 'I'm not going to call him M-Dog.'

Gareth laughed. 'I don't blame you.'

'Martin,' Billie said, raising her voice slightly as she addressed the sleeping patient.

Gareth shook his head. 'You don't have much experience with drunk teenage boys, do you? You need to be louder. You don't hear much in that state.'

She quirked an eyebrow. 'You talking from experience?'

He grimaced. 'Unfortunately, yes.'

Billie returned her attention to the patient. 'Martin!' she called, louder, firmer. But still nothing.

'Allow me,' said Gareth. He gave the teenager's shoulders a brisk hard shake and barked, 'Wake up, M-Dog.'

The teenager started, as did Billie, the demand cutting right through her. It was commanding, brooking no argument.

And *very* sexy.

Had he learned that in the military?

'Hmm? What?' the boy asked, trying to co-ordinate himself to sit up and failing.

Billie bit down on her cheek to stop from laughing. 'I'm Dr Keyes,' she said as Martin glanced at her through bloodshot eyes. 'I'm going to put some stitches in that nasty gash in your head.'

'Is there going to be a scar?' he asked, his eyes already closing again. 'Me mum'll kill me.'

Billie figured that M-Dog should have thought about that before he'd gone out drinking to excess. But, then, her sister Jessica had never been big on responsible drinking either. She guessed that was part and parcel of being a teenager.

For some, anyway.

'Martin, stay with me,' Billie said, her voice at the right pitch and command for M-Dog to force his bleary eyes open once again. 'I'm going to have to put a lot of local anaesthetic in your wound to numb it up. It's going to sting like the blazes.'

He gave her a goofy grin. 'Not feelin' nuthin' at the moment.'

Billie did laugh this time. 'Just as well,' she said, but the teenager was already drifting off. 'Okay,' she muttered, taking a deep breath and picking up the syringe. She glanced at Gareth. 'Here we go.'

Gareth nodded. She looked so much better now. She had pink in her cheeks, her freckles were less obvious and she'd lost that wide-eyed, freaked-out expression.

Billie's hand trembled as she picked up some gauze and started at the proximal end of the wound, poking the fine needle into the jagged edge and slowly injecting. M-dog twitched a bit and screwed up his face and Billie's heart leapt, her hand stilling as she waited for him to jerk and try and sit up. But he did nothing like that, his face settling quickly back into the passive droop of the truly drunk.

Clearly he *was* feeling no pain.

Gareth nodded at her encouragingly and Billie got back to work, methodically injecting lignocaine along the entire length of the wound, with barely a twitch from M-Dog. By the time she'd fully injected down to the distal end, the local had had enough time to start working at the beginning so she got to work.

Her stomach turned at the pull and tug of flesh, at the dull thread of silk through skin, and she peeked at Gareth.

'Talk to me,' she said, as he snipped the thread for her on her first neat suture.

He glanced at her, his gaze dropping to her mouth, and the memory of the kiss returned full throttle. 'What do you want me to talk about?'

Not that, Billie thought, returning her attention to the job at hand. *Anything but that.* The military. The *incident* that had caused his demotion, which Helen had hinted at earlier. But neither of those seemed appropriate either. Not that appropriateness hadn't already been breached tonight. But they needed to steer clear of the personal.

They'd already got *way* too personal.

'Tell me about the patients out there.'

And so he did, his deep steady voice accompanying her needlework as they wove and snipped as a team.

CHAPTER FIVE

THE REST OF the night and the two following were better than Billie could have hoped. The gore was kept to a minimum and she managed to get through them without any more near nervous breakdowns.

Or requiring any more resuscitative kissing.

Not that she wasn't aware of Gareth looking out for her. Which should probably have been annoying but which she couldn't help thinking was really sweet. *And* kind of hot.

She knew the last thing he needed was having a squeamish doctor to juggle as he ran the night shift with military-like efficiency—overseeing the nursing side as well as liaising with the medical side to ensure that the ER ran like a well-oiled machine. But he seemed to take it in his stride as just another consideration to manage.

He was clearly known and well respected by both nurses and doctors alike, he was faultlessly discreet, he knew everybody from the cleaning staff to the ward nurses, he knew where everything was and just about every answer to every procedure and protocol question any of them had.

By the time she'd knocked off on Sunday morning she was well and truly dazzled.

St Luke's was lucky to have Gareth Stapleton.

Which begged the question—why wasn't he *running* the department as he apparently used to? What had happened to cause his demotion? What was *the incident* Helen had made reference to? Annabel Pearce, the NUM, was good too, but from what Billie could see, Gareth ran rings around her.

Billie yawned as she entered the lift, pushing the button for the top floor. Her mind drifted, as it had done a little too often the last couple of days, to the kiss. She shut her tired eyes and revelled in the skip in her pulse and the heaviness in her belly as she relived every sexy nuance.

Not only could Gareth run a busy city emergency department but he could kiss like no other man she knew.

And Billie had been kissed some before.

She'd had two long-term relationships and a few shorter ones, not to mention the odd fling or two, including a rather risqué one with a lecturer, in the eight years since she'd first lost her virginity at university. She liked sex, had never felt unsatisfied by any of her partners and wasn't afraid to ask for what she wanted.

Essentially she'd been with men who knew what they were doing. Who certainly knew how to kiss.

But Gareth Stapleton had just cleared the slate.

She wet her lips in some kind of subconscious memory and grimaced at their dryness. Between winter and the hospital air-con they felt perpetually dry. She pulled her lip gloss out of her bag and applied a layer, feeling the immediate relief.

The lift dinged and she pushed wearily off the wall and headed to the fire exit for the last two flights of steps to the rooftop car park. She jumped as a figure loomed in her peripheral vision from the stairs below, her pulse leaping crazily for a second before she realised it was Gareth.

And then her pulse took off for an entirely different reason. 'You took the stairs?' she said in disbelief. '*All* eight floors?'

Of course he had. Super-nurse, freaked-out-doctor whisperer, kisser extraordinaire. What wasn't the man capable of?

'Of course.' He grinned. 'It's about the only exercise I get these days.'

Billie shook her head as they continued up the last two flights, which was torture enough for her tired body. By the time they'd reached the top and Gareth was opening the door, her thighs were grumbling at her and she was breathing a little harder.

Of course, that could just have been Gareth's presence.

Was it her overactive imagination or had his 'After you' been low and husky and a little too close to her ear?

She stepped out onto the roof, her brain a quagmire of confusion, thankful for the bracing winter air cooling her overheated imagination. She zipped up her hoody and hunched into it.

Gareth was hyper-aware of Billie's arms brushing against his as they walked across the car park to their vehicles. 'You on days off now?' he asked.

She nodded. 'Three. How about you?'

'Me too.' Which meant they'd be back on together on Wednesday. An itch shot up Gareth's spine.

Fabulous.

Three days didn't seem long enough to cleanse himself of the memory of the kiss and he really needed to do that because Billie, he'd discovered, was fast becoming the only thing he thought about.

And that wasn't conducive to his work. Or his life.

The last woman he remembered having such an instantaneous attraction to wasn't around any more, and it had taken a long time to get over that. In fact, he wasn't entirely sure he'd managed it yet. He grimaced just thinking about the black hole of the last five years.

Billie was in the ER for six months and the next few years of her life would be hectic, with a virtual roller-coaster of rotations and exams and killer shifts sucking up every spare moment of her time. She didn't have time to devote to a relationship, let alone one with a forty-year-old widower.

They were in different places in their life journeys.

They reached their cars, parked three spaces from each other, and he almost breathed a loud sigh of relief.

'Well…' he said, staring out at the Brisbane city skyline, 'I guess I'll be seeing you on Wednesday.'

She looked like she was about to say something but thought better of it, nodding instead, as she jingled her keys in her hand. 'Sure,' she murmured. 'Sleep well.'

Gareth nodded, knowing there was not a chance in hell of that happening. 'Bye.'

And he turned to walk to his vehicle, sucking in the bracing air and refusing to look back lest he suggest something *crazy* like her coming to his place and sleeping off her night shift there.

In his bed.

Naked.

Get in the car, man. *Get in the car and drive away.*

He opened the door, buckled up and started the engine. It took a while for his car to warm up and the windscreen to de-mist and he sat there trying not to think about Billie, or her sparkly dress, or her cute freckles.

Or that damned *ill-advised* kiss.

A minute later he was set to go and he reversed quickly, eager to make his escape. Except when he passed her car, it was still there and she was out of it, standing at the front with the bonnet open, looking at the engine.

He groaned out loud. No, no, no! *So close.* He sighed, reversing again and manoeuvring his car back into his car space. He disembarked with trepidation, knowing he shouldn't but knowing he couldn't not offer to help her.

'Problem?' he asked, as he strode towards her.

Billie looked at him with eyes that felt like they'd been marinating in formaldehyde all night. If possible he looked even better than before. 'It won't start,' she grumbled.

'Is it just cold?'

'No. I think the battery's flat.'

'Want me to give it a try?'

'Knock yourself out,' she invited.

Gareth slid into the plush leather passenger seat and turned the key. A faint couple of drunken whirrs could be heard and that was it. He placed his head on the steering-wheel. Yep. Dead as a doornail.

'Did you leave your lights on?' he asked, as he climbed out.

She shook her head. She'd taken her hair out of her pony-tail and it swished around her face, the tips brushing against the velour lettering decorating the front of her hoody. Her nose was pink from the cold.

'The car automatically turns them off anyway.'

Of course it did. It wasn't some twenty-year-old dinosaur. A pity, because if it had been he could have offered her a jump start. But with the newer vehicles being almost totally computerised, he knew that wasn't advisable.

'Do you have roadside assistance?'

'No. I know, I know…' Billie said, as he frowned at her. She rubbed her hands together, pleased for the warmth of her jeans and fleecy top in her unexpected foray into the cold. 'It expired a few months back and I keep meaning to renew it but…'

His whiskers looked even shaggier after three nights and his disapproving blue eyes seemed to leap out at her across the distance. 'You're a woman driving *alone* places, you should have roadside assistance.'

Billie supposed she should be affronted by his assumption that she was some helpless woman but, as with everything else, she found his concern for her well-being completely irresistible.

He sighed. 'I'll drive down to the nearest battery place and get you one,' he said.

Billie blinked as his irresistibility cranked up another notch. Was he crazy? 'It's *Sunday*, Gareth. Nothing's going to be open till at least ten and I don't know about you but

I'm too tired to wait that long.' She shut her bonnet. 'I'll get a taxi home and deal with the battery this afternoon after I've had a sleep.'

Gareth knew he was caught then. He couldn't let her get a taxi home. Not when he could easily drop her. Unless she lived way out of his way. 'I'll give you a lift,' he said. 'Where do you live?'

He hoped it was somewhere *really* far away.

Billie would have been deaf not to hear the reluctance in his voice. And she was too tired to decipher what it meant. Tired enough to be pissed off. 'You don't have to do that, Gareth,' she said testily, fishing around in her bag for her mobile phone. 'I'm perfectly capable of ringing and paying for a taxi. I could even walk.'

She watched a muscle clench in his jaw. 'Don't be stupid,' he dismissed. 'You've worked all night and I'm here with a perfectly functioning car. It makes sense. Now... Where. Do. You. Live?'

She glared at him. 'Only a really *stupid* man would call a tired woman stupid.'

Gareth shut his eyes and raked a hand through his hair, muttering, 'Bloody hell.' He glanced at her then. 'I apologise, okay? Just tell me where you live already.'

'Paddo.'

Paddington. *Of course she did.* Trendy, yuppie suburb as befitted her sparkly dress and expensive car. 'Perfect. You're on my way home.' He was house-sitting in the outer suburbs but she lived in his general direction.

She folded her arms. He could tell she was deciding between being churlish and grateful. 'If you're sure you don't mind?'

Gareth shook his head. 'Of course not,' he said, indicating that she should make her way to his car. 'As long as you don't mind slumming it?'

Billie shot him a disparaging look. 'I'm sure I'll manage.'

Gareth nodded as she passed in front of him. The question was, would he?

CHAPTER SIX

THEY DROVE IN silence for a while as Gareth navigated out of the hospital grounds and onto the quiet Sunday morning roads. He noticed she tucked her hands between her denim-clad thighs as he pulled up at the first red traffic light.

'Are you cold?' he asked, cranking the heat up a little more.

'Not too bad,' she murmured.

Gareth supposed the seats in her car were heated and this was probably a real step down for her. And maybe when he'd been younger, before life had dealt him a tonne of stuff to deal with, he might have felt the divide between them acutely.

But he'd since lived a life that had confirmed that possessions meant very little—from the pockmarked earth of the war-torn Middle East to the beige walls of an oncology unit—he'd learned very quickly that *stuff* didn't matter.

And frankly he was too tired and too tempted by her to care for her comfort.

Her scent filled the car. He suddenly realised that she'd been wearing the same perfume last Saturday night but he had been too focused on the accident to realise. Something sweet. Maybe fruity? Banana? With a hint of vanilla and something…sharper.

Great—she smelled like a banana daiquiri.

And now it was in his car. And probably destined to be so for days, taunting him with the memory.

She shifted and in his peripheral vision he could see two narrow stretches of denim hugging her thighs, her hands still jammed between them.

'So,' Gareth said out of complete desperation, trying to *not* think about her thighs and how good they might feel wrapped around him, 'you called yourself Dr Keyes…the other night. With M-Dog.'

Yep. Complete desperation. Why else would he even be remotely stupid enough to bring up *that* night when they were trapped in a tiny, warm cab together, only a small gap and a gearstick separating them, the kiss lying large between them?

But Billie didn't seem to notice the tension as she shrugged and looked out the window. 'It's easier sometimes to just shorten it. Ashworth-Keyes is a bit of a mouthful at times and, frankly, it can also sound a bit prissy. I tend to use it more strategically.'

'So drunk teenagers who go by the name of M-Dog don't warrant the star treatment?'

Billie turned and frowned at him, surprisingly stung by his subtle criticism. 'No,' she said waspishly. 'Some people respond better to a double-barrelled name. There are some patients, I've found, who are innately…snobbish, I guess. They like the idea of a doctor with a posh name. Guys called M-Dog tend to see it as a challenge to their working-class roots…or something,' she dismissed with a flick of her hand. 'And frankly…' she sought his gaze as they pulled up at another red light and waited till he looked at her '…I was a little too…confounded by our kiss to speak in long words. I'm surprised I managed to remember my name at all.'

Billie held his gaze. If he was going to call her on something, he'd better get it right or be prepared to be called on it himself. She might be helplessly squeamish, she might not be able to stand up to her family and be caught up in the sticky web of their expectations but she'd been taught how to hold her own by experts.

There was nothing more cutting than a put-down from a surgeon who thought the sun shone out of his behind.

'Yes,' he said after a moment or two, his throat bobbing as he broke eye contact and put the car into gear. 'That was... confounding.'

Billie almost laughed at the understatement. But at least he wasn't denying it. They'd studiously avoided any mention of the kiss since it had happened, but it *was* there between them and she knew he felt it as acutely as she did.

She'd spent the last couple of days telling herself that it hadn't meant anything. That it didn't *count*. That Gareth had used it only as a strategy to snap her out of her situation.

But it had still felt very real.

They accomplished the rest of the trip in silence, apart from her brief directions, and Gareth pulled up outside her place in under ten minutes.

'Thank you,' she said, unbuckling.

Gareth nodded. 'No problems,' he murmured, as he let the car idle.

He waited for her to reach for the door handle but she didn't. 'No. I mean for everything,' she said. 'For just now but also for the other night. For what you did. For how you helped...calm the situation. For the kiss.'

Gareth swallowed hard as Billie once again mentioned the one thing he was trying hard not to think about. She'd been right when she'd said it was confounding and he wished she'd just leave it alone so he could put it away in his mental too-hard-to-deal-with basket.

'Don't,' he said. 'Don't thank me for that.' Confounding or not, it hadn't been proper. 'What happened...it pretty much constitutes sexual harassment.'

Her snort was loud in the confined space between them, the world outside the warm bubble of the car forgotten.

'That's rubbish, Gareth,' she said. 'Kissing me at work is only sexual harassment if I didn't want or encourage it, if it was unwelcome, and while I appreciate you trying to give me a pass on my behaviour, you can be damned sure I wanted you to kiss me, very *very* much. We're not *just* two people who met at work, we're not *just* colleagues, and you know it. We're both adults here so let's not pretend there hasn't been a thing between us since the accident.'

Gareth looked at Billie, her brown eyes glowing at him fiercely, her chest rising and falling, stretching the fabric of her hoody in very interesting ways across her chest. He found it hard to reconcile this woman with the one who had been a pale wreck over a head lac or vomiting at the scene of an accident.

He nodded. 'Of course. You're right. I apologise.'

The *thing* pulsed between them and God knew he wanted her now.

He looked away, inspecting her house through the windscreen for a few moments, the heater pumping warm air into the already heated atmosphere. It was one of those old-fashioned worker cottages that had been bought for a song twenty years ago, renovated and sold for a goodly sum.

'Do you want to come in? For a coffee.'

Gareth shut his eyes against the temptation, feeling older and more tired than he had in a long time. 'Billie,' he murmured, a warning in his voice.

Billie looked at his profile. 'Don't trust yourself, Gareth?' she taunted.

He looked at her, her lip gloss smeared enticingly, a small smile playing on her mouth, a knowing look in her eyes, and his tiredness suddenly evaporated.

He didn't trust himself remotely.

'Billie… This isn't going to happen.'

She looked at him for long moments. 'Why not?'

The enquiry could have come across sounding petulant. If she'd pouted. If she'd injected any kind of whine into her voice. But she didn't. She just looked at him with that slight smile on her mouth and asked the very sensible, very reasonable question.

They wanted each other. They were both single and of age. *Why not indeed?*

Gareth sighed. 'You're, what, Billie? Twenty-seven?'

She shook her head. 'Twenty-six.'

Gareth groaned. Dear God, It was worse than he'd thought. 'I'm forty years old,' he said. 'I think you need to play with boys your own age.'

'You think I'm too young for you?'

He nodded. 'Yes.' *Way* too young. 'And…'

'And?' She skewered him with her gaze. 'You think I'm too forthright, don't you?'

'No! I don't care about that. I like forthright women.' His wife, a complete stranger at the time *and* stone-cold sober, had come right up to him in a bar and kissed the life out of him in front of everyone.

'Well, then?'

'Billie…' he sighed. 'I'm at a different stage of my life than you are. You've got many years ahead of you, with a lot of hard work and dedication to get where you're going. You don't have the time to devote to serious relationships and I'm—'

'It's *coffee*, Gareth,' she interrupted.

Gareth shook his head at her, his gaze drifting to her mouth, the gloss beckoning, then back to her earnest brown eyes. 'It's not just coffee and you know it.'

She shrugged then slid her hand onto his leg. 'Would that be such a bad thing?'

A hot jolt streaked up Gareth's thigh and he was instantly hard. His hand quickly clamped down on hers as it moved closer to ground zero. 'Give me a break here, Billie. I'm trying to do the right thing.'

'How very *noble* of you,' she murmured glancing at her hand held firmly in place by his before returning her attention to him. 'Look…I understand that you think I need kid gloves after the other night but I really don't need you looking out for me in *this* department. I think this *is* the right thing.'

Gareth's sense of self-preservation told him otherwise. There wasn't one part of him that believed their *coffee* session would be the end of it. And, despite her confidence right now, he'd met enough doctors in this stage of their careers to know how many relationships didn't make it.

His wife's death had left Gareth very wary. It had taken a huge chunk out of him. One that had never grown back. He had no intention of lining up for another pound of flesh. And something told him Billie could do exactly that.

So she wanted a fling? Not going to happen. Not when they worked together.

'I'm not into recreational sex.'

'Really?'

She smiled then, her voice clearly disbelieving. She tried to move her hand further north but he held tight for a few moments before finally giving away to her insistence. Gareth watched her palm move closer to his crotch, torn between stopping her again and grabbing her hand and putting it where his groin screamed for attention.

She halted just short of his happy zone and he tore his gaze away from her neat fingernails so very, very close to his zipper.

'I think you must be the only man in the world who doesn't see the value in a little harmless physical release,' she said.

Gareth absently noticed that the windscreen was fogging up on the inside and tuned in to the roughness of her voice and the heaviness of his own breathing as the pads of her fingers brushed awfully close to nirvana. He knew if he didn't stop this now, he wouldn't.

And with his normal self-control lulled due to lack of sleep, he was just weary enough to succumb.

'*I think* you're tired,' he said, turning his face to look at her. 'We're both tired. *I think* people can make bad decisions when they're tired.'

She slid her hand home and Gareth shut his eyes, biting

back a groan as pleasure undulated through the fibres deep inside his belly and thighs.

'I'm awake now,' she murmured, her voice husky in the charged atmosphere. 'And I gotta say…' she paused to give his erection a squeeze '…you don't feel that tired to me.'

God.

She was trying to kill him.

Gareth gave a half-laugh. 'Trust me,' he said, his eyes opening as he gathered his last scrap of self-control and re-moved her hand from his hard-on, '*that* is a really unreliable measure of tiredness. Of anything, for that matter.'

Billie's stomach plummeted, and not in a good way, as she placed her hand back between her thighs. She'd felt so sure that she'd be able to persuade Gareth to stay and she squirmed a little in the seat to ease the ache that had started to build between her legs in delicious anticipation.

'I'm sorry, Billie.'

She tossed her head and looked out the window. 'It's fine,' she said.

Billie supposed she should feel embarrassed or mortified. And perhaps if she'd been more mentally alert she might have been. Hell, if she'd been more mentally alert she probably wouldn't have propositioned him at all.

Or been so damned persistent.

No doubt the mortification was yet to come but for now she just felt disappointed.

'I just…don't want you to do something that you might regret tomorrow,' he continued. 'This kind of step needs to be taken when all your faculties are intact and I don't want to be on your dumb-things-I-did list, Billie. We have to work together for the next six months and I've been around long enough to see how awkward that can be in the workplace.'

Billie nodded. Just her luck to develop a thing for the first man she'd ever met who didn't think with his penis.

She turned to look at him. 'You have one of those?'

He frowned and his eyes crinkled and he looked all sexy

and sleepy and perplexed and she wanted to drag him into her house, into her bed *so freaking bad* even if it was just to snuggle and sleep. 'One of what?' he asked.

'A dumb-things-I-did list.'

His frowned cleared and then he laughed. 'Oh, hell, yeah.'

His laughter was deep and rich and warm, a perfect serenade in their intimate cocoon, so nearly tangible Billie felt as if she could pick it up and wrap it around her like a cloak. Interesting lines buried amidst all that stubble bracketed his mouth and she squeezed her thighs together tight, trapping her hands there.

Hands that wanted to touch him.

Billie didn't have that kind of list, although she suddenly wished she did. Even if it meant he was at the top. Although no doubt there were plenty who would think living out her sister's dreams to keep her parents happy was a really dumb thing to do.

The unhappy thought pierced the intimacy and Billie stirred. She didn't want it in here with them. She unbuckled her seat belt. 'Thanks for the lift.'

Billie reached for the handle and pulled; the door opened a crack and cold air seeped in as she half turned her body, preparing to exit. But Gareth's hand reached across the interior, wrapping gently around her upper arm.

'You understand it's not about *not* wanting you, right?'

Billie's heart almost stopped in her chest. She looked over her shoulder at him. He looked bleak and tired and *torn*.

'I know,' she murmured, and then, without thinking about it, she leaned across the short distance between them and kissed him quick and hard.

For a brief few seconds she felt him yield. Whiskers spiked her mouth and scraped her chin and she tasted the spice of his groan.

And then she pulled away—pulled away before she did something crazy like straddle him—and exited the car without looking back.

CHAPTER SEVEN

WORKING WITH GARETH on Wednesday wasn't as excruciating as Billie had thought it was going to be. She *had* suffered a degree of remorse over her behaviour and *had* been prone to episodes of acute embarrassment during her days off whenever she remembered how persistent she'd been, but he'd soon put her at ease with his brisk professionalism.

It helped that he didn't come on until the afternoon so she was already in the groove when she first fronted him. And then, of course, he was focused and businesslike as always and by teatime she'd almost forgotten that she'd groped him in his car and more or less invited him into her bed but been knocked back.

She didn't regret it, as he had predicted. She doubted she would have regretted it if he'd taken her up on her offer either.

But she was mindful of how it must look to him. How *she* must look. What he thought of her she had no idea. She'd known him for less than two weeks and in that time she'd swung wildly from being a vomiting, hyperventilating wreck to a penis-squeezing vamp.

That made her cringe.

He seemed so sophisticated, so *together,* compared to her.

Why it should be a concern she didn't want to think about. He was right—she had a tough few years ahead of her career-wise and being in a relationship had not been part of her plans.

Her parents and all the extended members of the Ash-worth-Keyes surgical dynasty had said the same thing. Specialising was hard on your social life and not a lot of relationships survived. Career first, personal life later.

So, yeah, Gareth's words of wisdom had resonated with her the other morning.

But still... He made her want things. And specialising wasn't one of them.

Gareth's mobile rang as he sat at the table in the staffroom. He was pleased for the reprieve. Billie was sitting opposite him and he swore she was just wearing that lip gloss now to drive him crazy. Thankfully Kate and Lindy, two of the junior nurses on the afternoon shift, were having their break as well and the three women were engaged in a conversation about television vampires.

Amber's picture flashed on the screen and he smiled as he slid the bar across to answer. 'Hey, sweetheart,' he said as he answered the phone. Billie glanced at him, a little frown drawing her brows together, and he got up and wandered over to the sink, his back to the table. 'Everything okay?'

Apparently not. His stepdaughter was crying so hard he could barely make out her garbled reply. A hot spike of concern lanced him. 'Amber?' he said, trying to keep his voice down and devoid of alarm. 'What's wrong?' he demanded.

He was pretty sure she was telling him she was outside. 'You're here?' he asked, already turning and heading for the door, aware on a subliminal level of Billie's interest but too worried about Amber for it to register properly.

'I'm coming now,' he said, as he hung up and pulled the door open.

Thirty seconds later he was stalking out into the main thoroughfare, spotting Amber looking red-faced and dishevelled near the triage desk, the long fringe of her pixie cut plastered to her forehead in a way that she usually wouldn't be seen dead wearing.

His heart leapt into his mouth. 'Amber?' He strode towards her.

When she flung herself against his chest and dissolved into even more tears, Gareth knew it had to be bad. His and Amber's relationship had been fairly tempestuous since her mother had died and public displays of affection had been strictly forbidden.

He didn't blame her. Amber had been fifteen when Catherine had been diagnosed and had died five months later from breast cancer. Being angry at him was easier than being angry at the entire world. Although she'd been there too.

Patients in the waiting area and members of staff looked on curiously as Amber's loud honking cries continued and didn't seem likely to abate any time soon. He led her into the nearby nurses' handover room, which was essentially a cubicle with three sides of glass. But it had a door he could shut, was relatively soundproof and with various posters stuck on the walls they were obscured somewhat from full view.

'What happened?' he asked, as he shut the door after them. 'Did you break up with Blaine?'

Amber's cries cut off as she glared at him. 'Only three months ago.'

He held up his hands in apology. 'Really?'

'Yes,' she snapped.

Amber had been a good kid but also, in many ways, a typical teenager—everything an overblown drama—and then she'd been a *grieving* teenager, which had put her into a whole different category. It had been like watching a train wreck and trying to be there to pick up the pieces, when she'd let him. Things had been particularly fraught.

And now she was a pissed-off young woman.

And he *still* couldn't tell when her tears were serious or just the I-broke-my-fingernail-and-it's-all-your-fault variety.

Catherine had always known.

Gareth realised suddenly he hadn't thought about Catherine in a while and, with Amber looking at him with those big green eyes the exact shade of her mother's, guilt punched him hard in the chest.

'Okay, so…what *is* the matter?'

Amber sniffled and dragged a ball of crumbled-up paper out of her bag and handed it to him. Gareth took it, hoping it wasn't some 'Dear John' letter that he really *did not* want to read. He unravelled it, the wrinkled page quickly revealing itself to be a lab report.

A sudden spike of fear sliced into his side. He looked at this kind of report every day in his job. But he and Amber had a history with these reports too—not one he ever wanted to repeat.

He ironed it out with his hands as he scanned it.

The top left-hand corner had Amber's personal details. Name. Address, Date of birth. Allergy status. The next line leapt out at him.

BRCA1—positive.

Gareth's breath caught in his throat. His heart thumped so hard his ribs hurt. His vision tunnelled, narrowed down to the stark brevity of that line.

She had tested positive for a faulty gene that dramatically increased her risk of developing breast cancer. The disease that had killed her mother.

Crap!

'I didn't think you wanted the test,' he said, looking at a red-eyed Amber as his brain scrambled to absorb the shocking news.

She shrugged in that belligerent way he was used to but it somehow lost its effectiveness when she looked so devastated. 'I changed my mind.'

Gareth sat down on the nearest chair. 'I thought we were going to talk about it together before you decided.'

'I…couldn't,' she said. 'And anyway it was…spur of the moment.'

Gareth looked down at the page again. 'I didn't want you to go through this by yourself, Amber.'

'I didn't…I had counselling. The cancer centre wouldn't let me do it without.'

He shook his head at the things she must have been going through these last few weeks. He rang or texted most days but Amber was busy at uni, living the college life. Occasionally she rang or texted back. Sometimes happy, sometimes not. Sometimes because she needed money or a place to crash for the night.

And he got that. But this…he would have thought she'd want him around for this.

'I could have been there for you.'

Gareth had had to stop himself five years ago from demanding she take the test there and then. Catherine's death had been devastating and the thought that Amber might have inherited the gene had been too much to bear. He hadn't been able to reach in and rip the cancer out of Catherine, but he could protect Amber from her mother's fate.

They could be forewarned. Forearmed.

But the oncologists and Amber's psychologist had counselled against it at such a young age. And he'd *known* they were right. Logically, he'd known that. She hadn't needed that extra burden at that point, not when she had probably been years away from making any concrete decisions over a potentially positive result.

But his fear hadn't been logical.

Amber may not have been his daughter by blood but he'd been with Catherine since Amber had been a cute five-year-old with two missing front teeth and he loved her as fiercely as if she were his own.

She shook her head. 'I didn't want to…worry you.'

He gave her his best don't-kid-me look. 'You think I don't worry about you, Amber?'

Her eyes filled with tears then, so like her mother's, and

his heart broke for the grief Amber had endured in such a short life.

'What am I going to do, Gareth? I have a forty to eighty per cent chance of developing breast cancer. Do I get a double mastectomy? Do I line up to have my uterus removed and never be able to have a baby?' She looked at him with those big green eyes swimming in tears. 'What man's going to want me with no boobs, Gareth?'

She started to cry again and Gareth stood, reaching for her and sweeping her into his arms. 'Shh,' he said, hugging her close just like when she'd been a kid and fallen off her bike, skinning her knee and denting her pride.

Back in the days when there hadn't been five years of angst and grief and blame between them.

'Hey,' he said, as he stroked her hair, letting her cry, raising his voice above the wrenching noise of it. 'Firstly, you and I are going back to the clinic together so we can have a nice long talk about options.'

He made a mental note to make the first available appointment. 'Secondly, these aren't decisions you're going to need to make for a long time, sweetheart. This just means we have to be more vigilant. And I'm going to be there for you every step of the way, okay?'

'Okay,' she said, and cried harder.

'Thirdly...' This was the hardest one. He didn't relish having to talk to Amber about sexuality and desire. She'd generally thought any topics like that were private and female and not up for discussion with her stepfather.

But if she'd been a patient asking these questions, searching for answers, he wouldn't have hesitated to reassure her.

Gareth prised her gently off his chest and looked down into her red swollen eyes. 'Do you think your mother losing a breast made me love her any less? Made her any less desirable to me as a woman?'

He half expected her to rebel. To screw up her face and say, 'Eww, gross, Gareth,' which had been pretty much her catchphrase from thirteen onwards. But she didn't, she just shook her head at him. 'But you already had a relationship with Mum. You had to love her regardless of her…boob situation.'

Gareth smiled at Amber's typical reluctance to use correct anatomical words. 'I loved your mother from the first moment I met her. And it had nothing to do with her *boobs*.'

'It's still not the same,' Amber dismissed.

Gareth squeezed her arms. 'Any man who can't see past your physical self to the amazing woman you are inside isn't worth your time, Amber. Life's short, sweetie, you don't need me to tell you that. Too short to waste on men who aren't worthy.'

Amber smiled up at him through her tears. She slid her hand onto his cheek and patted his stubble like she used to when she was little and had been endlessly fascinated by its scratchiness. She'd never known her father and Gareth's stubble had been intriguing. She dropped her hand.

'I don't think they make men like you any more.'

Gareth smiled down at Amber, feeling closer to her than he had in a long time. 'Yes, they do, sweetie,' he said. 'And I still have my service revolver for the others.'

She smiled again then pulled away, turning her back to him as she looked absently through the patches of glass to the hustle and bustle of the department.

'Do you think I'm vain for worrying about my boobs?' she asked eventually. 'About someone wanting me when so many women are dead? When Mum is dead?'

Gareth slid his hand onto her shoulder and gave it a squeeze. 'Of course not, Amba-San.' Her old nickname slipped out. She normally chided him for using it these days but not today. 'You can't think about something like this and not think about how it affects you in every way. But you are getting ahead of yourself sweetheart. Way ahead.'

Amber turned and nodded and Gareth's hand slipped

away. 'I'm sorry. I guess the results freaked me out a little. They tried to talk to me at the clinic about them but I just ran.'

'It's okay, we'll go back there together in the next couple of days, okay?'

Amber nodded. 'Just promise me you'll find me the best plastic surgeon in the country to give me new boobs if or when this whole thing becomes a reality.'

Gareth smiled, encouraged by her *if*. 'I promise I'll find you the best breast man I can.'

Amber screwed up her nose and said, 'Eww, gross, Gareth,' but she was smiling and she walked easily into his arms, accepting his hug.

When they pulled apart he slipped his hands either side of her face and cradled it like he used to. 'How about you come over tonight? I don't get off till nine but we can get takeaway and watch one of those dreadful chick flicks you like so much.'

Amber laughed. 'Oh, the sacrifice.' She rubbed her cheek into his big palm for long moments before pulling away. 'It's okay. Carly knows. I'm going out with her tonight and drinking way too much tequila.'

Gareth nodded. The father in him wanted to caution her against drinking to excess but he'd been twenty himself once. And Carly was a very sensible young woman. If she knew the circumstances then Gareth had absolute faith she wouldn't let Amber get too messy. Those two had had each other's backs since they'd been nine.

'Okay,' he said. 'Are you sure you're going to be all right?'

Amber nodded. 'Talking with you helped.'

He smiled. 'You can always talk to me, Amba-San.'

'I know. Sorry I can be such an ingrate sometimes. It just still…gets me sometimes and I just don't know what to do with it. It makes me so…angry, you know?'

'Yeah,' Gareth said. He knew *exactly* how she felt. 'I know.'

There was a brief knock on the door and it opened.

'Gareth,' the triage nurse said, peeking her head around the door, 'assault victim, multiple injuries, blunt chest trauma, in a bad way. Ten minutes out.'

He looked at Amber. 'Sorry.'

She smiled and gave him a quick hug. 'It's fine. I'm already late and Carly will be waiting for me.'

'I'll call you tomorrow,' he said.

'Okay.'

'I love you, Amber,' he said.

She gave his stubble a pat again. 'Love you too,' she said, as she departed the room.

Gareth's gaze followed her, his heart beating a steady determined tattoo. Cancer couldn't take her too.

Billie almost collided with Amber as she hurried out of the handover room. 'Sorry,' Billie called after the young woman, who continued on but not before Billie had noticed the tear-streaked face.

Billie glanced up to find a grim-looking Gareth standing in the open doorway, tracking the woman's progress. Clearly something had transpired between them. Was it another nurse she hadn't met yet? Or another colleague? Or a patient's relative?

Whatever it was, it was obviously intense.

Her stomach twisted hard.

CHAPTER EIGHT

'YOU READY FOR THIS?'

Billie looked up from staring down at her gloves, the ambulance siren loud as it screeched to a halt metres from them. It echoed around the concrete and steel bay, reverberating against her chest, drumming through her veins.

She stiffened at Gareth's propriety. 'Yes.'

He still looked all kinds of grim. Was that him mentally preparing for what they were about to see or was it to do with the mysterious woman? A hot knot of emotion lodged in her chest and Billie realised she felt jealous. Which was utterly insane. She had no claim over him to justify jealousy. And it was hardly an appropriate time to feel the hot claw in her gut.

An assault victim was fighting for his life in the back of an ambulance, for crying out loud.

But it was there. It just *was*.

And his *concern* for her rankled. It was courteous and kind and thoughtful. And she hated it.

She didn't need his pity, his propriety or his patience.

Well…she didn't *want* them anyway. She didn't want him looking at her as some cot case to coddle and hand-hold and treat with kid gloves.

She didn't want him to look at her as a chore.

Not when she saw him in an entirely different light.

A paramedic opened the back door of the ambulance. 'It's going to be messy,' Gareth warned.

Billie's irritation ramped up another notch despite the strong stir of nausea in her gut. 'I know,' she snapped.

Did he really think she *didn't* know?

And then it was action stations as the paramedics hauled the gurney out of the back and pushed it quickly towards them, the intensive care paramedic reeling off a handover as they all accompanied the briskly moving trolley.

'Corey Wilson, twenty-two-year-old male, found in an alley in the city with multiple injuries, presumed assault. Unresponsive, bradycardic, hypotensive. Pupils unequal but reactive to light. Intubated on the scene, a litre of Hartmann's given, wide-bore IV access both arms.'

They entered the resus bay and Billie's hands shook as she helped get the beaten and bloodied young man across to the hospital trolley. An endotracheal tube protruded from his mouth and a hard collar protected his neck during the process.

Within a trice the ambulance gurney was gone and Billie was staring into Corey's grotesquely bruised face. Dried blood was smeared everywhere, his eyes swollen and ringed in black and purple. Her stomach turned over.

His shirt, split up the middle by a pair of paramedic shears, hung down his side, revealing more blood and bruising on his chest as ECG dots were slapped in place.

Denise Haig, the emergency consultant, who hadn't yet gone home for the day, barked orders at everyone. 'Let's get him assessed and to CT,' she said.

The oxygen saturations on the monitor were decreased and Denise looked at Billie and said, 'Listen to his chest.'

Billie fought against the urge to turn away, fought the pounding in her own chest, concentrated on her breathing, staring at Corey's chest rather than his face as she shoved her stethoscope in her ears and listened. She felt Gareth's eyes on her but refused to look at him as she quickly assessed both lung fields.

She was part of this team and she would work with them

to save Corey, no matter how affected she was by his battered body.

'Chest sounds decreased on the right, almost absent,' Billie reported. 'Lot of crepitus.'

Which was hardly surprising. Corey looked like he'd taken a real beating to the chest, broken ribs were a given. The oxygen saturations fell further and Corey's heart rate, which had been worryingly slow, suddenly shot up.

'Check his JVP,' Denise said.

Billie was on autopilot now, the adrenaline in her system keeping her going, elevating her to a higher place, allowing her to do her work yet stay removed from the horror of it.

The hard collar obscured his neck veins from her view and she had to peer through the side window to assess it. His jugular bulged ominously. 'Pressure elevated,' Billie said. She flicked her gaze to his windpipe, which appeared, from what she could see, to be skewed to one side. 'Trachea's deviated.'

Denise nodded. 'Tension pneumo. Put in a chest tube, stat,' she ordered.

Billie's hands shook as someone thrust a pair of sterile gloves at her. No time for a proper surgical scrub. This was *emergency* medicine with a capital E. The build-up of air in Corey's chest from a fractured rib puncturing his lung was affecting his venous return and he needed urgent chest decompression.

She looked up as she shoved her right hand into the right glove. *Gareth.* He nodded and smiled at her. 'Good to go?'

Concern radiated from his eyes and Billie was determined to dispel it immediately. She nodded back. 'You got the pack?'

He dragged a small mobile trolley over with all she would need already laid out. He reached over and squirted some liquid antibiotic on Corey's chest and briskly cleaned a section of skin mid-axilla with some gauze. When it was reasonably clear of dried blood he doused the area again with the brown antiseptic agent.

'Your turn,' he said.

Billie moved closer, reaching for the scalpel. In a normal clinical setting she'd be gowned and masked, she'd inject local, the patient would be draped. But Corey didn't have that time, this was down and dirty. This was life and death.

She was conscious of the screaming of alarms around her and the battering of her pulse through her head as she quickly located the right spot. This wasn't her first chest tube, although it was her first tension pneumo.

Billie made a small incision. Blood welled from the cut and she forced her shaking knees to lock.

'Forceps,' she said, concentrating hard on keeping her voice steady as she handed the scalpel back to Gareth.

He passed her the forceps and she bluntly dissected down to the pleura, puncturing it with the tip of the forceps. She inserted her finger into the hole and swept away a soft clot she could feel there, her stomach revolting at the action.

'Tube,' she said, not looking at Gareth, not looking at anything other than her finger in someone's chest and concentrating on not throwing up. He handed it to her and she placed the tip into the hole, using the forceps to feed it in, advancing it until all the drainage holes lining the tip were inside the chest cavity.

The whole procedure was accomplished in less than a minute and her hands shook as she stripped the gloves off.

The oxygen sats improved almost immediately and Corey's heart rate decreased.

'Well done,' Gareth murmured, just loud enough amidst the chaos for only the two of them to hear. He handed her a pair of regular gloves and connected a drain bottle to the end of the tube.

Their celebration of her competency was short-lived, however, as suddenly a torrent of blood flowed out the tube, draining quickly into the collection device. Before Billie's eyes it filled to halfway and she swallowed back a retch as more rushed in, forming a thick red sludge.

'Haemo-pneumo,' Gareth said.

Denise nodded. 'Not surprising. Push two units of O-neg.'

'Pupils are blown.'

'Right,' Denise said to Gareth. 'Get on to Cat Scan. Tell them we're coming around. Where the hell is Neuro?' she asked no one in particular.

They were snapping the side rails in place when the monitor alarmed again. The heart rate, which had started to slow down again after the chest tube insertion, suddenly flicked into a dangerous tachy-arrythmia. Denise felt through the side windows in the collar. 'We've lost his pulse.'

The rails came down again as Denise issued another rapid-fire set of orders, rattling off some drug doses.

Billie couldn't stop looking at the drainage from the chest, the bottle was three-quarters full now. She couldn't block out the screaming of the alarms. Corey's life was literally draining away.

Just like Jessica's had that night.

He was twenty two and dying. It was too cruel. She wanted to throw up, faint *and* burst into tears.

'Billie!'

Denise's shrill command broke through her inertia. Billie looked at her. 'I said start chest compressions.'

Billie nodded. She faltered as she placed her gloved hands on Corey's chest, looking down at the dried blood streaking his ribs and belly. 'I'll do it,' Gareth said, stepping forward.

'No!' Gareth's interference suddenly snapped Billie out of it. She didn't care how much she wanted to stop and throw up right now. She needed to prove she could do this. To Denise. *To Gareth.* To her long-dead sister.

And most especially to herself.

She had to know she could get past her physical reaction to the gore and rawness of emergency medicine. She had to know that she could pigeonhole the human tragedy that threatened to overwhelm and cripple her and do what needed to be done.

* * *

They worked on Corey for forty-five minutes. Billie sought and found her earlier state of removal as she pounded on his chest. Going through the motions, following directions but all the time placing her mental side, her emotional self, elsewhere. Buried somewhere at the back of her brain.

Not thinking about Corey or his age or what his last moments must have been like or that he was dying surrounded by strangers. Not thinking about the drainage bottle being changed. Or the repeated unsuccessful zaps to the chest. Removing herself from the arrival of his mates and the shouting and loud angry sobs as they were told he was critical and they had to wait.

Just doing her job.

Her arms ached. Her muscles screamed at her. Gareth offered to take over but she declined. Several others offered as well but she refused.

And even when Denise called time of death and everyone stopped and stepped away, it took a moment or two for Billie to realise, continuing the compressions until Gareth touched her arm and said, 'You can stop now, Billie.'

She'd been so focused on the action, on breathing with each one, on the way her gloved fingers looked against Corey's sternum, she'd zoned out everyone else.

Billie looked around at the defeated faces, the downcast eyes and stepped back herself.

Denise stripped off her gloves. 'Thanks, everyone,' she said.

Half an hour later Denise approached Gareth. 'I need you in on the chat with the relatives,' she said.

Gareth nodded. They'd been waiting for Corey's parents to arrive. His mates were still in the waiting room, subdued now as they waited for news about their friend, but as it was against hospital policy to provide information to people who weren't relatives, they hadn't yet been told of Corey's passing.

'You going to do it now?' he asked.

'No.' She shook her head. 'Billie's going to do it. But I'll be there. And so will you.'

Gareth glanced over at Billie, who was writing up Corey's notes. He'd sat in on one too many of these not to know how harrowing they were—he wouldn't wish them on his worst enemy. He certainly wouldn't wish it on a woman he'd come perilously close to bedding a handful of days ago.

'Come on, Denise,' he murmured, 'do you really think she's up to it? Don't you think she's been through enough trauma today?'

Demise nodded briskly. 'I know. But if she wants to do this job, then talking to relatives is all part and parcel of it. Better to get the first one over and done with.'

He quirked an eyebrow at her. He'd worked with Denise for five years. She was good. Fair. Shrewd. And a little old school. 'Tough love?'

'Got to sort the wheat from the chaff.'

'You don't have to do it tonight. She should have knocked off thirty minutes ago.'

Denise shrugged. 'Billie's a good doctor but she's not cut out for this. I know it and I suspect you know it too. It's better that she figures that out early than waste years of her life specialising in a field that doesn't suit her talents because she watched too many ER dramas on TV.'

Gareth shot her a look full of recrimination. 'Steady on.'

'Oh, come on, Gareth, don't tell me you haven't seen them year after year, lining up to work here because it's been glamorised on television.'

Sure, he had, but those residents rarely lasted the distance. 'I think her reasons are a little deeper than that.'

'Okay. Maybe you're right. Maybe it's because she felt a calling or because Mummy and Daddy hot-shot surgeons want her to do it. Whatever the reason is behind her wanting to screw up her life, it's still a bad idea.'

Gareth had to admit that Denise made very valid points

but he believed there were some things that people just had to work out for themselves. And that Billie's reasons for setting her sights on emergency medicine *were* a lot more complicated than watching too much television medical drama.

'I think she'll figure it out,' he said.

'This should help.'

'She's due off,' he reiterated.

'She can do this then go home,' Denise said briskly, her mind clearly made up. 'You coming or do you want me to grab one of the other nurses who were in there?'

Gareth sighed. No way could he abandon Billie to Denise's tough love. He put down his pen. 'I'm coming.'

CHAPTER NINE

BILLIE LOOKED DOWN at the notes. Her hands were still trembling and there was a persistent numbness inside but writing the notes helped.

And when she got home—which *could not* be soon enough—there was a bottle of wine in the fridge that would also help.

But for now it was pen on paper.

And she took comfort in that. Writing notes she *could* do. She could be clinical and detached in notes. She could look back at the situation and couch it in neat medical terms. The words formed a mental barrier between the chronology of the event and the *emotion* of the event. They allowed her to report the frantic last moments of Corey Wilson's life in a simple, detached way that she only hoped stayed with her when she got home tonight.

'Billie.'

Billie looked up from the chart as Denise approached, with Gareth hovering behind. They looked very serious and a prickle shot up her spine as she wondered what kind of hell they had in store for her now.

'Corey's parents are here. I know your shift finished half an hour ago but as you were involved in the resus I thought it would be good experience for you to talk to them.'

Billie stilled. Watching Corey Wilson die had been hard enough. Now she had to deliver the dreadful news to his parents too? She'd rather stick herself in the eye with a poker than have to tell these people their twenty-two-year-old son was dead.

She glanced at Gareth, whose face was carefully neutral.

'His parents are going to want to talk to people who were there at the end,' Denise said. 'And it's vital that we provide that for them. That we put aside our emotions and feelings and do whatever we can to make it a little bit easier for them.'

Denise stopped for a moment, as if she was allowing some time for that message to sink in.

'One of the most important things you'll ever do as a doctor is tell someone that their loved one has died,' Denise said. 'It's never easy, especially in sudden death, and it doesn't get any easier, no matter what anyone tells you. But it is a skill you need to learn. I'll be there,' she said. 'So will Gareth.'

Billie nodded. She knew Denise was right. That whatever she was feeling was nothing compared to what those two strangers waiting in that room off the triage desk with the mismatched furniture and the bland prints on the wall were feeling.

'Okay,' she murmured huskily, and rose on legs that felt like cement.

Billie sat on her couch two hours later, her hand still trembling as she sipped on her third glass of wine. She'd been home for an hour, and apart from turning on the fire and collecting the wine bottle and a glass she hadn't moved from this position.

Feelings of helplessness hit her in waves and she blinked back tears, rocking slightly as she fanned her face, breathing in and out through pursed lips as if she were running an ante-natal class. And then the words that she'd written in Corey's chart would come back to her and she would calm down again, holding onto every sentence like she had when she'd been in with his parents, repeating what she'd memorised from the notes to cut herself off from the emotion, to stop herself from breaking down in front of them.

But then the echo of Chantelle Wilson's wounded howl would break through the cool clinical words and the waves would buffet her again. It had been chilling. And the way she'd crumpled, folded in on herself...Billie had seen her mother do that when her sister had died and hated that she was the one inflicting the wound on another mother.

Billie had seen a few deaths in her first year but they'd been elderly people or terminal patients. Not like this.

Not this total waste of a human life that had barely begun.

She'd never looked into the eyes of a mother and had to use the D word. Denise had cautioned about using euphemisms for death as they'd walked to the room. People were in a highly emotional state, they needed clarity, she said.

But even so it had dropped like a stone into the atmosphere of that room and then the howl had sucked all the oxygen away.

A loud knock at the door interrupted her pity party and she flinched, dragging her gaze away from the fire. 'Billie, it's Gareth.' Another knock. 'Open up.'

Tears formed in her eyes again and she concentrated on whistling air in and out of her lips. She was barely hanging on here. If she saw him, if he was kind, she'd break down for sure.

'Billie!' Another sharp rap on the door. 'I know you're in there. I swear I'm going to kick this door in if you don't open it.'

Billie believed him. Unfortunately, Mrs Gianna next door was probably already calling the police due to Gareth's insistent knocking.

The last thing she needed was a police car pulling up in her driveway.

She took another fortifying sip of her wine before rising on legs that felt like wet string, desperately reaching for the cool detachment of her notes. She scrubbed a hand over her face to dispel the dampness on her cheeks as she walked to the door.

Billie drew in a steadying breath as she placed her hand on the knob. *You can do this.*

'Hi,' she said, as she opened the door, the cold night air like a perfect balm on her simmering emotions.

Gareth had expected to find a tear-stained wreck. But Billie looked exactly the same as when she'd left the hospital. Same jeans and shirt clinging in all the right places, a little on the pale side, her freckles standing out but a look of stoic resolve embedded on her features.

'Hi,' he said. 'I called by to check on you.'

She nodded. 'I'm fine.'

Except the tiny crack in her husky voice and the way she had to quell the tremble of her bottom lip with her teeth told him differently.

Gareth's heart went out to her. Incidents like this took their emotional toll on everyone involved. They left a little chink in a person's soul. And those chinks could build up if they were ignored.

'Billie…' he said softly. 'His head injuries were too massive. He probably coned. Nobody could have saved his life.'

'I know that,' she said testily.

He inclined his head. 'I know you do.'

He watched as Billie's throat bobbed. 'Don't be nice to me,' she warned. 'I can't deal with that.'

'Okay…' Gareth buried his hands in the pockets of his leather jacket. 'What are you doing?'

'Getting drunk.'

He smiled. 'Very Australian of you.' He earned a ghost of a smile back. 'You know, you could have joined us at Oscar's. A bunch of us went there at the end of the shift.'

Oscar's was the bar across the street from St Luke's. A very profitable business, especially after shifts like these.

She shrugged. 'I didn't feel like company.'

Gareth understood the sentiment but he'd learned through

his years in the military that drinking alone after the kind of day she'd had was not good.

What she needed was camaraderie. To be with people who understood the horror of what she'd been through.

'It helps to talk it out with people who know, you know?'

Billie nodded. 'Yeah. But I *really* didn't feel like company.'

And Ashworth-Keyes' did not break down in front of people.

Gareth regarded her for long moments—it looked like *he* was going to be her sounding board tonight. He knew he could sure as hell do with some alcoholic fortification. Between Amber's news and the bloodied trauma of Corey's death, a beer would really hit the spot right now.

And, besides, there was no way he could leave her to drown her sorrows solo.

'Do you have beer?' he asked.

'Yes.'

'Can I join you?'

'If you want.' She shrugged.

Billie turned on her heel and left him to follow her. She was already feeling stronger for the distraction of something else, someone else to think about.

'Take a seat,' she threw over her shoulder, as she passed the lounge room and headed for the kitchen. The house was dark, she hadn't bothered with lights, but she knew the low glow from the fire provided enough radiance for Gareth to see where he was going.

She opened the fridge door and plucked a beer from the back. She didn't know what type it was. Some boutique beer her father favoured and had left in her fridge for the odd time he dropped around. Usually to check how she was going with her studies and whether she was being a good little Ashworth-Keyes. Telling her how proud they were of her, how proud *Jessica* would be of her.

Billie entered the lounge room, noting Gareth had suc-

cumbed to the toastiness of the room and slipped out of his
jacket. He was wearing a long-sleeved knit shirt like she was,
except his had a round neck as opposed to her V. It obscured
the fascinating hollow at the base of his throat, the one she'd
used to ground herself during her harrowing talk with the
Wilsons whenever emotion had threatened to overwhelm her.

She also noticed he'd chosen to sit on the three-seater
where she'd been sitting, and not on one of the single chairs.

Billie handed him the beer as she plonked down next to
him, leaving a discreet *just two colleagues talking* distance
between them. She picked up her glass of wine and turned
slightly side on to him. He followed suit so they were facing each other.

She raised her glass towards him. 'To traumatic shifts.'

Gareth smiled. 'To *getting through* traumatic shifts,' he
said, tapping his beer bottle against the side of her glass.

They both drank, their gazes turning to the fake flames
of the gas fire bathing the room in a cosy glow. For long moments silence filled the space between them.

Billie looked down into the deep red of her Merlot, the
flame reflected in the surface. 'I can't do it,' she announced
quietly.

Gareth turned his head. 'You were fine, Billie. And you
were great with the Wilsons.'

At another time his praise might have filled her with pride
but it was little consolation right now. She looked at him.
'Denise knows I can't do it.'

He shrugged. 'So prove her wrong.'

Billie shook her head. 'She thrives on it. *You* thrive on it.'

'And you don't?'

She shook her head. 'It turns my stomach.'

Gareth watched the reflection of the flames glow in her
eyes as he asked her the same question he'd asked her before.
'So…why *are* you doing it, Billie?'

Blind Freddie could see that her heart wasn't in it.

'Oh…now,' she said, taking a sip of her wine. 'That's…'

'Long and complicated?' he said, repeating her answer from the last time he'd asked.

She gave a half-smile. 'Yes.'

Gareth held his beer up to the light. The fluid level had barely moved from the top after his two mouthfuls. 'I'm not going anywhere for a while.'

Billie looked into the fire. Where did she even start? She'd spent so much of her life pretending this was what she wanted that it was hard to remember sometimes why it wasn't.

'My sister died when she was sixteen. In a car accident. She was quite the rebel, always in trouble for something. She sneaked out of her window one night and went joy riding with some friends and never came back again.'

Gareth shut his eyes at the news. What an awful time that must have been for Billie. For her family. 'I'm sorry,' he murmured.

'Thank you.'

'What was her name?'

'Jess,' Billie said. 'Jessica.'

'Were you close?'

Billie nodded. 'She was two years older than me but, yeah…we were close. Close enough to confide in me that not only didn't she want to carry on the mighty Ashworth-Keyes tradition of being a surgeon, she didn't want to be a doctor at all. She wanted to be a kindy teacher.'

'And she couldn't tell your parents that?'

Billie snorted. 'Ashworth-Keyes' are *not* kindergarten teachers.'

'Even if it makes them happy?'

She shook her head. 'What on earth has happiness got to do with it? Ashworth-Keyes' are *surgeons*. My parents, my uncles, an assortment of cousins, my grandfather, my great-grandfather. From the cradle our glorious future in a gleaming operating theatre is talked about and planned incessantly. Everything revolves around that. There is no other career path in my family.'

'Oh, I see,' Gareth said, even though he really didn't.

As a father all he cared about was Amber being happy and well adjusted and contributing to society. But he *was* beginning to understand the conditioning that Billie had been subjected to.

'Of course, my father thought he would have sons, like all of his brothers had, to carry on the family tradition, but unfortunately he was saddled with girls. Still, to give him his due, he took it on the chin and settled into indoctrinating us too. He wasn't going to be *the* Ashworth-Keyes to break with tradition just because he had *girls* who might want to do something unpredictable and girly.'

'It sounds like there was a lot of pressure on you.'

Billie nodded. 'Jessica didn't know how to tell them. And she didn't want to be a disappointment to them. So she just kept telling them what they wanted to hear. That she was going to do medicine. That she was going to become a cardiothoracic surgeon just like them.'

'And would she have eventually, do you think, had she lived?'

Billie shrugged. 'I don't know. She was certainly bright enough. Straight As, even with no studying. Not like me, who had to work for my As. But she was very strong-headed. I doubt she would have done anything she didn't want to do. She was just keeping them sweet, I guess, putting off the inevitable confrontation.'

'Sounds like she was trying to tell them something with her rebellion.'

Billie nodded. 'Yes. I think all her reckless behaviour was really just a cry for help. I think it was her way of trying to goad them into disowning her and then she'd be free to do what she wanted.'

'But it didn't work out so well?'

Billie thought about that awful night. The police. Waking to crying at midnight. Her crumpled mother, a lot like Mrs Wilson. Her disbelieving father. 'No. It didn't.'

Gareth waited for a few moments. Took a mouthful of his beer. 'And so you decided to step into her shoes,' he said eventually. 'To be the daughter they thought she was going to be.'

Billie looked at him sharply. 'Yes.'

He nodded. 'Did you even want to be a doctor at all?'

'Of course,' she said derisively. 'I'm an Ashworth-Keyes, aren't I?'

'Billie.'

The reproach in his voice pulled her up. 'Yes,' she said. 'I did. I've always wanted to be one.'

'But not a cardiothoracic surgeon, right?'

Billie shook her head. 'Not a surgeon at all, I'm afraid. Or an ER consultant. I wanted to be a GP.'

CHAPTER TEN

GARETH LOOKED AT HER, surprised. A general practitioner? The complete opposite of an emergency physician. But he knew, instantly, it was the right fit for her.

Billie was an *excellent* doctor. He'd watched her with patients. She liked to take her time with them, which they loved but wasn't always conducive to the ER. And it wasn't laziness, it was thoroughness.

And her bedside manner was one of the best he'd ever witnessed.

She enjoyed the little stuff that the others had no patience for, the attention to detail, and she loved a medical mystery, loved getting to the bottom of what was making a person sick.

He knew without a shadow of doubt that she'd make a brilliant GP. And, God knew, there weren't enough of them.

'What's wrong with being a GP? They're just as vital to the health care system.'

Billie snorted. Her father would have apoplexy at hearing such sacrilege. 'Ashworth-Keyes' aren't—'

'GPs,' Gareth finished off with a grimace. 'And you never told them either?'

She shook her head. 'I was relying on Jessica being the trail blazer. Rocking the boat first, upsetting the apple cart, and then I could sneak in behind, wanting to be a GP. I figured they'd be so grateful I still wanted to be in the medical profession at all that they'd give me a pass. But then my mother…she completely fell apart after Jessica died. She didn't operate for an entire year.'

Billie paused and rubbed her arms, feeling suddenly cold again. 'She was just this…shell, this…husk. She'd just sit for hours and stare at the wall. Apart from looking at my sister's dead body, it was the most frightening thing I've ever seen.'

Gareth slid his hand onto hers. He thought back to how emotionally whammied he'd been when Catherine had died. It had only been his duty to Amber, her emotional distress and neediness that had kept him from spiralling into his own pit of despair. Amber had looked at him sometimes with fear in her eyes, fear that he just might sink into depression and then what would she do?

So he didn't. But there had been days when it had been very hit and miss.

'I'm sure it was,' he murmured.

'Finally, she came out of it. Finally, she came back to her old self, started seeing patients, resumed her surgical schedule, but she never seemed quite as robust again, like she could still break at any second. And somewhere along the way she decided that *I* was going to take Jessica's place. That *I* was going to live the life that Jessica had supposedly wanted because that would be the perfect way to honour my sister. She became obsessed with it and there were so many times when she seemed so fragile I just couldn't tell her the truth so I…went along with it. I couldn't bear the thought of her…going back to that dark place… Pretty pathetic, huh?'

Gareth shook his head. He understood the weight of parental expectations and the things people did to live up to them, and that was without a tonne of grief behind it all.

His father had never quite forgiven him for eschewing a job as his building apprentice to become a nurse. *Real men weren't nurses,* according to him. It was only joining the military that had made it more respectable in his eyes.

And, he guessed, GPs weren't real doctors to Billie's high-flying parents. 'I think we all do things we don't want to in order to keep from disappointing the people we love,' he said.

Billie nodded. It sounded like Gareth had some experience in that department too. 'What did you do?' she asked.

Gareth withdrew his hand and looked away from her as he took a long drag on his beer. When he was done he rolled it back and forth in his hands, watching the firelight catch the gold in the label.

'I became NUM of the ER,' he said eventually.

Billie blinked. He hadn't *wanted* to be NUM? Now, *that* she hadn't been expecting. She'd have thought that would be the pinnacle of his civilian career.

'For who?' she asked his downcast head, as his inspection of the shiny label continued.

Gareth glanced up at Billie. The firelight gilded the warm brown of her eyes and added pink to her cheeks. 'My wife.'

Billie stilled. His *wife?* He was *married?* But…she'd been in the tearoom when a couple of the junior nurses had been swooning over him and had gleaned there that he wasn't married. *And* he didn't wear a ring. Neither did he have a white mark where one had recently been taken off.

So then he must be divorced.

He had to be. Gareth had been nothing but honourable. She couldn't believe that he would have kissed her—no matter what psychological state she'd been in—if he hadn't been free and clear to do so.

She felt ill just thinking about it.

And the way she'd come on to him. His frankness about the…*thing* between them. He wouldn't have allowed that, acknowledged their vibe, if he'd been married.

He wouldn't be here now, surely?

Billie swallowed hard, battling against the invective raring to leap from her throat, and simply asked, 'Why?'

He frowned. 'Why did I do it for her?'

Billie nodded, still fighting the urge to demand he clarify his marital status immediately.

Gareth steeled himself to answer. He didn't talk about Catherine often, especially to colleagues or people he barely knew. But he did know Billie. Probably better than a lot of people he'd worked with for years.

And he knew her even better after the events of today, after their talk tonight.

Besides…there was just something about a fire that encouraged confidences.

'Because she was dying,' he said, capturing Billie's gaze. 'And she was happy and proud and excited for me and because she knew it would be more regular working hours for Amber after she was gone.'

'Amber?'

'Our daughter.'

It all clicked into place then for Billie. He was a widower. He had a daughter. Suddenly she knew Amber was the young woman she'd seen him with at teatime. 'She was there today…Amber…'

'Yes.'

Relief flooded through her. Cool and soothing. 'I'm sorry…about your wife. How long ago?'

'Five years.

'What cancer was it?'

'Breast,' Gareth said. 'From diagnosis to her death was five months.'

Billie shook her head sadly. Cancer was a real bitch. 'How old was she?'

'Catherine,' Gareth said. He wanted Billie to know her name. 'Her name was Catherine and she was forty. We'd been married for ten years.'

'How did Amber take it?'

He shrugged. 'She was fifteen. She blamed me.'

Fifteen. About the same age Billie had been when Jessica had died. Not the same thing as losing your mother but still an utterly devastating experience.

'Why did she blame you?'

'I was on tour in the Middle East when Catherine found the lump. She waited until I came home almost two months later before she did anything about it.'

Billie couldn't contain the gasp that escaped her throat at that particular piece of information. 'Why did she wait that long?'

Gareth felt the old resentment stir. 'For a lot of reasons—none of them very sound. She didn't want to worry me or Amber. She didn't want to cause a fuss and have me brought home over something she was sure was nothing. She didn't really think it was anything because she'd always had lumpy breasts. She didn't want to go through the investigations alone...'

Billie watched as he ticked each one off on a finger. The firelight caressed the spare planes of his face, picking up the grooves on either side of his mouth, the whiskers shadowy there. She almost reached out and traced the fascinating brackets.

'The list goes on,' Gareth continued, and he sounded so grim and bleak Billie had the strangest urge to put her arms around him. 'Not that it would apparently have mattered that much, the cancer was so aggressive. But, in her bad moments, Amber felt betrayed by Catherine. She felt that her mother had put me and my job—*"the stinking army"*, I believe were her exact words—first. That Catherine had loved me more than her own flesh and blood.'

Billie winced. 'That must have been rough.'

He shrugged. 'She was a grieving teenager. She was lashing out. I was just the dad. The stepdad at that.'

'She's not your biological child?'

He took a sip of his beer, shaking his head. 'No. She was five when Catherine and I met. Cute as a button. Both of them were.'

He grinned suddenly, raising the bottle once more, his lips pressed to the rim, still smiling. And it was so sexy, so masculine her stomach took a little dive. He obviously had wonderful memories.

'You loved her.'

He nodded as he looked directly at her. 'Of course. She filled up my heart.'

Billie was touched by his sincerity. Not some stupid fake Valentine's Day sentiment but something deep and honest.

She'd never known love like that.

'I'm sorry,' she said again, topping up her wine and taking a sip, watching him over the rim of her glass.

He shrugged and looked back at his beer but not before she glimpsed a dark shadow eclipsing the blue of his eyes. It spoke of pain and grief and *stuff* that hid in dark recesses, hijacking a person when they least expected it.

How long had the grief consumed him? And was that what had caused the incident that Helen had spoken about on her first day, the one that had seen him demoted?

She knew it was none of her business but sipping on her wine, feeling warm and floaty, she knew she was sufficiently lubed to ask. 'So why aren't you still NUM? I understand there was some kind of…incident that resulted in your demotion?'

Gareth looked up at her sharply. An *incident?* 'Where'd you hear that?'

She shrugged. 'The grapevine.'

Gareth was speechless for a moment then he laughed. It was good to know that some things at St Luke's never changed. Clearly it didn't matter if there was no ammunition for gossip—people would just make it up.

He drained his beer. 'There was no *incident*,' he said, as he placed his empty bottle on the table. 'Amber became independent. She graduated from high school, went off to college, got a car and a part-time job. I stepped down because I didn't need to work regular hours any more.'

Billie frowned. 'You just…stepped down?'

'Yep.'

'But…why? Surely managing an emergency department in a tertiary hospital is a prestigious career opportunity? How do you just walk away from that?'

Gareth could hear the incredulity in her voice. He guessed for someone who had grown up where prestige mattered above everything else, it was a big deal.

'It's easy when you don't care about prestige.'

Billie blinked. She'd had prestige rammed down her throat from a very early age. No matter how many times she'd fantasised about telling her parents where they could stick their aspirations for her, she'd never for a moment imagined that she'd walk away from them. And Jessica's death had made that near on impossible anyway.

She wished she had even an ounce of Gareth's resolve.

'But you must be highly qualified?'

'Sure. I spent a decade in field hospitals, triaging the wounded fresh from battle. I did multiple tours in the Middle East.'

'And you really didn't want to be NUM with all *that* experience?'

He shook his head. 'Nope, I *really* didn't. Being in charge of a civilian unit is not like being in the military. There's too much paperwork and being stuck in an office or going to round after round of meetings.'

Billie nodded. Gareth had obviously been very hands-on during his overseas tours. He exuded vitality and energy and she could just imagine him in head-to-toe khaki under the blades of a chopper with an injured soldier lying on a gurney as the sand whipped up around him.

He certainly strode around St Luke's like a man very comfortable in his environment. Like there was nothing that could be thrown at him that he hadn't already seen.

Somehow she couldn't quite picture him sitting in a white-walled office at some dreary quality or bed-management meeting.

'I guess St Luke's must be a little tame for you.'

'Nah. I've had more than enough excitement to last a lifetime.'

'But you thrive on it.' She'd said it earlier and it seemed even more so now. 'Why didn't you join up again?'

'I have to be here. For Amber.'

Especially now. Amber needed him to be here more than ever at the moment.

'It was okay being away for long periods of time while Catherine was still alive but I'm *it* now. I'm her only family. I can't abandon her even if she is independent and doesn't need me like she did when she was fifteen. And besides…' he rubbed his fingers along his jaw '…trauma medicine, field medicine…it's tough. Mentally tough. I have enough images in my head to fuel nightmares for the rest of my days. I don't see the point in adding to them.'

Goosebumps broke out on Billie's arms at the rasp of scraped whiskers. Her nipples followed suit. He was looking at her with shadows in his eyes again. Her heart almost stopped in her chest as she thought about the things he must have seen. The danger he'd been in.

'Were you scared?'

Gareth shook his head at Billie's husky question. 'I was never near the action. I was safe.'

She quirked an eyebrow. 'Are you ever truly safe in a war zone?'

He gave her a half-smile. 'We were safe.'

The smile played on his mouth and her gaze dropped to inspect it. Orange glow from the flames licked across his lips and she had the sudden urge to try them out. See if they were cool like the beer or scorching hot like the fire.

Billie had her money on the latter and suddenly felt pretty hot herself. 'Do you want another beer?' she asked, as the silence grew between them.

Gareth roused himself. Two beers around this woman would not be a wise move. He'd been dreaming about her in his bed for days now. The last thing he needed was anything that loosened his inhibitions and ruined his common sense. 'No. I should get going.'

Billie quelled the urge to protest the notion out loud.

She didn't want him to go. And she didn't think he wanted to go either.

He hadn't come in and sat opposite her and spent the whole time lecturing her about getting too involved in her job while drinking tea. He'd sat next to her, drunk a beer, listened to her talk.

And he'd been right. It was better to be around people who understood how you were feeling after a particularly harrowing day at work. People who had been right there, side by side with you.

They were debriefing. Being human.

But she wanted more. And maybe, for tonight—after everything she'd been through today—that was possible?

His palm was flat against his leg and Billie tentatively slid her hand onto his. 'Don't go.'

CHAPTER ELEVEN

GARETH LOOKED DOWN at Billie's hand. It was pale compared to his. There were no rings. No nail polish. No fuss. Just like the rest of her.

His heart thrummed in his chest. Not just at her touch but at what she was offering. He swallowed hard. His interest was already making itself felt inside his underwear.

There were only so many denials in him.

He looked up at her, his speech ready to go on his lips, the words he'd said to her the other morning in the car about being in different places easy to repeat. But she didn't give him the chance. She'd edged closer, pushed her hand higher.

'Gareth,' she murmured.

And any words he'd been about to say died on his lips as she pressed her mouth to his.

He sucked in a breath at her boldness and his senses filled with her. Not banana daiquiri this time. Something much more seductive. Red wine and lip gloss. Every nerve ending in his belly snapped taut as her mouth opened, her tongue touched his bottom lip. She pressed herself closer, her thigh aligning with his, her shoulder brushing his.

'Kiss me,' she whispered, her lips leaving his, travelling along the line of his jaw, nuzzling his earlobe, pulling it into her mouth. A hot flush of goosebumps prickled at his skin and he shut his eyes to their seduction.

'Kiss me,' she repeated, her breath hot in his ear, her

voice a sexy whimper, full and wanton. 'I know I shouldn't want you,' she groaned, her lips heading back to his mouth. 'But I can't stop.'

Her mouth claimed his again and there was nothing light and teasing about it. She opened her mouth and dragged him in, sucking him into the kiss and dumping him in the middle of a thousand carnal delights.

The slim thread of his resistance snapped so loudly Gareth swore it could be heard ricocheting off the walls. He groaned, stabbed his fingers into her hair and yanked her head closer.

'Damn it, Billie.'

And then *he* had the con.

The kiss was his to master and he did, taking control, steering the course, opening his mouth wide and demanding she do the same. Seeking her tongue and finding it, duelling with it. He grabbed her then, sliding his hands around her waist, pulling her towards him, putting his hand on a knee, parting her legs, urging her to straddle him, which she did with complete abandon, rubbing herself against him as their hips aligned perfectly.

Her hands glided to his cheeks as he settled her onto him and from her vantage point above him she returned his kiss. Twisting her head to meet his demands, moaning when his tongue thrust inside her. Would this be how she sounded when his tongue thrust inside her at a point significantly lower than her mouth?

Would she moan? Would she whimper? Would she gasp?

Would she squirm against him like she was now, trying to ramp up the friction between them by rubbing herself back and forth along the length of his erection?

He didn't know. But he wanted to find out.

'Shirt,' she gasped, against his mouth.

Shirt.

A one-word cold shower.

Gareth dug his fingertips into her hips as she reached for the hem of his shirt, battling the demons that told him this was a bad idea, praying they wouldn't win, hoping they would.

He held fast, trapping her between his body and the barrier of his arms. She squirmed in protest, trying to move, to strip him of his shirt. His pants. His sanity.

But he knew if he didn't stop this now, he wouldn't stop at all. Once her hands were on his bare, naked flesh, once his were on hers, he was going to be a goner for sure.

'Billie,' he panted, 'stop.'

Billie shook her head. 'No, no.' She kissed his neck, her hot tongue running up the length of it. 'Please…no.'

Gareth shut his eyes, trying not to think about how good her tongue would feel running up the length of something else.

Her hands reached for his pecs and he covered them with his own, capturing them against his chest and refusing to let them move, to cause any kind of rub or friction.

His libido just wasn't that strong at the moment.

'Billie…' he murmured in her ear, as she collapsed against him in frustration, 'we can't do this.'

Billie couldn't believe what she was hearing. They were so close to getting naked and doing the wild thing. And he wanted it as much as she did, she knew he did.

Why couldn't they do this? Why was he being so damn honourable?

'Why not?' she asked. 'I know you want to.'

Gareth shut his eyes and asked the universe for patience to be forthcoming—ASAP.

'Of course I want to, Billie,' he said, keeping his voice low, turning his head so his lips brushed her hair. He sat with her there for long moments. He needed her to know that this wasn't about what he wanted.

He shifted then, applying pressure to her hips, urging her to sit back a little. Somehow along the way her ponytail had loosened from its clasp, her hair falling forward to form a curtain around her face, and he pushed it back so he could see her.

'But you've been drinking,' he said, peering into her face. With her back to the fire it was heavily shadowed. Her eyes were dark, taupe puddles and he couldn't tell what she was thinking. 'So have I. This isn't the kind of decision we should be making now.'

Billie snorted. 'I've had three glasses of wine, Gareth. I'm hardly messy drunk.'

'And as you well know, consent can't be given under the influence of drugs or alcohol.'

She crossed her arms. 'You want me to sign a waiver?'

'Billie…'

Gareth shut his eyes briefly as she moved, swinging her leg off him and sitting back on the couch, taking care to leave a good distance between them. What seemed like an acre of orange glow flickered between them. He raked a hand through his hair.

She was furious.

'I'm sorry. I just don't want you to regret this tomorrow.'

Billie laughed. She couldn't help herself. She was beginning to wonder about his prowess between the sheets. 'Are you that bad, Gareth?' She almost laughed again at the affronted look he shot her.

'I've never had any complaints,' he said stiffly, and Billie had to admire his restraint. Any other man would have bragged. Any other man might have been tempted to make her retract her deliberately bold statement by resuming what they'd started. But she was fast coming to realise that Gareth Stapleton was not like any other man.

Billie rose from the couch and stalked to the fire. She couldn't sit a moment longer. Not next to him anyway. He was driving her mad and she needed to pace.

She stared into the fake orange flames for a few moments, trying to come up with the right words that would give him some insight into her feelings.

'I think I'm the best judge of what I will and won't regret,' she said eventually.

Gareth stared at the dip at the small of her back and the way it arched up so elegantly to the span of her ribs. He admired the straight line of her shoulders.

'You think I like this?' he murmured. 'You think I think that self-denial is some bloody balm for the soul? Because I don't. But not only are you under the influence, you've also been through some heavy emotional stuff tonight. Using sex as some kind of emotional eraser *isn't* the right way to handle it.'

Billie turned to face him, her arms folded. 'Well, *gee whiz*, Gareth, thanks for the lecture, but how about you let me handle my stuff my way and you handle yours your way, okay?'

'I have had some experience with this, you know.'

He looked kind of grim again and Billie wondered what experience he meant. His time in the military? The horror of the things he must have seen there? Or the things he'd seen during five years in a busy city emergency department?

Or was he thinking about his wife?

Had he used sex after his wife's death to *handle* it?

Had he had a bevy of women, mistresses, who had helped him through it or had his transactions been more…random? Had he preferred hook-ups to any further potential emotional entanglements?

'Okay. So what is the right way to handle it?'

Gareth stood. 'Believe it or not, talking about it with someone who knows.' He shoved his hands in his pockets as he moved closer lest he do something really dumb like think *Screw it* and drag her into his arms. 'Which is exactly what we were doing before we went and…'

'Complicated it?' she supplied.

'Okay…sure.' Gareth had been going to say 'ruined it'. Complicated was far less severe.

'Fine,' Billie said. 'But you should know I'm about all talked out now. I'm going to sit here and finish the bottle of wine. You can either stay and watch me or you can leave. But I must warn you if you stay I *will* be outrageously provocative. I'll probably get grabby. I may even take off my clothes. Because…' she pulled her shirt away from her tummy and fanned it back and forth a couple of times '…it's getting kind of hot in here, you know?'

Gareth nodded. He was burning up.

'So…' She gave him a half-smile. 'Probably best you leave now, unharassed and unmolested.'

Gareth smiled back, glad that she was trying to make light of the situation. 'I think plan B sounds like the wisest choice.'

She raised a derisive eyebrow. 'Imagine my surprise.'

He laughed. 'I'll be off now, then.'

Gareth was relieved, as he followed her to the door, that their earlier antipathy seemed to have dissolved and they were back on a more even footing.

'Thanks for coming over,' she said, as she opened the door and stood aside for him to exit.

It was his turn to lift a derisive eyebrow. 'Really?'

Billie laughed. 'Yes. Really. It did help, doing that talking stuff you're so big on.'

'Really?' He grinned.

Billie rolled her eyes. 'Really. Just don't come over again unless you plan on doing an Elvis.'

'An Elvis?'

She grinned. 'A little less conversation, a little more action.'

Gareth chuckled. Billie Ashworth-Keyes was an intriguing woman. She was a strange mix of smart and unsure, vulnerable and strong, funny and sober. He knew, standing on her threshold tonight, a warm orange glow behind her gilding her chestnut hair, soft yellow from the streetlight caressing her face, that sooner or later he and Billie were going to end up in bed.

Just not tonight.

Sure, he'd been telling himself since they'd met that it

wasn't going to happen but denial seemed useless now. He could feel the power of their attraction in the stir of his loins and the thrum of his pulse. And he knew, even though it was wisest, he wasn't going to be able to ignore the dictates of his body for ever.

He was, after all, only a man. And he wanted her.

He just needed to remember that they couldn't have anything permanent. That underneath her cool, funny façade Billie was a mess. A ticking time bomb ready to explode, and he'd had enough of bombs—metaphorical and actual—to last a lifetime.

She had a lot of things to work out in her life or she was going to wind up completely miserable, and most of it, unfortunately, she was going to have to figure out by herself.

And he didn't want to be collateral damage while she did.

He stared at her mouth for long moments—it really was utterly kissable—before he dragged his gaze back up to hers.

'When we do finally do it, Billie, and I promise you *we will*, I will Elvis your brains out.'

And while she was standing there, blinking up at him, her mouth forming a delicious little O, he smiled and said, 'Goodnight.'

CHAPTER TWELVE

TWO DAYS LATER Gareth sat in a counsellor's office at the cancer clinic with Amber. They were listening to the pros and cons of double mastectomy versus regular intensive screening and hyper-vigilance.

'In short, Amber, we don't recommend such a radical step at such a young age,' Margie, the counsellor, said regarding the mastectomy. 'Certainly not without extensive counselling and taking some time to really think through the implications.'

Margie was a breast cancer survivor herself. She looked to be in her sixties, her hair grey, short and spiky, and Gareth could tell that Amber valued her opinion. It was also clear that Amber was desperate to be told what to do, clutching at all advice as an absolute.

'So you're saying I shouldn't?' Amber asked.

Margie glanced at Gareth before addressing Amber. 'No.' She shook her head. 'I'm saying that you're young, that there is currently no sign of breast cancer on any of your scans or blood tests. I'm saying this is a big decision and that you have time to make it. I'm saying that you should take that time. No decisions have to be made straight away, Amber. You might not have to do anything about it for years yet.'

Amber turned to him, a tonne of indecision in her eyes. 'What do you think?'

'I think Margie's being very sensible. She's urging caution and that you take your time. I think that's wise.'

'So you don't think I should either?'

Gareth leaned forward in his chair and placed his hands on top of Amber's fidgeting ones. 'This isn't up to me, sweetie. Or Margie. All she's saying, all we're both saying is you don't need to feel pressured into making such a huge decision right now.'

'But if I did go ahead, you'd support me, right?'

Amber's huge eyes filled with unshed tears that punched him hard in the gut. She'd looked at him with those eyes the day the oncologist had told them Catherine was terminal. Eyes that said, What the hell are we going to do?

Gareth squeezed her hands, he could not have loved this young woman any more than he did at this moment, standing at this truly horrible crossroads with her. She may not have been his from the beginning but she'd been the centre of his world from the moment she'd grinned at him with her gappy, five-year-old smile and called him Carrot.

'Of course I will, honey,' he said, and when she nodded the tears spilled from her eyes and he pulled her close, tucking her head under his chin like he used to when she was little.

'Amber,' Margie said after a few moments, having given them some time to hold each other. 'There's a really good support group here for women who deal with familial breast cancer. A lot of them are your age, facing the same kind of dilemma and questions that you are. How about I hook you up with them? You can listen to what they have to say, to their stories. It might help.'

Amber broke out of the embrace. 'Okay,' she sniffled. 'That sounds good, right?' she said, turning to look at Gareth.

He nodded. 'It sounds great.'

They walked out of the building fifteen minutes later with another appointment for a further counselling session, a bunch of pamphlets and the details for the support group Margie had recommended.

'You okay?' Gareth asked.

Amber nodded. 'Yeah. I think so. This will be good, I think,' she said, brandishing the card with the support group details.

'Yes,' he agreed. 'Fabulous that there's a meeting Saturday week too. Not that long to wait. Will you be able to get to it?'

'Yep, I should be able to.'

'You want me to see if I can swap my shift next Saturday and drive you there? I can hang around. We can grab a bite to eat after, if you want.'

She shook her head. 'Nah. I'll be fine.'

'Well, come over for tea Saturday night and tell me about it.'

'Can't,' she said. 'Carly's organised a pub crawl for Del's twenty-first.'

Gareth winced. Carly's stamina could kill an ox. 'Okay. Why don't you come around for breakfast on the Sunday after the meeting, then? Bring Carly if you want to. Sounds like you're going to need the resuscitative qualities only bacon can provide and you know I cook it better than anyone.'

Amber smiled at him and then suddenly her eyes were full of tears again as she stood on tiptoe and hugged him. 'Deal,' she whispered.

That Sunday afternoon Gareth was getting some details from his patient in cubicle three when Billie slid the curtain partially back and stepped inside.

He nodded at her, slipping on his cool, professional mask. They had only seen each other in passing since their impulsive passion the other night. The department had been busy and he was fairly certain she'd been avoiding him.

Which was fine by him.

Thinking about her every night as he drifted off to sleep, having extremely inappropriate erotic dreams about her, was hard enough. It was imperative he didn't let any thoughts of the way she'd rubbed herself against him, the way she'd kissed him the other night enter his head. They were at work and John deserved their full, undivided attention.

'Hi,' he said.

'Hi.'

She was dressed in requisite scrubs, her normal ponytail—not one hair out of place—falling down her back. She looked like any other doctor here.

Except he wasn't treading water with any of them.

He dragged his gaze away from the gloss on her mouth. 'This is Dr Ashworth-Keyes,' Gareth said to John.

'Call me Billie,' she said, smiling at her patient.

Gareth watched John's mouth drop open. He sympathised with the guy.

'This is twenty-two-year-old John Sutton. John was kicked in the testicles during a basketball match and has what appears to be a large haematoma on his left testicle.' He looked at John. 'Dr Ashworth-Keyes will be assessing your injury.'

John's eyes practically bulged out of his head and he cast Gareth a stricken look. '*She's* going to be looking at my nuts? Don't you have a dude doctor?'

Gareth quelled an inappropriate urge to laugh as he sympathised with John again. He doubted his junk would behave itself if Billie was down there, poking and prodding, either.

'I'm sorry, Billie is it. But don't worry. She's highly qualified. Seen a thousand testicles,' he joked.

'Uh...okay.'

Billie saw John swallow visibly as a dull red glow stained his cheekbones. She cringed inwardly. The guy was already embarrassed and she hadn't even lifted the green surgical towel placed strategically across his lap.

This was going to be bad.

John was going to get an erection and die of complete mortification. She would then, in turn, also want the floor to swallow her whole.

No amount of saying it was a perfectly normal biological reaction was going to make this job any easier.

'Gareth?' A nurse opened the curtain a little and stuck her head in. 'Mrs Berkley's asking for you.'

Gareth sighed. 'Okay,' he said as the nurse disappeared. He looked at Billie. 'I'd better go check on her. Just yell when you're done.'

John's alarmed gaze darted to Gareth before giving Billie an extra stricken look. Billie felt for him. This had to be an embarrassing situation for him. Some guys would relish it, brag about it to their mates come Monday morning, but John didn't look like a bragger. John looked like he was already mentally trying to conjure up the least sexual things in the world.

Cane toads. Dental extraction. Burnt toast.

Billie stepped in front of Gareth, barring his exit, a forced smile on her lips. 'Can I…talk to you outside for a moment?'

Gareth frowned. 'Okay…'

Billie turned to John, her smile feeling utterly fake. 'We'll be right back.'

They stepped outside the curtain and Gareth pulled it closed. The department was busy and people bustled around them. Billie waited for a nurse to pass before she started. 'You can't leave me in there with him,' she said, her voice low. 'You have to stay.'

Gareth blinked. 'What? Why?'

'Because!' Her voice dropped. 'The guy is clearly worried that…' She switched to a whisper, '*Things* are going to happen as soon as I examine him, and I'd rather save him and myself the embarrassment.'

'The guy's got a black and blue testicle,' Gareth whispered in reply. 'I don't think *anything's* going to happening down there any time soon.'

'Maybe. But the point is, *he* thinks it will,' she murmured, still keeping her voice hushed but not whispering any longer.

'And how is me being in there with you going to help?'

'Because you're a *guy*. You can distract him with guy things.'

He quirked his eyebrow. 'Guy things?'

'Yes. You know. Beer and football and…'

Billie wasn't sure what men talked about. The men in her family talked about the latest surgical technique. She didn't think that was what John needed to hear, considering he was probably going to be under a surgeon's knife by night's end.

'…mountain climbing.'

Gareth laughed. Beer and football he could manage. Everest not so much. 'Mountain climbing?'

His low chuckle was equal parts sexy and irritating and Billie glared at him. 'Sporty stuff.'

Gareth shoved his hands on his hips. 'And what would you do if I wasn't here?'

'I'd find another male on staff to accompany me.'

'And what would happen if there were only female staff on?'

'Then, of course, I'd do it myself,' Billie said. 'But you *are* here and I don't have to. Now, can you please help a fellow male out and distract him for me?'

'With all my mountain-climbing stories?'

Billie rolled her eyes. 'With whatever you like.'

'Okay. But only if you help me with Mrs Berkley after.'

She narrowed her eyes. 'What's wrong with Mrs Berkley?'

'She's an eighty-four-year-old PFO with a fractured wrist.'

Billie frowned. 'PFO?'

'Pissed and fell over.'

'I *know* what it means, Gareth,' she said. She may have only have been in the ER for a couple of weeks but she'd picked up the vernacular quickly.

Medicine was full of acronyms. Both official and unofficial. 'But…eighty-four?'

He grinned. 'Yup.'

'Do I want to know what she was doing?'

'I believe it was the Chicken Dance at her great-grandson's wedding.'

Billie whistled. 'Go, Mrs Berkley.'

'Easy for you to say. She's a little high and...' Gareth searched for the right word and smiled as their conversation from the other night came back to him. 'Grabby.'

Billie regarded him for a moment as he plunged her straight back into the middle of that night, their kiss, his erection pressing hard and urgent at the juncture of her thighs.

Crap.

She'd been doing just fine pretending it hadn't happened but suddenly she was there again—the firelight, the confidences, the wine.

'Please, Billie.'

Billie dragged herself out of the sexual morass. Gareth looked more than a little desperate and it was almost comical to see such an experienced nurse worried about a little old lady. 'Since when did the big military guy have problems fending off a sweet old lady with a broken wrist?'

'I don't have a problem,' he said firmly. 'I'd just rather have a female member of staff there while she's not in her right mind. Between the alcohol and the happy juice the ambos gave her, she's not quite herself.'

Billie laughed at the picture Gareth was creating. 'Well, at least she's not feeling anything.'

'Oh, she's not feeling a thing. She's singing sea shanties.'

'She sounds a hoot.' Billie grinned.

'A hoot with wandering hands.'

Billie laughed again. She couldn't blame Mrs Berkley. Gareth was utterly grab-worthy. 'Okay, fine.' She checked her watch. 'John first then the irrepressible Mrs Berkley.'

'Deal,' he said, as he pulled back the curtain and they both trooped back in.

'Right, John,' Billie said, approaching the nervous patient briskly, professionally, reaching for some gloves that were in a dispenser attached to the wall behind the gurney and quickly snapping them on. 'Let's see what you've done to yourself.'

As she pulled up the corner of the green towel she heard Gareth say, 'So, done any mountain climbing, John?' and it took all her willpower not to laugh.

The urge died quickly as the extent of John's bruising was revealed. Gareth was right—it was black and blue. And very, very swollen. She winced.

'He's had some pain relief?' she asked.

Gareth nodded. 'Morphine.'

She looked at John, who was looking anywhere but at her. 'How's the pain?'

'It's better,' he said, the blush darkening on his cheeks as he spoke to a spot just beyond her ear.

'Okay, good, but I'm sorry…I have to have a feel, okay?'

John swallowed. 'Okay.'

Billie carried out the examination as gently as she could, feeling both testicles methodically. Gareth prattled on about Sherpas and carabineers. She flipped the towel back over when she was done and stripped off her gloves.

'Right. We're going to get the surgical doctor on call to come and see you but I think you've got yourself a nasty haematoma down there that'll need to be evacuated.'

John, a nice colour of beetroot now, nodded, looking at his toes. 'The surgical doctor, is it a…woman?'

Billie bit the inside of her cheek. It was heartening if somewhat foolish to meet a guy who was more concerned about the sex of the doctor than the fact his testicle looked like a battered plum.

She patted his foot. 'Dr Yates is very much male.'

John's sigh of relief was audible.

CHAPTER THIRTEEN

'AH, THERE YOU ARE, you gorgeous young man.' The elderly woman lying on the exam table located in the middle of the room had a twinkle in her eyes as she waggled her fingers at Gareth and Billie almost laughed out loud at her greeting. 'I thought you'd skipped out on me.'

'Me? Skip out on you, Mrs Berkley?' Gareth murmured, and Billie blinked at the low, easy, flirty tone to his voice. 'Never.'

'Oh, and you've bought a pretty young woman with you.' Mrs Berkley beamed at Billie. 'Come in, my dear.' She gestured with her good arm. 'My goodness, how *do* you young people get things done around here with so much to distract you?'

He glanced at Billie. Their gazes locked and her breath hitched for a second.

'It's a challenge, Mrs B., I can't deny that,' Gareth said, before switching his attention to the patient, sitting himself down on the stool beside the table and swinging slightly from side to side.

Mrs B. cackled merrily. 'I can imagine. I remember when me and my Ted were going around. Couldn't pass each other without wanting to tear each other's clothes off.'

Billie blinked at the frank admission and Gareth stopped swivelling on the stool as the room filled with a pregnant silence.

'Hah.' The octogenarian cracked up again. 'That shocked the cotton socks off you, didn't it? What, you think you young people invented sex?'

Gareth recovered quite quickly. 'Absolutely not, and I thank you and your generation most earnestly for your pioneering ways.'

Mrs B. grinned from ear to ear. 'You're welcome,' she said, her hand covering Gareth's and giving it a pat. 'I could tell you some stories that would make you blush right to the roots of your hair.'

Billie's mind boggled but Gareth had her measure. 'I don't embarrass easily, Mrs B. We nurses aren't prone to being shocked.'

Billie was pleased Gareth wasn't shocked because she had to admit to feeling just the tiniest bit so. She didn't know if Mrs B. was always this outrageous or if it was the combination of alcohol and drugs but Billie wasn't used to such freeness of expression *in eighty-year-olds*.

But it appeared Mrs Berkley was on a roll. The older woman gave Gareth a secretive smile and tapped the side of her nose three times. 'I still reckon I could teach you a thing or two, young man.'

Gareth, looking completely unconcerned by the flirting, grinned and said, 'I'll bet you could.'

Mrs B. turned her eyes on Billie. 'Isn't he marvellous, dear? I mean, really, do they have those nudie calendars for male nurses…you know, like they do for the firefighters? This young man could be the centrefold.'

Now Billie really was at a loss for words and not just because they'd been uttered by a great-grandmother. The illicit thought of Gareth stripped nude made her lose her train of thought.

She glanced at Gareth, who was looking at her with a quirked eyebrow. 'Yes,' he mused. 'Why don't we do calendars?'

Billie really felt like she'd leapt into an alternate universe.

She needed to get them out of this bizarre conversation immediately. Why was Gareth encouraging her? Hadn't he asked her in here to defend his honour?

'Inappropriate perhaps?' she said, smiling sweetly.

Mrs B. nudged Gareth and said in a stage whisper they could probably hear out in the ambulance bay, 'Ooh. She's a bit of a spoilsport, that one.'

Gareth, his gaze still locked with hers, a small smile playing on his lips, nodded. 'Yes, she is.'

Billie almost choked on his statement. She wasn't going to stand by and be defamed when nothing could be further than the truth. 'Don't listen to a word he says, Mrs Berkley. The only spoilsport around here is Gareth.'

She raised an eyebrow back at him. It hadn't been her who had knocked him back. *Twice.* He had the good grace to look away.

'Right,' he said, turning back to his patient. 'Let's get this cast on, shall we? A nice light fibreglass one for you today.'

'Ooh, can I have a purple one?' Mrs Berkley asked. 'My great-granddaughter Kahlia had one last year.' She glanced at Billie. 'It looked very groovy.'

Gareth nodded. They had a selection of colours for paediatric patients so why not? 'Purple it is. Let me get set up.'

She beamed at him and patted his cheek. 'Such a good boy.'

Gareth smiled and extracted himself. He rummaged through the supply cupboard and found some rolls of purple. 'Can I help?' Billie asked, appearing at his elbow.

'Sure. Fill this halfway,' he said, thrusting a stainless-steel basin at her.

'What are you doing?' she whispered under her breath as she took it. 'Why am I here if you keep encouraging her?'

'Because I just spent twenty minutes talking to a very confused guy about hiking boots and grappling hooks.'

She rolled her eyes. 'You didn't have to talk to him about mountain climbing and you know it.'

Gareth grinned at her. 'Now, where would the fun have been in that?' He nodded his head to the right. 'Sink over there.'

A few minutes later they were set up. Gareth had the rolls of plaster soaking in the basin that had been set on a trolley, and he was sitting back on his stool, pulled in close to the table. Billie was sitting on the other side of Mrs Berkley, also on a stool.

He positioned her arm correctly and started to apply the padded underlay. His hair flopped forward as he worked his way up to her elbow and Mrs Berkley reached out her unbroken hand and pushed it back off his forehead.

Gareth looked up at her, startled. 'I miss running my hands through a man's hair,' she said wistfully.

'Okay, Mrs B.,' Billie said, taking the older woman's hand and bringing her arm back down beside her. She intertwined her fingers with the patient's and gave the gnarled old hand a squeeze. 'How about we let Gareth finish his job?'

'Yes, of course, dear,' Mrs Berkley said, and tutted to herself a couple of times. 'I guess I'm probably making a bit of an old fool of myself. I just so rarely get to hang out with younger people these days.'

Billie squeezed her hand again. 'Of course not,' she murmured. 'You're just keeping Gareth on his toes.' She glanced across at him. 'Men need that.'

'Damn straight,' Mrs Berkley hooted, her crinkly face splitting into a hundred different ravines, deep and beautiful.

Once the padding was in situ Gareth plunged his gloved hand into the basin and removed the first roll. 'You sure about purple?' he asked.

Mrs Berkley nodded her head enthusiastically. 'Quite.'

He squeezed the roll out gently, removing the excess water, and started applying the first layer. 'You should ask this young lady out,' Mrs Berkley said, out of the blue.

Billie's alarmed gaze met Gareth's across the top of their

patient. Gareth returned his to the job at hand, but not before murmuring, 'You don't say?'

'Oh, yes.' Mrs Berkley nodded. 'You'd look good together. Make *beautiful* babies. Her hair and complexion, your eyes and strapping physique. Perfect.'

'But we work together, Mrs B. You know they say you should never mix business with pleasure.'

Mrs Berkley snorted. 'What a load of old tosh. What do *they* know? They are the cat's mother. And what do cats have to do with it?'

Billie frowned. What indeed? she thought as she tried to follow the muddled ponderings. But somehow in this very strange conversation nothing seemed too bizarre.

'What do you reckon, Billie? You fancy a date?'

Mrs Berkley gave a horrified gasp. 'Young man, that is no way to ask a young lady out. Where are your manners? Now, do it again. Properly this time!'

Billie glanced at Gareth, who was looking suitably chastised, and she bit down on her lip to stop laughing.

'You do know how to ask, don't you?' Mrs Berkley said, clearly not done with her disapproval.

'To be honest,' Gareth said, the smile slipping from his face, 'it's been a while for me.'

A shiver wormed its way up Billie's spine at Gareth's sudden grimness. Been a while since what? He'd gone on a date? It certainly hadn't been a while since he'd kissed a woman—she could attest to that. Or did he mean it had been a while since he'd taken a woman to bed?

Had he slept with anyone since his wife had died?

'You say,' Mrs Berkley said in a voice that was half imperious, half exasperated, '"Would you do me the honour of accompanying me to dinner?" Or wherever you're going.'

His patient's disgust brought Gareth back from the edge of the familiar darkness that had overwhelmed him for a long time. He laughed.

Mrs B. was so affronted it was hard not to.

'Of course, you're right, Mrs B.' He unwound the last of the first roll then looked across at Billie as he picked up the second. 'Willamina Ashworth-Keyes, will you do me the honour of having a drink with me after work tonight?'

His blue eyes sparkled playfully, the shadows she'd seen there moments ago banished, making it hard for Billie to ascertain if he was serious or just humouring Mrs Berkley. It worked anyway as the octogenarian nodded approvingly.

'Good. Now you...' she looked at Billie '...say, "Why, thank you, I'd be delighted to have a drink with you after work tonight."'

Billie glanced at Gareth, who gave her an encouraging little wink before returning to the cast. So they were just humouring their patient, then...?

Disappointment trickled down her spine.

'Why...thank you, Gareth Stapleton,' she said, forcing an equally light tone to her voice. 'I'd be delighted to have a drink with you after work tonight.'

He chuckled as he worked and Billie's disappointment grew. Mrs Berkley clapped. 'There, see. Perfect. My work here is done.'

'And so,' Gareth announced as he unrolled the last of the roll, smoothing the end down thoroughly, 'is mine. There you go.' He stood. 'All pretty in purple.'

Mrs Berkley looked at Gareth's handiwork. 'I love it,' she said, grinning.

'Another happy customer,' he said, smiling at Mrs Berkley with such genuine affection it took Billie's breath away. Was there nothing the man couldn't do? Pull heart-attack victims out of wrecks, run an emergency room with military efficiency, while calming freaked out residents *and* charm little old ladies.

'Now, let's get you up and outside for a while. You'll need to stick around for an hour or so in case there's swelling, then you can be on your way.'

'Right you are,' Mrs Berkley said, as Gareth ushered her

into a wheelchair. 'Hand me my bag, will you, dear?' she asked Billie. 'I'll text my granddaughter to come and get me in an hour.'

Billie handed Mrs Berkley her handbag, still trying to wrap her head around an eighty-four-year-old with a smartphone. Gareth flipped the brake off with his foot. 'Hold tight,' he said.

'It was nice meeting you, Mrs B.,' Billie said, as the wheelchair drew level with her. 'Maybe no more chicken dancing for a while.'

Mrs Berkley smiled at her. 'I'm old, my dear. I'm going to chicken dance while I can.' She patted Billy's hand. 'Gotta make hay before those chickens hatch. Enjoy your date.'

Gareth grinned and winked, pushing the chair past her before Billie had a sensible reply. She watched them go, Mrs Berkley saying, 'I don't suppose you could round me up a cuppa, could you, dear? I'm desperate for one,' as Gareth pushed her down the corridor.

His deep 'Of course I can, anything for you, Mrs B.,' as they disappeared from sight was typical Gareth. From CPR to cups of tea, he was a regular knight in shining armour.

He'd certainly saved her ass more than once.

CHAPTER FOURTEEN

A FEW HOURS LATER, Billie changed out of her scrubs in the female locker room. It had been a long day and her feet were killing her. She needed a hot shower, a glass of wine and her bed. Slipping into her trendy, buckle-laden boots, she threw her Italian leather jacket over her arm, grabbed her bag and headed out.

Gareth was lounging against the opposite wall when she opened the door. He was wearing jeans that looked old and worn and soft as butter, some kind of duffle coat and a smile. The coat was open to reveal a snug-fitting shirt and he looked all warm and rugged and just a little bit wild, like he was about to throw his leg over a motorbike. Billie had to grind her heels into the ground to stop herself from slipping her arms inside his coat and snuggling into the broad expanse of his chest.

'I thought you were never coming out,' he said, as he pushed off the wall and moved closer.

'Sorry,' she said, puzzled. 'Did I miss signing something?'

'Nah.' He indicated that she should walk and they fell into step. 'Mrs B. just rang to make sure that I was collecting you for our date.'

Billie stopped for a moment. 'She did?'

He grinned and nodded, also stopping. 'She did.'

'Wow,' Billie murmured, as they commenced walking again, conscious of Gareth's arm casually brushing hers.

'I'm surprised she can even remember through all that happy juice.'

'I have a feeling that Mrs B. doesn't miss much at all.'

Billie laughed. 'I think you may be right.'

They got to the end of the corridor and Billie went to turn right for the lifts and the car park.

'Hey, where are you going?' Gareth asked. 'What about our date?'

Billie's breath caught in her throat. He was looking at her with a tease in those blue eyes and something else, something very *frank*. His promise to Elvis her brains out echoed around her head but that had been a few days ago and nothing he'd done since had indicated that the event was likely to happen, much less imminently.

'Oh…I didn't think that was real,' she stalled.

He shrugged. 'It wasn't but…I'm pretty sure Mrs B. has this place bugged and when she rings tomorrow looking for me—and she *assures* me she's going to—I'll be able to put my hand on my heart and tell her I was the epitome of a gentleman.'

Billie didn't think he looked remotely gentlemanly right now. He looked all whiskery and hunky and she could suddenly picture him beneath the rotors of a chopper, accepting a wounded soldier. She certainly didn't want him to act all gentlemanly. She wanted him to push her against the wall in the deserted corridor and kiss her until she didn't have any breath left in her chest.

She wanted a quick, hard military incursion.

Billie blushed and covered her embarrassingly real fantasy with a spot of mocking. 'You? *You're* frightened of a little old lady.'

'*That* little old lady?' Gareth grinned. 'Hell, yeah. What do you say? A quick drink at Oscar's for Mrs B.'s sake?'

Billie knew she should say no. But Gareth was hard to resist when he was being all charming and he-man. And who was she to disappoint an octogenarian?

'Okay, sure. But I expect you to be on your very best behaviour or I'll tell Mrs Berkley.'

'Yes, ma'am,' he murmured, saluting her, and Billie's pulse just about ratcheted off the scale.

Billie was very pleased as they entered Oscar's that she'd decided to dress nicely that morning. She was wearing her designer jeans and a fluffy-on-the-outside, fleecy-on-the-inside zip-up jumper that pulled nicely across her breasts and showed off a decent hint of cleavage.

She knew that this was just them humouring an old woman but it didn't hurt to be looking her best either.

Gareth held out a chair for her and Billie smiled. 'Very gallant,' she murmured. 'Keep this up and I'll expect you to throw your cloak over a puddle for me.'

Gareth grinned. 'Sorry, I'm fresh out of cloaks. But I will buy you a drink. Wine?'

Billie nodded. 'Red.'

She watched him walk away. He'd removed his jacket and the way his jeans hung to the long, lazy stride of his legs should have been illegal. Billie felt a little flutter in her chest. They weren't even on a real date and Gareth was already doing better than any other man she'd been out with.

She watched him laughing with the guy behind the bar as he picked up their drinks and brought them over. Everything seemed easy with him. From his laid-back chuckle to the looseness of his stride, to the slow spread of his lazy grin.

'Baz recommends the Merlot, apparently,' he said as he placed the glass of ruby liquid in front of her.

Billie smiled. Of course he knew the name of the guy behind the bar—Gareth knew everyone. He sat and raised his glass towards her. 'To Mrs Berkley,' he said, smiling as they clinked their glasses.

Some froth from Gareth's beer clung to his top lip and Billie had to drag her gaze away from it as she groped around for a distraction. 'So…what now?' she asked.

'Well, I guess we should do that getting-to-know-you stuff that dates are for.'

Billie gave a half-laugh. 'You already know about my dead sister, my fragile mother, my pompous father, my inability to deny them anything and my pathological dislike of gore. I know about your wife, your stepdaughter, the way you handle yourself in an emergency and what you've been doing for the last decade or so. What else is there to know?'

Gareth laughed. That was a very good question. 'We have done the big stuff, haven't we?'

He was sure there was more for both of them—hell, they both had a tonne of baggage. But Gareth wasn't in the mood for heavy tonight. Suddenly he wanted to know the little stuff.

'What's your favourite colour?'

Billie blinked. 'My favourite colour?'

'Sure. Let's do the pop-quiz version.'

Okay…that could be fun. 'Um…yellow,' she said. 'What's yours? No…hang on, let me guess…khaki?'

Gareth laughed. 'Ha. Funny girl. Definitely not.' He looked at her hair then back at her. 'Chestnut,' he said, taking a sip of his beer.

Billie's pulse skipped a beat.

He took another swig of his beer, taking care this time to remove any errant foam, for which Billie was exceedingly grateful. 'Favourite food,' he said.

'Jam on toast.'

Gareth threw back his head and laughed. '*That's* your favourite food?'

Billie raised an eyebrow at him. 'You got a problem with that?'

'Nope. Just find it hard to believe that Willamina Ashworth-Keyes eats jam on toast.'

'Well, *she* doesn't. But plain old Billie Keyes loves it!' She took a mouthful of her wine. 'I suppose yours is caviar? No, wait…quiche!'

He grinned at her deliberate goading. 'A steak. Big, thick and juicy.'

'How very tough guy of you.'

Gareth laughed some more. 'You don't like tough guys?'

Billie's gaze wandered to where the hem of his sleeve brushed his biceps. She raised her eyes to his face and warmth flooded her cheeks. She'd had no experience of tough guys whatsoever. The men she'd been with had been cultured and urbane.

'I'm liking them more and more.'

Their gazes locked for long moments then Gareth smiled. 'You're good for my ego.'

Billie pulse fluttered as she dragged herself back from the compelling blueness of his eyes and reminded herself this wasn't a real date. 'Well...we won't tell Mrs B. that.'

Gareth found himself laughing again. It felt good to talk and laugh with a woman—really good. It had been a long time since he felt this *all over* good and he was suddenly overwhelmed by how easy it was.

Billie put him at ease.

When she wasn't tying him in knots.

His smiled faded a little as he contemplated the implications. 'I like you, Willamina Ashworth-Keyes.'

Everything stilled inside Billie as the sudden, serious admission fell from his lips. She didn't know what to say but she knew she felt the same way. 'I like you too, Gareth Stapleton.'

The bar noises faded into the background as they stared at each other, their drinks forgotten in front of them.

'Hey, guys, Gareth and Billie are here.'

The words yanked them out of their little bubble and they turned to see a bunch of emergency nurses heading their way.

'Uh-oh,' Gareth said. 'Date's over.'

Billie nodded. 'Leave this bit out when you speak to Mrs B. tomorrow.'

Gareth smiled. 'Good idea.'

And then they were being swamped with company as

half a dozen colleagues descended and Billie gave herself up to the mayhem.

Because it wasn't a real date anyway.

The following Saturday, Gareth watched Billie through a crack in cubicle four's curtain. He was supposed to be doing paperwork so he could finish up and get out of there but his gaze continued to be drawn to her.

She was examining a nasty cellulitic arm from an infected scratch. She said something to her patient, a fifty-two-year-old male, and he laughed. Billie laughed with him and he admired the effortless way she put people at ease.

They responded to her.

And Gareth knew that patients who liked and trusted the doctors they saw were more likely to take their advice.

He liked seeing her at ease. It was her natural habitat and a far cry from the woman she became when confronted with the rawness of a medical emergency. There was something compelling about her. She looked cool and confident. Sure of herself.

And that was very, very sexy.

He'd tried hard not to dwell on their *date* this past week and had failed miserably. It seemed to be the only thing he *had* thought about and he was thinking about it again now as she charmed her patient. The teasing and the banter had been fun and he realised he wanted to see more of her.

Sure, there were a lot of reasons why seeing her outside work was dumb. They both knew that. But right from the beginning there'd been an inevitability about them, he'd felt it and so had she. Hell, he'd told her that night at her place that something would happen between them sooner or later.

And the time for fighting it was over.

He wanted to see her, touch her, kiss her. He didn't want to keep his distance, push her away again. He wanted her in his bed. For however long it lasted.

And he hadn't felt this way since Catherine.

So forget the rest of it.

Billie glanced up and Gareth realised he'd been caught staring. Their gazes held for a long moment before she turned back and said something to her patient, and Gareth felt as if his chest wall had just been released from a vice.

When she strode towards him a minute later, he was still recovering.

'Shouldn't you have knocked off by now?' she said, as she took the chair beside him at the work station, her voice casual but he could tell she was being deliberately so.

'Yep,' Gareth said. 'Just finishing up some charting.'

'Ah,' she murmured, as she opened the chart in front of her, 'the never-ending paperwork.'

He laughed. 'Yes.' They continued their charting in silence for a moment. Gareth glanced sideways at her, briefly admiring her neat handwriting. They were the only two at the work station for now. 'I think we should go on a proper date,' he said.

She looked up and her ponytail swished to the side. She frowned at him, which emphasised her freckles. 'R-really?'

Gareth nodded. 'Yes.'

Her throat bobbed and his gaze followed the tantalising movement. 'When?'

'Tonight?' Why not. *Seize the day.*

There was a drawn-out silence as she regarded him solemnly. 'There seem to be a lot of reasons why we shouldn't.'

She was looking at him as if she was remembering the last two times she'd tried to reach out to him and he'd rejected her. 'Yes, there are.' He nodded. 'But I don't care any more.'

Gareth took her nervous swallow as a good sign. A nurse swished past the desk and Billie faked interest in the chart until they were alone again.

'Could I take a raincheck?' she asked, lifting her gaze from the chart. 'I'm not off for a couple of hours yet and I'm beat. The thought of having to go home and get dressed up and go out…'

Gareth tried really hard *not* to think about her getting dressed up. For him. 'That's okay. Just come to my place straight from work. I'll cook you dinner and you don't have to get dressed up.'

Also, if he didn't do this now, he was frightened he'd chicken out altogether. That common sense would win out.

'Oh.' Billie looked back at the chart again and Gareth wasn't sure if that was a good thing or a bad thing. Was she weighing up the pros and cons or freaking out?

When she lifted her eyes there was a directness to her gaze that was utterly compelling. 'Thank you. I'd love to.'

Gareth hadn't realised how much had been mentally riding on her acceptance until she'd uttered it and he sagged a little.

'Can I bring something?' she asked, her gaze unwavering. 'Beer, wine, dessert?' She looked around surreptitiously and lowered her voice. 'Condoms?'

Gareth blinked but their gazes still held. She wanted to know the lie of the land—he could understand that. He shook his head. 'I'm good. For *everything.*'

Her mouth quirking up at the side was the only indication that they were talking about something they probably shouldn't have been, considering where they were. And it added to the anticipation of the moment.

'In that case, I look forward to it very much, thank you,' she murmured.

Gareth's mouth quirked up too. 'My pleasure.'

She held his gaze for a little longer. 'I hope so,' she said, then returned her attention to the chart.

CHAPTER FIFTEEN

BILLIE WAS NERVOUS when she pulled up at Gareth's just after eight-thirty. She couldn't quite believe how up front she'd been about her expectations of this night and she cringed a little now, thinking about it.

But she was a grown woman, a fully qualified doctor, for crying out loud—she knew what she wanted and she wasn't ashamed to ask for it. It was past time for them to stop beating around the bush. This wasn't some fake date for the sake of an old lady.

This was the real thing.

And there was something between her and Gareth. She'd felt the pull from the beginning and that hadn't lessened. Every time she looked at him, every time he was near she felt it and she knew he did too.

Okay, she had a lot going on in her life at the moment. She was struggling with decisions in her life she didn't feel she had any control over. But she didn't care about that right now because she did have control over this. Tonight she needed to be with him and that's all she cared about.

And Gareth, thankfully, had agreed.

Billie's breath misted into the air as she climbed the five stairs and put her foot on the wide veranda that continued all the way in both directions, typical of the old Queenslander style of architecture.

She rapped on the door, wishing again she'd thought to

wear something a little more elegant to work this morning instead of a pair of track pants, a turtleneck sweater and her seen-better-days college jumper.

Yes, it had been freezing, as it was now, but she could have at least worn something more along the lines of what she'd worn the day they'd ended up on their fake date.

She wasn't even wearing matching underwear.

Sure, he'd seen her looking worse—in plain baggy scrubs at half past stupid o'clock in the morning, tired and cold and hungry and feeling like death—but he'd also seen her in her best sparkly cocktail dress with full make-up and hair in curls.

Of course, she'd thrown up on him then too so maybe that didn't count…

Billie heard footsteps and she could see his shape coming towards her in the glass side panes of the door. Her pulse sped up. The light flicked on overhead and she quickly pulled her hair out from the constraints of her standard workwear ponytail and fluffed it a little as the door opened.

'Hi,' Gareth murmured, a smile tugging at the corners of his mouth.

He was wearing jeans and a long-sleeved button-up shirt, left undone at the neck, and his hair was damp. He looked so good and clean and warm and laid-back, casual sexy, she couldn't decide if she wanted to snuggle him or jump him.

'Hi,' she said, suddenly realising she was staring.

They didn't say anything or do anything for a few moments. Gareth just looked at her and Billie's stomach twisted in a knot.

'You look good,' he murmured.

Billie laughed then because she knew good was stretching it. 'It's okay. You don't have compliment me,' she said. 'Trust me, I'm a sure thing.'

He shook his head, slid his hand onto her hip and pulled her in close to him, bringing his mouth to within millimetres of hers, hovering it oh-so-close. So close she could feel the warmth of his breath and smell the mint of his toothpaste.

'You look good,' he repeated, his husky voice reaching inside, plucking at the fibres of her belly deep and low.

Then he dropped his mouth to hers and Billie felt the impact to her system like a lightning bolt. She moaned as he opened his mouth over hers and demanded she do the same. And she did. He urged her body closer and she went.

She wrapped her arms around his neck, flattened her breasts against his chest, aligned her pelvis with his and then somehow she was inside and the door was shut and a warm wall was hard behind her and he was hard in front of her and he groaned her name like it was torn from the depth of his soul and she never wanted to let him go.

And when he broke the kiss off she mewed in protest, their breathing harsh in the sudden silence.

'Sorry,' he murmured, pulling away slightly to look at her. 'I promised myself I'd wait but I've been fantasising about doing that for hours.'

Billie shrugged. His lips were wet from her mouth and she wanted them back on hers again. 'Don't stop on my behalf.'

'Oh, no, if I don't stop now I won't stop at all and what would Mrs Berkley think if I invited a young lady to dinner and then she didn't get any?'

Billie laughed. 'I think she'd disapprove. I'd think she'd think you quite ungentlemanly.'

He grinned. 'Me too.' He dropped his hands from her hips and took a reluctant step back. 'Come on, I've even cooked for you.' He held out his hand and she took it. 'I hope you're hungry.'

'*Very*,' she murmured, as he led the way through the house, his completely asexual touch doing funny things to her legs anyway.

He chuckled at her emphasis, leaving her in no doubt he knew she wasn't talking about food. 'I made a basil and cherry-tomato pasta.'

They entered the kitchen. 'Glass of wine?'

'Yes, please.' If he was determined that they eat first then she was going to need to do something with her hands other than putting them all over him.

'Take a seat,' he said, gesturing to the stools along the far side of the wide central kitchen bench.

'This is a nice place,' she said, looking up at what she figured had to be a twelve-foot ceiling. That, combined with the panelled walls and the wraparound veranda, confirmed its architectural heritage.

'Yes,' Gareth, said as he poured a glass of red wine for her and cracked the lid of a beer for himself. 'It's not mine, I'm just house-sitting, but I believe it's almost one hundred years old. The owners had it moved from a homestead out west.'

'You're house-sitting? For friends?'

Gareth shook his head as he handed over her glass of wine. 'No. It's what I do. I house-sit for people.'

'You don't have a…permanent home?'

'Nope,' Gareth said, as he went and checked the food on the stove. 'I sold our house a couple of years after Catherine died, when Amber headed to uni, so I could put half of it in trust for her.'

'Oh.'

He turned and lounged against the oven. His jeans pulled tight against his thighs as he casually sipped his beer. He looked calm and comfortable in his skin and that cranked the sexy up another notch.

Billie was thankful there was a bench separating them.

'Catherine didn't really have anything of monetary value to leave Amber. Only what we had together, like the house and cars. And I wanted Amber to be able to have a legacy from her mother, something that could help her get a good start in life when she was ready.'

'So you sold your house?'

Gareth shook his head. 'It was our house. And, besides, it felt empty, not like a home any more. Catherine was gone and Amber was at college. Without them to fill it up it was just four walls and a roof.'

He stared into his drink for long moments, suddenly sombre, and Billie was pleased anew for the bench separating them. She wanted to go to him. Go to him, comfort him.

Which would probably embarrass the hell out of him. And herself. But the urge was there nonetheless.

'The house sold much faster than I'd anticipated so I was going to rent until I found something, but at the same time a friend of mine was going away for a few months and asked if I wanted to house-sit and it sort of snowballed from there. I'm with an agency now and I haven't been without a place to stay since. These owners have moved to Switzerland for a year.'

Billie's heart broke a little for Gareth. She loved her house—the one thing she'd accomplished without any help from her parents after she'd refused their monetary assistance.

Because she'd wanted to do it herself but mostly because of the guilt strings that came attached.

She loved how it grounded her. How she walked into it after a shift and it felt familiar and right; it felt like a home. She couldn't imagine walking into her house and it not feeling like a home any more.

She couldn't imagine walking away from it.

'Isn't it strange, having nowhere to call your own? Eating in someone else's kitchen, sitting on someone else's couch, sleeping in someone else's bed'

'Nah. I'm used to moving around from my years in the military. It feels right.'

'So you'll never get your own place again?'

He shook his head. 'I will…one day, I guess. The money's there. I could have done it at any point. But I liked the gypsy lifestyle. I've felt very…cast adrift these last few years, I guess…so this suits me for now.'

Billie sipped her wine. 'And how does Amber feel about that?'

'Amber has her own life. As she should. And she has financial security that she wouldn't have if I was still in the house. And as long as there's a spare bed for her when she needs it, she doesn't care where I live.'

'She sounds like an extraordinary young woman.'

'Yes.' He nodded. 'She is. Considering what she's been through.'

'She sounds like she's lucky to have you.'

Gareth shook his head. 'No. *I'm* lucky to have *her.*'

Billie's throat clogged with emotion. She'd never met a man like Gareth. A man who was unashamedly frank about his feelings, who had his priorities straight. She thought about her own father, who'd never told her how lucky he was to have her. He *had* told her *frequently* how lucky she was to have him, though.

His experience, his influence, his name.

He'd never even cried at Jessica's funeral.

'I hope you tell her that,' Billie murmured.

'Yep, as often as I can.' He smiled at her. 'I'll serve up.'

Gareth took their plates through to the formal dining room and set them down at the large table that seated twelve.

'Wow,' Billie said, looking above her at the imposing chandelier. 'Do you eat in here?'

'Nah, I usually eat in the lounge room in front of the telly; I like to catch up on the news but I figured an Ashworth-Keyes is used to formal dining,' he teased.

Billie grimaced. She *had* grown up with formal dining. In fact, they'd had a chandelier quite similar to this one.

'I vote for the lounge,' she said. 'This Ashworth-Keyes prefers relaxed and casual.'

Gareth's gaze met and held hers for a brief moment. He smiled at her and her breath hitched. 'There is nothing casual about you.'

Billie blushed. She didn't know what he meant by that exactly. Did he mean that she was too serious, too much of a mess? Or did he mean she wasn't going to be casual in his life?

She looked down to hide her confusion, her daggy jumper staring back at her. 'I don't know,' she said, looking back at him. 'I'm not exactly dressed for the opera.'

He grinned as he picked up the plates. 'All the better to undress you.'

Billie's insides quivered as she followed.

Gareth put some music on low and they chatted as they ate. Billie seemed stilted at first—not that he could blame her after his blatant statement of intent in the dining room—but she soon warmed up.

Conversation quickly drifted to his time in the military and they talked long after they'd set their bowls aside. He told her a bit about his postings and she asked him about the things he'd seen that had given him faith in the human race.

The question surprised him. Most people wanted to know the gory details. But he guessed, given Billie's abhorrence of gore, she was positioned to ask an atypical question.

'Was it hard to leave?' she asked.

Gareth shook his head. 'I loved being in the military. Putting on that uniform made me feel proud and worthy. It took me places and gave me opportunities to make a difference I wouldn't have had otherwise, but I was away from home a lot and if someone had told me that I was going to lose Catherine after only ten years together, I would have ditched the military in an instant and spent every one of those years by her side. We thought we'd have decades.'

Billie slid her hand onto his. 'Life's shorter than we think sometimes,' she whispered.

Gareth glanced at her. Moisture shimmered in her eyes. Was she thinking about her sister? 'I'm never making that mistake again,' he said, turning his hand over, her fingers automatically interlocking with his.

'She didn't mind you being away so much?' Billie asked.

'No. She knew how much I loved my job and Catherine was the most self-reliant woman I'd ever met. She'd been a single mother for five years, she could look after herself and she didn't mind being on her own.'

'She sounds great.'

Gareth nodded. 'You would have liked her.' He looked down at their hands. '*She* would have liked you.' The silence grew between them and Gareth glanced up. Billie looked wistful and a little sad. 'Sorry… God…' He shook his head. 'Way to kill a mood…talk incessantly about your dead wife.'

She laughed then. 'No, it's fine. I don't mind. I wish I could talk more about Jess. But she's such a taboo topic at home.'

'It's too painful for your parents still?'

'Yes,' Billie said. 'Mum can't even bear to hear her name uttered. And I think Dad feels this sense of…failure. My father comes from a long line of successful, ground-breaking surgeons; everything the Ashworth-Keyes clan have ever attempted has ended in success. And they like to talk about their successes, celebrate them. They don't talk about their failures. And I think he feels like he failed with Jess most of all.'

'I'm sorry,' Gareth said.

She shrugged. 'It is what it is.'

Gareth put his arm around her and snuggled her into the crook of his shoulder. Her head fitted under his chin, the silky strands of her hair brushing his skin. Their legs were already stretched out in front of them, their bare feet propped on the coffee table. He inched his foot closer to hers and rubbed it gently against her.

'What *was* she like?' he asked, as he absently dropped a kiss on the top of her head.

Billie didn't answer for a while and he could feel the tension across her shoulders as if the memories had been kept inside for so long it was taking an effort to drag them out and dust them off. But he didn't mind waiting. The music was nice and she was snuggled in close and he knew the benefits of talking about those you'd loved and lost.

He and Amber often talked about Catherine.

'She had this mad laugh,' Billie said after a while. 'Like… really loud…*honking*, my father called it. He always thought Jess did it deliberately to annoy him.'

'And did she?'

'No. Well…maybe she took some pleasure in emphasising it.'

He chuckled. 'What else?'

'She was beautiful. And *fun*. And she loved kids. She wanted a dozen. I think she would have too, you know,' she said, shifting to look up at him, her eyes misting. 'She'd have made a great mother.'

Gareth's heart swelled in his chest. 'It sucks.'

'Yes. It does.'

'It helps to talk, though.'

She nodded. 'Yes. It does. And sometimes…' her gaze zeroed in on his mouth and it tingled so hard it hurt '…it helps not to talk at all.'

Gareth sucked in a breath. He couldn't agree more.

CHAPTER SIXTEEN

BILLIE WHIMPERED WHEN Gareth's mouth took hers in an achingly tender kiss. It was sweet and soft, warm and gentle, exploring the contours of her mouth in unhurried detail.

It broke her and healed her all at once.

When he pulled away, Billie's head was swimming from its intensity. 'No,' she murmured, reaching for him. Needing him to do it again.

'Shh,' he whispered against her mouth, as he dropped another gentle kiss on her lips. 'Not here,' he said, extricating himself and standing, holding his hand out to her. 'I want to lay you out on my bed. I want to look at you.'

Billie's stomach dropped right out as his words washed over her. She slid her hand into his and stood, her legs trembling in anticipation. Gareth smiled at her and led her though the house, down a darkened hallway, until they reached the double doors at the end.

He pushed one open and tugged her in after him.

The low-lit room was beautiful but Billie didn't notice the expensive furnishings or the plush carpet underfoot, she only had eyes for Gareth, who was turning and taking her in his arms again, kissing her mouth and her eyes and her nose. Nuzzling her ear and her neck, his hands stroking down her back, pushing underneath her jumper and her top to find her bare flesh.

'Off,' he muttered in her ear, pushing both pieces of clothing up. 'I want to kiss you all over.'

Billie didn't have to be asked twice as she ducked her head out of the clothing and Gareth flung them on the floor.

His breath hissed out as she stood before him in her bra and track pants. His gaze devoured her and her nipples beaded before his thorough inspection. He traced a finger from the hollow of her throat to the cleavage of her bra.

'I knew you'd be this beautiful,' he whispered, his eyes never leaving her, his fingers stroking lightly along her collarbones. 'I haven't been able to stop thinking about you.'

Billie's eyes fluttered closed under his silky caress.

'I've dreamed about being inside you,' he said, and her eyes opened at his frank admission. He sank on his knees before her and kissed her belly. She sank her hand into his crinkly hair as his tongue dipped into her navel.

'Gareth,' she moaned, her legs threatening to give away.

He grabbed her other hand and placed it on his shoulder and Billie held on for dear life, bunching his shirt in her hands as his tongue traced from one hip to the other.

'Damn…you taste good.' She felt his groan hot against her belly.

Billie whimpered at the want and ache in his voice. Ached for him too. Wanted to touch him, put her mouth to him as he was to her. She grabbed at his shirt, hauled it up, yanking him up with it, whipping it off, her greedy hands going to his chest, feeling the heat, her palms revelling in the rough smatter of hair as he plundered her mouth, squeezing her buttocks, urging her closer.

And then his palms were sliding beneath the waistband of her track pants, sizzling against the bare flesh of her bottom, and she moaned against his mouth as his thumbs hooked into the band sitting on her hips and pulled it down, her underwear going too. He eased them over her hips, his palms pushing them down her legs.

Billie kicked out of them and then she was completely naked, conscious of the erotic scrape of denim against the bare skin of her thighs and the smooth play of his hands as they caressed her buttocks, kneading and stroking, urging her closer to him.

'Bed,' he said, pulling away slightly to walk her closer to the mattress, stopping when the backs of her thighs hit the edge, urging her to sit, to lie back.

She sat. She lay.

She stretched her arms above her head and looked right at him.

'God…Billie…' he said, his breath rough, 'the things I want to do to you.'

Billie smiled, her nipples peaking under his hot gaze. She lifted her leg and hooked it around the back of his thighs. 'Bit hard to do it from all the way up there,' she murmured.

He slid a hand onto her thigh. 'I just want to look at you some more.'

Billie's cheeks warmed as he did exactly that. Pinned to the bed by the raw sexuality in his blue gaze, her neck flushed, her nipples ruched into tight, hard pebbles, her belly tightened.

The tingling at the juncture of her thighs went from buzz to burn.

'Gareth,' she complained, her voice almost a pant. She was going to die from the anticipation if he didn't do something. 'You promised me Elvis.'

His hand tightened on her thigh and he grinned. 'Do you see me talking?'

'You're talking with your eyes.'

He laughed then. 'Damn straight. Do you know what they're saying?'

'No.' She grimaced. 'But I'm guessing you're going to tell me.'

He grinned again. 'They're saying…where do I start first? Do I stroke? Do I kiss? Do I lick?'

Billie bit back a full-blown moan. 'I'm good with any combination.'

'Do I start at your mouth and work down?' he mused, following that path with his eyes. 'Or do I start at your toes and head up? Or do I just zero in on one bit. And, if so, which bit? Your neck?' His gaze dropped to her breasts, 'Your nipples?' It lingered there for long moments and Billie suppressed the urge to arch her back. 'Or do I start a little further south?'

His gaze moved down to the juncture of her thighs and Billie swallowed—hard.

'You're like a smorgasbord,' he murmured, staring at her there. 'And I'm really, really hungry.'

Billie's leg clamped hard around his thigh. 'Damn it, Gareth,' she groaned. 'A little less conversation.'

He chuckled, cranking her frustration up another notch. 'Where do you want me first?'

'Just kiss me,' she half moaned, half begged, reaching for him. 'Kiss me anywhere.'

And then he crawled on the bed over top of her and kissed her. Long and deep and so exquisitely Billie wanted to cry for the beauty of it. It sucked away her breath and twenty-six years of being an Ashworth-Keyes as she linked her arms around his neck and fell headlong into the perfect insanity.

They kissed for an age. Universes were born and died and still he kissed her. Taking his time, savouring her taste and her moans and sighs. Billie let him lead, followed him eagerly as her own hands explored the contours of his neck, his shoulders, his back. Her fingers brushed the denim waistband of his jeans and pushed beneath, finding other contours, better contours to squeeze and knead.

Suddenly, impatient with any barrier between them, her fingers came around to the front, delving between their bodies, nudging open his button and his zip and pushing at the fabric, taking his underwear as well, easing them both down over his hips as he had done to her.

He lifted, shifted to give her access, wriggled and kicked

out of the denim, not breaking his lip lock once, and then he was naked, settling between her thighs, taunting her mercilessly with a slow rub, the long, hard length of him easing through all her slick heat.

'God…you feel so good. So wet…' he groaned against her mouth. 'I want to be inside you.'

'*Gareth*,' Billie gasped, at the strained urgency of his words and the slow erotic grind. She dug her nails into his back. 'Yes,' she panted. 'God…please…yes.'

He lifted away from her and Billie was momentarily bereft. 'No,' she protested, grabbing for him.

He came back to her, kissed her. 'It's okay,' he murmured, dropping soothing kisses against her mouth, her nose, her eyelids. 'Just getting a condom.'

And then he was gone again but he was back quickly and sheathing himself and settling between her legs again and she was opening wide to him, lifting her hips, locking her legs around his waist, blatantly inviting him inside.

She gasped at the first thick nudge of him and when he entered her completely, sliding all the way in, she arched her back and cried out.

'Billie,' he panted, burying his face in her neck.

Billie slid her hands onto his buttocks, clenching them hard in her hands, holding him tight, right where he was as he pressed and stretched all the right spots. 'Feels so good,' she muttered.

He chuckled into her neck and it was sweet and sexy all at once, fanning hot breath onto her sensitised skin. Then he planted the flats of his arms on either side of her head and lifted himself up, rearing over her, their chests apart, their hips joined, his eyes looking right down into hers.

'Hold on,' he said. 'It's going to feel better.'

He moved then, flexing his hips, and she gasped again, gripping his back as he pulled out and slid back in, thick and sure. Billie shut her eyes as pleasure shimmied through the nerve fibres in her belly and thighs.

He was right, it felt *so* much better.

'Look at me.'

Billie opened her eyes and saw his blue gaze piercing her. 'I want to watch you come,' he said, pulling out. 'I want you to be…' he eased into her oh-so-slowly '…looking right at me.'

Billie nodded but her eyes closed involuntarily as his hardness stretched every last millimetre of her and everything clenched inside.

'Billie.' They snapped open at the raw command. 'I said…' he pulled out '…open.' He pushed in.

Billie fought the urge to close them again as pleasure pulled at her eyelids. She groaned, gripped his buttocks, as the maddeningly slow pace continued. 'Come on, Gareth, faster.'

'No.' He grimaced, the veins in his neck standing out. 'I'm going to make you come so slowly you're going to feel every…' he eased in '…single…' he eased out '…second.'

He eased all the way in again.

And it was working. A flutter pulsed low in her belly as she gripped the hard length of him.

'You're beautiful,' he murmured, looking down at her, burying his fingers in her hair as he kept up the slow and easy pace. 'I've wanted you since that first night, at the accident. I could hardly take my eyes off you.'

'Oh, yeah?' she panted. 'Was that before or after I tossed my cookies?' He hit a sweet spot and she gasped, anchoring her hands to his shoulders and flexing her hips. 'Oh, God, yes, just there,' she said, all high and breathy.

He obliged, angling himself just right, massaging the spot back and forth with the same steady thrusts, cranking up the flutter.

'God, Billie,' he groaned, as he thrust and held tight, seating himself deep. 'You make me crazy. I can't believe I kissed you in the tearoom…I so should not have done that.'

'Yes,' she moaned, as she flexed her hips some more, encouraging him to go deeper. 'You should have.' She looked into his eyes. 'I wanted it.' She locked her legs around his waist, lifting her hips again. 'I *needed* it.'

It was satisfying to see his eyes shut, hear the hiss of his breath. 'Damn it, Billie,' he groaned, his eyes flashing open, piercing her with hungry eyes as he clamped a hand to her hip. 'Stop wriggling like that.'

Billie shook her head, circling her hips again, daring him with her gaze. 'You've kept me waiting for weeks, Gareth.' She clenched internal muscles around him. 'Enough already.'

Gareth groaned then dropped his head, kissing her hard, surging inside her as he released her hip, his elbows digging into the bed either side of her head, giving him greater purchase. 'I wanted to go inside with you that morning in the car,' he said, pulling away from her mouth, his own moist from their passion. He rocked into her. 'And that night, at your place…'

Billie could see his biceps flexing in her peripheral vision as he slid in and out. 'You're here now,' she said, lifting her head, nuzzling his lips. 'So do me already.'

And she kissed him, hot and hard, putting every ounce of herself into it. Showing him the extent of her need, the depths of her desperation. Whimpering, 'Please,' against his mouth. Laying herself bare. Making herself vulnerable to him in a way she'd never done with another man. Needing his possession as much as she needed oxygen.

Did he want her to beg? Because she'd do that too.

Billie was breathing hard when she pulled out of the kiss. So was he.

Gareth looked down at her, his gaze roving over her face, her neck, her breasts, his chest heaving. 'Like this?' he asked, pumping his hips a little quicker.

Billie moaned as he hit all the right spots. 'God…yes.' Her head dropped back, her belly tightened.

He sped up some more. 'You want it like this?' he demanded.

Billie whimpered. 'Yes,' she gasped. 'More.'

'Like this?' he panted, his gaze snagging hers as his thrusts steadily picked up tempo, rocking her head, driving her higher and higher.

The flutter turned into a ripple.

She grabbed his buttocks. 'Yes.'

'You want it hard and fast?' he demanded.

Billie moaned, finding his blue gaze utterly compelling. 'God, yes.' Meaty muscles flexed in her hands with each thrust and she held them fast, anchored herself there.

'More?'

'Yes.' Her heart thundered, her breath rasped. The ripple became a contraction. 'Don't stop,' she gasped. 'Don't. Ever. Stop.'

He didn't. He drove into her relentlessly, their bodies meshed as one, their gazes locked. The contractions multiplied, rippling out, her consciousness slowly fraying at the edges. 'Yes, yes,' she sobbed, her eyes widening, as a wave of pleasure washed over her.

'Yes,' he muttered triumphantly, as she tightened around him. 'That's it…yes. Hold on, I've got you.'

And then as more waves broke he slowed it right down. Billie whimpered as he pulsed in and out slowly, rocking her gently, sweetly, wringing every ounce of pleasure out of each contraction, prolonging it to an unbearable intensity.

She shut her eyes. It was too much. It was going to kill her. She was going to die, die here in his arms, gasping in pleasure. 'Look at me, damn it, Billie,' he demanded.

She looked at him as she slowly came apart.

'Look at what you do to me.'

He groaned then, long and low, his blue gaze heating to flame, his arms trembling, his hips thrusting hard, jerking to a standstill as he cried out.

Billie gripped him hard, his pleasure feeding hers, the honesty in his eyes overwhelming. 'Yes,' she whispered, snaking a hand up into his hair, twisting her fingers hard into his wavy locks, dragging his head down. 'More,' she said against his lips.

'Yes,' he said, kissing her, moving his hips again.

Billie moaned into his mouth as the pulsing continued unabated, her entire body buffeted by waves of intense pleasure. 'Good,' she whispered. 'So good.'

'Yes,' he agreed.

And he kissed her all the way to the end. Until he collapsed on top of her and they were both gasping and sated.

CHAPTER SEVENTEEN

GARETH WOKE A few hours later with Billie spooning him, her hand lightly stroking his hip. His groin was already well and truly awake. He smiled. 'A little lower.'

Billie laughed as his low rumble vibrated along muscle fibres already in a state of excitability. She slid her hand onto his solid thigh and then down onto his erection.

'Lower?'

Gareth grunted, shutting his eyes as she slid her hand up and down. 'No,' he said, shunting in a ragged breath. 'That's just right.'

She played a little longer before sliding her hand up to his shoulder and urging him onto his back. She threw her leg across his body and claimed his lips and then, before she knew it, he was pulling her over on top of him, settling the slick juncture of her thighs against the hot, hard length of him.

She rubbed herself against his delicious thickness, pleasure pouring heat into the cauldron of her pelvis.

'Mmm,' he murmured, stroking her back. 'That feels good.'

Billie sighed, stilling against him, enjoying the feel of his girth, hard and good, pressing into all her softness. She rested her cheek on his pec, the thud of Gareth's heart and the slow, lazy patterns he was stroking over her back lulling her eyes shut.

Gareth shut his eyes too, remembering how nice this part was. Lying with a woman afterwards. Touching her. Snuggling in the glow. Every nerve ending sated and energised at the same time. Feeling lazy and heavy but also light and floaty.

He opened his eyes after a while. Billie's breathing was deep and even and he wondered if she was asleep. 'Thank you,' he said into the dark. 'I've missed this.'

Billie stirred from the trancelike state she'd entered. She lifted her head to look at him. 'Am I your first…I mean, since Catherine…? Has there been anyone else?'

He smiled at her, his hand stroking down the side of her face, tucking a strand of hair behind her ear. 'Why? Was I that rusty?'

Billie laughed as she made two fists on his chest and propped her chin on them. 'If that was you rusty I hope I'm around for when you're well oiled.'

He grinned at her and Billie's heart hitched a little. 'If we keep going this way, that should be by morning.'

She smiled. 'Lucky me.'

Gareth picked up another lock of her hair and sifted it through his fingers. Lying in the dark with her, her body warm and supple, her breasts pressed against his chest, he felt like he could tell her anything.

'I've had a couple of brief liaisons since Catherine died. One was at a conference. A one-night stand thing. The other was a mother from Amber's school, who'd just been through a rough divorce and was after a little revenge sex.'

Billie smiled, despite the spike of jealousy niggling at her chest. 'She chose well.'

He chuckled. 'It was good. Fun. The first time was only a couple of months after Catherine had died. I was…lost, I guess.' He sought her gaze as he rubbed a copper lock between his finger pads. 'I missed her so much. I wanted to stop feeling so awful, to forget for a while. But…I felt even more awful after, like I'd cheated on her. The second time,

Laura, was much later. I was more emotionally ready for it. And I…needed it. I needed to feel like a man again, a fully functioning man.'

Billie sobered. She understood what he was telling her. It was only natural for a man who had lost the love of his life to go through the entire gamut of emotional responses to that loss.

But it beggared the question—what was she? Was she just another signpost on his journey through grief?

She absently traced her finger around his nipple, the hairs tickling. 'Is that was this is? Am I helping you feel like a man again?'

Gareth frowned. Her tone was light but her eyes had gone all serious. 'What? No.' He grabbed her hand. He couldn't concentrate when she was touching him like that. 'No,' he re-iterated, bringing her fingers to his mouth and kissing them.

He shifted then, taking her with him as he rolled over, rolling her under him, his body half on, half off her, his thigh parting her legs, pinning them to the bed. He propped him-self up on an elbow.

He needed her to understand what she meant. What their coming together tonight meant to him.

Gareth pushed his hand into her hair and stroked his thumb along her cheekbone as he looked into her eyes.

'You're the first woman since my wife died that's meant *anything* to me. For the first time in five years this isn't about me or my grief or what I want or need. I'm attracted to you, because of *you*. And I know the way you know things deep down in your gut that this can't possibly last but I really *like* you, Billie.'

'Yes.' She smiled. 'You told me already.'

'No.' This wasn't the same thing as their fake-date thing. 'I *like you* like you.'

Billie's heart squeezed in her chest at his sudden serious-ness. It wasn't the L word that most women her age seemed to long for but it was such an earnest, heartfelt sentiment that

Billie drank it up. Gareth had been through so much, lost so much. That he was even capable of feeling anything again was a miracle. And she cherished it.

She smiled at him. 'I *like* you too.'

'It's okay, I don't expect a reciprocal admission. That wasn't why I said it. I just know I feel very deeply for you already. And I wanted you know it too. I wanted you to know that you're not some way for me to prove that I still have all my working bits or that you're some diversion to keep the blackness at bay. You're not *just* my two-yearly roll in the hay.'

He kissed her then, slow and gentle. Kissed her until she moaned and clung and begged him for more.

They finally woke around nine. Slow and easy at first as they drifted up through layers of sleep then hot and heavy as their bodies woke and desire, sweet and heady, surged through their systems.

'I think I could get used to this,' he murmured.

Billie sighed. She could definitely get used to waking up with Gareth. It would be *no* hardship. She snuggled into him. 'Me too.'

Gareth's hands found her breasts and his groin perked up again. He was surprised it was still physically able after last night. He was about to suggest going again when a loud growl emanated from her stomach. Gareth laughed.

'Wow. That's a helluva belly rumble. I'm impressed.'

Billie blushed at her noisy innards. 'Sorry.' She slid her hand over her navel. 'It must be all that physical activity you put me through. I'm starving.'

'Put you through.' He chuckled again. 'Didn't seem like a chore when you were screaming my name all night,' he murmured, nipping at the patch of skin where shoulder met neck. She sucked in a breath and her nipples beaded in his palm. 'I make some mean French toast. Or would you prefer jam on toast?'

Billie smiled as her stomach rumbled again. 'I *love* French toast. Do you have banana?'

'Yes. And bacon. And maple syrup'

'You are a god amongst men.'

He grinned. 'Damn straight.' He kissed her neck then extricated himself, dropping his head down to kiss her hip before leaving the bed. He grabbed his underwear off the floor and climbed into it before turning to look at her. She'd rolled onto her back, not bothering to pull the sheet up. His gaze wandered up and down the length of her and his recipe for French toast slipped away.

Her stomach growled again and he shook his head. 'Why don't you come and keep me company?'

Billie arched an eyebrow. 'Like this?'

He nodded. 'Exactly like that. You could be my muse while I create food for you. Of course, I couldn't promise that you won't end up covered in maple syrup.'

Billie's head filled with a very erotic image of her spread out on the kitchen bench while he licked maple syrup out of her belly button. And other places. Thinking about where she could lick it off him was equally erotic.

She rolled up onto her elbow and she liked the way his gaze wandered to the fall of her breasts. 'Let me take a shower first. Maybe bring it back to bed after?'

Gareth liked the way she thought. He particularly liked the way she thought when she was naked in his bed. 'Good thinking.' His gaze drifted down to where the sheet cut across low on her hips, hiding one of her best bits from his view.

A fine spot for maple syrup if ever there was one.

Billie was pretty sure she knew where his mind was and her toes curled beneath the sheet. 'You could always, of course, join me?' she suggested, slowly trailing her palm down the middle of her belly, bringing it to a halt where sheet met skin. His gaze snagged on the movement and she smiled as she slid her fingers under the edge slightly. 'You could make sure I get all those *nooks and crannies* clean?'

Gareth dragged in a shaky breath. He wanted to rip that sheet back and dive between her legs. Make her come so loud she'd be sure to think twice about teasing him so blatantly.

For sure he wanted to take her against the tiles of his shower.

He dragged his gaze to her face. 'Do you want to eat at some stage today? Because if I get you in the shower all wet and slippery, there's no way I'm letting you out for a *very long time*.'

Billie smiled as he snatched up his jeans and left without a backward glance.

She sighed. The man really did have a spectacular butt.

CHAPTER EIGHTEEN

GARETH HAD CLIMBED into his jeans and was whistling by the time he hit the kitchen. He shouldn't be. He had a hunch, despite them both admitting to having feelings for each other, that things with Billie weren't going to run smoothly. She was pretty messed up about her life direction and grief had made him wary, more cautious with his heart.

But today he didn't much care about any of that.

He flicked the radio on. Rock music blared out loud and perfect and he bopped his head to the exhilarating beat as he clanged around in the kitchen, barefoot, bare-chested and one hundred per cent lord of all he surveyed.

He felt indomitable. He felt like a freaking king.

He felt like throwing his head back and crying out Tarzan-style as he beat his chest.

Gareth, King of the Jungle!

He smiled at the notion as he cracked the eggs into a bowl. He couldn't remember the last time he'd felt this good. He certainly hadn't felt this deep down happy with either of his last two liaisons.

Sure, Laura had been fun, a brief superficial distraction that he'd enjoyed very much, but she hadn't left him feeling this bone-deep satisfaction.

This feeling that all was right with the world.

Maybe he was getting ahead of himself. Maybe hormones and endorphins were making him delirious.

But nothing could erase his happy this morning.

* * *

Billie towelled off and headed back into the bedroom for her clothes. They lay scattered around the floor and her stomach dropped just remembering everything that had happened since she'd shed those suckers last night.

She picked them up, figuring she could get back into her track pants and turtleneck. She didn't want to get back into her undies but she could go without. If she played her cards right they'd be back in bed before too much longer anyway.

She smiled as she plotted how she might drop her commando state into their breakfast conversation. Or was that brunch?

She quickly jammed a foot into the leg of her track pants, her gaze taking in her surroundings properly for the first time as she stuck her other foot in and pulled the track pants up. The dishevelled bed dominated the room. Off one wall was the en suite. Off the other a walk-in wardrobe.

Billie grinned to herself. Oh, the possibilities!

She sauntered over. Maybe she could find something clean of Gareth's to get into instead?

The wardrobe was extensive but most of it was empty except for a small section of hanging clothes and some occupied drawers. She figured the owners must have taken all their clothes with them and what was left was Gareth's.

She riffled through his hanging clothes and found a russet-coloured business shirt that matched her hair perfectly. She inhaled the sunshine and soap-powder smell of it before removing it from the hanger and shoving her arms through the sleeves.

She turned and inspected herself in the full-length mirror. Her hair was still knotted on top of her head and she quickly released it, shaking it out, watching as it fell down around her shoulders.

She stripped off her track pants and she liked what she saw—pink cheeks, glowing skin, sparkling eyes. She didn't look tired as she probably should be, considering how little sleep she'd had. On the contrary, she looked like a woman who had been kept up all night in the best possible way.

She looked thoroughly sated.

On impulse, Billie undid the top two and bottom two buttons, leaving only two in the middle holding the shirt together. An enticing slice of bare breasts and a glimpse of shadow at the juncture of her thighs looked back at her.

She put her hand on her hip and pouted at her reflection. The action drew the hem of the shirt up even higher, revealing a much bigger glimpse of what was below her navel.

Not the effect she was going for.

She turned to his drawers and searched for some underwear, smiling when she found a pair of fluro green boxers. *Perfect.*

She slipped them on. They were on the baggy side but she rolled the waistband low on her hips and it anchored there well enough. She went back to the mirror, giving herself a once-over. A barely recognisable woman stared back at her. With her hair all loose, her mouth all pouty and cleavage to burn, she looked far from a responsible emergency medicine doctor.

She certainly didn't look like an Ashworth-Keyes.

No. She looked like one of those old-fashioned sex kittens from the magazines of the forties and fifties.

Billie smiled. She hoped Gareth *liked* it too.

Gareth was so engrossed in the music, juggling the cooking of the French toast and the bacon and thinking about how good Billie would look all wet and naked in the shower, he didn't hear the key in the lock or the door open.

He was well and truly in his happy place.

So much so he actually startled when Amber appeared in front of him, saying, 'God, that smell's amazing. Remind me to flip out more often, would you?'

He blinked at his daughter uncomprehendingly for a few moments. 'Amber?'

She laughed. 'Correct. Are you okay? You're looking weird.' She stepped forward and kissed him on the cheek, swiping a piece of piping-hot, crispy bacon off the plate.

Gareth couldn't think for a moment. Crap!

Amber.

She'd been to that support group yesterday and he'd forgotten he'd invited her for breakfast this morning!

'Ooh, French toast?' she murmured, oblivious to his turmoil. 'You've outdone yourself. Great timing too. It's as if you knew I was about to walk through the door.'

He smiled as he gathered his scattered wits. He needed to talk and fast. Billie was bound to be showing her face any time soon. 'Yes. About that…'

Billie followed the sound of music and the smell of frying bacon all the way to the kitchen. Her mouth watered and her stomach rumbled louder.

'Hope you've made double,' she announced as she entered the kitchen. 'You wore me out last night, I need sus—'

Billie stopped abruptly when she realised Gareth wasn't alone in the kitchen.

Amber?

'Oh.' She looked from Gareth to a shocked Amber then back to Gareth again. 'I'm sorry. I didn't realise you had… company…'

Billie wished the floor would open up and swallow her in the tense silence that followed. Suddenly her forties sex-kitten look seemed cheap and tawdry. Or at least that must be how it looked to Gareth's daughter.

Amber looked at her father. 'Who the hell is *she*?'

Gareth grimaced at the poison in Amber's words. She was looking at him with eyes full of anger and confusion and he'd give anything to rewind the last couple of minutes. He and Amber had never talked about what would happen when this day swung around. When he became involved with another woman.

He'd always figured when—*if*—it did, that it would be a gradual thing and Amber would be along for the ride.

He hadn't expected to be sprung fresh out of bed by his twenty-year-old daughter.

He held up both his hands. Amber looked like she was going to bolt and he didn't want her leaving without knowing that this wasn't what she was thinking. 'I'm sorry, Amber. I forgot you were coming over this morning.'

Clearly the wrong thing to say as Amber went from frosty anger to visible hurt. But she recovered quickly, her wounded eyes turning as hard as stone. 'I just bet you did,' she snapped, whirling away.

'Amber…' he said, striding across the room to stop her exit. He grabbed her arm. 'Let me explain.'

'What are you going to tell me?' she demanded, whirling back to face him. 'That this isn't what I think it is? That this… woman isn't wearing the shirt I bought you for Christmas last year and you haven't been *screwing h*er all night long?'

Billie's audible gasp sliced through him. 'Amber, that's enough.' This had obviously come as a shock to her and it certainly wasn't the way he'd have hoped Amber found out about his private life but he wouldn't let her cheapen what had happened between him and Billie either.

Amber glared at him. 'Screw you too,' she said, jerking her arm out of his grasp and storming out of the house.

Fabulous. Beautifully handled.

Not.

He turned back to Billie, his brain churning with a hundred different things to say, none of them particularly adequate in the face of her stillness or pallor. She was standing, apparently frozen to the spot in the middle of the kitchen, every cute freckle dusting the bridge of her nose standing out.

The fact that she looked so incredibly sexy in his shirt was a particular irony. Amber's impromptu arrival had blown any chance of him getting her out of it now.

He raked a hand through his hair. 'Sorry about that.'

His words prodded Billie out of her inertia. She shook her head. 'It's fine.'

'I…forgot.' He rubbed his eyes. 'I forgot I invited her over.'

Billie nodded. She didn't think Gareth had deliberately set this up for some fairy-tale meet-cute. If he had, it had seriously backfired.

'It's fine,' she said again.

'She's just found out that she has the BRCA1 gene,' he said. 'She went to some support group yesterday. We were supposed to be debriefing this morning but—'

But.

Billie didn't need him to fill in the blanks. She was the *but*. It was *her* fault he'd forgotten. S*he'd* distracted him from his parental responsibilities.

'I'm sorry to hear that,' she said, hugging herself as she sucked in a breath around the painful lump in the centre of her chest. It was stupid to feel slighted—this wasn't about her. Amber must be reeling from the dreadful news. 'She must be feeling very vulnerable at the moment.'

If she kept this about Amber, Billie knew she could keep everything in perspective. And it should be about Amber. The twenty-year-old had just been dealt a huge whammy. It was nothing compared to whatever fledgling thing they had going on.

He rubbed the back of his neck. 'It's been a shock.'

Billie nodded. Of course it had. She only had to look at Gareth's face to know how much it was eating him up. 'I'm just…going to go,' she said.

Gareth looked at her in alarm. 'No…Billie…' He joined her in the kitchen in four easy strides, sliding his hands onto her waist.

He knew he'd gaffed with her too. This morning when

he'd woken up he'd felt bulletproof. And then Amber had thrown one hell of a spanner in the works.

'I didn't mean to imply that this Amber thing is your fault. *I* messed this up.'

Billie held up her hand. 'It's fine. *I'm* fine. You should go to her. You need to talk to Amber.'

And she needed some time and space. Billie was still struggling to assimilate what had happened. She guessed it was inevitable that reality would intrude into their bubble sooner or later but she'd figured she'd have a little more time. And reality would come in the form of work or her family, not in the form of Gareth's rightfully furious daughter.

The reality of Gareth's life was that he was a forty-year-old father and that had to be the main priority in his life. The reality was that they *both* had other priorities in their life—how could it ever work?

Reality was a bitch like that.

Gareth sighed. He knew she was right. He had to go after Amber but he didn't want to leave it like this with Billie either. 'Can I see you tonight?'

She stepped out of his arms. 'I'm having dinner with my family tonight.'

It was the first time Billie had ever been grateful for one of the tediously long, pompous do's she was subjected to every month.

'I'll see you at work on Monday, though, right?' she added.

Gareth may have been off the market for a long time but he knew a brush-off when he saw it. Although, to be fair to Billie, this had to be a little overwhelming.

Maybe it was good to have some space.

'Sure,' he said.

'Okay… I'll just…' she looked over her shoulder '…grab my stuff, then.'

Gareth watched her go, thoughts churning around his head as he absently dealt with the half-cooked breakfast. She was back in the kitchen in under five minutes, wearing her clothes from last night. The brief goodbye peck on the cheek she gave him was not encouraging.

Neither was the way she didn't look back as she strode out of his house.

CHAPTER NINETEEN

GARETH WAS STANDING on Amber's doorstep an hour later. He'd showered and changed first, knowing from old that giving Amber some time to cool down always boded well.

Carly answered the door. 'You're in the doghouse,' she said in her usual blunt manner.

'Yes.' Gareth grimaced. 'Can I come in?'

'I think her exact words were, "If that rat shows up here, kick his butt to the kerb."'

Gareth ignored the insult, quirking an eyebrow. 'Is that what you're here to do?'

Carly was possibly the most petite female he knew. Sure, she made up for it with her big, ballsy personality but he could have pushed her aside with one finger.

Carly opened the door wider and stepped aside. 'Nope. She needs to talk to you. She just doesn't know it yet.'

He grinned. 'I've always liked you.'

'Got your back, Jack,' Carly quipped, as Gareth entered.

'So…how is she…really?' he asked, after Carly shut the door.

Carly shrugged. 'I think she's on her bed, sticking pins in an effigy of you.'

Gareth chuckled but quickly sobered. 'I messed up, Carly.'

'Yeah.' Carly nodded. 'She said. But you know what I told her?'

'No, what?'

'That any other hottie father who'd been through what you'd been through would probably have blown through a stack of sympathetic chicks by now and it was about time she stopped putting you on some exalted pedestal and realised you're just flesh and blood. And that Catherine wouldn't have wanted you to be alone for ever.'

Even as an eight-year-old, Carly had said stuff that had been designed to shock, so he ignored her *hottie father* reference. But she'd always been a wise little thing. 'Oh.'

'Yeah…I think she's sticking pins in an effigy of me too.'

Gareth chuckled. 'Well, thank you. That can't have been easy.'

Carly shrugged. 'Ya gotta know when to hand out the tissues and when to dish out some tough love. Breast cancer gene gets tissues. Daddy's got a girlfriend after being a widower for five long lonely years not so much.'

Gareth was grateful that Amber had such a good friend in Carly. He knew Catherine's death had devastated Carly too. He glanced down the hall at Amber's door.

'Going in, then. Wish me luck.'

'You won't need it,' Carly said, shaking her head. 'She can never stay mad at you for long.'

Gareth snorted. 'She was angry at me for two years.'

'That's different. Her mother had died. You think anything's worse than that?'

Gareth shook his head. 'Good point.'

Gareth knocked on the door but didn't wait for permission to enter. It was unlocked so he pushed it open.

'Go away,' Amber said, glaring at him from the bed. Her eyes were red-rimmed and puffy-looking but there were no effigies in sight.

'I think we should talk.'

'I don't want to talk to you.'

'Fine… I'll talk and you can listen.'

Amber stared at him mutinously, crossing her arms. 'How about you turn around and don't come back?'

Gareth shook his head, not easily deterred. 'I'm really sorry about earlier. You coming over had slipped my mind and—'

Amber's snort interrupted him. 'I wonder why?'

'Yes,' Gareth sighed. 'Billie being there distracted me.'

'Billie? That's a stupid name.'

Gareth would have laughed at the childish comeback had he not already been walking a delicate line. 'It's actually Willamina. Willamina Ashworth-Keyes. She's one of the new residents at work.'

'You think I should be impressed that you can pull a doctor?' she said scornfully.

'No, of course not...' Gareth sighed, risking sitting on the edge of Amber's bed. 'I just thought you might like to know more about her.'

'Why?' she flared back at him. 'Is she going to be my new mummy?'

Gareth took a breath and searched for the deeper meaning to the scathing question, like the hospital counsellors had urged him to do. 'You're angry because you think I'm replacing Catherine? That I'm forgetting her?'

'No,' Amber denied hotly, but Gareth could see the hurt in her eyes. 'I'm angry because we were supposed to spend the morning together but you *forgot* because you were too busy with your new girlfriend.'

'She's not my girlfriend, Amber. We've just met. It's just new...' He looked down at his hands as he remembered Billie's noncommittal departure. 'I'm not even certain it's going anywhere.'

'But you're in love with her.'

He glanced at Amber sharply. Her puffy eyes looked deadly serious and they were demanding the truth. 'We *just* met,' he repeated.

Amber shook her head at him, her lip curling. 'How *old* is she?'

'She's twenty-six.'

'Bloody hell, Gareth!'

'Yes.' The thought was depressing. 'That is one of the complications.'

'Didn't stop you sleeping with her, though, did it?'

'Amber,' he warned. 'I'm not going to talk about my sex life with you.'

'Oh…so you have a *sex life* now?' she demanded.

Gareth grimaced. 'Probably not after today, no…'

Amber didn't say anything for a long time, she just looked at him, her gaze roving over his face, searching for what, he didn't know. But slowly the anger drained from her face.

'You do love her.'

Gareth shook his head. He wished he knew how he felt. 'I don't know, Amba-san. I know I like her. I like her a lot. But it's complicated. She's at a different stage in her life to me.'

Another snort but this one was softer, more mocking than angry. 'No kidding.'

He gave a half-laugh, relieved that Amber's anger had dissipated. He could still see shadows in her gaze but she'd had them since she'd been fifteen.

Amber swung her legs over the side of the bed. 'I'm sorry. I didn't mean to flip out the way I did. I guess I'm doing that quite a bit lately,' she said quietly.

He shrugged. 'You're dealing with a lot.'

'I was…shocked. I guess part of me always thought you'd be faithful to Mum for ever. I know that's not fair to you, though. Carly says I need to cut you some slack and that you're just flesh and blood.'

Gareth smiled. He leaned in closer to her and nudged her arm with his. 'I think we should keep Carly.'

'As if we could get rid of her.'

They laughed then and it felt good after the emotionally charged morning. When they stopped Gareth looked down at his daughter. 'I'm always going to love your mum, Amba-san. No matter what my future holds, she'll always be...' he tapped his chest '...here.'

She turned her face to him and tears were swimming in her big eyes, so like her mother's. 'I have this dream every now and then... I can't remember what she looks like. What if I forget what she looks like, Gareth?'

Gareth put his arm around her shoulder and hugged her to his side. 'You won't forget. Her image is engraved on your heart. And, anyway, there are too many pictures of her around.'

'Don't you ever worry you will?'

Gareth shook his head. 'No. She's engraved on my heart too. And even if for some obscure reason I did and every single picture of the thousands we have were destroyed, I'd just need to look at you.'

They sat together for long moments. He kissed her on the head again. 'You okay now?'

Amber nodded, looking up at him. 'I guess we'd better go and let Carly know she's not going to need to bury a body.'

'Comforting to know she would, though,' Gareth said, smiling as he took Amber's hand and they stood together and headed for the door.

At nine-thirty Billie was ready to fake a heart attack to get away early from the family dinner. But dessert was yet to be served and an Ashworth-Keyes did not leave before dessert, coffee, liqueurs and every single grotesque medical story since the last time they had met had been told.

And it *was* only once a month.

In between grilling her about the emergency department at St Luke's, her grandfather, her parents, two uncles and three cousins were discussing a surgical case that had hit the news due to mismanagement. If she heard the words 'faecal peritonitis' one more time she was going to throw up her beef Wellington.

Did they really have to talk about such things while they were *eating?*

Of course, she should be used to it now—she'd grown up with medical chitchat forming the basis of most teatime conversation, but it all seemed so…clinical. Billie had an insane urge to mention Jessica—something they never talked about—just to get a human, non-medical reaction.

She didn't. *Of course.*

That would be very un-Ashworth-Keyes of her.

But her mind kept drifting to where she'd been this time last night, preferring the memory of being naked with Gareth than anything going on at the table. And when it wasn't there, it was reliving the nightmare of Amber's 'Who the hell is *she?*'

Coming face to face with the reality of Gareth's life had been a wake-up call. She hadn't handled it very well. But running away from things was what she did best.

'Billie?'

Billie blinked as her father's harsh voice dragged her out of the events of this morning. All eyes were on her. 'I'm sorry?'

He sighed impatiently. 'What on earth is the matter with you tonight? Why are you so distracted?' he demanded.

The whole table was looking at her, apparently waiting for her response. 'I'm just…tired,' she said lamely, dismissing her father's query with a wave of her hand.

'*Tired!*' her father snorted, as if it was something only lazy people suffered. If only he knew how very little sleep she'd had last night. 'A good doctor pushes through that barrier.'

And then he went off on a tangent about his days of training and how many hours they'd worked and how little time off they'd had, and then her grandfather and uncles joined in and Billie let her mind drift again.

Her phone vibrated in her pocket and she leapt for it as

if it was a lifeline and she was drowning. Her father glared at her as she checked the text message. She didn't care. She knew it was bad table manners but so was talking about gruesome surgeries, as far as she was concerned.

Sorry about this morning. Things better with Amber. Thinking of you. Hope you are having a nice dinner with your family. Gareth x

Billie's heart thundered in her chest. She'd been worried about the fallout with Amber all day and had almost texted him a dozen times but had forced herself not to. Gareth needed to focus on his daughter—this mess was not about her. Not really anyway.

She stared at the screen. Her heart fluttered as she read and re-read *'Thinking of you'*. And that little 'x'. What the hell did that mean?

Her fingers shook as she tapped in a quick response.

Am going mad. Rescue me?

Her thumb hovered over the send button. Should she? Shouldn't she?

'Amber.' Her mother's gentle reprimand pulled all Billie's strings.

That was it. She needed to get out of here and the text left the ball in his court. He could send something flippant and noncommittal or he might just help.

She hit send.

Billie nervously placed the phone on the table, ignoring her mother's pursed lips. Would Gareth come to her rescue?

The phone vibrated almost instantly. She picked it up and swiped her thumb across the screen to read the new message.

Getting in car now. I'll be at yours in twenty. Plead a headache.

Billie smiled. She stood abruptly, cutting her father off in midstream as everyone jumped. 'I'm sorry. I have a head-ache,' she announced. She grabbed her bag from where it was hanging over the back of her chair. 'I'm going home.'

'That was sudden,' her father, who never liked being in-terrupted, said waspishly as he half stood.

'No, don't get up,' Billie dismissed, waving him back into his chair. She whipped around the table, doling out kisses. 'I'm fine. Just need to lie down in a dark room.'

With a very hot nurse.

'I'll see everyone next month.'

And before anyone could catch their breath she was prac-tically running out of the house, her fingers flying over her phone keyboard.

See you soon.

She hesitated about putting an 'x' there as he had done. After last night it seemed natural but then, after everything this morning, she wasn't sure...

After dithering for a few seconds Billie decided against it, hitting send exactly as it was as she climbed into her car and reversed in a flurry of gravel down the driveway.

CHAPTER TWENTY

FORTY MINUTES LATER Gareth rolled onto his back in the middle of Billie's hallway, half-clothed, and groaned.

'Well…that was intense…'

Billie, her head still spinning, laughed as she slid her head onto his shoulder. 'Only what you deserved for rescuing a damsel in distress.'

Gareth gave a half-laugh. 'Well…you know what they say…you can take the guy out of the military…'

'Mmm,' Billie murmured, inhaling the smell of his skin, revelling in the warmth of his meaty pectoral muscle against her cheek. 'That blew my mind.'

Gareth shut his eyes as her nuzzling streaked hot arrows to his groin. How was that even *possible* so soon? 'A little on the fast side,' he murmured, thinking about their mad dash from the driveway to the door then collapsing to the floor once they'd got inside.

Billie turned her head until her chin was resting on his chest. Her gaze travelled up his whiskery throat to the downward sweep of his eyelashes. 'I don't know,' she murmured. 'I like it that you couldn't wait to have me. It's good for my ego.'

His smile did funny things to her pulse. A pulse that was barely back to its normal rhythm. He opened his eyes and their gazes locked and the humour she saw dancing in all that blueness bubbled in her heart.

'Trust me, your ego is going to be well and truly pandered to tonight.'

Gareth shifted then, displacing her, sat first before vaulting to his feet, adjusting his clothing as he went. He turned to look down at her. Her skirt was rucked right up, her blouse was half-undone and her breasts had been removed from her bra cups. Her cheeks were flushed and her hair lay in disarray around her head.

'Damn, you're sexy,' he muttered, offering her his hand.

Billie grinned as she took it and before she knew it she wasn't just on her feet but was swept up in his arms.

'I'm going to need directions,' he said.

She wound her arms around his neck as a nice buzz settled into her bones. She nuzzled his throat. 'You are the last man who needs *any* direction,' she sighed.

He chuckled and she could feel it reverberate through his windpipe. 'I mean to your room.'

Billie blushed, feeling foolish. 'Oh, yes…straight ahead, third door on the right.'

Gareth made it to her room in ten seconds, throwing her on the bed. He watched as her breasts bounced enticingly. 'I'm going to use your en suite,' he said. 'When I get back I'm going to be naked. You'd better be too.'

She quirked an eyebrow at him. 'Or what?'

Gareth grinned. She looked so sexy barely dressed, her mouth a little swollen from their passion, a flirty little dare sparkling in her eyes. He shoved his hands on his hips and let his eyes rake over her. 'I may have to spank you.'

Billie's breath hitched. She'd never been into that kind of thing but Gareth made it sound enticing. 'Maybe I'll stay dressed.'

He chuckled. 'Up to you.'

But when he strode out of the en suite she'd pulled the covers down and she was lying in the middle of the bed gloriously naked. It was his turn to quirk an eyebrow.

'I think I'm too squeamish for S and M.'

Gareth laughed at her slightly defensive tone. 'It's too much hard work anyway.'

Billie relaxed. 'I agree. Dinner with my parents was hard enough.' And she reached over and flicked out the light.

There was a desperation to Billie this time. In the hallway it had been all about burning off the tsunami of lust that had swamped them when they'd first laid eyes on each other again. This time, it seemed to Gareth, it was as if she was using it to obliterate everything else.

Dinner *must* have been a bust.

She clung to him in the aftermath and Gareth held her tight. Their breathing slowly returned to normal and eventually he said, 'Tell me about dinner.'

Billie stirred as Gareth's words sunk in. 'Nothing to tell.'

He trailed his fingers up and down her arm. 'I feel like we just had exorcism sex and that somehow it was related to dinner, and you won't spill the beans?'

'It's the same as it always is,' Billie dismissed. 'Tales of surgical glory interspersed with grilling me about what I'm doing. And tonight, for a lovely added extra, we got a graphic discussion on faecal peritonitis. *While we ate.*'

Gareth chuckled. He couldn't help himself. He could only imagine how that had gone down with Billie's volatile constitution.

'It's not funny,' Billie grouched. 'Give me a patient with a complex web of medical conditions any day.'

Gareth's fingers stilled on her arm. Surely Billie understood that being a GP came with its own set of gruesome realities?

'You do know that GPs deal with some fairly grotesque stuff too, right? They see their fair share of hideous wounds and unsightly conditions. The GP is usually the first place people seek help and it can be pretty raw there at the coalface. You'll still have to tell your patients they're dying. And they *will* die, Billie. In fact, you'll be the one there for them and their family right at the end.'

Billie rolled on her stomach and propped her chin on his chest. She shot him a reproachful look. 'Do I look naive to you?'

'No. Definitely not after that thing you just did anyway.' He grinned.

Billie whacked him playfully on the arm. 'Of course I know I'll come across stuff that will turn my stomach. That I'll have to look a patient in the eye and tell them they've only got a certain amount of time to live. I know that. And it'll be awful.'

Billie didn't even want to think about how awful some of those moments were going to be.

'But at least I'll *know* that patient. I'll have a relationship, a rapport with them. It won't be a stranger telling them.'

Gareth picked up a strand of her hair and rubbed the tip with the pads of his fingers. 'And you think that'll make it *easier*?'

'For them, yes. And also for me…I think. It'll never be easy, of course, but one of the hardest things to take about Corey's death was the fact that he died in a roomful of strangers. *I* had to tell his parents he'd died. *Me.* Who didn't know them from a bar of soap. It shouldn't happen like that, Gareth.'

Billie searched his face earnestly—he understood, didn't he? 'How many men have you seen die from combat wounds far away from the people who loved them?'

She watched him as he stared at the strand of her hair he had in his fingers. 'Too many,' he murmured.

'*Exactly.*' Billie continued. 'People should die with loved ones around them, not strangers. Their relatives shouldn't be told such devastating news by someone who doesn't know them. And I get that that's the way it is in emergency departments and when you're deployed to a war zone. Of course it is. But I don't want to spend the rest of my life imparting bad news to strangers.'

Gareth's gaze cut to Billie as he let the strand of hair drop. 'So don't.'

Billie stared at him. He made it sound so simple. Could she really get out from under twenty-six years of conditioning and manipulation and dare to reach for *her* dream?

'Tell your parents what you want. You're a big girl now. Billie. What's the worst that could happen?'

'A lot of yelling—my father. And tears—my mother. A lot of guilt tripping and subtle threats.'

'Are they going to stop loving you?'

Billie blinked. It had been a lot of years since she'd felt loved by them. She'd felt tolerated and pushed and pressured but love? She was fairly certain her parents were afraid to love too much again.

'They'll stop inviting me to dinner so I guess there'll be an upside,' she joked, her heart not in it.

'But…' he traced her bottom lip with his thumb '…you'll have what you want. You can be what *you* want.'

'You don't understand. I don't do this kind of thing. I'm the good daughter. The peacekeeper. It was hard enough to sell them on emergency medicine. I think my father may well have a heart attack if I tell him I've decided to become a GP. And my mother…'

Billie didn't want to be the one to kill Jessica twice.

'So you're just going to go along with their vision for you? Even if it means you'll be miserable?'

'I won't be miserable,' Billie protested, no idea now why she was defending the thing she didn't want to Gareth. 'I'll just not be one hundred per cent happy. I'll still see a lot of the stuff I like to deal with. A lot of emergency department stuff is GP territory and you know it.'

'Billie.'

She dropped her gaze from his, staring at the strong pulse beating in his throat. She couldn't bear to see the reproach, the disappointment in his eyes. 'You didn't see my mother the night Jess died. She was so gutted. And in those awful months afterwards she looked at me like I was their lifeline.'

Gareth bit back his reply. He wanted to push more. Push her to see she couldn't live someone else's life for them. But he didn't want to be that person. The one who swooped in and tried to fix everything. It could backfire badly and Billie needed to figure it out for herself.

She glanced up at him. 'You think I should tell them to stick it?'

Gareth gave her a half-smile, his fingers sifting through her hair. 'I think…' *I think I have to choose my words very carefully.* 'You have to make the decision that's right for you. And you've got time to do it. You were going to have to do a few years in a hospital anyway before you branched off into GP land, including time in emergency medicine, so none of this is wasted.'

Billie traced her index finger around his mouth, his whiskers tickling. 'Are you always this wise?'

Gareth rubbed his mouth against the pad of her finger. 'I just want you to be happy, Billie. Life's too short to be miserable.'

Billie thought about Corey. And Jess. And Catherine. And Amber staring down a potential death sentence. He was right. It was far too short to be having hypothetical conversations about her career that even she didn't know the answers to when she had a sex god in her bed.

She shifted, crawling on top of him, pushing up into a sitting position, straddling him. 'I know something that makes me happy,' she said, rubbing herself against him.

He sucked in a quick breath clamping his hands on her hips. 'Coincidentally it makes me pretty damn happy too,' he murmured.

Billie smiled. 'Excellent.'

Gareth had to make a mad dash out of Billie's bed the next morning after sleeping through his alarm and dodging her sleepy advances. 'I'll be quick,' she protested, pulling the sheet back to entice him to stay. 'Like in the hallway.'

Gareth chuckled as he covered her up and kissed her hard on the mouth. It was all right for her, she started at eight, which gave her a whole extra hour to get to St Luke's.

'How about I join you in the shower?' she said from the bed as he headed for the en suite.

'I'm locking the door,' he threw over her shoulder. He'd be late for sure if she was in there with him all wet and slippery and determined.

When Gareth stepped out of the en suite the bed was empty and he could smell coffee and toast. His mouth watered and he followed the intoxicating aromas.

His mouth watered a little more as he entered the kitchen to find Billie standing at the bench in a polar fleece dressing gown, her hair swept up on top of her head, licking jam off her fingers.

'Mmm,' he said, reaching her in three easy strides, slipping his arms around her waist and nuzzling her neck. 'Something smells good.'

'The toast,' she said, picking up a slice and shoving it towards his mouth.

Gareth bit into it. Butter and jam melted against his tongue in some kind of orgasmic mix and he grabbed the slice as she let it go. He stepped back from her, moving to her side, his butt coming to rest against the bench, their hips almost touching.

'Coffee's done,' she said, as the toaster popped and she reached for the freshly cooked slices.

Gareth spied the percolator and headed for it as he downed the last large bite. He pulled two mugs off a nearby stand and filled them both. He knew without asking that she took it black with sugar—the same as him. A sugar bowl sat beside the percolator.

He fixed the coffees and passed hers over. He watched as

she took her first sip and gave a happy little sigh. He'd heard that a lot last night and he laughed.

She smiled at him over the rim of the mug and he noticed she had a smear of butter on her top lip. He was just about to lean down and lick it off when a loud knock sounded on the door.

Gareth frowned down at her. 'Do you usually get visitors at six-thirty in the morning?'

Billie shook her head but her eyes held a little twinkle. 'No. I told my other lover to wait until after you'd left.'

He gave her a wry smile as she placed the mug on the bench but he grabbed her and kissed her hard. Pretend lover or not, he wanted her to know who she'd spent the night with.

Billie's head was spinning as she floated to the door, a goofy smile on her face. It was still there when she opened the door seconds later.

Seeing her visitor on the doorstep killed it dead.

'Dad?'

CHAPTER TWENTY-ONE

'HELLO, WILLAMINA.' HER father pecked her on the cheek.

Billie accepted the kiss automatically. 'Oh… Hi. You're here…early…'

'Morning rounds before my theatre list. Like to stay on top of things.'

'Oh…right.'

'Have you got a moment to chat?' he asked, rubbing his hands together vigorously, and Billie noted absently how nippy it was outside.

'Ah…actually…' she said, trying desperately to think of a way to get him to leave. 'I'm running late for work…'

Her father checked his watch and frowned. 'I thought you said you started at eight this morning? Don't worry,' he dismissed in that way of his that wrote off a person's concerns as trivialities. 'This won't take long.'

He indicated that she should let him pass and Billie stepped back out of deference and habit more than anything. 'I feel like you were distracted last night. Pour me a cup of that coffee I can smell and we can talk. You can't afford to be distracted.'

Billie realised suddenly he was charging ahead and she scrambled to get to the kitchen before him but it was too late. By the time she'd followed him in, her father and Gareth were already eyeing each other.

Her father turned to look at her with ice in his eyes. '*This* is your distraction, I take it?'

For the second morning in a row Billie found herself wishing the floor would open up and swallow her. First Gareth's twenty-year-old daughter had sprung them. And now her father.

'Mr Ashworth-Keyes, sir,' Gareth said, coming forward, his hand extended. 'I'm Gareth Stapleton.'

Billie watched her father reluctantly shake Gareth's hand, finally finding her voice. 'Gareth's a...' She glanced at Gareth, who was looking at her with questioning eyes.

How the hell did she explain Gareth to her father, who thought nurses were handmaidens there to serve doctors' needs and fade into the background at all other times? She was too busy fighting the obvious disapproval that there was a man in her apartment distracting her from the hallowed calling of medicine without facing any more judgement.

'We work together in the ER at St Luke's,' she said, suddenly unable to look at the man who'd warmed her bed all night.

Charles crossed his arms across his chest. 'I take it you're some kind of emergency specialist, although...' his brow puckered as he obviously searched his memory banks '... the name's not familiar...'

Gareth glanced at Billie, who had turned pleading eyes on him. Her cheeks were flushed and he knew what she was asking him to do. But he'd been around enough to know that playing it straight was the best policy. If Billie wanted to lie to her father about her own stuff, that was her prerogative. But he wouldn't.

'Actually, sir, I'm a nurse.'

Had Gareth not been in the middle of this awkward conversation he might have found Billie's father's double-take quite comical. But he was.

Charles turned to Billie. 'A nurse? A *male* nurse.'

Gareth almost laughed out loud. The Ashworth-Keyes'

and the Stapletons may have been miles apart in socio-economic status but Charles had just sounded exactly like his own father when Gareth had told him what he was going to do.

Billie scrambled to Gareth's side. 'He's ex-military, Dad. He did several tours to Africa and the Middle East.'

Gareth looked down at Billie. He understood what she was trying to do but he didn't need her to talk him up. He was proud of what he did and he was damn good at it. He couldn't care less what the Charles Ashworth-Keyes' of the world thought. He met men like him all the time. But he did care what Billie thought. And that, apparently, was embarrassment.

Maybe he shouldn't have expected anything too much, given their brief liaison, but he'd never thought she found what he did for a living lacking in any way.

And he wasn't sure he could be with someone who did.

'I should go,' Gareth announced picking up his coffee mug and draining it.

Billie's father clearly thought so too, folding his arms and looking down his imperious nose at Gareth.

'Okay,' Billie said nervously. 'I'll see you out.'

'No.' Gareth shook his head. 'You stay. I'll see you at work.' He turned to her father. 'Nice meeting you, sir.'

Billie watched as Gareth strode out of the kitchen and she desperately wanted to call him back. The door shut firmly behind him and she knew she'd blown it.

But…it was complicated with her father.

The morning sure hadn't ended the way she'd thought it would. Clearly they sucked at mornings. They needed to stick to the nights.

That was if Gareth ever spoke to her again.

'*A male* nurse?'

'Would you prefer it if I'd slept with a female nurse?' Billie asked waspishly.

Her father glared at her. 'Don't get sassy with me, young lady.'

Billie gathered her wits and girded her loins. She so did not want to talk about Gareth. Not when there was so much she didn't know herself. She turned away, busying herself with pouring his coffee.

'I take it he's the reason you suddenly developed a headache last night?'

Billie doubted her father would understand that she'd walked away from many a family dinner with a splitting headache.

'He's a little old for you, isn't he?'

Billie turned and handed him the mug. 'It's really none of your business.'

He scowled at her. 'I'm the one who paid your exorbitant school fees and tutor fees and university and college fees and bought you a car and got you the residency at St Luke's. If you're about to mess it all up then damn right it's my business.'

And here came the guilt trip. 'Gareth has nothing to do with any of that.'

'You can do better than him,' he announced pompously.

Billie gaped at her father. 'Dad...you don't even know him!'

'I know how it's going to look.'

She shook her head wearily, knowing what was about to follow. 'Maybe I don't care how it looks?'

'You will.'

Billie sighed. God help her if her father ever found out Gareth was a single father who drove a twenty-year-old car and didn't even own his own home.

'I keep forgetting what an incredible snob you are.'

Charles gaped at her and even Billie blinked at her audacity to finally give voice to her criticism. It was the first time she'd ever uttered her innermost thoughts.

'It's them and us, Billie.' He looked down at her the way

he looked down on all non-surgeons, like he had some kind of divine right to walk the earth and everyone else deserved his pity. 'It's better for everyone if the status quo is maintained.'

Billie cringed, just listening to his pompous dribble. But she did what Jess had taught her to do when dealing with their father and his *opinions*—take a deep breath and imagine him in the operating theatre dressed only in his underwear and theatre cap.

Billie almost smiled at the thought. 'Plenty of doctors date nurses, Dad, hell, they even marry them, and you know it.'

'Yes, male doctors and female nurses. Not the other way round. If you ever want to be taken seriously as a specialist, you date other specialists. You marry another specialist.'

Suddenly he frowned, his coffee mug halfway to his lips. 'Wait…you're not thinking of marrying this man, are you?'

Oh, good Lord, would this *never* end? 'Dad…I just met Gareth.'

He gave her evasive answer an approving nod—the first time he'd softened since he'd blustered his way into her house and, like Pavlov's dog, she felt herself responding to it. Being the least bright out of her and Jessica, she'd always striven hard for his approval and even more so since she'd announced she wasn't becoming a surgeon.

She really didn't want to ruin the moment by voicing the truth. She had *feelings* for Gareth.

'Good. You don't need this kind of distraction right now. I'll tell you the same thing I tell all my residents, dating and doctoring don't mix. Concentrate on your work until you've settled into your specialty. There's plenty of time for that love nonsense after that.'

Her father put his coffee mug down. 'Right…must dash. I'm pleased we've had this chat.' He patted her on the shoulder. 'You'll see I'm right, Willamina.' He pecked her on the cheek. 'I'll see myself out, you need to get ready for work, don't want to get a reputation for being late. Punctuality is everything.'

And with that he was striding out of the kitchen and disappearing out her front door.

Billie felt too drained from the conversation to move.

Don't want a reputation for being late. Don't want a reputation for dating nurses.

Her father sucked all the joy out of everything.

And now she had to go and face Gareth, *who was angry with her.* And rightly so.

She wished she could blame that one on her father. Only it was all on her. She'd chosen to deny what Gareth did and invalidate it in one fell swoop. Her father may have been the catalyst but she'd made her own bed on that one.

She'd been a coward and had probably ruined everything.

Billie gripped the bench at the thought. She didn't want to ruin it with Gareth.

Please, let me be able to fix it.

Billie hit the ground running as soon as she got to work. She'd glimpsed Gareth briefly and he'd nodded at her politely but that had been the extent of their interaction. She'd fought back disappointment. After the last two nights she'd have expected one of those secret, knowing smiles, a silent communiqué conveying all kinds of sexy messages, like how pleased he was to see her, or how he couldn't wait to get her alone, or he was picturing her naked and screaming his name.

But, then, she only had herself to blame for its absence.

She made a pact with herself to talk to him this morning before their shift was done. To apologise. Although, if he was avoiding her, as she suspected he was, that might be a little difficult.

But she wasn't going to let this fester. No matter what, she *would* talk to Gareth today—even if she had to lock him in the supply cupboard until he heard her out.

* * *

With that course of action decided on, the *last* person Billie expected to be talking to entered the staffroom at lunchtime and introduced herself. 'Hi. I'm Amber.'

'Oh…yes… Hi,' Billie said, pausing, a sandwich halfway to her lips. 'If you're looking for Gareth he's up in Outpatients for a few hours.'

'No. It's you I want. Do you think we could go somewhere and talk?' Amber looked around at the three other occupants of the room. 'It won't take long.'

A knot of nervous tension screwed tight in Billie's stomach as she forced a smile to her face. 'Of course. We can use one of the offices.'

Billie located the nearest empty office and walked in, with Amber close behind. It was small, with enough room for a desk, a chair and a narrow exam table against the wall. She shut the door and turned to face Gareth's daughter, her nervousness increasing now they were alone.

'I'd like to apologise for Sunday morning,' Amber said, looking defiant, as if she was daring Billie to contradict her. 'I was rude and out of line.'

Billie blinked. That she hadn't expected. 'It was a shock,' Billie dismissed. 'Don't worry about it.'

'No. Well…yes, it was a shock…but my mother taught me better manners than that.'

Billie tensed at the mention of Catherine. Where was this going? 'Like I said…it's fine.'

Amber eyed her for long moments. 'Gareth told you about my mother?'

Billie nodded. 'Yes. I'm very sorry for your loss.'

Amber grunted. 'Why do people always think those words help somehow?'

Billie blushed at Amber's belligerence. She felt like she was walking on eggshells. 'I'm sorry…you're right. They don't. Nothing helps.'

Amber eyed her sharply. 'You talking from *actual* experience or just doctor experience?'

Billie almost laughed at Amber's prioritising. Her father would have had apoplexy to hear Amber dismissing her doctoring in preference to real life. 'My sister died when I was fourteen. I know that's not the same as a mother but it was the single most devastating thing that's ever happened to me.'

Gareth's daughter didn't say anything for long moments as she regarded Billie. 'How old was she? What happened?'

'She was sixteen. A car accident. Joy riding with friends.'

Amber's shoulders sagged as her defiance and belligerence dissipated. 'I'm sorry.'

Billie nodded. 'Thank you.'

There were more long moments of silence as Amber obviously mentally recalculated. 'I came to say that I'm pretty sure Gareth is in love with you and…that's been a lot to take in…'

Whoa! Billie blinked. That was a different kind of L word. But conviction rang in Amber's voice and shone in her gaze.

Had Gareth *told* his daughter that?

'But it's been five years since my mother died and Carly… that's my friend…reckons any other guy would have found someone else a long time ago…so I'm trying to be grown up about this but…he said that you were both at different stages of your lives and it struck me that he might be more…into you than you are to him so…I just wanted to say, if you hurt him, you'll have me to answer to.'

Billie couldn't quite believe she was being threatened by a twenty-year-old but her admiration for Amber grew tenfold.

'Amber…Gareth's a wonderful man and I don't want to hurt him. But he's right. There are complications.' She thought back to that morning. 'I'm…trying.'

'Well, try harder,' she said. 'Or let him go now, before you break his heart. I don't want to watch that again.'

Amber's words sliced right to Billie's core. Maybe Amber was right. How could she be any kind of equal partner to

Gareth when she couldn't even stand up for the things she wanted?

Maybe she should end it. Whatever *it* was.

Her pager beeped, she pulled it off the waistband of her scrubs and looked at the screen.

Incoming trauma.

Bile rose in Billie's throat at the mere thought. 'I'm sorry,' she said. 'I have to go.'

Amber nodded. 'Just think about what I said, okay? After all he'd been through he deserves to be happy. He deserves to be with someone who wants to be with him too.'

Billie nodded. Amber was right. The truth sucked.

CHAPTER TWENTY-TWO

GARETH WAS IN the same cubicle with Billie as they attended to the traumatic amputation of a leg. It was bloody and gory, the male patient having lost a lot of blood—most of it over himself. She did well with holding it together but he was probably the only one in the cubicle who really knew how much it cost her.

How much it had to be turning her stomach.

In fact, when it was done and the patient had been whisked to Theatre, she quickly excused herself. His gaze followed her as she disappeared into the staff restrooms and emerged five minutes later looking very pale and shaky, pressing some paper towels to her mouth.

Gareth would bet his last cent she'd just thrown up.

Their eyes met and she gave him a helpless little shrug.

And his simmering anger cranked up another notch. He'd been furious with her that morning, with the way she'd been uncomfortable about telling her father what he did. But part of him understood she was between a rock and a hard place with her old man.

He understood how fraught those relationships could be. And he understood Billie being reluctant to rock the boat and potentially jeopardise her mother's mental health.

But this…

This…pretence was utter madness. How could she even

contemplate not being true to herself over this? This was the rest of her life.

She was hiding behind a mask that was so thin in places it was slowly cracking. And he couldn't stand by and watch it any longer. It had to stop. He didn't want any part of a woman who had to lie and hide her true self from the people who mattered most. Who was okay with living a lie.

Gareth stepped down from the central work station and stalked towards her. He collected her arm on the way past, spinning her around. 'We need to talk,' he muttered.

Billie should have been annoyed at the firm hold Gareth had on her arm but, frankly, she'd been that close to collapsing it felt good to lean into him. 'Where are we going?'

'In here,' Gareth said, opening the door to one of the back examination rooms that was rarely used. He switched on the light and dragged her inside. 'Sit,' he ordered. She looked like she was about to keel over, for crying out loud.

Billie sat gratefully. 'Before you say anything,' she said, eyeing him as he paced, 'I want to apologise for this morning. My father was rude and insulting and—'

'It's fine,' Gareth dismissed. 'He was taken by surprise, just like Amber was.'

Billie blinked. She hadn't expected him to defend her father. 'Amber's twenty. My father doesn't have that excuse.'

'I don't care about that. Well, I do, but I'm not ashamed of what I am. I was more insulted that *you* felt you had to conceal that than anything your father said. I don't want to be your dirty little secret, Billie, but…that's not what this is about.'

A wave of shame washed over Billie, chasing away the last vestiges of her nausea. She had insulted him. This man who had been nothing but supportive and encouraging.

'You have to tell them you can't be an emergency doctor, Billie. You can't keep going on like this.'

Billie blanched at his suggestion. Her father had just found out about Gareth. *One bombshell at a time, please!* She shook her head. 'I don't think that would be very wise.'

'If you don't, you're going to end up here for ever. Throwing up in that loo for ever.'

'I'm fine now,' she dismissed.

Gareth shook his head. 'You're not *fine.*'

'They're not ready to hear it yet.'

Gareth snorted. 'They're never going to be ready, Billie. C'mon…maybe it won't be as bad as you think. Just rip the plaster off, get it over and done with.'

'I've never been a ripper,' she said, shaking her head. 'I'm more an "ease the plaster off bit by bit" girl. And you said it yourself last night. I have to be doing what I'm doing now anyway before I can go down the GP path so why cause a problem before I need to? In a few years I'll face the choice, the *real* choice, and I can upset the applecart then. Why borrow trouble?'

Billie knew it was classic Jess behaviour—tell her parents what they wanted to hear then spring the bad news on them at the last moment. But it had worked for her sister. Jess had gone to her grave with her parents completely unaware of her plans outside medicine.

The perfect daughter, as far as they were concerned.

And now it was she who had to be the perfect daughter.

Gareth shoved his hands on his hips. 'Because I'm worried you *won't* upset the applecart when the moment comes. The longer you put it off the harder it will be, Billie. And why should you *have* to pretend? This is your *family.* You should be able to *be yourself* around your family and expect their support.'

Billie could see the frustration in Gareth's stance, hear it in his voice, but she knew how best to handle her life, not him. 'Look…' She stood, walking over to him, her legs feeling much stronger now. She stopped when he was an arm's length away. 'I appreciate your concern but I've been dealing with my father for a lot of years and I know how to handle him.'

Gareth couldn't believe it. She was really going to suppress what she wanted for a little peace and quiet? 'So you're just going to keep being a…*coward*, like you were this morning when you couldn't even tell your father I was a nurse?'

Heat rushed to Billie's face at his "coward" taunt. 'I prefer to think of it as self-preservation,' she said waspishly.

Gareth raked a hand through his hair. 'Okay, well…that's fine. But I can't do this, Billie.' His hand dropped to his side. 'I don't think we should do this any more.'

Billie frowned, her heart in her mouth. 'This?'

'You and me,' Gareth said. 'I don't want to be around to watch you grow unhappier and unhappier until you self-destruct from the weight of it all.'

Billie's pulse was thundering through her head as the reality of what he was saying sank in. He was ending whatever it was between them before it had even begun.

So much for thinking it was something *she* was going to decide.

She searched his blue gaze for signs of reluctance or disingenuousness. But it was clear and firm.

A flutter of panic swarmed in her stomach. She didn't want it to be over. 'So that's it? Two nights together with the chemistry between us off the charts and you pull the plug?'

Gareth grimaced. He didn't need to be reminded what he was giving up. It hadn't been easy to start this thing with Billie after five years alone and it was frightening how deeply he already felt.

Which was precisely why he needed to get out now.

'All I have as a man is my self-respect, Billie, and I get that by being true to myself. And I want to be with a woman who's also true to herself. I didn't think I'd find another woman I wanted to be with, to share my life with, after Catherine, but then you came along and you made me smile and I felt good and I started to hope…'

His gaze swept over the freckles on the bridge of her nose and the twin glossy pillows of her mouth. He was going to miss that mouth.

'Now you've got to do what you've got to do. That's fine, I can respect that. But I've got to do what's right for me too and that's not being with someone who still lets her parents dictate her life. I think it's best if we get out now before we're in too deep.'

Billie took a step back. He'd been thinking of a future with her? Something small and fragile fluttered in the vicinity of her heart but the grim line of his mouth quashed it. She'd ruined her chances with him by being such a basket case.

'I'll try and roster myself on opposite shifts to you for your remaining time here but it will be inevitable that some shifts will clash. Can I suggest we try and keep things as civil as possible in that eventuality?'

Billie frowned. Did he think she was going to go all me-doctor-you-nurse on him? 'Of…course.'

Gareth hardened his heart to the catch in her voice. He'd seen the collateral damage broken work relationships could inflict and he didn't want either of them to fall prey to that. But he needed to get away from her now before the catch in her voice had him changing his mind and he hauled her into his arms.

'Well…' He stepped to the side. 'I guess I'll see you around, then.'

Billie nodded but didn't bother to turn and face him. The door clicked shut behind her and she groped for the exam bed in front of her, holding onto it for dear life.

That was it. Over before it had truly begun. Her heart ached already.

It didn't improve at all over the next couple of weeks. They worked a few shifts together but, true to his word, Gareth and Billie passed mostly like ships in the night.

Billie knew it was insane to miss him this much after such

a short time together. It wasn't like they had even been *in* a relationship. They'd had two nights together.

That had been it.

But she did miss him.

Lying in bed at night, she craved him. At work, she listened for his voice. She got all fluttery in the chest when he was there and when he walked by she didn't seem to be able to take her eyes off him.

She felt like a teenager mooning over a screen idol.

But she couldn't stop it either and there were times when she swore he found it difficult to drag his eyes off her too.

They may not be together but he was still under her skin. She only hoped the itch wouldn't be permanent.

Another week passed and Billie found herself working a Saturday day shift with Gareth. It was frantically busy so there wasn't any time for idle chit-chat. Not that they indulged in that any more.

Or ever had, for that matter.

As thrilling as it was to work the odd shift with Gareth, the days she did usually ended up being total downers—a case of look, don't touch and the vague feeling that Gareth was judging her for her choices.

She had had one triumph today, though, and she did a little jig as she snapped cubicle eight's curtain back in place, practically running into Gareth as he bowled past.

'Whoa, there,' he said, reaching out his hands to steady her, and Billie was sure they lingered a little longer than necessary.

'You look like you've had a win,' he said, so politely she wanted to scream.

She smiled at him despite his formality. 'I finally diagnosed this obscure skin condition. The patient's been back three times this last week and we finally nailed it. And, best of all, it's totally treatable!'

Gareth sucked in a breath as Billie literally glowed. Her cheeks were pink and her eyes glittered with excitement.

She was so sexy he wanted to kiss her until they both couldn't breathe.

But they had a trauma coming in.

'That's great,' he said, his tone brisk. 'Unfortunately we have a gunshot victim coming in. Head, chest and abdo wounds. GCS nine. ETA seven minutes. Helen wants you in Resus.'

Billie felt everything deflate inside her. *Crap.* Her smile slid right off her face. 'Oh, God, really?'

'Yep. Really.' He paused for a moment and Billie thought he was going to commiserate with her for a second and her pulse fluttered. 'Remember this feeling, Billie. It's not all skin conditions and surgical abdos.'

Gareth felt like an utter bastard as he walked away. But they were in an emergency department, not a dermatology clinic, for crying out loud.

She wanted this? Well, *this* was the reality.

CHAPTER TWENTY-THREE

BILLIE GOT THROUGH the trauma with her usual degree of bluff. It was raw and bloody and the patient died, and the only thing that prevented her from losing her lunch afterwards was the fact she had to sit with the man's wife and tell her.

And all she could hear in her head the whole time was, *Remember this feeling, Billie.*

Remember it? How could she forget it? She *hated* this feeling. But she was trying her best here—surely he could see that?

She knew he didn't owe her anything but at heart Gareth was a compassionate man and she certainly hadn't deserved his condescension.

And she was damn well going to tell him so.

She spied him from the desk, heading out of the department, his backpack slung over his shoulder, and she checked her watch. His shift had finished.

Before she knew what she was doing, she was following him—no time like the present for giving him a piece of her mind.

She caught sight of him as he turned a corner ahead of her and she realised he was heading for the fire escape that led to the rooftop car park. She rounded that corner and stopped abruptly as the sight of Amber and Gareth embracing in the distance greeted her.

Billie fell back, feeling like she was intruding on their

privacy. She couldn't hear what they were saying but Amber laughed at something her father had said and was looking at Gareth like he hung the moon. They hugged again then Gareth slipped his arm around Amber's waist and they entered the fire escape together.

She'd never felt that with her own father.

Never had a moment like that where they'd just laughed and loved and revelled in their family connection. Charles Ashworth-Keyes just wasn't the touchy-feely kind.

She was overwhelmed as she stood and stared at the closing fire-escape door. She wanted that.

She wanted to feel loved.

And she wanted to love back.

She wanted kids to hug and kiss and be there for. She wanted a man who was going to be there for her too. And her children.

And she wanted to feel the exhilaration of solving a complex medical puzzle and improving somebody's life. And she *never* wanted the feeling of dread that the piercing tone of a siren elicited.

And if a woman with a skin condition and a dead gunshot victim had taught her anything today, it had taught her where her strengths lay.

If Gareth had taught her anything, it was time she stood up for that. And she was tired of pretending.

She was pretty sure Jessica would have kicked her up the butt a long time ago.

She pulled her mobile out of her pocket and tapped off a quick text as she returned to the work station and the last few hours of her shift.

Four hours later Billie was parked in her car outside her parents' house, waiting. Gareth had texted to say he'd be here but he was late and she was running out of bravado.

Headlights flashed in her rear-view mirror and she breathed a sigh of relief when they pulled in behind her.

She got out of the car on shaky legs. The shutting of the door seemed loud in a street full of high walls and immaculately groomed lawns.

'Hi,' she said, as Gareth joined her, and he looked so sexy in his jeans and hoody, like the first time they'd met, she wanted to fling herself at him and beg his forgiveness.

But that wasn't why she was here.

'Hi.' He smiled at her and she felt encouraged. 'What's this about, Billie?'

'I'm telling my parents I'm going to study to be a GP and I needed moral support.'

Gareth regarded her seriously for a few moments. The news made him want to leap in the air but he was aware he'd treated her badly that afternoon. He didn't want her doing it because he'd guilted her into it. If she was going to do something so monumental then she needed to do it for the right reasons.

'Are you sure?'

Billie nodded. 'Yes. I realised today that I'm much better at diagnosing skin conditions than I am at treating gunshot victims. That treating Sally Anders gave me a much bigger rush than treating Danny Wauchope. I don't get the rush that people like you thrive on during a full-on resus. And I think you need that, I think you have to be wired that way to survive in that kind of environment.'

A cold wind blew strands of her loose hair across her face and Billie pushed them back. 'I saw you and Amber together near the fire escape this afternoon and I realised I don't have that kind of relationship with my father and that just seemed…sad. And wrong. Do you want more kids, Gareth?'

Gareth blinked at the unexpected question. 'I'd always thought I'd have more kids…yes.'

Billie nodded. Her future was becoming clearer. 'Can you please come with me while I break the news to my parents? I've tried so many times in the past and failed. I need someone there who's in my corner. Who will also call me on it if I chicken out.'

Gareth smiled. 'Okay. But I'm pretty sure your father isn't going to be happy to see me.'

Billie looked at the ground. Even the bitumen in this street was perfect. 'I know I'm putting you in an awkward position,' she said, raising her head.

Gareth waved his hand. 'You think I care about that? I just need you to be certain.'

'I have never been surer of anything.'

'Okay, then.' He smiled, holding out his hand. 'Let's do this.'

Waiting for the door to open was nerve-racking and she thanked her lucky stars for the warmth and calm, anchoring assurance of Gareth's hand at her back. Her mother answered the door with a puzzled expression but ushered them in anyway after Billie had performed a quick introduction. It was clear from her mother's wary gaze that her father had already mentioned Gareth.

Once the token politeness of drinks and offering of chairs—which they both declined—had been dispensed with her father came right to the point. 'What's this all about, Willamina?'

'I'm here to tell you that I'm not going to pursue a career in emergency medicine. I want to be a GP.'

The silence in the room was tense and lengthy.

'General practice!'

Her father made wanting to be a GP sound like wanting to be a prostitute but Billie was done with backing down.

'Yes.'

Her father slammed his heavy crystal glass down on the coffee table. 'No.'

'Dad. It doesn't matter what you—'

'I said no!' he snapped, advancing on her. 'This is the most preposterous thing I have ever heard. He…' Charles pointed his finger at Gareth as he came closer '…is dumbing you down.'

'He has a name,' Billie retorted, as Gareth swiftly stepped in front of her, blocking her father's progress.

'I think we need to calm down,' Gareth said.

Charles glowered at him. 'Don't tell me how to talk to my daughter.'

Gareth did not budge. 'You need to step back, sir.'

'I will do *no such thing*!'

Billie was quaking internally at the confrontation. She had expected her father to be upset, but not like this. There was a film of spittle coating his lips and he'd gone a very startling shade of red.

She shifted closer to Gareth, who wasn't giving an inch. He was staring at her father with absolute chilling authority.

'Step. Back. Sir.'

Her father halted at the ruthless determination in Gareth's eyes.

'Your daughter is trying to tell you something important, sir. You need to listen.'

'Don't presume to tell me about my daughter,' Charles snapped. 'You don't know her.'

Billie watched Gareth's jaw clench. 'I know that Billie's a brilliant doctor. I know she can't bear blood and gore yet she's working in an emergency department to please you when all she wants to be is a GP.'

'She's always been squeamish,' her father dismissed. 'But she never wanted it until you came along.'

Billie shook her head, coming out from behind Gareth. 'That's not true, Dad. I've *always* wanted to be a GP. I was just never brave enough to tell you.'

'But, Billie…how can you do this?'

Her mother, who had been silent up till now, grasped Billie by her forearms. 'Do you think Jess would have wanted you to *squander* the opportunities you've been given? She wanted to be a cardiothoracic surgeon and she didn't get the chance.

And here you are, alive and well and *spitting* on her memory. First this emergency medicine nonsense and now...*a GP?*'

Billie dragged in a ragged breath at her mother's verbal attack. She was torn between the old habit of shutting her mouth and taking it and the sudden rage inside that demanded her parents know the truth and to hell if it destroyed them.

She'd been silent for far too long.

She wrenched out of her mother's grip. 'Jessica *never* wanted to be a surgeon, cardiothoracic or otherwise,' Billie snapped. 'She wanted to be a kindergarten teacher. But she couldn't tell you that so she...'

Billie didn't realise that tears had sprung to her eyes and were falling down her cheeks until Gareth's arm came around her, and even then she just dashed them away and kept going because she knew if she stopped she wouldn't get this off her chest and after ten years it needed saying.

'...she went out drinking and yahooing and staying out late and she drove in fast cars, hoping that you'd disown her so she could do what *she* wanted.'

Her mother gasped but Billie didn't care about her emotional distress for a moment. It just felt so good to finally get it off her chest.

'You're lying,' her mother said, tears tracking down her face now.

'No.' Billie shook her head. 'I'm not. We talked about everything, Mum. *Everything.*'

Her mother sagged on the couch in a dreadful moment of déjà vu. Her father, to his credit, joined her, putting his arm around his wife's shoulders. Billie wished it didn't have to be this way. But she couldn't sacrifice what she wanted any more in the name of her sister.

And she was pretty sure Jessica—the ultimate free spirit—wouldn't have wanted her to either.

'I'm sorry, Mum...Dad. I didn't want you to find out like this. I didn't want to...upset you. But it's the truth.'

They didn't say anything for long moments. 'So you're

just going to throw everything away…all that education and invaluable career advantage?' her father demanded.

'I'm not the kind of doctor you two are,' Billie said, looking down at her confused parents. 'But that doesn't mean my contribution to medicine will be any less important or that you failed. I'm just not interested in the specialty limelight. I'm going to be a damn good GP and that's enough for me. I hope it can eventually be enough for you.'

'And where does *he* fit in?' her father said, nodding his head at Gareth like he was some kind of new species that needed explaining.

'I love him,' Billie said, her heart hammering in her chest as she looked at the man who had turned her whole world upside down.

'He's going to let me be what I need to be, he's going to be the glue that holds me together when I think I can't do it, and one day soon, I hope, he's going to be the father of your grandchildren, who I *will* take time out of work to raise. And you're going to love him too because he's awesome but also because *I* love him and we come as a package from now on.'

Billie held her breath for long moments as Gareth's blue eyes stared back at her. Somewhere deep inside she'd always known she loved him. But him showing up here tonight despite all the stuff she'd put him through had removed her blinkers. All the impossibilities fell by the wayside and they were just a man and a woman who were meant to be together.

'I love you too,' he said, sliding his arm around her.

Billie's heart cracked wide open as she smiled at him. She knew they had a lot to sort out, a lot of *stuff,* and declaring her love for him in front of two people who weren't exactly amenable to the match was a little unorthodox, but it had felt right.

And she'd waited long enough.

Gareth had helped her see so many truths about herself and she didn't want to spend even a second of her life without him in it.

She looked at her parents. 'I want you to meet the man I love,' she said.

Gareth smiled down at Billie, his heart exploding with a wellspring of emotion. In a million years he hadn't expected this outcome.

But in so many ways it was perfect.

He'd been falling in love with her for weeks, not letting himself sink into it completely, not trusting that it could happen twice in his life. But standing here, looking down at her in front of the people who loved her most, he'd never been more certain of anything.

She had shown him it was possible to love again.

He glanced at Billie's parents, who looked like they'd both been struck by lightning. 'Mr and Mrs Ashworth-Keyes, you have my word that I will make Billie happy to the end of her days. I understand that you're more concerned about her career prospects at the moment and hooking up with a man who isn't of the pedigree you'd imagined. But I promise you, I will be her champion, whatever way she wants to jump.'

Billie's heart just about floated right out of her chest. Her parents were clearly still trying to wrap their heads round things but right now she didn't care if they never got it. She'd spent far too long worrying about them and their expectations.

It was time for her.

She glanced at Gareth. 'I love you,' she murmured.

He smiled at her. 'I love you too.'

And right there, in front of her parents, he kissed her. Long and hard. And Billie didn't give a fig what they thought. She wrapped her arms around his neck and kissed him back.

This was her man. Life was short. And she was never letting him go.

* * * * *

FROM FLING
TO FOREVER

AVRIL TREMAYNE

This book is dedicated to my fellow writer PTG
Man and Dr John Sammut with many, many
thanks for the generous medical advice. Thanks
also to Dr John Lander and Dr Hynek Prochazka.
Any errors that snuck in despite their best efforts
are mine, all mine!

I would also like to acknowledge the amazing
Angkor Hospital for Children (AHC) – a
non-profit pediatric teaching hospital that
provides free quality care to impoverished
children in Siem Reap, Cambodia. All the
characters, settings and situations in *From Fling
to Forever* are fictional – however, during the
course of my research, I learned so much from
AHC, which has provided over one million
medical treatments, education to thousands
of Cambodian health workers, and prevention
training to thousands of families since it opened
in 1999. You can find out more about the hospital
at www.angkorhospital.org

CHAPTER ONE

WEDDINGS.

Ella Reynolds had nothing against them, but she certainly didn't belong at one. Not even this one.

But her sister, Tina, had insisted she not only attend but trick herself out as maid of honour in this damned uncomfortable satin gown in which there was *no* stretch. Add in the ridiculous high heels and hair twisted into a silly bun that was pinned so tightly against her scalp she could practically feel the headache negotiating where to lunge first.

And then there was the stalker. Just to top everything off.

She'd first felt his stare boring into her as she'd glided up the aisle ahead of her sister. And then throughout the wedding service, when all eyes should have been on the bride and groom. And ever since she'd walked into the reception.

Disconcerting. And definitely unwanted.

Especially since he had a little boy with him. Gorgeous, sparkly, darling little boy. Asian. Three or four years old. Exactly the type of child to mess with her already messed-up head.

Ella looked into her empty champagne glass, debating whether to slide over the legal limit. Not that she was driving, but she was always so careful when she was with her family. Still… Tina, pregnant, glowing, deliriously happy, was on the dance floor with her new husband Brand—and not paying her any attention. Her parents were on the other side of the room, catching up with Brand's family on this rare visit to Sydney—and not paying her any attention. She was alone at the bridal table, with *no one* paying her any attention. Which was just fine with her. It was much easier to hold it all together when you were left to yourself. To not let anyone see the horrible, unworthy envy of Tina's pregnancy, Tina's *life*.

And—she swivelled around to look for a waiter—it made it much easier to snag that extra champagne.

But a sound put paid to the champagne quest. A cleared throat.

She twisted back in her chair. Looked up.

The stalker. *Uh-oh.*

'Hi,' he said.

'Hello.' Warily.

'So…you're Ella,' he said.

Oh, dear. *Inane* stalker. 'Yep. Sister of the bride.'

'Oh.' He looked surprised. And then, 'Sorry, the accent. I didn't realise…'

'I speak American, Tina speaks Australian. It does throw people. Comes of having a parent from each country and getting to choose where you live. I live in LA. Tina lives in Sydney. But it's still all English, you know.' Good Lord—*this* was conversation?

He laughed. 'I'm not sure the British see it that way.'

Okay—so now what? Ella wondered.

If he thought she was going to be charmed by him, he had another think coming. She *wasn't* going to be charmed. And she was *not* in the market for a pick-up tonight. Not that he wasn't attractive in a rough sort of way—the surfer-blond hair, golden tan and bursting muscles that looked completely out of place in a suit was a sexy combination. But she'd crossed the pick-up off her to-do list last night— and that had been a debacle, as usual. And even if she hadn't crossed it off the list, and it hadn't been a debacle, her sister's wedding was not the place for another attempt. Nowhere within a thousand *miles* of any of her relatives was the place.

'Do you mind if I sit and talk to you for a few minutes?' he asked, and smiled at her.

Yes, I do. 'Of course you can sit,' she said. Infinitesimal pause. 'And talk to me.'

'Great.' He pulled out a chair and sat. 'I think Brand warned you I wanted to pick your brains tonight.'

She frowned slightly. 'Brand?'

He smiled again. 'Um…your brother-in-law?'

'No-o-o, I don't think so.' Ella glanced over at Brand, who was carefully twirling her sister. 'I think he's had a few things on his mind. Marriage. Baby. Imminent move to London. New movie to make.'

Another smile. 'Right, let's start again and I'll introduce myself properly.'

Ella had to give the guy points for determination. Because he had to realise by now that if she really wanted to talk to him, she would have already tried to get his name out of him.

'I'm Aaron James,' he said.

Ella went blank for a moment, before the vague memory surfaced. 'Oh. Of course. The actor. Tina emailed me about a…a film?' She frowned slightly. 'Sorry, I remember now. About malaria.'

'Yes. A documentary. About the global struggle to eradicate the disease. Something I am very passionate about, because my son… Well, too much information, I guess. Not that documentaries are my usual line of work.' Smile, but looking a little frayed. 'Maybe you've heard of a television show called *Triage*? It's a medical drama. I'm in that.'

'So…' She frowned again. 'Is it the documentary or the TV show you want to talk to me about? If it's the TV show, I don't think I can help you—my experience in city hospital emergency rooms is limited. And I'm a nurse—

you don't look like you'd be playing a nurse. You're playing a doctor, right?'

'Yes, but—'

'I'm flying home tomorrow, but I know a few doctors here in Sydney and I'm sure they'd be happy to talk to you.'

'No, that's not—'

'The numbers are in my phone,' Ella said, reaching for her purse. 'Do you have a pen? Or can you—?'

Aaron reached out and put his hand over hers on the tiny bronze purse. 'Ella.'

Her fingers flexed, once, before she could stop them.

'It's not about the show,' he said, releasing her hand. 'It's the documentary. We're looking at treatments, mosquito control measures, drug resistance, and what's being done to develop a vaccine. We'll be shooting in Cambodia primarily—in some of the hospitals where I believe you've worked. We're not starting for a month, but I thought I should take the chance to talk to you while you're in Sydney. I'd love to get your impression of the place.'

She said nothing. Noted that he was starting to look impatient—and annoyed.

'Brand told me you worked for Frontline Medical Aid,' he prompted.

She controlled the hitch in her breath. 'Yes, I've worked for them, and other medical aid agencies, in various countries, including Cambodia. But I'm not working with any agency at the moment. And I'll be based in Los Angeles for the next year or so.'

'And what's it like? I mean, not Los Angeles—I know what— Um. I mean, the aid work.'

Ella shifted in her seat. He was just not getting it. 'It has its highs and lows. Like any job.'

He was trying that charming smile again. 'Stupid question?'

'Look, it's just a job,' she said shortly. 'I do what every

nurse does. Look after people when they're sick or hurt. Try to educate them about health. That's all there is to it.'

'Come on—you're doing a little more than that. The conditions. The diseases that we just don't see here. The refugee camps. The landmines. Kidnappings, even.'

Her heart slammed against her ribs. Bang-bang-bang. She looked down at her hands, saw the whitened knuckles and dropped them to her lap, out of Aaron's sight. She struggled for a moment, getting herself under control. Then forced herself to look straight back up and right at him.

'Yes, the conditions are not what most medical personnel are used to,' she said matter-of-factly. 'I've seen the damage landmines can do. Had children with AIDS, with malnutrition, die in my arms. There have been kidnappings involving my colleagues, murders even. This is rare, but…' She stopped, raised an eyebrow. 'Is that the sort of detail you're looking for?' She forced herself to keep looking directly into his eyes. 'But I imagine you'll be insulated from the worst of it. They won't let anything happen to you.'

'I'm not worried about that,' Aaron said, with a quick shake of his head. Then, suddenly, he relaxed back in his chair. 'And you don't want to talk about it.'

Eureka! 'It's fine, really,' she said, but her voice dripped with insincerity.

The little boy Ella had seen earlier exploded onto the scene, throwing himself against Aaron's leg, before the conversation could proceed.

'Dad, look what Tina gave me.'

Dad. So, did he have an Asian wife? Or was the little boy adopted?

Aaron bent close to smell the small rose being offered to him.

'It's from her bunch of flowers,' the little boy said, blinking adorably.

'Beautiful.' Aaron turned laughing eyes to Ella. 'Ella, let me introduce my son, Kiri. Kiri, this is Tina's sister, Ella.'

Kiri. He was Cambodian, then. And he'd had malaria—
that was Aaron's TMI moment. 'Nice to meet you Kiri,'
Ella said, with a broad smile, then picked up her purse.
'Speaking of Tina and flowers, it must be time to throw
the bouquet. I'd better go.'

She got to her feet. 'Goodbye Aaron. Good luck with
the documentary. Goodbye Kiri.'

Well, that had been uncomfortable, Ella thought as she left
the table, forcing herself to walk slowly. Calm, controlled,
measured—the way she'd trained herself to walk in moments of stress.

Clearly, she had to start reading her sister's emails more
carefully. She recalled, too late, that Tina's email had said
Aaron was divorced; that he had an adopted son—although
not that the boy was Cambodian, because *that* she would
have remembered. She'd made a reference to the documentary. And there probably had been a mention of talking
to him as a favour to Brand, although she really couldn't
swear to it.

She just hadn't put all the pieces together and equated
them with the wedding, or she would have been better
prepared for the confrontation.

Confrontation. Since when did a few innocent questions
constitute a confrontation?

Ella couldn't stop a little squirm of shame. Aaron wasn't
to know that the exact thing he wanted to talk about was
the exact thing she couldn't bring herself to discuss with
anyone. Nobody knew about Sann, the beautiful little Cambodian boy who'd died of malaria before she'd even been
able to start the adoption process. Nobody knew about
her relationship with Javier—her colleague and lover, kidnapped in Somalia and still missing. Nobody knew because
she hadn't *wanted* anyone to know, or to worry about her.
Hadn't wanted anyone to push her to talk about things, relive what she couldn't bear to relive.

So, no, Aaron wasn't to be blamed for asking what he thought were standard questions.

But he'd clearly sensed something was wrong with her. Because he'd gone from admiration—oh, yes, she could read admiration—to something akin to dislike, in almost record time. Something in those almost sleepy, silver-grey eyes had told her she just wasn't his kind of person.

Ella's head had started to throb. The damned pins.

Ah, well, one bouquet-toss and last group hug with her family and she could disappear. Back to her hotel. Throw down some aspirin. And raid the mini-bar, given she never had got that extra glass of champagne.

Yeah, like raiding the mini-bar has ever helped, her sub-conscious chimed in.

'Oh, shut up,' she muttered.

Well, that had been uncomfortable, Aaron thought as Ella Reynolds all but bolted from the table. Actually, she'd been walking slowly. Too slowly. Unnaturally slowly.

Or maybe he was just cross because of ego-dent. Because one woman in the room had no idea who he was. And didn't *care* who he was when she'd found out. Well, she was American—why *would* she know him? He wasn't a star over there.

Which wasn't the point anyway.

Because since when did he expect people to recognise him and drool?

Never!

But celebrity aside, to be looked at with such blank dis-interest…it wasn't a look he was used to from women. Ella Reynolds hadn't been overwhelmed. Or deliberately *under*-whelmed, as sometimes happened. She was just…hmm, was 'whelmed' a word? Whelmed. Depressing.

Ego, Aaron—so not *like you.*

Aaron swallowed a sigh as the guests started position-ing themselves for the great bouquet toss. Ella was in the thick of it, smiling. Not looking in his direction—on purpose, or he'd eat the roses.

She was as beautiful as Tina had said. More so. Staggeringly so. With her honey-gold hair that even the uptight bun couldn't take the gloss off. The luminous, gold-toned skin. Smooth, wide forehead. Finely arched dusky gold eyebrows and wide-spaced purple-blue eyes with ridiculously thick dark lashes. Lush, wide, pouty mouth. No visible freckles. No blemishes. The body beneath the figure-hugging bronze satin she'd been poured into for the wedding was a miracle of perfect curves. Fabulous breasts—and silicone-free, if he were any judge. Which he was, after so many years in the business.

And the icing on the cake—the scent of her. Dark and musky and delicious.

Yep. Stunner.

But Tina had said that as well as being gorgeous her sister was the best role model for women she could think of. Smart, dedicated to her work, committed to helping those less fortunate regardless of the personal danger she put herself in regularly.

Well, sorry, but on the basis of their conversation tonight he begged to differ. Ella Reynolds was no role model. There was something wrong with her. Something that seemed almost…dead. Her smile—that dazzling, white smile—didn't reach her eyes. Her eyes had been beautifully *empty*. It had been almost painful to sit near her.

Aaron felt a shiver snake down his spine.

On the bright side, he didn't feel that hot surge of desire—that bolt that had hit him square in the groin the moment she'd slid into the church—any more. Which was good. He didn't want to lust after her. He didn't have the time or energy or emotional availability to lust after anyone.

He turned to his beautiful son. 'Come on, Kiri—this

part is fun to watch. But leave the bouquet-catching to the girls, huh?'

We're not going down that road again, bouquet or not, he added silently to himself.

CHAPTER TWO

ELLA HAD BEEN determined to spend a full year in Los Angeles.

But within a few weeks of touching down at LAX she'd been back at the airport and heading for Cambodia. There had been an outbreak of dengue fever, and someone had asked her to think about helping out, and she'd thought, *Why not?*

Because she just hadn't been feeling it at home. Whatever 'it' was. She hadn't felt right since Tina's wedding. Sort of restless and on edge. So she figured she needed more distraction. More work. More…something.

And volunteering at a children's hospital in mosquito heaven is just the sort of masochism that's right up your alley, isn't it, Ella?

So, here she was, on her least favourite day of the year—her birthday—in northwest Cambodia—and because it *was* her birthday she was in the bar of one of the best hotels in town instead of her usual cheap dive.

Her parents had called this morning to wish her happy birthday. Their present was an airfare to London and an order to use it the moment her time in Cambodia was up. It was framed in part as a favour to Tina: stay with her pregnant sister in her new home city and look after her health while Brand concentrated on the movie. But she knew Tina would have been given her own set of orders: get Ella to rest and for goodness' sake fatten her up—because her mother always freaked when she saw how thin and bedraggled Ella was after a stint in the developing world.

Tina's present to Ella was a goat. Or rather a goat in Ella's name, to be given to an impoverished community in India. Not every just-turned-twenty-seven-year-old's cup of tea, but so totally perfect for this one.

And in with the goat certificate had been a parcel with a note: 'Humour me and wear this.' 'This' was sinfully expensive French lingerie in gorgeous mint-green silk, which Ella could never have afforded. It felt like a crime wearing it under her flea-market gypsy skirt and bargain-basement singlet top. But it did kind of cheer her up. Maybe she'd have to develop an underwear fetish—although somehow she didn't think she'd find this kind of stuff digging around in the discount bins the way she usually shopped.

A small group of doctors and nurses had dragged her out tonight. They'd knocked back a few drinks, told tales about their life experiences and then eventually—inevitably—drifted off, one by one, intent on getting some rest ahead of another busy day.

But Ella wasn't due at the hospital until the afternoon, so she could sleep in. Which meant she could stay out. And she had met someone—as she always seemed to do in bars. So she'd waved the last of her friends off with a cheerful guarantee that she could look after herself.

Yes, she had met someone. Someone who might help make her feel alive for an hour or two. Keep the nightmares at bay, if she could bring herself to get past the come-on stage for once and end up in bed with him.

She felt a hand on her backside as she leaned across the pool table and took her shot. She missed the ball completely but looked back and smiled. Tom. British. Expat. An…engineer, maybe? *Was* he an engineer? Well, who cared? Really, who cared?

He pulled her against him, her back against his chest. Arms circled her waist. Squeezed.

She laughed as he nipped at her earlobe, even though she couldn't quite stop a slight shudder of distaste. His breath was too hot, too…moist. He bit gently at her ear again.

Ella wasn't sure what made her look over at the entrance to the bar at that particular moment. But pool cue in one hand, caught against Tom's chest, with—she realised in one awful moment—one of the straps of her top hanging off her shoulder to reveal the beacon-green silk of her bra strap, she looked.

Aaron James.

He was standing still, looking immaculately clean in blue jeans and a tight white T-shirt, which suited him way more than the get-up he'd been wearing at the wedding. Very tough-guy gorgeous, with the impressive muscles and fallen-angel hair with those tousled, surfer-white streaks she remembered very well.

Actually, she was surprised she remembered so much!

He gave her one long, cool, head-to-toe inspection. One nod.

Ah, so he obviously remembered her too. She was pretty sure that was not a good thing.

Then he walked to the bar, ignoring her. *Hmm.* Definitely *not a good thing*.

Ella, who'd thought she'd given up blushing, blushed. Hastily she yanked the misbehaving strap back onto her shoulder.

With a wicked laugh, Tom the engineer nudged it back off.

'Don't,' she said, automatically reaching for it again.

Tom shrugged good-humouredly. 'Sorry. Didn't mean anything by it.'

For good measure, Ella pulled on the long-sleeved, light cotton cardigan she'd worn between her guesthouse accommodation and the hotel. She always dressed for modesty outside Western establishments, and that meant covering up.

And there were mosquitoes to ward off in any case.

And okay, yes, the sight of Aaron James had unnerved her. She admitted it! She was wearing a cardigan because Aaron James had looked at her in *that* way.

She tried to appear normal as the game progressed, but every now and then she would catch Aaron's gaze on her and she found it increasingly difficult to concentrate on the game or on Tom. Whenever she laughed, or when Tom let out a whoop of triumph at a well-played shot, she would feel Aaron looking at her. Just for a moment. His eyes on her, then off. When Tom went to the bar to buy a round. When she tripped over a chair, reaching for her drink. When Tom enveloped her from behind to give her help she didn't need with a shot.

It made her feel…dirty. Ashamed. Which was just not fair. She was single, adult, independent. So she wanted a few mindless hours of fun on her lonely birthday to take her mind off sickness and death—what was wrong with that?

But however she justified things to herself, she knew that tonight her plans had been derailed. All because of a pair of censorious silver eyes.

Censorious eyes that belonged to a friend of her sister. Very sobering, that—the last thing she needed was Aaron tattling to Tina about her.

It was probably just as well to abandon tonight's escapade. Her head was starting to ache and she felt overly hot. Maybe she was coming down with something? She would be better off in bed. Her bed. Alone. As usual.

She put down her cue and smiled at Tom the engineer. Her head was pounding now. 'It's been fun, Tom, but I'm going to have to call it a night.'

'But it's still early. I thought we could—'

'No, really. It's time I went home. I'm tired, and I'm not feeling well.'

'Just one more drink,' Tom slurred, reaching for her arm.

She stepped back, out of his reach. 'I don't think so.'

Tom lunged for her and managed to get his arms around her.

He was very drunk, but Ella wasn't concerned. She'd been in these situations before and had always managed to extricate herself. Gently but firmly she started to prise Tom's arms from around her. He took this as an invitation to kiss her and landed his very wet lips on one side of her mouth.

Yeuch.

Tom murmured something about how beautiful she was. Ella, still working at unhooking his arms, was in the middle of thanking him for the compliment when he suddenly wasn't there. One moment she'd been disengaging herself from his enthusiastic embrace, and the next—air.

And then an Australian accent. 'You don't want to do that, mate.'

She blinked, focused, and saw that Aaron James was holding Tom in an embrace of his own, standing behind him with one arm around Tom's chest. How had he got from the bar to the pool table in a nanosecond?

'I'm fine,' Ella said. 'You can let him go.'

Aaron ignored her.

'I said I'm fine,' Ella insisted. 'I was handling it.'

'Yes, I could see that,' Aaron said darkly.

'I was,' Ella insisted, and stepped forward to pull futilely at Aaron's steel-band arm clamped across Tom's writhing torso.

Tom lunged at the same time, and Ella felt a crack across her lip. She tasted blood, staggered backwards, fell against the table and ended up on the floor.

And then everything swirled. Black spots. Nothing.

The first thing Ella noticed as her consciousness returned was the scent. Delicious. Clean and wild, like the beach in winter. She inhaled. Nuzzled her nose into it. Inhaled again. She wanted to taste it. Did it taste as good as it smelled? She opened her mouth, moved her lips, tongue. One small lick. Mmm. Good. Different from the smell but…good.

Then a sound. A sharp intake of breath.

She opened her eyes. Saw skin. Tanned skin. White next to it. She shook her head to clear it. Oh, that hurt. Pulled back a little, looked up. Aaron James. 'Oh,' she said. 'What happened?'

'That moron knocked you out.'

It came back at once. Tom. 'Not on purpose.'

'No, not on purpose.'

'Where is he?'

'Gone. Don't worry about him.'

'I'm not worried. He's a big boy. He can take care of himself.' Ella moved again, and realised she was half lolling against Aaron's thighs.

She started to ease away from him but he kept her there, one arm around her back, one crossing her waist to hold onto her from the front.

'Take it easy,' Aaron said.

A crowd of people had gathered around them. Ella felt herself blush for the second time that night. Intolerable, but apparently uncontrollable. 'I don't feel well,' she said.

'I'm not surprised,' Aaron replied.

'I have to get home,' she said, but she stayed exactly where she was. She closed her eyes. The smell of him. It was him, that smell. That was…comforting. She didn't know why that was so. Didn't care why. It just was.

'All right, people, show's over,' Aaron said, and Ella realised he was telling their audience to get lost. He said something more specific to another man, who seemed to be in charge. She assumed he was pacifying the manager. She didn't care. She just wanted to close her eyes.

'Ella, your lip's bleeding. I'm staying here at the hotel.

Come to my room, let me make sure you're all right, then I'll get you home. Or to the hospital.'

She opened her eyes. 'Not the hospital.' She didn't want anyone at the hospital to see her like this.

'Okay—then my room.'

She wanted to say she would find her *own* way home *immediately*, but when she opened her mouth the words 'All right' were what came out. She ran her tongue experimentally over her lip. *Ouch*. Why hadn't she noticed it was hurting? 'My head hurts more than my lip. Did I hit it when I fell?'

'No, I caught you. Let me...' He didn't bother finishing the sentence, instead running his fingers over her scalp. 'No, nothing. Come on. I'll help you stand.'

Aaron carefully eased Ella up. 'Lean on me,' he said softly, and Ella didn't need to be told twice. She felt awful.

As they made their way out of the bar, she noted a few people looking and whispering, but nobody she knew. 'I'm sorry about this,' she said to Aaron. 'Do you think anyone knows you? I mean, from the television show?'

'I'm not well known outside Australia. But it doesn't matter either way.'

'I don't want to embarrass you.'

'I'm not easily embarrassed. I've got stories that would curl your hair. It's inevitable, with three semi-wild younger sisters.'

'I was all right, you know,' she said. 'I can look after myself.'

'Can you?'

'Yes. I've been doing it a long time. And he was harmless. Tom.'

'Was he?'

'Yes. I could have managed. I *was* managing.'

'Were you?'

'Yes. And stop questioning me. It's annoying. And it's hurting my head.'

They were outside the bar now and Aaron stopped. 'Just one more,' he said, and turned her to face him. 'What on earth were you thinking?'

Ella was so stunned at the leashed fury in his voice she *couldn't* think, let alone speak.

He didn't seem to need an answer, though, because he just rolled right on. 'Drinking like a fish. Letting that clown slobber all over you!'

'He's not a clown, he's an engineer,' Ella said. And then, with the ghost of a smile, 'And fish don't drink beer.'

He looked like thunder.

Ella waited, curious about what he was going to hurl at her. But with a snort of disgust he simply took her arm again, started walking.

He didn't speak again until they were almost across the hotel lobby. 'I'm sorry. I guess I feel a little responsible for you, given my relationship with Brand and Tina.'

'That is just ridiculous—I already have a father. And he happens to know I can look after myself. Anyway, why are you here?' Then, 'Oh, yeah, I remember. The documentary.' She grimaced. '*Should* I have known you'd be here now?'

'I have no idea. Anyway, you're supposed to be in LA.'

'I was in LA. But now— It was a sudden decision, to come here. So it looks like we've surprised each other.'

'Looks like it.'

Aaron guided Ella through a side door leading to the open air, and then along a tree-bordered path until they were in front of what looked like a miniature mansion. He *would* be in one of the presidential-style villas, of course. He didn't look very happy to have brought her there, though.

'How long will you be in town?' she asked, as he unlocked the door.

'Two weeks, give or take.'

'So, you'll be gone in two weeks. And I'll still be here, looking after myself. Like I've always done.' She was pleased with the matter-of-factness of her voice, because in reality she didn't feel matter-of-fact. She felt depressed. She blamed it on the birthday.

Birthdays: misery, with candles.

'Well, good for you, Ella,' he said, and there was a definite sneer in there. 'You're doing such a fine job of it my conscience will be crystal clear when I leave.'

Hello? Sarcasm? Really? Why?

Aaron drew her inside, through a tiled hallway and into a small living room. There was a light on but no sign of anyone.

'Is your son with you?' she asked. *Not that it's any of your business, Ella.*

'Yes, he's in bed.'

'So you've got a nanny? Or is your wife—?' *Um, not your business?*

'Ex-wife. Rebecca is in Sydney. And, yes, I have a nanny, whose name is Jenny. I don't make a habit of leaving my four-year-old son on his own in hotel rooms.'

Oh, dear, he really did *not* like her. And she was well on the way to actively disliking *him*. His attitude was a cross between grouchy father and irritated brother—without the familial affection that would only just make that bearable.

Aaron gestured for Ella to sit. 'Do you want something to drink?'

Ella sank onto the couch. 'Water, please.'

'Good choice,' Aaron said, making Ella wish she'd asked for whisky instead.

He went to the fridge, fished out a bottle of water, poured it into a glass and handed it to her. She didn't deign to thank him.

She rubbed her forehead as she drank.

He was watching her. 'Head still hurting?'

'Yes.'

'Had enough water?'

Ella nodded and Aaron took the glass out of her hand,

sat next to her. He turned her so she was facing away from him. 'Here,' he said tetchily, and started kneading the back of her neck.

'Ahhh…' she breathed out. 'That feels good.'

'Like most actors, I've had a chequered career—massage therapy was one of my shorter-lived occupations but I remember a little,' Aaron said, sounding not at all soothing like a massage therapist.

'Where's the dolphin music?' she joked.

He didn't bother answering and she decided she would *not* speak again. She didn't see why she should make an effort to talk to him, given his snotty attitude. She swayed a little, and he pulled her closer to his chest, one hand kneading while he reached his other arm around in front of her, bracing his forearm against her collarbone to balance her.

She could smell him again. He smelled exquisite. So clean and fresh and…yum. The rhythmic movement of his fingers was soothing, even if it did nothing to ease the ache at the front of her skull. She could have stayed like that for hours.

Slowly, he finished the massage and she had to bite back a protest. He turned her to face him and looked at her lip. 'It's only a small tear. I have a first-aid kit in the bathroom.'

'How very *Triage* of you, Aaron.' He looked suitably unimpressed at that dig.

'Just some ice,' she said. 'That's all I need. And I can look after it myself. I'm a nurse, remember?'

But Aaron was already up and away.

He came back with a bowl of ice and the first-aid kit.

Ella peered into the kit and removed a square of gauze, then wrapped it around an ice cube. 'It's not serious and will heal quickly. Mouth injuries do. It's all about the blood supply.'

Not that Aaron seemed interested in that piece of medical information, because he just took the wrapped ice from her impatiently.

'I promise you I can do it myself,' Ella said.

'Hold still,' he insisted. He held the ice on her bottom lip, kept it pressed there for a minute.

'Open,' he ordered, and Ella automatically opened her mouth for him to inspect inside. 'Looks like you bit the inside of your lip.' He grabbed another square of gauze, wrapped it around another cube of ice and pressed it on the small wound.

He was looking intently at her mouth and Ella started to feel uncomfortable. She could still smell that heavenly scent wafting up from his skin. Why couldn't he smell like stale sweat like everyone else in that bar? She blinked a few times, trying to clear her fuzzy head.

Her eyes fell on his T-shirt and she saw a smear of blood on the collar. Her blood. Her fingers reached out, touched it. His neck, too, had a tiny speck of her blood. Seemingly of their own volition her fingers travelled up, rubbing at the stain. And then she remembered how it had got there. Remembered in one clear flash how she had put her mouth there, on his skin. She felt a flare of arousal and sucked in a quick breath.

He had gone very still. He was watching her. Looking stunned.

CHAPTER THREE

'SORRY,' ELLA SAID. 'It's just… I—I bled on you.'

'Ella, I don't think it's a good idea for you to touch me.'

'Sorry,' Ella said again, jerking her fingers away.

Aaron promptly contradicted himself by taking the hand she'd pulled away and pressing it against his chest. He could actually *hear* his heart thudding. It was probably thumping against her palm like a drum. He didn't care. He wanted her hand on him. Wanted both her hands on him.

He could hear a clock ticking somewhere in the room, but except for that and his heart the silence was thick and heavy.

I don't even like her. He said that in his head, but something wasn't connecting his head to his groin, because just as the thought completed itself he tossed the gauze aside and reached for her other hand, brought it to his mouth, pressed his mouth there, kept it there.

Okay, so maybe you didn't have to like someone to want them.

He really, really hadn't expected to see her again. She was supposed to be in LA. Their 'relationship' should have begun and ended with one awkward conversation at a wedding.

And yet here he was. And here she was. And he had no idea what was going to happen next.

When he'd walked into that bar tonight and seen her

with that idiot, he'd wanted to explode, drag her away, beat the guy senseless.

And he *never* lost his temper!

He'd been so shocked at his reaction he'd contemplated leaving the bar, going somewhere else—a different bar, for a walk, to bed, anything, anywhere else. But he hadn't.

He'd only been planning on having one drink anyway, just a post-flight beer. But nope. He'd stayed, sensing there was going to be trouble. She'd laughed too much, drunk too much, Tom the idiot engineer had fondled her too much. Something was going to give.

And something definitely had.

And of course he'd been there smack bang in the middle of it, like he couldn't get there fast enough.

And then his arms had been around her. And she'd snuggled against him. Her tongue on his neck. And he'd wanted her. Wanted her like he'd never wanted anyone in his life.

And it had made him furious.

Was making him furious now.

So why was he moving the hand he'd been holding to his mouth down to his chest, instead of letting it go?

His hands were only lightly covering hers now. She could break away if she wanted to. Bring him back to sanity. *Please.*

But she didn't break away.

Her hands moved up, over his chest to his collarbones then shoulders. Confident hands. Direct and sure.

He stifled a groan.

'You don't want me.' She breathed the words. 'You don't like me.' But her hands moved again, down to his deltoids, stopping there. Her fingers slid under the short sleeves of his T-shirt, stroked.

This time the groan escaped as his pulse leapt.

Ella moved closer to him, sighed as she surrounded him with her arms, rested the side of her face against his chest then simply waited.

He battled himself for a long moment. His hand hovered over her hair. He could see the tremor in his fingers. He closed his eyes so the sight of her wouldn't push him over the edge. That only intensified the sexy smell of her. Ella Reynolds. Tina's *sister*. 'I can't,' he said. 'I can't do this.' Was that his voice? That croak?

He waited, every nerve tingling. Didn't trust himself to move. If he moved, even a fraction...

Then he heard her sigh again; this time it signalled resignation, not surrender.

'No, of course not,' she said, and slowly disentangled herself until she was sitting safely, separately, beside him.

Whew. Catastrophe averted.

'A shame,' she said. Her voice was cool and so were her eyes as she reached out to skim her fingernail over his right arm, at the top of his biceps where the sleeve of his T-shirt had been pushed up just enough to reveal the lower edge of a black tattoo circlet. Her lips turned up in an approximation of a smile. 'Because I like tattoos. They're a real turn-on for me. Would have been fun.'

He stared at her, fighting the urge to drag her back against his chest, not quite believing the disdainful humour he could hear in her voice, see in her eyes. Wondering if he'd imagined the yielding softness only moments ago.

At Tina and Brand's wedding he'd sensed that there was something wrong with her. It had made him uncomfortable to be near her. Made him want to get away from her.

He had the same feeling now. Only this time he couldn't get away. He would be damned if he'd let Tina's sister stagger home drunk and disorderly, with a pounding head and a split lip. *Oh, yeah, that's the reason, is it? Tina?*

Ella shrugged—a dismissive, almost delicate gesture. 'But don't worry, I won't press you,' she said calmly. 'I've never had to beg for it in my life and I won't start now, tattoos or not.'

She stood suddenly and smiled—the dazzling smile that didn't reach her eyes. 'I'd better go,' she said.

'I'll take you home,' he said, ignoring the taunt of all those men she hadn't had to beg. None of his business.

'I'll walk.'

'I'll take you,' Aaron insisted.

Ella laughed. 'Okay, but I hope we're not going to drag some poor driver out of bed.'

'Where are you staying?'

'Close enough. I can walk there in under ten minutes.'

'Then we'll walk.'

'All right, then, lead on, Sir Galahad,' Ella said lightly, mockingly.

And that was *exactly* why he didn't like her.

Because she was just so unknowable. Contrary. Changeable. Ready to seduce him one moment and the next so cool. Poised. Amused. They made it to the street without him throttling her, which was one relief. Although he would have preferred a different relief—one for inside his jeans, because, heaven help him, it was painful down there. How the hell did she *do* that? Make him both want her and want to run a mile in the opposite direction?

Ella led off and Aaron fell into step beside her, conscious of her excruciatingly arousing perfume. The almost drugging combination of that scent, the damp heat, the sizzle and shout of the street stalls, the thumping music and wild shouts from the tourist bars, was so mesmerisingly exotic it felt almost like he was in another world. One where the normal rules, the checks and balances, didn't apply.

The minutes ticked by. A steady stream of motorbikes puttered past. A short line of tuk-tuks carrying chatty tourists. Jaunty music from a group of street musicians. Sounds fading as he and Ella walked further, further.

'Needless to say, tonight's escapade is not something Tina needs to hear about,' Ella said suddenly.

'Needless to say,' he agreed.

A tinkling laugh. 'Of course, you wouldn't want it getting back to your wife either. At least, not the latter part of the evening.'

'Ex-wife,' Aaron corrected her. He heard a dog barking in the distance. A mysterious rustle in the bushes near the road.

'Ah.' Ella's steps slowed, but only very briefly. 'But not really ex, I'm thinking, Sir Galahad.'

Aaron grabbed Ella's arm, pulling her to the side of a dirty puddle she was about to step into. 'It's complicated,' he said, when she looked at him.

She pulled free of the contact and started forward again.

'But definitely ex,' he added. And if she only knew the drug-fuelled hell Rebecca had put him through for the past three years, she would understand.

'Oh, dear, how inconvenient! An ex who's not really an ex. It must play havoc with your sex life.'

She laughed again, and his temper got the better of him. The temper that he *never* lost.

'What is wrong with you?' he demanded, whirling her to face him.

She looked up at him, opened her mouth to say—

Well, who knew? Because before he could stop himself he'd slapped his mouth on hers in a devouring kiss.

Just what he *didn't* want to do.

And she had the audacity to kiss him back. More than that—her arms were around him, her hands under his T-shirt.

Then he tasted blood, remembered her lip. Horrified, he pulled back. 'I'm sorry,' he said.

She ran her tongue across her lower lip, raised her eyebrows. '*Definitely* would have been fun,' she said.

'I'm not looking for a relationship,' he said bluntly. And where had that come from? It seemed to suggest he *was* after *something*. But what? What was he after? Nothing— nothing from her.

It seemed to startle her, at least. 'Did I ask for one?'
'No.'

'That's a relief! Because I'm really only interested in
casual sex. And on that note, how fortunate that we're here.
Where I live. So we can say our goodbyes, and both pretend tonight didn't happen. No relationship. And, alas, no
casual sex, because you're married. Oh, no, that's right,
you're not. But no sex anyway.'

'I should have left you with the engineer.'

'Well, I would have seen a lot more action,' she said.
She started forward and then stopped, raised her hand to
her eyes.

'What is it?' Aaron asked.

'Nothing. A headache,' she answered. 'I'll be fine.'

'Goodbye, then,' he said, and turned to walk back to
the hotel.

A lot more action! Ha! Aaron was quite sure if he ever
let himself put his hands on Ella Reynolds she wouldn't be
able to think about another man for a long time. Or walk
straight either.

But he was not going to touch her, of course. *Not.*

Ella made her way to her room, cursing silently.

Her head was throbbing and her joints were aching and
she longed to lapse into a thought-free coma. She'd just realised she'd contracted either malaria or dengue fever. She
wasn't sure which, but either way it sucked.

But when she'd taken two paracetamol tablets and clam-
bered into bed, praying for a mild dose of whatever it was,
it wasn't the pain that made the tears come. It was shame.
And regret. And a strange sense of loss.

Aaron James had wanted her. Ordinarily, a man wanting her would not cause Ella consternation. Lots of men
had wanted her and she'd had no trouble resisting them.

But Aaron was different. He'd kissed her like he was

pouring his strength, his soul into her. And yet he'd been able to fight whatever urge had been driving him.

Why? How?

She manhandled her pillow, trying to get it into a more head-cradling shape.

Not looking for a relationship—that's what he'd said. How galling! As though it were something she would be begging for on the basis of one kiss. All right, one *amazing* kiss, but—seriously! What a joke. A relationship? The one thing she *couldn't* have.

Ella sighed as her outrage morphed into something more distressing: self-loathing. Because she was a fraud and she knew it. A coward who used whatever was at her disposal to stop herself from confronting the wreck her life had become since Javier had been kidnapped in Somalia on her twenty-fifth birthday.

She'd been in limbo ever since. Feeling helpless, hopeless. Guilty that she was free and he was who-knew-where. In the year after his kidnapping she'd felt so lost and alone and powerless she'd thought a nervous breakdown had been on the cards.

And then she'd found Sann in a Cambodian orphanage, and life had beckoned to her again. Two years old, and hers. Or so she'd hoped. But he'd been taken too. He'd died, on her twenty-sixth birthday.

And now here she was on her twenty-*seventh* birthday. Still in limbo, with no idea of what had happened to Javier. Still grieving for Sann.

Panicking at the thought of seeing an Asian child with an adoptive parent.

Unable to entertain even the thought of a relationship with a man.

Pretending she was calm and in control when she was a basket case.

Her life had become a series of shambolic episodes. Too many drinks at the bar. Getting picked up by strange

men, determined to see it through then backing out. *Always*
backing out, like the worst kind of tease, because no matter how desperate she was to feel *something*, the guilt was
always stronger. Coping, but only just, with endlessly sad
thoughts during the day and debilitating dreams at night.

She knew that something in her was lost—but she just
didn't know how to find it. She hid it from the people she
cared about because she knew her grief would devastate
them. She hid it from her colleagues because they didn't
need the extra burden.

And she was just…stuck. Stuck on past heartbreaks.
And it was starting to show.

No wonder Aaron James abhorred the idea of a 'relationship' with her.

Ella rubbed tiredly at her forehead. She closed her eyes,
longing for sleep, but knowing the nightmares would come
tonight.

Dr Seng slapped his hand on the desk and Aaron's wandering mind snapped back to him. 'So—we've talked about
malaria. Now, a few facts about the hospital.'

Kiri had been whisked off to do some painting—one of
his favourite pastimes—on arrival at the Children's Community Friendship Hospital, so Aaron could concentrate
on this first meeting.

But he wasn't finding it easy.

He had a feeling… A picture of Ella here. Was this
where she was working? He wasn't sure, but he kept expecting her to sashay past.

Dr Seng handed over an array of brochures. 'Pre-Pol
Pot, there were more than five hundred doctors practis-
ing in Cambodia,' Dr Seng said. 'By the time the Khmer
Rouge fled Cambodia in 1979 there were less than fifty.
Can you imagine what it must have been like? Rebuilding
an entire healthcare system from the ground up, with al-

most no money, no skills? Because that's what happened in Cambodia.'

Aaron knew the history—he'd made it his business to know, because of Kiri. But he could never come to terms with the brutal stupidity of the Khmer Rouge. 'No, I can't imagine it,' he said simply. 'And I'd say this hospital is something of a miracle.'

'Yes. We were started by philanthropists and we're kept going by donations—which is why we are so happy to be associated with your documentary: we need all the publicity we can get, to keep attracting money. It costs us less than twenty-five dollars to treat a child. Only fifty dollars to operate. Unheard of in your world. But, of course, we have so many to help.'

'But your patients pay nothing, right?'

'Correct. Our patients are from impoverished communities and are treated free, although they contribute if they can.'

'And your staff…?'

'In the early days the hospital relied on staff from overseas, but today we are almost exclusively Khmer. And we're a teaching hospital—we train healthcare workers from all over the country. That's a huge success story.'

'So you don't have any overseas staff here at the moment?'

'Actually, we do. Not paid staff—volunteers.'

'Doctors?'

'We have a group of doctors from Singapore coming in a few months' time to perform heart surgeries. And at the moment we have three nurses, all from America, helping out.'

'I was wondering if…' Aaron cleared his throat. 'If perhaps Ella Reynolds was working here?'

Dr Seng looked at him in surprise. 'Ella? Why, yes!'

Ahhhhh. Fate. It had a lot to answer for.

'I—I'm a friend. Of the family,' Aaron explained.

'Then I'm sorry to say you probably won't see her. She's not well. She won't be in for the whole week.'

Aaron knew he should be feeling relieved. He could have a nice easy week of filming, with no cutting comments, no tattoo come-ons, no amused eyebrow-raising.

But...what did 'not well' mean? Head cold? Sprained toe? Cancer? Liver failure? Amputation? 'Not well?'

'Dengue fever—we're in the middle of an outbreak, I'm afraid. Maybe a subject for your next documentary, given it's endemic in at least a hundred countries and infects up to a hundred million people a year.'

Alarm bells. 'But it doesn't kill you, right?'

'It certainly can,' the doctor said, too easily, clearly not understanding Aaron's need for reassurance.

Aaron swallowed. 'But...Ella...'

'Ella? No, no, no. She isn't going to die. The faster you're diagnosed and treated the better, and she diagnosed herself very quickly. It's more dangerous for children, which Ella is not. And much more dangerous if you've had it before, which Ella has not.'

Better. But not quite good enough. 'So is she in hospital?'

'Not necessary at this stage. There's no cure; you just have to nurse the symptoms— take painkillers, keep up the fluids, watch for signs of internal bleeding, which would mean it was dengue haemorrhagic fever—very serious! But Ella knows what she's doing, and she has a friend staying close by, one of the nurses. And I'll be monitoring her as well. A shame it hit her on her birthday.'

'Birthday?'

'Two days ago. Do you want me to get a message to her?'

'No, that's fine,' Aaron said hurriedly. 'Maybe I'll see her before I head home to Sydney.'

'Then let's collect Kiri and I'll have you both taken on a tour of our facilities.'

It quickly became clear that it was Kiri, not Aaron, who

was the celebrity in the hospital. He seemed to fascinate people with his Cambodian Australian-ness, and he was equally fascinated in return. He got the hang of the *satu*— the graceful greeting where you placed your palms together and bowed your head—and looked utterly natural doing it. It soothed Aaron's conscience, which had been uneasy about bringing him.

They were taken to observe the frenetic outpatient department, which Aaron was stunned to learn saw more than five hundred patients a day in a kind of triage arrangement.

The low acuity unit, where he saw his first malaria patients, a sardine can's worth of dengue sufferers, and children with assorted other conditions, including TB, pneumonia, malnutrition, HIV/AIDS and meningitis.

The emergency room, where premature babies and critically ill children were treated for sepsis, severe asthma, and on and on and on.

Then the air-conditioned intensive care unit, which offered mechanical ventilation, blood gas analysis and inotropes—not that Aaron had a clue what that meant. It looked like the Starship *Enterprise* in contrast to the mats laid out for the overflow of dengue sufferers in the fan-cooled hospital corridors.

The tour wrapped up with a walk through the basic but well-used teaching rooms, some of which had been turned into makeshift wards to cope with the dengue rush.

And then, to Aaron's intense annoyance, his focus snapped straight back to Ella.

Tina and Brand would expect him to check on her, right?

And, okay, *he* wanted to make sure for himself that she was going to recover as quickly and easily as Dr Seng seemed to think.

One visit to ease his conscience, and he would put Ella Reynolds into his mental lockbox of almost-mistakes and double-padlock the thing.

And so, forty minutes after leaving the hospital, with Kiri safely in Jenny's care at the hotel, he found himself outside Ella's guesthouse, coercing her room number from one of the other boarders, and treading up the stairs.

CHAPTER FOUR

AARON FELT SUDDENLY guilty as he knocked. Ella would have to drag herself out of bed to open the door.

Well, why not add another layer of guilt to go with his jumble of feelings about that night at the bar?

The boorish way he'd behaved—when he was *never* boorish.

The way he'd assumed her headache was the result of booze, when she'd actually been coming down with dengue fever.

The door opened abruptly. A pretty brunette, wearing a nurse's uniform, stood there.

'Sorry, I thought this was Ella Reynolds's room,' Aaron said.

'It is.' She gave him the appreciative look he was used to receiving from women—women who weren't Ella Reynolds, anyway. 'She's in bed. Ill.'

'Yes, I know. I'm Aaron James. A…a friend. Of the family.'

'I'm Helen. I'm in the room next door, so I'm keeping an eye on her.'

'Nice to meet you.'

She gave him a curious look and he smiled at her, hoping he looked harmless.

'Hang on, and I'll check if she's up to a visit,' Helen said.

The door closed in his face, and he was left wondering whether it would open again.

What on earth was he doing here?

Within a minute Helen was back. 'She's just giving herself a tourniquet test, but come in. I'm heading to the hospital, so she's all yours.'

It was gloomy in the room. And quiet—which was why he could hear his heart racing, even though his heart had no business racing.

His eyes went first to the bed—small, with a mosquito net hanging from a hook in the ceiling, which had been shoved aside. Ella was very focused, staring at her arm, ignoring him. So Aaron looked around the room. Bedside table with a lamp, a framed photo. White walls. Small wardrobe. Suitcase against a wall. A door that he guessed opened to a bathroom, probably the size of a shoebox.

He heard a sound at the bed. Like a magnet, it drew him.

She was taking a blood-pressure cuff off her arm.

'I heard you were ill,' he said, as he reached the bedside. 'I'm sorry. That you're sick, I mean.'

'I'm not too happy about it myself.' She sounded both grim and amused, and Aaron had to admire the way she achieved that.

'Who told you I was sick?' she asked.

'The hospital. I'm filming there for the next week.'

She looked appalled at that news. 'Just one week, right?'

'Looks like it.'

She nodded. He imagined she was calculating the odds of having to see him at work. Flattering—not.

He cleared his throat. 'So what's a tourniquet test?'

'You use the blood-pressure machine—'

'Sphygmomanometer.'

'Well, aren't you clever, Dr *Triage*! Yes. Take your BP, keep the cuff blown up to halfway between the diastolic and systolic—the minimum and maximum pressure—wait a few minutes and check for petechiae—blood points in the skin.'

'And do you have them? Um…it? Petechiae?'

'Not enough. Less than ten per square inch.'

'Is that…is that bad?'

'It's good, actually.'

'Why?'

Audible sigh. 'It means I have classic dengue—not haemorrhagic. As good as it gets when every bone and joint in your body is aching and your head feels like it might explode through your eyeballs.'

'Is that how it feels?'

'Yes.'

Silence.

Aaron racked his brain. 'I thought you might want me to get a message to Tina.'

Her lips tightened. Which he took as a no.

'That would be no,' she confirmed.

A sheet covered the lower half of her body. She was wearing a red T-shirt. Her hair was piled on top of her head, held in place by a rubber band. Her face was flushed, a light sheen of sweat covering it. And despite the distinct lack of glamour, despite the tightened lips and warning eyes, she was the most beautiful woman he'd ever seen.

'Shouldn't you keep the net closed?' he asked, standing rigid beside the bed. Yep—just the sort of thing a man asked a nurse who specialised in tropical illnesses.

'Happy to, if you want to talk to me through it. Or you can swat the mosquitoes before they get to me.'

'Okay—I'll swat.'

She regarded him suspiciously. 'Why are you really here? To warn me I'll be seeing you at the hospital?'

'No, because it looks like you won't be. I just wanted to make sure you were all right. See if you needed anything.'

'Well, I'm all right, and I don't need anything. So thank you for coming but…' Her strength seemed to desert her then and she rolled flat onto her back in the bed, staring at the ceiling, saying nothing.

'I heard it was your birthday. That night.'

An eye roll, but otherwise no answer.

He came a half-step closer. 'If I'd known…'

Aaron mentally winced as she rolled her eyes again.

'What would you have done?' she asked. 'Baked me a cake?'

'Point taken.'

Trawling for a new topic of conversation, he picked up the photo from her bedside table. 'Funny—you and Tina sound nothing alike, and you look nothing alike.'

Silence, and then, grudgingly, 'I take after my father's side of the family. Tina's a genetic throwback.' She smiled suddenly, and Aaron felt his breath jam in his throat. She really was gorgeous when she smiled like that, with her eyes as well as her mouth—even if it was aimed into space and not at him.

He gestured to the photo. 'I wouldn't have picked you for a Disneyland kind of girl.'

'Who doesn't like Disneyland? As long as you remember it's not real, it's a blast.'

Aaron looked at her, disturbed by the harshness in her voice. Did she have to practise that cynicism or did it come naturally?

Ella raised herself on her elbow again. 'Look, forget Disneyland, and my birthday. I *do* need something from you. Only one thing.' She fixed him with a gimlet eye. 'Silence. You can't talk about that night, or about me being sick. Don't tell Tina. Don't tell Brand. My life here has nothing to do with them. In fact, don't talk to anyone about me.'

'Someone should know you've got dengue fever.'

'*You* know. That will have to do. But don't worry, it won't affect you unless I don't make it. And my advice then would be to head for the hills and forget you were ever in Cambodia, because my mother will probably kill you.' That glorious smile again—and, again, not directed at him, just at the thought. 'She never did like a bearer of bad tidings—quite medieval.'

'All the more reason to tell them now.'

Back to the eye roll. 'Except she's not really going to kill you and I'm not going to drop dead. Look…' Ella seemed to be finding the right words. 'They'll worry, and I don't want them worrying about something that can't be changed.'

'You shouldn't be on your own when you're ill.'

'I'm not. I'm surrounded by experts. I feel like I'm in an episode of your TV show, there are so many medical personnel traipsing in and out of this room.'

Aaron looked down at her.

'Don't look at me like that,' Ella said.

'Like what?' Aaron asked. But he was wincing internally because he kind of knew how he must be looking at her. And it was really inappropriate, given her state of health.

With an effort, she pushed herself back into a sitting position. 'Let me make this easy for you, Aaron. I am not, ever, going to have sex with you.'

Yep, she'd pegged the look all right.

'You have a child,' she continued. 'And a wife, ex-wife, whatever. And it's very clear that your…encumbrances… are important to you. And that's the way it *should* be. I understand it. I respect it. I even admire it. So let's just leave it. I was interested for one night, and now I'm not. You were interested, but not enough. Moment officially over. You can take a nice clear conscience home to Sydney, along with the film.'

'Ella—'

'I don't want to hear any more. And I really, truly, do not want to see you again. I don't want— Look, I don't want to get mixed up with a friend of my sister's. Especially a man with a kid.'

Okay, sentiments Aaron agreed with wholeheartedly.

So he should just leave it at that. Run—don't walk—to the nearest exit. Good riddance. So he was kind of surprised to find his mouth opening and 'What's Kiri got to do with it?' coming out of it.

'It's just a…a thing with children. I get attached to them, and it can be painful when the inevitable goodbyes come around—there, something about me you didn't need to know.'

'But you're working at a children's hospital.'

'That's my business. But the bottom line is—I don't want to see Kiri. Ergo, I don't want to see you.' She stopped and her breath hitched painfully. 'Now, please…' Her voice had risen in tone and volume and she stopped. As he watched, she seemed to gather her emotions together. 'Please go,' she continued quietly. 'I'm sick and I'm tired and I— Just please go. All right?'

'All right. Message received loud and clear. Sex officially off the agenda. And have a nice life.'

'Thank you,' she said, and tugged the mosquito net closed.

Aaron left the room, closed the door and stood there.

Duty discharged. He was free to go. *Happy* to go.

But there was some weird dynamic at work, because he couldn't seem to make his feet move. His overgrown sense of responsibility, he told himself.

He'd taken two steps when he heard the sob. Just one, as though it had been cut off. He could picture her holding her hands against her mouth to stop herself from making any tell-tale sound. He hovered, waiting.

But there was only silence.

Aaron waited another long moment.

There was something about her. Something that made him wonder if she was really as prickly as she seemed…

He shook his head. No, he wasn't going to wonder about Ella Reynolds. He'd done the decent thing and checked on her.

He was not interested in her further than that. Not. Interested.

He forced himself to walk away.

Ella had only been away from the hospital for eight lousy days.

How did one mortal male cause such a disturbance in so short a time? she wondered as she batted away what felt like the millionth question about Aaron James. The doctors and nurses, male and female, Khmer and the small sprinkling of Westerners, were uniformly goggle-eyed over him.

Knock yourselves out, would have been Ella's attitude; except that while she'd been laid low by the dengue, Aaron had let it slip to Helen—and therefore everyone!—that he was a close friend of Ella's film director brother-in-law. Which part of 'Don't talk to anyone about me' didn't he understand?

As a result, the whole, intrigued hospital expected her to be breathless with anticipation to learn what Aaron said, what Aaron did, where Aaron went. They expected Ella to marvel at the way he dropped in, no airs or graces, to talk to the staff; how he spoke to patients and their families with real interest and compassion, even when the cameras weren't rolling; the way he was always laughing at himself for getting ahead of his long-suffering translator.

He'd taken someone's temperature. Whoop-de-doo!

And had volunteered as a guinea pig when they'd been demonstrating the use of the rapid diagnostic test for malaria—yeah, so one tiny pinprick on his finger made him a hero?

And had cooked alongside a Cambodian father in the specially built facility attached to the hospital. Yee-ha!

And, and, and, *and*—give her a break.

All Ella wanted to do was work, without hearing his name. They'd had their moment, and it had passed. Thankfully he'd got the message and left her in peace once she'd laid out the situation. She allowed herself a quick stretch before moving onto the next child—a two-year-old darling named Maly. *Heart rate. Respiration rate. Blood pressure. Urine output. Adjust the drip.*

The small hospital was crowded now that the dengue fever outbreak was peaking. They were admitting twenty additional children a day, and she was run off her still-wobbly legs. In the midst of everything she should have been too busy to sense she was being watched...and yet she knew.

She turned. And saw him. Aaron's son, Kiri, beside him.

Wasn't the hospital filming supposed to be over? Why was he here?

'Ella,' Aaron said. No surprise. Just acknowledgement.

She ignored the slight flush she could feel creeping up from her throat. With a swallowed sigh she fixed on a smile and walked over to him. She would be cool. Professional. Civilised. She held out her hand. 'Hello, Aaron.'

He took it, but released it quickly.

'And *sua s'day*, Kiri,' she said, crouching in front of him. 'Do you know what that means?'

Kiri shook his head. Blinked.

'It means hello in Khmer. Do you remember me?'

Kiri nodded. '*Sua s'day*, Ella. Can I go and see her?' he asked, looking over, wide-eyed, at the little girl Ella had been with.

'Yes, you can. But she's not feeling very well. Do you think you can be careful and quiet?'

Kiri nodded solemnly and Ella gave him a confirming nod before standing again. She watched him walk over to Maly's bed before turning to reassure Aaron. 'She's not contagious. It's dengue fever and there's never been a case of person-to-person transmission.'

'Dr Seng said it deserved its own documentary. The symptoms can be like malaria, right? But it's a virus, not a parasite, and the mosquitoes aren't the same.'

Ella nodded. 'The dengue mosquito—' She broke off. 'You're really interested?'

'Why wouldn't I be?'

'I just…' She shrugged. 'Nothing. People can get bored with the medical lingo.'

'I won't be bored. So—the mosquitoes?'

'They're called *Aedes aegypti*, and they bite during the day. Malaria mosquitoes—*Anopheles*, but I'm sure you know that—get you at night, and I'm sure you know that too. It kind of sucks that the people here don't get a break! Anyway, *Aedes aegypti* like urban areas, and they breed in stagnant water—vases, old tyres, buckets, that kind of thing. If a mosquito bites someone with dengue, the virus will replicate inside it, and then the mosquito can transmit the virus to other people when it bites them.' Her gaze sharpened. 'You're taking precautions for Kiri, aren't you?'

'Oh, yes. It's been beaten it into me. Long sleeves, long pants. Insect repellent with DEET. And so on and so forth.'

'You too—long sleeves, I mean. Enough already with the T-shirts.'

'Yes, I know. I'm tempting fate.'

Silence.

He was looking at her in that weird way.

'So, the filming,' she said, uncomfortable. 'Is it going well?'

'We're behind schedule, but I don't mind because it's given me a chance to take Kiri to see Angkor Wat. And the place with the riverbed carvings. You know, the carvings of the genitalia.' He stopped suddenly. 'I—I mean, the…um…Hindu gods…you know…and the—the…ah… Kal…? Kab…?'

Ella bit the inside of her cheek. It surprised her that she could think he was cute. But he sort of was, in his sudden embarrassment over the word genitalia. 'Yes, I know all about genitalia. And it's Kbal Spean, you're talking about, and the Hindu God is Shiva. It's also called The River of a

Thousand Lingas—which means a thousand stylised phalluses,' she said, and had to bite her cheek again as he ran a harassed hand into his hair.

'So, the filming?' she reminded him.

'Oh. Yeah. A few more days here and then the final bit involves visiting some of the villages near the Thai border and seeing how the malaria outreach programme works, with the volunteers screening, diagnosing and treating people in their communities.'

'I was out there a few years ago,' Ella said. 'Volunteers were acting as human mosquito bait. The mosquitoes would bite them, and the guys would scoop them into test tubes to be sent down to the lab in Phnom Penh for testing.'

'But wasn't that dangerous? I mean...*trying* to get bitten?'

'Well, certainly drastic. But all the volunteers were given a combination drug cocktail, which meant they didn't actually develop malaria.'

'So what was the point?'

'To verify whether the rapid treatment malaria programme that had been established there was managing to break the pathways of transmission between insects, parasites and humans. But you don't need to worry. That was then, this is now. And they won't be asking to roll up your jeans and grab a test tube.'

'Would you have rolled up your jeans, Ella?'

'Yes.'

'And risked malaria?'

'I've had it. Twice, actually. Once in Somalia, once here.'

'Somalia?'

Uh-oh. She was not going there. 'Obviously, it didn't kill me, either time. But I've *seen* it kill. It kills one child every thirty seconds.' She could hear her voice tremble so she paused for a moment. When she could trust herself, she added, 'And I would do anything to help stop that.'

Aaron was frowning. Watching her. Making her feel uncomfortable. Again. 'But you're not— Sorry, it's none of my business, but Kiri isn't going with you up there, right?'

'No.' Aaron frowned. Opened his mouth. Closed it. Opened. Closed.

'Problem?' she prompted.

'No. But… Just…' Sigh.

'Just…?' she prompted again.

'Just—do you think I made a mistake, bringing him to Cambodia?' he asked. 'There were reasons I couldn't leave him at home. And I thought it would be good for him to stay connected to his birth country. But, like you, he's had malaria. Before the adoption.'

'Yes, I gathered that.'

'I'd never forgive myself if he got it again because I brought him with me.'

Ella blinked at him. She was surprised he would share that fear with her—they weren't exactly friends, after all— and felt a sudden emotional connection that was as undeniable as it was unsettling.

She wanted to touch him. Just his hand. She folded her arms so she couldn't. 'I agree that children adopted from overseas should connect with their heritage,' she said, ultra-professional. And then she couldn't help herself. She unfolded her arms, touched his shoulder. Very briefly. 'But, yes, we're a long way from Sydney, and the health risks are real.'

'So I shouldn't have brought him?'

'You said there were reasons for not leaving him behind—so how can I answer that? But, you know, these are diseases of poverty we're talking about. That's a horrible thing to acknowledge, but at least it can be a comfort to you. Because you know your son would have immediate attention, the *best* attention—and therefore the best outcome.'

He sighed. 'Yes, I see what you mean. It is horrible, and also comforting.'

'And it won't be long until you're back home. Meanwhile, keep taking those precautions, and if he exhibits any symptoms, at least you know what they are—just don't wait to get him to the hospital.'

She swayed slightly, and Aaron reached out to steady her.

'Sorry. Tired,' she said.

'You're still not fully recovered, are you?' he asked.

'I'm fine. And my shift has finished so I'm off home in a moment.'

Ella nodded in Kiri's direction. The little boy was gently stroking the back of Maly's hand. 'He's sweet.'

'Yes. He's an angel.'

'You're lucky,' Ella said. She heard the...thing in her voice. The wistfulness. She blinked hard. Cleared her throat. 'Excuse me, I need to— Excuse me.'

Ella felt Aaron's eyes on her as she left the ward.

Ella was doing that too-slow walk. Very controlled.

She'd lost her curves since the wedding. She'd been thin when he'd visited her a week ago, but after the dengue she was like a whippet.

But still almost painfully beautiful. Despite the messy ponytail. And the sexless pants and top combo that constituted her uniform.

And he still wanted her.

He'd been furious at how he'd strained for a sight of her every time he'd been at the hospital, even though he'd known she was out of action. Seriously, how pathetic could a man be?

He'd tried and tried to get her out of his head. No joy. There was just something...something under the prickly exterior.

Like the way she looked at Kiri when he'd repeated her Cambodian greeting. The expression on her face when she'd spoken about diseases of the poor. It was just so hard to reconcile all the pieces. To figure out that *something* about her.

He caught himself. Blocked the thought. Reminded himself that if there *was* something there, he didn't want it. One more week, and he would never have to see or think of her again. He could have his peace of mind back. His libido back under control.

He called Kiri over and they left the ward.

And she was there—up the corridor, crouching beside a little boy who was on one of the mattresses on the floor, her slender fingers on the pulse point of his wrist.

Arrrggghhh. This was *torture*. Why wasn't she on her way home like she was supposed to be, so he didn't have to see her smile into that little boy's eyes? Didn't have to see her sit back on her heels and close her eyes, exhausted?

And wonder just who she really was, this woman who was prickly and dismissive. Knowledgeable and professional. Who wouldn't think twice about letting mosquitoes bite her legs for research. Who looked at sick children with a tenderness that caused his chest to ache. Who made him feel gauche and insignificant.

Who made him suddenly and horribly aware of what it was like to crave something. Someone. It was so much more, so much *worse*, than purely physical need.

'Ow,' Kiri protested, and Aaron loosened his hold on Kiri's hand.

Ella looked up, saw them. Froze. Nodding briefly, she got to her feet and did that slow walk out.

This was not good, Aaron thought.

A few days and he would be out of her life.

Ella felt that if only she didn't have to converse with Aaron again, she would cope with those days.

But she hadn't banked on the *sight* of him being such a distraction. Sauntering around like a doctor on regular rounds, poking his nose in everywhere without even the excuse of a camera. Not really coming near her, but always *there*.

It was somehow worse that he was keeping his distance, because it meant there was no purpose to the way she was perpetually waiting for him to show up.

Him and the boy, who reminded her so much of Sann.

It was painful to see Kiri, even from a distance. So painful she shouldn't want to see him, shouldn't want the ache it caused. Except that alongside the pain was this drenching, drowning need. She didn't bother asking why, accepting that it was a connection she couldn't explain, the way it had been with Sann.

On her fourth day back at work, after broken sleep full of wrenching nightmares, the last thing she needed was Aaron James, trailed by his cameraman, coming into the outpatient department just as a comatose, convulsing two-year-old boy was rushed up to her by his mother.

The look in Ella's eyes as she reached for the child must have been terrible because Aaron actually ran at her. He plucked the boy from his mother's arms. 'Come,' he said, and hurried through the hospital as though he'd worked there all his life, Ella and the little boy's mother hurrying after him.

This was a child. Maybe with malaria. And Aaron was helping her.

How was she supposed to keep her distance now?

CHAPTER FIVE

AARON SIGNALLED FOR the cameraman to start filming as what looked like a swarm of medical people converged on the tiny little boy in the ICU.

Ella was rattling off details as he was positioned in the bed—name Bourey, two years old, brought in by his mother after suffering intermittent fever and chills for two days. Unable to eat. Seizure on the way to the hospital. Unable to be roused. Severe pallor. Second seizure followed.

Hands, stethoscopes were all over the boy—pulling open his eyelids, taking his temperature. Checking heart rate, pulse and blood pressure. *Rash? No.* Feeling his abdomen.

I want a blood glucose now.

Into Bourey's tiny arm went a canula.

Blood was taken, and whisked away.

Intravenous diazepam as a slow bolus to control the seizures.

The doctor was listening intently to Bourey's breathing, which was deep and slow. The next moment the boy was intubated and hooked up to a respirator.

Every instruction was rapid-fire.

'Intravenous paracetamol for the fever.'

'Intravenous artesunate, stat, we won't wait for the blood films—we'll treat for falciparum malaria. Don't think it's menigococcus but let's give IV benzylpenicillin. We'll hold

off on the lumbar puncture. I want no evidence of focal
neuro signs. What was his glucose?'

'Intravenous dextrose five per cent and normal saline
point nine per cent for the dehydration—but monitor his
urine output carefully; we don't want to overdo it and end
up with pulmonary oedema, and we need to check renal
function. And watch for haemoglobinuria. If the urine is
dark we'll need to cross-match.'

Overhead an assortment of bags; tubes drip, drip, dripping.

How much stuff could the little guy's veins take?

A urinary catheter was added to Bourey's overloaded
body. Empty plastic bag draped over the side of the bed.

A plastic tube was measured, from the boy's nose to
his ear to his chest, lubricated, threaded up Bourey's nose,
taped in place.

'Aspirate the stomach contents.'

'Monitor temp, respiratory rate, pulse, blood pressure,
neuro obs every fifteen minutes.'

*Hypoglycaemia, metabolic acidosis, pulmonary oedema,
hypotensive shock. Watch the signs. Monitor. Check. Observe.*

Aaron's head was spinning. His cameraman silent and
focused as he filmed.

And Ella—so calm, except for her eyes.

Aaron was willing her to look at him. And every time
she did, she seemed to relax. Just a slight breath, a soften-
ing in her face so subtle he could be imagining it, a lessen-
ing of tension in her shoulders. Then her focus was back
to the boy.

The manic pace around Bourey finally eased and Aaron
saw Ella slip out of the ICU. Aaron signalled to his cameraman to stop filming and left the room.

They had enough to tell the story but they needed a
face on camera.

He went in search of Dr Seng, wanting to check the

sensitivity of the case and get suggestions for the best interviewee.

Dr Seng listened, nodded, contemplated. Undertook to talk to Bourey's family to ascertain their willingness to have the case featured. 'For the interview, I recommend Ella,' he said. 'She knows enough about malaria to write a textbook, and she is highly articulate.'

Aaron suspected the ultra-private Ella would rather eat a plate of tarantulas and was on the verge of suggesting perhaps a doctor when Ella walked past.

Dr Seng beckoned her over, asked for her participation and smiled genially at them before hurrying away.

Ella looked at Aaron coolly. 'Happy to help, of course,' she said.

They found a spot where they were out of the way of traffic but with a view through the ICU windows. The cameraman opted for handheld, to give a sense of intimacy.

Great—intimacy.

'Well?' she asked, clearly anxious to get it done.

'Don't you want to…?' He waved a hand at his hair. At his face.

'What's wrong with the way I look?'

'Nothing. It's just that most people—'

'What's more important, how my hair looks or that little boy?'

'Fine,' Aaron said. 'Tell me about the case.'

'This is a two-year-old child, suffering from cerebral falciparum malaria. Blood films showed parasitaemia—'

'Parasitaemia?'

'It means the number of parasites in his blood. His level is twenty-two per cent. That is high and very serious. Hence the IV artesunate—a particular drug we use for this strain—which we'll administer for twenty-four hours. After that, we'll switch to oral artemisinin-based combination therapy—ACT for short. It's the current drug regime

for falciparum. We'll be monitoring his parasitaemia, and
we'd expect to see the levels drop relatively quickly.'

She sounded smart and competent and in control.

'And if they don't drop?' Aaron asked.

Her forehead creased. 'Then we've got a problem. It
will indicate drug resistance. This region is the first in the
world to show signs of resistance to ACTs, which used to
kill the parasites in forty-eight hours and now take up to
ninety-six hours. It was the same for previous treatments
like cloroquine, which is now practically useless—we're
like the epicentre for drug resistance here.'

'How does it happen, the resistance?'

'People take just enough of the course to feel better. Or
the medicines they buy over the counter are substandard,
or counterfeit, with only a tiny fraction of the effective
drug in it. Or they are sold only a fraction of the course.
Often the writing on the packet is in a different language,
so people don't know what they're selling, or buying. And
here we have highly mobile workers crossing the borders—
in and out of Thailand, for example. So resistant strains
are carried in and out with them. The problem is there's
no new miracle drug on the horizon, so if we don't address
the resistance issue…' She held out her hands, shrugged.
Perfection for the camera. 'Trouble. And if the resistance
eventually gets exported to Africa—as history suggests it
will—it will be catastrophic. Around three thousand children die of malaria every day in sub-Saharan Africa, which
is why this is a critical issue.'

He waited. Letting the camera stay on her face, letting
the statistic sink in. 'Back to this particular case. What
happens now?'

'Continuous clinical observation and measuring what's
happening with his blood, his electrolytes. I could give you
a range of medical jargon but basically this is a critically ill
child. We hope his organs won't fail. We hope he doesn't

suffer any lifelong mental disabilities from the pressure on his brain. But, first, we hope he survives.'

A forlorn hope, as it turned out.

One minute they had been working to save Bourey's life, preparing for a whole-blood transfusion to lower the concentration of parasites in Bourey's blood and treat his anaemia. The next, Ella was unhooking him from the medical paraphernalia that had defined his last hours.

She left the ICU and her eyes started to sting. She stopped, wiped a finger under one eye, looked down at it. Wet. She was crying. And what was left of the numbness—one year's worth of carefully manufactured numbness—simply fell away.

She heard something and looked up. She saw Aaron, and tried to pull herself together. But her body had started to shake, and she simply had no reserves of strength left to pretend everything was all right.

A sobbing sort of gasp escaped her, a millisecond before she could put her hand over her mouth to stop it. Her brain and her heart and her body seemed to be out of synch. Her limbs couldn't seem to do what she was urging them to do. So the horrible gasp was followed by a stumble as she tried to turn away. She didn't want Aaron to see her like this. Didn't want anybody to see her, but especially not Aaron. He knew her sister. He might tell her sister. Her sister couldn't know that she was utterly, utterly desolate.

'I'm fine,' she said, as she felt his hand on her shoulder, steadying her.

Aaron withdrew his hand. 'You don't look fine,' he said.

Ella shook her head, unable to speak. She took one unsteady step. Two. Stopped. The unreleased sobs were aching in her chest. Crushing and awful. She had to get out of the hospital.

She felt Aaron's hand on her shoulder again and found

she couldn't move. Just couldn't force her feet in the direction she wanted to go.

Aaron put his arm around her, guiding her with quick, purposeful strides out of the hospital, into the suffocating heat, steering her towards and then behind a clump of thick foliage so they were out of sight.

Ella opened her mouth to tell him, again, that she was fine, but… 'I'm sorry,' she gasped instead. 'I can't— Like Sann. My Sann. Help me, help me.'

He pulled her into his arms and held on. 'I will. I will, Ella. Tell me how. Just tell me.'

'He died. He died. I c-c-couldn't stop it.'

Aaron hugged her close. Silence. He seemed to know there was nothing to say.

Ella didn't know how long she stood there, in Aaron James's arms, as the tears gradually slowed. It was comforting, to be held like this. No words. Just touch. She didn't move, even when the crying stopped.

Until he turned her face up to his. And there was something in his eyes, something serious and concerned.

A look that reminded her Aaron James could not be a shoulder to cry on. He was too…close, somehow. She didn't want anyone to be close to her. Couldn't risk it.

Ella wrenched herself out of his arms. Gave a small, self-conscious hunch of one shoulder. 'It shouldn't upset me any more, I know. But sometimes…' She shoved a lank lock of hair behind her ear. 'Usually you think if they had just got to us faster…they are so poor, you see, that they wait, and hope, and maybe try other things. Because it is expensive for them, the trip to the hospital, even though the treatment is free. But in this case I think…I think nothing would have made any difference… And I…I hate it when I can't make a difference.'

She rubbed her tired hands over her face. 'Usually when I feel like this I donate blood. It reminds me that things that cost me nothing can help someone. And because the hospital always needs so much blood. But I can't even do that now because it's too soon after the dengue. So I've got nothing. Useless.'

'I'll donate blood for you,' Aaron said immediately.

She tried to smile. 'You're doing something important already—the documentary. And I didn't mind doing that interview, you know. I'd do anything.'

She started to move away, but he put his hand on her arm, stopping her.

'So, Ella. Who's Sann?'

Ella felt her eyes start to fill again. Through sheer will power she stopped the tears from spilling out. He touched her, very gently, his hand on her hair, her cheek, and it melted something. 'He was the child I wanted to adopt,' she said. And somehow it was a relief to share this. 'Here in Cambodia. A patient, an orphan, two years old. I went home to find out what I had to do, and while I was gone he…he died. Malaria.'

'And you blame yourself,' he said softly. 'Because you weren't there. Because you couldn't save him. And I suppose you're working with children in Cambodia, which must torture you, as a kind of penance.'

'I don't know.' She covered her face in her hands for one long moment. Shuddered out a breath. 'Sorry—it's not something I talk about.' Her hands dropped and she looked at him, drained of all emotion. 'I'm asking you not to mention it to Tina. She never knew about Sann. And there's no point telling her. She doesn't need to know about this episode today either. Can I trust you not to say anything?'

'You can trust me. But, Ella, you're making a mistake. This is not the way to—'

'Thank you,' she said abruptly, not wanting to hear advice she couldn't bear to take. 'The rain…it's that time of the day. And I can feel it coming. Smell it.'

'So? What's new?'

'I'd better get back.'

'Wait,' he called.

But Ella was running for the hospital.

She reached the roof overhang as the heavens opened. Looked back at Aaron, who hadn't moved, hadn't taken even one step towards shelter. He didn't seem to care that the gushing water was plastering his clothes to his skin.

He was watching her with an intensity that scared her.

Ella shivered in the damp heat and then forced her eyes away.

The next day Helen told Ella that Aaron James had been in and donated blood.

For her. He'd done it for her.

But she looked at Helen as though she couldn't care less. The following day, when Helen reported that Aaron had left for his visit to the villages, same deal. But she was relieved.

She hoped Aaron would be so busy that any thought of her little breakdown would be wiped out of his mind.

Meanwhile, she would be trying to forget the way Aaron had looked at her—like he understood her, like he knew how broken she was. Trying to forget *him*.

There was only one problem with that: Kiri.

Because Kiri and Aaron came as a set.

And Ella couldn't stop thinking, worrying, about Kiri. Knowing that the cause was her distress over Bourey's death didn't change the fact that she had a sense of dread about Kiri's health that seemed tied to Aaron's absence.

Which just went to prove she was unhinged!

Kiri has a nanny to look after him. It's none of your business, Ella.

She repeated this mantra to herself over and over.

But the nagging fear kept tap-tapping at her nerves as she willed the time to pass quickly until Aaron could whisk his son home to safety.

When she heard Helen calling her name frantically two days after Aaron had left, her heart started jackhammering.

'What?' Ella asked, hurrying towards Helen. But she knew. *Knew*.

'It's Aaron James. Or rather his son. He's been taken to the Khmer International Hospital. Abdominal pains. Persistent fever. Retro-orbital pain. Vomiting. They suspect dengue fever.'

Ella felt the rush in her veins, the panic.

'They can't get hold of Aaron,' Helen said. 'So the nanny asked them to call us because she knows he's been filming here. I thought you should know straight away, because— Well, the family connection. Ella, what if something goes wrong and we can't reach Aaron?'

Ella didn't bother to answer. She simply ran.

Aaron had been unsettled during his time in the monsoonal rainforest.

Not that it hadn't been intriguing—the medical challenges the people faced.

And confronting—the history of the area, which had been a Khmer Rouge stronghold, with regular sightings of people with missing limbs, courtesy of landmines, to prove it.

And humbling—that people so poor, so constantly ill, should face life with such stoic grace.

And beautiful, even with the daily downpours—with the lush, virgin forest moist enough to suck at you, and vegetation so thick you had the feeling that if you stood still for half an hour, vines would start growing over you, anchoring you to the boggy earth.

But!

His mobile phone was bothering him. He'd never been out of contact with Kiri before, but since day two, when they'd headed for the most remote villages that were nothing more than smatterings of bamboo huts on rickety stilts, he'd had trouble with his phone.

He found himself wishing he'd told Jenny to contact

Ella if anything went wrong. But Jenny, not being psychic, would never guess that was what Aaron would want her to do—not when she'd never heard Ella's name come out of his mouth. Because he'd been so stupidly determined *not* to talk about Ella, in a misguided attempt to banish her from his head. And what an epic fail *that* had been, because she was still in his head. Worse than ever.

He'd hoped being away from the hospital would cure it. Not looking likely, though.

Every time he saw someone with a blown-off limb, or watched a health worker touch a malnourished child or check an HIV patient, he remembered Ella's words at the wedding reception. *I've seen the damage landmines can do. Had children with AIDS, with malnutrition, die in my arms.* He hadn't understood how she could sound so prosaic but now, seeing the endless stream of injuries, illness, poverty, he did.

And anything to do with malaria—well, how could he not think of her, and that searing grief?

The malaria screening process in the villages was simple, effective. Each person was registered in a book. *Ella, in the outpatient department, recording patient details.*

They were checked for symptoms—simple things like temperature, spleen enlargement. *Ella's hands touching children on the ward.*

Symptomatic people went on to the rapid diagnostic test. Fingertip wiped, dried. Squeeze the finger gently, jab quickly with a lancet. Wipe the first drop, collect another drop with a pipette. Drop it into the tiny well on the test strip. Add buffer in the designated spot. Wait fifteen minutes for the stripes to appear. *Ella, soothing children as their blood was siphoned off at the hospital.*

Aaron helped distribute insecticide-impregnated mosquito nets—a wonderfully simple method of protecting against malaria and given out free. *Ella, blocking him out so easily just by tugging her bed net closed.*

Arrrggghhh.

But relief was almost at hand. One last interview for the documentary and he would be heading back to Kiri. Jenny would have already packed for the trip home to Sydney. Ella would be out of his sight, out of his reach, out of his life once they left Cambodia.

Just one interview to go.

He listened closely as the village volunteer's comments were translated into English. There were three thousand volunteers throughout Cambodia, covering every village more than five kilometres from a health centre, with people's homes doubling as pop-up clinics. Medication was given free, and would be swallowed in front of the volunteers to make sure the entire course was taken. People diagnosed with malaria would not only have blood tested on day one but also on day three to assess the effectiveness of the drug treatment. *Ella, explaining drug resistance. Mentioning so casually that she'd had malaria twice.*

Half an hour later, with the filming wrapped up, they were in the jeep.

Twenty minutes after that his phone beeped. Beeped, beeped, beeped. Beeped.

He listened with the phone tight to one ear, fingers jammed in the other to block other sounds.

Felt the cold sweat of terror.

If he hadn't been sitting, his legs would have collapsed beneath him.

Kiri. Dengue haemorrhagic fever. His small, gentle, loving son was in pain and he wasn't there to look after him.

His fault. All his. He'd brought Kiri to Cambodia in the middle of an outbreak. Left him while he'd traipsed off to film in the boondocks, thinking that was the safer option.

He listened to the messages again. One after the other. Progress reports from the hospital—calm, matter-of-fact, professional, reassuring. Jenny—at first panicked, tearful. And then calmer each time, reassured by one of the nurses.

Rebecca frantic but then, somehow, also calmer, mentioning an excellent nurse.

Three times he'd started to call the Children's Community Friendship Hospital to talk to Ella, wanting her advice, her reassurance, her skills to be focused on Kiri. Three times he'd stopped himself—he *had* expert advice, from Kiri's doctor and a tropical diseases specialist in Sydney he'd called.

And Ella had made it clear she wanted nothing to do with him.

And his son wasn't Ella's problem. Couldn't be her problem.

He wouldn't, couldn't let her mean that much.

The hospital where Kiri had been taken was like a five-star hotel compared with where Ella worked, and Kiri had his own room.

Ella knew the hospital had an excellent reputation; once she'd satisfied herself that Kiri was getting the care and attention he needed, she intended to slide into the background and leave everyone to it.

There was no reason for her to be the one palpating Kiri's abdomen to see if his liver was enlarged, while waiting to see if Kiri's blood test results supported the dengue diagnosis. Hmm, it was a little tender. But that wasn't a crisis and she didn't need to do anything *else* herself.

The blood tests came back, with the dengue virus detected. Plus a low white cell count, low platelets and high haematocrit—the measurement of the percentage of red blood cells to the total blood volume—which could indicate potential plasma leakage. Serious, but, as long as you knew what you were dealing with, treatable. He was still drinking, there were no signs of respiratory distress. So far, so good.

Hands off, Ella, leave it to the staff.

But… There was no problem in asking for a truckle to

be set up for her in Kiri's room, was there? At her hospital, the kids' families always stayed with them for the duration.

So all right, she wasn't family, but his family wasn't here. And kids liked to have people they knew with them. And Ella knew Kiri. Plus, she was making it easier for his nanny to take a break.

She'd got Aaron's cell number from Jenny, and was constantly on the verge of calling him. Only the thought of how many panicked messages he already had waiting for him stopped her. And the tiny suspicion that Aaron would tell her she wasn't needed, which she didn't want to hear—and she hoped that didn't mean she was becoming obsessive about his son.

By the time she'd started haranguing the doctors for updated blood test results, double-checking the nurses' perfect records of Kiri's urine output, heart and respiratory rates, and blood pressure, taking over the task of sponging Kiri down to lower his fever and cajoling him into drinking water and juice to ensure he didn't get dehydrated, she realised she was a step *beyond* obsessive.

It wasn't like she didn't have enough to do at her own place of work, but she couldn't seem to stop herself standing watch over Kiri James like some kind of sentinel—even though dashing between two hospitals was running her ragged.

Kiri's fever subsided on his third day in hospital—but Ella knew better than to assume that meant he was better because often that heralded a critical period. The blood tests with the dropping platelet levels, sharply rising white cells and decreasing haematocrit certainly weren't indicating recovery.

And, suddenly, everything started to go wrong.

Kiri grew increasingly restless and stopped drinking, and Ella went into hyper-vigilant mode.

His breathing became too rapid. His pulse too fast. Even

more worryingly, his urine output dropped down to practically nothing.

Ella checked his capillary refill time, pressing on the
underside of Kiri's heel and timing how long it took to go
from blanched to normal: more than six seconds, when it
should only take three.

His abdomen was distended, which indicated ascites—
an accumulation of fluid in the abdominal cavity. 'I'm just
going to feel your tummy, Kiri,' she said, and pressed as
gently as she could.

He cried out. 'Hurts, Ella.'

'I'm so sorry, darling,' she said, knowing they needed
to quickly determine the severity of plasma leakage. 'You
need some tests, I'm afraid, so I'm going to call your nurse.'

Ella spoke to the nurse, who raced for the doctor, who
ordered an abdominal ultrasound to confirm the degree
of ascites and a chest X-ray to determine pleural effusion,
which would lead to respiratory distress.

'As you know, Ella,' the doctor explained, drawing her
outside, 'a critical amount of plasma leakage will indicate he's going into shock, so we're moving Kiri to the
ICU, where we can monitor him. We'll be starting him
on intravenous rehydration. We'd expect a fairly rapid improvement, in which case we'll progressively reduce the
IV fluids, or they could make the situation worse. No improvement and a significant decrease in haematocrit could
suggest internal bleeding, and at that stage we'd look at a
blood transfusion. But we're nowhere near that stage so no
need to worry. I'll call his father now.'

'Aaron's phone's not working,' Ella said mechanically.

'It is now. He called to tell us he's on his way. I know
you're a close friend of the family, so...'

But Ella had stopped listening. She nodded. Murmured
a word here and there. Took nothing in.

The doctor patted her arm and left. The orderly would
be arriving to take Kiri to ICU. This was it. Over. She

wasn't needed any more. And she knew, really, that she had never been needed—the hospital had always had everything under control.

Ella braced herself and went to Kiri's bedside. 'Well, young man,' she said cheerfully, 'you're going somewhere special—ICU.'

'I see you too.'

Ella felt such a rush of love, it almost choked her. 'Hmm. In a way that's exactly what it is. It's where the doctors can see you every minute, until nobody has to poke you in the tummy any more. Okay?'

'Are you coming?'

'No, darling. Someone better is coming. The best surprise. Can you guess who?'

Kiri's eyes lit up. 'Dad?'

'Yep,' she said, and leaned over to kiss him.

The door opened. The orderly. 'And they'll be putting a special tube into you here,' she said, touching his wrist. 'It's superhero juice, so you're going to look like Superman soon. Lucky you!'

A moment later Ella was alone, gathering her few possessions.

Back to reality, she told herself. Devoting her time to where it was really needed, rather than wasting it playing out some mother fantasy.

Ella felt the tears on her cheeks. Wiped them away. Pulled herself together.

Walked super-slowly out of the room.

Ella was the first person he saw.

Aaron was sweaty, frantic. Racing into the hospital. And there she was, exiting. Cool. Remote.

He stopped.

If Ella is here, Kiri will be all right. The thought darted into his head without permission. The relief was immediate, almost overwhelming.

A split second later it all fell into place: Ella was the nurse who had spoken to Rebecca. His two worlds colliding. Ex-wife and mother of his child connecting with the woman he wanted to sleep with.

No-go zone.

He reached Ella in three, unthinking strides. 'It was you, wasn't it?'

His sudden appearance before her startled her. But she looked at him steadily enough, with her wedding face on. 'What was me?'

'You spoke to Rebecca.'

'Yes. Jenny handed me the phone. I wasn't going to hang up on a worried parent. I had no *reason* to hang up on her.'

'What did you tell her?'

She raised an eyebrow at him. 'That you and I were having a torrid affair.'

She looked at him, waiting for something.

He looked back—blank.

'Seriously?' she demanded. '*Seriously?*' She shook her head in disgust. 'I told her what I knew about dengue fever, you idiot. That it was a complex illness, and things did go wrong—but that it was relatively simple to treat. I shared my own experience so that she understood. I said that early detection followed by admission to a good hospital almost guaranteed a positive outcome. I explained that, more than anything else, it was a matter of getting the fluid intake right and treating complications as they arose.'

'Oh. I—I don't—'

'I told her Kiri was handling everything bravely enough to break your heart, and that Jenny and I were taking shifts to make sure he had someone familiar with him at all times. I didn't ask her why she wasn't hotfooting it out here, despite the fact that her son was in a lot of pain, with his joints aching and his muscles screaming, and asking for her, for you, constantly.'

'I—'

'Not interested, Aaron.'

'But just—he's all right, isn't he? In ICU, right?'

A look. Dismissive. And then she did that slow walk away.

'Wait a minute!' he exploded.

But Ella only waved an imperious hand—not even bothering to turn around to do it—and kept to her path.

CHAPTER SIX

WELL...IT BOTHERED Aaron.

Ella's saunter off as though he wasn't even worth talking to.

Followed by Jenny's report of Ella's tireless care: that Ella had begged and badgered the staff and hadn't cared about anyone but his son; the fact that she of all people had been the only one capable of reassuring Rebecca.

He had to keep things simple.

But how simple could it be, when he *knew* Ella would be visiting Kiri—and that when she did, he would have to tell her that, all things considered, she would have to stay away from his son.

Two days. The day Kiri got out of ICU. That's how long it took her.

Aaron had left Kiri for fifteen minutes to grab something to eat, and she was there when he got back to Kiri's room, as though she'd timed it to coincide with his absence.

It wrenched him to see the look on Ella's face as she smoothed Kiri's spiky black hair back from his forehead. To experience again that strange combination of joy and terror that had hit him when he'd seen her coming out of the hospital.

He would *not* want her. He had enough on his plate. And if Ella thought she got to pick and choose when their lives could intersect and when they couldn't—well, no! That was all. No.

She looked up. Defensive. Defiant. *Anxious?*

And he felt like he was being unfair.

And he was *never* unfair.

No wonder she made him so mad. She was changing his entire personality, and not for the better.

After a long, staring moment Ella turned back to Kiri. 'I'll see you a little later, Kiri. Okay?' And then she walked slowly away.

Kiri blinked at his father sleepily, then smiled. 'Where's Ella gone?'

'Back to her hospital. They need her there now. And you've got me.'

Kiri nodded.

He was out of danger, but he looked so tired. 'Are you okay, Kiri? What do you need?'

'Nothing. My head was hurting. And my tummy. And my legs. But Ella fixed me.'

'That's good. But I'm here now.'

'And I was hot. Ella cooled me down.'

'How did she do that?'

'With water and a towel.'

'I can do that for you, sport.'

'I'm not hot any more.' Kiri closed his eyes for a long moment, then blinked them open again and held out his skinny forearm, showing off the small sticking plaster. 'Look,' he said.

'You were on a drip, I know.'

'Superhero juice, Ella said.'

'To get you better.'

A few minutes more passed. 'Dad?'

'What is it, sport?'

'Where's Ella?'

Aaron bit back a sigh. 'She has a lot of people to look after. I'm back now. And Mum will be coming soon.'

'Mum's coming?'

'Yes, she'll be here soon.'

Kiri's eyes drifted shut.

The elation at knowing Kiri was out of danger was still with him. Even the prospect of calling Rebecca again to reinforce his demand that she get her butt on a plane didn't daunt him—although he hoped that, this time, Rebecca wouldn't be off her face.

Of course, breaking the other news to her—that he and Kiri would be heading to LA for his audition after Kiri's convalescence, and then straight on to London—might set off a whole new word of pain. He knew Rebecca was going to hate the confirmation that Aaron had landed both the audition and a plum role in Brand's film, because she resented every bit of career success that came his way.

He suspected she would try to guilt him into leaving Kiri in Sydney with her, just to punish him—for Kiri's illness and for the role in Brand's film—but that wasn't going to happen. Until Rebecca got herself clean, where he went, Kiri went.

So he would call Rebecca, get her travel arrangements under way so she could spend time with Kiri while he got his strength back, and tell her that London was all systems go.

Then he would have only two things to worry about: Kiri's convalescence; and figuring out how to forget Ella Reynolds and the way she had looked at his son.

Rebecca wasn't coming.

It was a shock that she would forego spending time with Kiri, knowing she wouldn't see him for months.

Aaron was trying to find the right words to say to Kiri and had been tiptoeing around the subject for a while.

The last thing he needed was Ella breezing in—triggering that aggravating, inexplicable and entirely inappropriate sense of relief.

Not that she spared Aaron as much as a look.

'You don't need to tell me how you are today,' she said to Kiri, leaning down to kiss his forehead. 'Because you look like a superhero. I guess you ate your dinner last night! And are you weeing? Oops—am I allowed to say that in front of Dad?'

Kiri giggled, and said, 'Yes,' and Ella gave his son that blinding smile that was so gut-churningly amazing.

She looked beautiful. Wearing a plain, white cotton dress and flat leather tie-up sandals, toting an oversized canvas bag—nothing special about any of it. But she was so…lovely.

She presented Kiri with a delicately carved wooden dragonfly she'd bought for him at the local market and showed him how to balance it on a fingertip.

Then Kiri asked her about the chicken game she'd told him about on a previous visit.

'Ah—you mean Chab Kon Kleng. Okay. Well they start by picking the strongest one—that would be you, Kiri—to be the hen.'

'But I'm a boy.'

'The rooster, then. And you're like your dad—you're going to defend your kids. And all your little chickens are hiding behind you, and the person who is the crow has to try and catch them, while everyone sings a special song. And, no, I'm not singing it. I'm a terrible singer, and my Khmer is not so good.'

'You asked me something about *ch'heu*. That's Khmer.'

'Yes—I was asking if you were in pain and forgot you were a little Aussie boy.'

'I'm Cambodian too.'

'Yes, you are. Lucky you,' Ella said softly.

Aaron was intrigued at this side of Ella. Sweet, animated, fun.

She glanced at him—finally—and he was surprised to see a faint blush creep into her cheeks.

She grabbed the chart from the end of Kiri's bed, scanning quickly. 'You will be out of here in no time if you keep this up.' Another one of those smiles. 'Anyway, I just wanted to call in and say hello today, but I'll stay longer next time.'

'Next time,' Kiri piped up, 'you'll see Mum. She's coming.'

'Hey—that's great,' she replied.

Aaron sucked in a quick, silent breath. Okay, this was the moment to tell Kiri that Rebecca wasn't coming, and to tell Ella that she wasn't welcome. 'Er...' *Brilliant start.*

Two pairs of eyes focused on him. Curious. Waiting.

Aaron perched on the side of Kiri's bed. 'Mate,' he said, 'I'm afraid Mum still can't leave home, so we're going to have to do without her.'

Kiri stared at him, taking in the news in his calm way.

'But she knows you're almost better, and so you'll forgive her,' Aaron continued. 'And I have to give you a kiss and hug from her—yuckerama.'

Kiri giggled then. 'You always kiss and hug me.'

'Then I guess I can squeeze in an extra when nobody's looking.'

'Okay.'

'Right,' Ella said cheerily. 'You'd better get yourself out of here, young man, so you can get home to Mom. You know what that means—eat, drink, do what the doctor tells you. Now, I'm sure you and Dad have lots to plan so I'll see you later.'

That smile at Kiri.

The usual smile—the one minus the eye glow—for him.

And she was gone before Aaron could gather his thoughts.

See you later? No, she would *not*.

With a quick 'Back soon' to Kiri, Aaron ran after her.

'Ella, wait.'

Ella stopped, stiffened, turned.

'Can we grab a coffee?'

Ella thought about saying no. She didn't want to feel that uncomfortable mix of guilt and attraction he seemed to bring out in her. But a 'no' would be an admission that he had some kind of power over her, and that would never do. So she nodded and walked beside him to the hospital café, and sat in silence until their coffee was on the table in front of them.

'I wanted to explain. About Rebecca.' He was stirring one sugar into his coffee about ten times longer than he needed to.

'No need,' she said.

'It's just she had an audition, and because Kiri was out of danger…'

She nodded. 'And he'd probably be ready to go home by the time she arrived anyway…'

Aaron looked morosely at the contents in his cup, and Ella felt an unwelcome stab of sympathy.

'Actually, the audition wasn't the main issue,' he said. 'I know the director. He would have held off for her.'

Ella waited while he gave his coffee another unnecessary stir.

'Has Tina told you about Rebecca?' he asked, looking across at her.

'Told me what?'

'About her drug problem?'

'Ah. No. I didn't know. I'm sorry.' That explained the not-really-divorced divorce; Sir Galahad wasn't the type to cut and run in an untenable situation.

'Things are…complicated,' he said. 'Very.'

'I'm sure.'

'It doesn't mean Rebecca isn't anxious about Kiri. I mean, she's his mother, and she loves him.'

'I understand. But he should recover quickly now. At this stage—the recovery phase—all those fluids that leaked out of his capillaries are simply being reabsorbed by his body. Like a wave—flooding, receding, balancing. But he'll be tired for a while. And there may be a rash. Red and itchy, with white centres. Don't freak out about it. Okay?'

Silence. Another stir of the coffee.

'Are you going to drink that, or are you just going to stir it to death?' Ella asked, and then it hit her: this was not really about Rebecca. 'Or…do you want to just tell me what this all has to do with me?'

Aaron looked at her. Kind of determined and apologetic at the same time. 'It's just…he's very attached to you. *Too* attached to you. I don't know how, in such a short time, but he is.'

'It's an occupational hazard for doctors and nurses.'

'No, Ella. It's you. And that makes things more complicated, given he won't be seeing you again once we leave the hospital. I—I don't want him to miss you.'

'Ahhh,' she said, and pushed her cup away. 'I see. Things are complicated, and he already has a mother, so stay away, Ella.'

'It's just the flip side of what you said to me—that you don't like saying goodbye to a child when a relationship goes south.'

'We don't have a relationship. And the fact you're a father didn't seem to bother you when you were kissing me, as long as we weren't *in* a "relationship".'

'Don't be naïve, Ella. It's one thing for us to have sex. It's another when there are two of us sitting together at my son's bedside.'

The hurt took her by surprise. 'So let me get this straight—you're happy to sleep with me, but you don't want me anywhere near your son?'

'We haven't slept together.'

'That's right—we haven't. And calm yourself, we won't. But the principle is still there: it would be *okay* for you to have sex with me, but because you *want* to have sex with me, it's *not* okay for me to be anywhere near your son. And don't throw back at me what I said about not wanting to get mixed up with a man with a kid—which would be my problem to deal with, not yours. Or tell me it's to protect him from the pain of missing me either. Because this is about *you*. This is because *you're* not comfortable around me. I'd go so far as to say you disapprove of me.'

'I don't know what to think of you.' He dragged a hand through his hair. 'One minute you're letting a drunk guy in a bar paw you and the next you're hovering like a guardian angel over sick kids. One minute you're a sarcastic pain in the butt, and the next you're crying like your heart's breaking. Do I approve of you? I don't even know. It's too hard to know you, Ella. Too hard.'

'And you're a saint by comparison, are you? No little flaws or contradictions in your character? So how do you explain your attraction to someone like me?'

'I don't explain it. I can't. That's the problem.' He stopped, closed his eyes for a fraught moment. 'Look, I've got Rebecca to worry about. And Kiri to shield from all that's going on with her. That's why I told you I couldn't develop a relationship with you. To make it cl—'

'I told *you* I didn't want one. Or are you too arrogant to believe that?'

'Wake up, Ella. If Kiri has developed an affection for you, that means we're *in* a relationship. Which would be fine if I didn't—'

'Oh, shut up and stir your coffee! This is no grand passion we're having.' Ella was almost throbbing with rage, made worse by having to keep her voice low. A nice yelling match would have suited her right now but you didn't yell at people in Cambodia.

She leaned across the table. 'Understand this: I'm not interested in you. I'm not here, after having worked a very long day, to see you. I'm here to see Kiri, who was in this hospital parentless. No father. No mother. Just a nanny. And me. Holding his hand while they drew his blood for tests. Coaxing him to drink. Trying to calm him when he vomited, when his stomach was hurting and there was no relief for the pain. Knowing his head was splitting and that paracetamol couldn't help enough. So scared he'd start bleeding that I was beside myself because what the hell were we going to do if he needed a transfusion and you weren't here? How dare you tell me after that to stay away from him, like I'm out to seduce you and spoil your peace and wreck your family?'

She could feel the tears ready to burst, and dashed a hand across her eyes.

He opened his mouth.

'Just shut *up*,' she said furiously. 'You know, I'm not overly modest about my assets, but I somehow think a fine upstanding man like you could resist making mad passionate love to a bottom feeder like me in front of Kiri, so I suggest you just get over yourself and stop projecting.'

'Projecting?'

'Yes—your guilty feelings on me! I have enough guilt of my own to contend with without you adding a chunky piece of antique furniture to the bonfire. It's not my fault your wife is a drug addict. It's not my fault you got a divorce. It's not my fault your son got dengue fever. It's not my fault you find me attractive, or a distraction, or whatever. I am not the cause or the catalyst or the star of your documentary, and I didn't ask you to lurk around hospital corners, watching me.'

She stood, pushing her chair back violently. 'I'm no saint, but I'm not a monster either.'

She headed for the door at a cracking pace, Aaron scrambling to catch up with her.

He didn't reach her until she was outside, around the corner from the hospital entrance.

'Wait just a minute,' he said, and spun her to face him.

'This conversation is over. Leave me *alone*,' she said, and jerked free, turned to walk off.

His hand shot out, grabbed her arm, spun her back. 'Oh, no, you don't,' he said, and looked as furious as she felt. 'You are not running off and pretending I'm the only one with a problem. Go on, lie to me—tell me you don't want me to touch you.'

He wrenched her up onto her toes and smacked her into his chest. Looked at her for one fierce, burning moment, and then kissed her as though he couldn't help himself.

In a desperate kind of scramble, her back ended up against the wall and he was plastered against her. He took her face between his hands, kissed her, long and hard. 'Ella,' he whispered against her lips. 'Ella. I know it's insane but when you're near me I can't help myself. Can't.'

Ella was tugging his shirt from his jeans, her hands sliding up his chest. 'Just touch me. Touch me!'

His thighs nudged hers apart and he was there, hard against her. She strained against him, ready, so ready, so—

Phone. Ringing. His.

They pulled apart, breathing hard. Looked at each other.

Aaron wrenched the phone from his pocket. Rebecca.

The phone rang. Rang. Rang. Rang. Stopped.

And still Ella and Aaron stared at each other.

Ella swallowed. 'No matter what you think of me—or what I think of myself right now, which isn't much—I don't want to make things difficult. For you, for Kiri. Or for me.' She smoothed her hands down her dress, making sure everything was in order. 'So you win. I'll stay away.'

'Maybe there's another way to—'

Ella cut him off. 'No. We've both got enough drama in our lives without making a fleeting attraction into a Shakespearean tragedy. I just...' Pause. Another swallow.

'I don't want him to think I don't care about him. Because he might think that, when I don't come back.'

Aaron pushed a lock of her hair behind her ear. It was a gentle gesture that had her ducking away. 'That's not helping,' she said.

'Don't think I don't know how lucky I am to have had you watching over Kiri. He knows and I know that you care about him. And I know how much, after Sann—'

'Don't you dare,' she hissed. 'I should never have told you. I regret it more than I can say. So we'll make a deal, shall we? I'll stay away and you don't ever, *ever* mention Sann again, not to anyone. I don't need or want you to feel sorry for me. I don't need or want *you*. So let's focus on a win-win. You go home. I'll go...wherever. And we'll forget we ever met.'

Ella walked away, but it was harder than it had ever been to slow her steps.

The sooner Aaron James was back in Sydney the better.

She was putting Sydney at number three thousand and one on her list of holiday destinations—right after Afghanistan.

CHAPTER SEVEN

'ELLA!'

Tina was staring at her. Surprised, delighted. 'Oh, come in. Come in! I'm so glad you're here. I was wondering when you'd use that ticket. Brand,' she called over her shoulder.

Ella cast appreciative eyes over the grand tiled entrance hall of her sister's Georgian townhouse. 'Nice one, Mrs. McIntyre,' she said.

Tina laughed. 'Yes, "nice".'

'So I'm thinking space isn't a problem.'

'We have *oodles* of it. In fact, we have other g—. Oh, here's Brand. Brand, Ella's here.'

'Yes, so I see. Welcome,' Brand said, pulling Tina backwards against his chest and circling her with his arms.

Ella looked at Brand's possessive hands on Tina's swollen belly. In about a month she would be an aunt. She was happy for her sister, happy she'd found such profound love. But looking at this burgeoning family made her heart ache with the memory of what she'd lost, what she might never have.

Not that Ella remembered the love between her and Javier being the deep, absorbing glow that Tina and Brand shared. It had been giddier. A rush of feeling captured in a handful of memories. That first dazzling sight of him outside a makeshift hospital tent in Somalia. Their first tentative kiss. The sticky clumsiness of the first and only time they'd made love—the night before the malaria had hit her; two nights before he was taken.

Would it have grown into the special bond Tina and Brand had? Or burned itself out?

Standing in this hallway, she had never felt so unsure, so…empty. And so envious she was ashamed of herself. Maybe it had been a mistake to come. 'If you'll show me where to dump my stuff, I'll get out of your hair for a couple of hours.'

Tina looked dismayed. 'But I *want* you in my hair.'

'I'm catching up with someone.'

'Who? And where?'

Ella raised her eyebrows.

Tina made an exasperated sound. 'Oh, don't get all frosty.'

Ella rolled her eyes. 'She's a nurse, living in Hammersmith. We're meeting at a pub called the Hare and something. Harp? Carp? Does it matter? Can I go? Please, please, pretty please?'

Tina disentangled herself from her laughing husband's arms. 'All right, you two, give it a rest,' she said. 'Brand— show Ella her room. Then, Ella, go ahead and run away. But I don't expect to have to ambush you every time I want to talk to you.'

Ella kissed Tina's cheek. 'I promise to bore you rigid with tales of saline drips and bandage supplies and oxygen masks. By the time I get to the bedpan stories, you'll be begging me to go out.'

London in summer, what was there not to like? Aaron thought as he bounded up the stairs to Brand's house with Kiri on his back.

He went in search of Brand and Tina and found them in the kitchen, sitting at the table they used for informal family dining.

'Good news! We've found an apartment to rent,' he announced, swinging Kiri down to the floor.

Tina swooped on Kiri to kiss and tickle him, then settled him on the chair beside her with a glass of milk and a cookie. She bent an unhappy look on her husband. 'Why do all our house guests want to run away the minute they step foot in the place?'

'We've been underfoot for two weeks!' Aaron protested. 'And we're only moving down the street.'

'It's her sister,' Brand explained. 'Ella arrived today, stayed just long enough to drop her bag and ran off to some ill-named pub. Princess Tina is *not* amused.'

Aaron's heart stopped—at least that's what it felt like—and then jump-started violently. He imagined himself pale with shock, his eyes bugging out. He felt his hair follicles tingle. What had they said while he'd been sitting there stunned? What had he missed? He forced himself to take a breath, clear his mind, concentrate. Because the only coalescing thought in his head was that she was here. In London. In this house.

He'd thought he would never see her again. Hadn't wanted to see her again.

But she was here.

'...when we weren't really expecting her,' Tina said.

Huh? What? What had he missed while his brain had turned to mush?

'You know what she's like,' Brand said.

What? What's she like? Aaron demanded silently.

'What do you mean, what she's like?' Tina asked, sounding affronted.

Bless you, Tina.

'Independent. Very,' Brand supplied. 'She's used to looking after herself. And she's been in scarier places. Somehow I think she'll make it home tonight just fine.'

'Yes, but what time? And she hasn't even told me how long she's staying. Mum and Dad are going to want a report. How can I get the goss if she runs away when she should be talking to me?'

Brand gave her a warning look. 'If you fuss, she *will* go.' He turned to Aaron, changing the subject. 'So, Aaron, when do you move in?'

'A week,' Aaron said, racking his brain for a way to get the conversation casually back to Ella. 'Is that all right? I mean, if your sister is here…' he looked back at Tina '…maybe Kiri and I should leave earlier.' He'd lost it, obviously, because as the words left his mouth he wanted to recall them. 'We can easily move to a hotel.' Nope. That wasn't working for him either.

He caught himself rubbing his chest, over his heart. Realised it wasn't the first time he'd thought of Ella and done that.

'No way—you're not going any earlier than you have to,' Tina said immediately, and Aaron did the mental equivalent of swooning with relief.

And that really hit home.

The problem wasn't that he didn't want to see Ella—it was that he did.

On his third trip downstairs that night, Aaron faced the fact that he was hovering. He hadn't really come down for a glass of water. Or a book. Or a midnight snack.

Barefoot, rumpled, and edgy, he had come down looking for Ella.

On his fourth trip he gave up any pretence and took a seat in the room that opened off the dimly lit hall—a library-cum-family room. From there he could hear the front door open and yet be hidden. He turned on only one lamp; she wouldn't even know he was there, if he chose the sensible option and stayed hidden when the moment came.

He was, quite simply, beside himself.

Aaron helped himself to a Scotch, neat, while he waited.

His blood pressure must have been skyrocketing, because his heart had been thumping away at double speed all day.

And he had *excellent* blood pressure that *never* skyrocketed.

He knew precisely how long he'd been waiting—an hour and thirteen minutes—when he heard it.

Key hitting the lock. Lock clicking. Door opening.

A step on the tiled floor. He took a deep breath. Tried—failed—to steady his nerves. Heard the door close. Then nothing. No footsteps. A long moment passed. And then another sound. Something slumping against the wall or the door or the floor.

Was she hurt? Had she fallen?

Another sound. A sort of hiccup that wasn't a hiccup. A hitched breath.

He got to his feet and walked slowly to the door. Pushed it open silently. How had he ever thought he might sit in here and *not* go to her? And then he saw her and almost gasped! He was so monumentally unprepared for the punch of lust that hit him as he peered out like a thief.

She was sitting on the floor. Back against the door, knees up with elbows on them, hands jammed against her mouth. He could have sworn she was crying but there were no tears.

He saw the complete stillness that came into her as she realised someone was there.

And then she looked up.

CHAPTER EIGHT

AARON WALKED SLOWLY towards Ella. She was wearing a dark green skirt that had fallen up her thighs. A crumpled white top with a drawstring neckline. Leather slide-on sandals. Her hair was in loose waves, long, hanging over her shoulders—he'd never seen it loose before.

He felt a tense throb of some emotion he couldn't name, didn't want to name, as he reached her. He stood looking down at her, dry-mouthed. 'Where have you been?' he asked.

'Why are you here?' she countered, the remembered huskiness of her voice scattering his thoughts for a moment.

The way her skirt was draping at the top of her thighs was driving him insane. *Concentrate*. 'Here? I've been staying here. I'm working here. In London, I mean. Brand's film.' He couldn't even swallow. 'Didn't they tell you?'

'No,' Ella said, sighing, and easily, gracefully, got to her feet. 'Well, that's just great. I guess you're going to expect me to move out now, so I don't corrupt Kiri—or you.'

'No. I don't want you to move out. We'll be leaving in a week, anyway.'

'Oh, that makes me feel *so* much better. I'm sure I can avoid doing anything too immoral for one lousy week.'

Her silky skirt had settled back where it was supposed to be. It was short, so he could still see too much of her thighs. He jerked his gaze upwards and it collided with her breasts. He could make out the lace of her bra, some indistinguishable pale colour, under the white cotton of her top.

His skin had started to tighten and tingle, so he forced his eyes upwards again. Jammed his hands in his pockets as he caught the amused patience in her purple eyes.

'Why are you waiting up for me?' she asked.

He had no answer.

She sighed again—an exaggerated, world-weary sigh. 'What do you want, Aaron?'

'I want you,' he said. He couldn't quite believe he'd said it after everything that had gone on between them, but once it was out it seemed so easy. So clear. As though he hadn't spent agonising weeks telling himself she was the *last* thing he needed in his life and he'd been right to put the brakes on in Cambodia. 'I haven't stopped wanting you. Not for a second.'

Her eyebrows arched upwards. Even her eyebrows were sexy.

'I think we've been through this already, haven't we?' she asked softly, and started to move past him. 'One week— I'm sure you can resist me for that long, Sir Galahad.'

His hand shot out. He saw it move, faster than his brain was working. Watched his fingers grip her upper arm.

She turned to face him.

He didn't know what he intended to do next—but at least she wasn't looking amused any more.

She looked hard at him for a moment. And then she took his face between her hands and kissed him, fusing her mouth to his with forceful passion. She finished the kiss with one long lick against his mouth. Pulled back a tiny fraction, then seemed to change her mind and kissed him again. Pulled back. Stepped back. Looked him in the eye.

'Now what?' she asked, her breathing unsteady but her voice controlled. 'This is where you run away, isn't it? Because of Rebecca. Or Kiri. Or just because it's me.'

That strange other being still had control of him. It

was the only explanation for the way he jerked her close, crushed his arms around her and kissed her. He broke the contact only for a second at a time. To breathe. He wished he didn't even have to stop for that. His hands were everywhere, couldn't settle. In her hair, on her back, gripping her bottom, running up her sides. And through it all he couldn't seem to stop kissing her.

He could hear her breathing labouring, like his. When his hands reached her breasts, felt the nipples jutting into his palms through two layers of clothing, he shuddered. He finally stopped kissing her, but kept his mouth on hers, still, reaching for control. 'Now what?' He repeated her question without moving his mouth from hers, after a brief struggle to remember what she'd asked. Kissed her again.

Ella wrapped her arms around his waist and he groaned. He looked down into her face. 'There doesn't seem to be much point in running away, because you're always there. So now, Ella, I get to have you.'

One long, fraught moment of limbo.

He didn't know what he'd do if she said no, he was so on fire for her.

But she didn't say no. She said, 'Okay. Let's be stupid, then, and get it done.'

Not exactly a passionate acquiescence, but he'd take it. Take her, any way he could get her.

He kissed her again, pulling her close, letting her feel how hard he was for her, wanting her to know. Both of his hands slipped into her hair. It was heavy, silky. Another time he would like to stroke his fingers through it, but not now. Now he was too desperate. He dragged fistfuls of it, using it to tilt her head back, anchoring her so he could kiss her harder still. 'Come upstairs,' he breathed against her mouth. 'Come with me.'

'All yours,' Ella said in that mocking way she had—but Aaron didn't care. He grabbed her hand and walked quickly to the staircase, pulling her up it at a furious pace.

'Which way to your room?' he asked.

Silently, she guided him to it.

The room next to his.

Fate.

The moment they were inside he was yanking her top up and over her head, fumbling with her skirt until it lay pool-like at her feet. The bedside lamp was on and he said a silent prayer of thanks because it meant he could see her. She stood before him in pale pink underwear so worn it was almost transparent, tossing her hair back over her shoulders. He swallowed. He wanted to rip her underwear to shreds to get to her. It was like a madness. Blood pounding through his veins, he stripped off his T-shirt and shoved his jeans and underwear off roughly.

She was watching him, following what he was doing as she kicked off her sandals. Aaron forced himself to stand still and let her see him. He hoped she liked what she saw.

Ella came towards him and circled his biceps with her hands—at least, partly; his biceps were too big for her to reach even halfway around. Aaron remembered that she liked tattoos. His tattooed armbands were broad and dark and intricately patterned—and, yes, she clearly did like what she saw. The tattoos had taken painful hours to complete and, watching her eyes light up as she touched them, he'd never been happier to have them. He hoped during the night she would see the more impressive tattoo on his back, but he couldn't imagine taking his eyes off her long enough to turn around.

He couldn't wait any longer to see her naked. He reached for her hips, and she obligingly released his arms and stepped closer. She let him push her panties down, stepped free of them when they hit the floor. Then she let him work the back fastening of her bra as she rested against him, compliant. As he wrestled with the bra, he could feel her against him, thigh to thigh, hip to hip. The tangle of soft hair against his erection had his heart bashing so hard and fast in his chest he thought he might have a coronary. Oh, he liked the feel of it. She was perfect. Natural and perfect. His hands were shaking so badly as he tried to undo her bra he thought he was going to have to tear it off, but it gave at last. Her breasts, the areoles swollen, nipples sharply erect, pressed into his chest as he wrenched the bra off. He was scared to look at her in case he couldn't stop himself falling on her like a ravening beast…but at the same time he was desperate to see her.

'Ella,' he said, his voice rough as he stepped back just enough to look. With one hand he touched her face. The other moved lower to the dark blonde hair at the apex of her thighs. He combed through it with trembling fingers. Lush and beautiful. He could feel the moisture seeping into it. Longed to taste it. Taste her. He dropped to his knees, kissed her there.

Aaron loved the hitch in her voice as his fingers and tongue continued to explore. 'I do want you, Aaron. Just so you know. Tonight, I do want you,' Ella said, and it was like a flare went off in his head. He got to his feet, dragged her into his arms, holding her close while his mouth dived on hers. He moved the few steps that would enable him to tumble her backwards onto the bed and come down on her.

The moment they hit the bed he had his hands on her thighs and was pushing her legs apart.

'Wait,' she said in his ear. 'Condoms. Bedside table. In the drawer.'

Somehow, Aaron managed to keep kissing her as he fumbled with the drawer, pulled it open and reached inside. His fingers mercifully closed on one quickly—thankfully they were loose in there.

He kissed her once more, long and luscious, before breaking to free the condom from its packaging. Kneeling between her thighs, he smoothed it on, and Ella raised herself on her elbows to watch. She looked irresistibly wicked, and as he finished the job he leaned forward to take one of her nipples in his mouth. She arched forward and gasped and he decided penetration could wait. She tasted divine. Exquisite. The texture of her was maddeningly good, the feel of her breasts as he held them in his hands heavy and firm. He could keep his mouth on her for hours, he thought, just to hear the sounds coming from her as his tongue circled, licked.

But Ella was shifting urgently beneath him, trying to position him with hands and thighs and the rest of her shuddering body. 'Inside,' she said, gasping. 'Come inside me. Now.'

With one thrust he buried himself in her, and then he couldn't seem to help himself. He pulled back and thrust deeply into her again. And again and again. He was kissing her mouth, her eyes, her neck as he drove into her over and over. The sound of her gasping cries urged him on until he felt her clench around him. She sucked in a breath, whooshed it out. Again. Once more. She was coming, tense and beautiful around him, and he'd never been so turned on in his life. He slid his arms under her on the bed, dragged her up against him and thrust his tongue inside her mouth. And with one last, hard push of his hips he came, hard and strong.

As the last waves of his climax receded, the fog of pure lust cleared from Aaron's head and he was suddenly and completely appalled.

Had he hurt her? Something primal had overtaken him, and he hadn't felt in control of himself. And he was *never, ever* out of control.

He kissed her, trying for gentleness but seemingly unable to achieve it even now, because the moment his mouth touched hers he was out of control again.

Aaron couldn't seem to steady his breathing. It was somehow beautiful to Ella to know that.

He sure liked kissing. Even now, after he'd exhausted

both of them and could reasonably be expected to roll over and go to sleep, he was kissing her. In between those unsteady breaths of his. He seemed to have an obsession with her mouth. Nobody had ever kissed her quite like this before. It was sweet, and sexy as hell, to be kissed like he couldn't stop. It was getting her aroused again. She'd sneered at herself as she'd put those condoms in the drawer, but now all she could think was: did she have enough?

He shifted at last, rolling onto his back beside her. 'Sorry, I know I'm heavy. And you're so slender,' he said.

'It's just the—' She stopped. How did you describe quickly the way long hours, fatigue and illness sapped the calories out of you at breakneck speed? 'Nothing, really. I'm already gaining weight. It happens fast when I'm not working.'

'So you can lose it all over again the next time,' Aaron said, and Ella realised she didn't have to explain after all.

His eyes closed as he reached for her hand.

Okay, so now he'll go to sleep, Ella thought, and was annoyed with herself for bringing him to her room. If they'd gone to his room she could have left whenever she wanted; but what did a woman say, do, to get a man to leave?

But Aaron, far from showing any signs of sleep, brought her hand to his mouth and rolled onto his side, facing her. He released her hand but then pulled her close so that her side was fitted against his front, and nuzzled his nose into the side of her neck. He slid one of his hands down over her belly and between her legs. 'Did I hurt you, Ella?'

Huh? 'Hurt me?'

'Yes. I was rough. I'm sorry.'

As he spoke his fingers were slipping gently against the delicate folds of her sex. It was like he was trying to soothe her. Her heart stumbled, just a little, as she realised what he was doing. And he was looking at her so seriously while he did it. He had the most remarkably beautiful eyes. And, of course, he was ridiculously well endowed, but she'd been so hot and ready for him it hadn't hurt. It had been more erotic than anything she could have dreamed.

How did she tell him that his fingers, now, weren't soothing? That what he was doing to her was gloriously *good*, but not soothing?

'No, Aaron, you— Ah...' She had to pause for a moment as the touch of his fingers became almost unbearable. 'I mean, no. I mean, you didn't hurt me.' She paused again. 'Aaron,' she said, almost breathless with desire, 'I suggest you go and get rid of that condom. And then hurry back and get another one.'

He frowned, understanding but wary. 'You're sure? I mean— Oh,' as her hands found him. 'I guess you're sure.' He swung his legs off the side of the bed and was about to stand but Ella, on her knees in an instant, embraced him from behind. Her mouth touched between his shoulder blades then he felt her tongue trace the pattern of the dragon inked across his back.

'I don't want to leave you,' he said huskily. 'Come with me.'

Ella, needing no second invitation, was out of the bed and heading for the en suite bathroom half a step behind him.

Ella trailed the fingers of one hand along his spine and snapped on the light with the fingers of her other. 'Oh, my, it's even better in the full light.'

Aaron discarded the condom and started to turn around. She imagined he thought he was going to take her in his arms.

'No, you don't. It's my turn,' Ella said.

She turned on the shower, drew Aaron in beside her, and as he reached for her again she shook her head, laughing, and dodged out of the way. 'I'm glad this is such a small shower cubicle,' she said throatily. 'Close. Tight.' She spun Aaron roughly to face the tiled wall, slammed him up against it and grabbed the cake of soap from its holder.

Lathering her hands, his skin, she plastered herself against his back, moving her breasts sensually against his beautiful tattoo as she reached around to fondle him. 'I love the size of you,' she said, as his already impressive erection grew in her hands. 'I want to take you like this, from behind.'

'I think I'd take you any way I could get you,' Aaron said, groaning as she moved her hands between his legs. He was almost panting and Ella had never felt so beautiful, so powerful.

At last.

She could have this, at last.

As her hands slid, slipped, squeezed, Aaron rested his forehead against the shower wall and submitted.

Aaron watched as Ella slept. She'd fallen into sleep like a stone into the ocean.

No wonder. Aaron had been all over her from the moment they'd left the shower. Inexhaustible. He didn't think he'd understood the word lust until tonight. If he could have breathed her into his lungs, he would have.

He didn't know why he wanted her so badly. But even having had her three times, he couldn't get her close enough. She was in his blood. What a pathetic cliché. But true.

The bedside light was still on, so he could see her face. She looked serious in her sleep. Fretful. Aaron pulled her closer, kissed one of her wickedly arched eyebrows. He breathed in the scent of her hair. Looking at her was almost painful. The outrageous loveliness of her.

Sighing, he turned off the bedside light. It was past five in the morning and he should go back to his room, but he wanted to hold her.

He thought about their last meeting, in Cambodia. The horrible things they'd said to each other. They'd made a pact to forget they'd ever met. How had they gone from that to being here in bed now?

What had he been thinking when he'd left the library, when he'd seen her slumped against the front door with her fists jammed against her mouth?

On a mundane level, he'd thought she must have been drinking. Or maybe he'd hoped that, so he could pigeon-hole her back where he'd wanted to.

Oh, he had no doubt she regularly drank to excess—it fitted with the general wildness he sensed in her. But to-night she'd smelled only like that tantalising perfume. And her mouth had tasted like lime, not booze. It was obvious, really, when he pieced together what he knew about her, what he'd seen of her: she wouldn't let Tina see her out of control. She would be sober and serene and together in this house. The way her family expected her to be. The way she'd been described to him before he'd ever met her.

He thought about the day he'd held her as she'd cried over Bourey's death. And the other boy, Sann, whose death had been infinitely painful for her. Things she didn't want anyone to know.

She was so alone. She chose to be, so her fears and sorrows wouldn't hurt anyone else.

Aaron pulled her closer. She roused, smiled sleepily at him. 'You should go,' she said, but then she settled herself against him and closed her eyes, so he stayed exactly where he was.

Wondering how he could both have her and keep things simple.

CHAPTER NINE

ELLA ROLLED RESTLESSLY, absent-mindedly pulling Aaron's pillow close and breathing in the scent of him, wondering what time he'd left.

She didn't know what had come over her. She'd finally managed to get past second base—way past it, with a blistering home run. And it had been with her brother-in-law's friend under her sister's roof. Not that there had seemed to be much choice about it. It had felt like…well, like fate.

And Aaron wouldn't tell, she reassured herself.

She got out of bed, reached for her robe, and then just sat on the edge of the bed with the robe in her lap. She didn't want to go downstairs. Because downstairs meant reality. It meant Tina and Brand. And Aaron—not Lover Aaron but Friend-of-her-sister Aaron. Daddy Aaron.

She stood slowly and winced a little. It had been a very active night. A fabulous night. But she would have been relieved even if it had been the worst sex of her life instead of the best. Because she had needed it.

Yesterday she'd forced herself to think about Sann. Tina's pregnancy was an immutable fact, and Ella knew she had to come to terms with it; she couldn't run away every time a pang of envy hit her. So she had deliberately taken the memories out of mothballs and examined them one by one. A kind of desensitisation therapy.

But forcing the memories had been difficult. So when

she'd come home to find Aaron there, sex with him had offered an escape. A talisman to keep her sad thoughts at bay, hopefully ward off the bad dreams.

She had been prepared to make a bargain with herself—sex and a nightmare-free night, in exchange for guilt and shame today.

And she did feel the guilt.

Just not the shame.

What did that mean?

Get it together, Ella. It was just a one-night stand. People do it all the time. Simple.

Except it was *not* simple. Because she hadn't managed it before. And she recalled—too vividly—Aaron walking towards her in the hallway, and how much she'd wanted him as their eyes had met. She was deluding herself if she thought she'd only been interested in a nightmare-free night. Oh, he had certainly materialised at a point when she'd been at her lowest ebb and open to temptation, but she had wanted him, wanted the spark, the flash of almost unbearable attraction that had been there in Cambodia.

But now what?

Nothing had really changed. All the reasons not to be together in Cambodia were still there. Kiri. Rebecca. Javier.

Definitely time to return to reality.

Ella tossed the robe aside and strode into the bathroom.

She looked at herself in the mirror. Her mouth looked swollen. Nothing she could do to hide that, except maybe dab a bit of foundation on it to minimise the rawness. She could see small bruises on her upper arms—easily covered. There were more bruises on her hips, but nobody would be seeing those. She sucked in a breath as more memories of the night filled her head. Aaron had been insatiable—and she had loved it. She had more than a few sore spots. And, no doubt, so did he. Like the teeth marks she'd left on his inner thigh.

Ella caught herself smiling. Aaron had called her a vampire, but he hadn't minded. He hadn't minded at all, if the passionate lovemaking that had followed had been any indication.

The smile slipped.

He would have come to his senses by now. Remembered that he didn't like her. Didn't want her near his son.

Time to store the memory and move on.

Tina checked the clock on the kitchen wall as Ella walked in. 'So lunch, not breakfast.'

'Oh, dear, am I going to have to punch a time clock whenever I come and go?'

'Oh, for heaven's sake!'

'Well, sorry, Tina, but really you're as bad as Mom. Just sit down and tell me stories about Brand as a doting father while I make us both something to eat.'

Ella forced herself to look at Tina's stomach as she edged past her sister. Bearable. She could do this.

Tina groaned as she levered herself onto a stool at the kitchen counter. 'I am so over the doting father thing. We've done the practice drive to the hospital seven times. And he's having food cravings. It's not funny, Ella!'

But Ella laughed anyway as she laid a variety of salad vegetables on a chopping board. 'Where is he now?'

'On the set, thank goodness. Which reminds me—I didn't tell you we have other guests.'

Ah. Control time. Ella busied herself pulling out drawers.

'What are you looking for?' Tina asked.

Ella kept her head down and pulled open another drawer. 'Knife.'

'Behind you, knife block on the counter,' Tina said, and Ella turned her back on her sister and took her time selecting a knife.

'Where was I?' Tina asked. 'Oh yes, Aaron. Aaron James and his son. You know them, of course.'

Indistinct mumble.

'Aaron is in Brand's movie,' Tina continued. 'That's why he's in London. They've been staying with us, but they're only here for another week.'

'Why's that?' Ella asked, desperately nonchalant, and started chopping as though her life depended on the precision of her knife action.

'Aaron was always intending to find a place of his own, and yesterday he did.'

'So...would it be easier if I moved out for the week? Because I have friends I was going to see and I—'

'What is wrong with you people? Everyone wants to move out. We've got enough room to house a baseball team! And, anyway, I need you to help me look after Kiri.'

Uh-oh. 'What? Why?'

'Kiri's nanny had some crisis and can't get here until next week. Aaron's due on set tomorrow so I volunteered. I told him it would be good practice. And Kiri is adorable.'

Ella's hand was a little unsteady so she put down the knife. Kiri. She would be looking after Kiri. Aaron wouldn't want that. 'But what about—? I mean, shouldn't he have stayed in Sydney? With his mother?' *Drugs, Ella, drugs.* 'Or—or...someone?'

Tina looked like she was weighing something up. 'The thing is—oh, I don't know if... Okay, look, this is completely confidential, Ella.'

Tina put up her hands at the look on Ella's face. 'Yes, I know you're a glued-shut clam. Aaron is just sensitive about it. Or Rebecca is, and he's respecting that. Rebecca is in rehab. Drugs. Apparently, she auditioned for a role in a new TV show while Aaron was in Cambodia, but didn't get it. The director told her if she didn't get things under control, she'd never work again.'

'That's...tough. How—how's Kiri coping with the separation?'

'Aaron does all the parenting, so it's not as big a deal as you'd think. He has sole custody. But that's not to say

Rebecca doesn't see Kiri whenever she wants. It's just that the drugs have been a problem for some time.'

'Oh. *Sole* custody. Huh.' Ella scooped the chopped salad vegetables into a large bowl. 'But should he...Aaron... should he be here while she's there?'

'Well, they *are* divorced, although sometimes I wonder if Rebecca really believes that. But in any case, it's not a case of him shirking responsibility. Aaron found the clinic—in California, while he was over there auditioning for a new crime show—because Rebecca wanted to do it away from her home city where it might have leaked to the press. And he got her settled in over there, which pushed back filming here so it's all over the place, but what can you do? And of course he's paying, despite having settled a fortune on her during the divorce. He'll be back and forth with Kiri, who thinks it's a spa! But there are strict rules about visiting. Anyway, I hope it works, because Aaron needs to move on, and he won't until Rebecca gets her act together.' She slanted an uncomfortably speculative look at Ella.

'Don't even!' Ella said, interpreting without difficulty.

'Come on, Ella. He's totally, completely hot.'

Ella concentrated on drizzling dressing over the salad.

'Hot as Hades,' Tina said, tightening the thumbscrews. 'But also sweet as heaven. He is amazingly gentle with Kiri. And with me, too. He took me for an ultrasound last week. I had a fall down the stairs and I was petrified.'

Ella hurried to her sister's side, hugged her. 'But everything's all right. You're fine, the baby's fine, right?'

'Yes, but Brand was filming, and I couldn't bring myself to call him. Because I'd already had one fall on the stairs, and he was furious because I was hurrying.'

'Well *stop* hurrying, Tina.' Tentatively, Ella reached and placed a hand on Tina's stomach. The baby kicked suddenly and Ella's hand jerked away—or would have, if Tina hadn't stopped it, flattened it where it was, kept it there.

Tina looked at her sister, wonder and joy in her eyes, and Ella felt her painful envy do a quantum shift.

'So anyway, Aaron,' Tina said. 'He was home. Actually, he saw it happen. I don't know which of us was more upset. He must have cajoled and threatened and who knows what else to get the ultrasound arranged so quickly. He knew it was the only way I'd believe everything was all right. And he let me talk him into not calling Brand until we got the all clear and I was back home.' Tina smiled broadly. 'Unbelievably brave! Brand exploded about being kept in the dark, as Aaron knew he would, but Aaron took it all in his stride. He just let Brand wear himself out, and then took him out for a beer.'

Ella tried not to be charmed, but there was something lovely about the story. 'Well I'm here now to take care of you,' she said, navigating the lump in her throat.

'And I'm very glad.' Tina took Ella's left hand and placed it alongside the right one that was already pressed to her stomach. 'It really scared me, Ella. But I'm not telling you all this to worry you—and don't, whatever you do, tell Mum and Dad.'

'I wouldn't dream of it.'

'I just wanted you to know. I mean, you're my sister! And a nurse. And...well, you're my sister. And I wanted to explain about Aaron. Don't disapprove of him because of Rebecca. He takes his responsibilities very seriously. He practically raised his three young sisters, you know, after his parents died, and he was only eighteen. They idolise him. So does Kiri. And so do I, now. He'll do the right thing by Rebecca, divorced or not, and—more importantly—the right thing by Kiri.'

Ella moved her hands as Tina reached past her to dig into the salad bowl and extract a sliver of carrot.

'You're going to need more than salad, Ella,' Tina said. 'You're like a twig.'

'Yes, yes, yes, I know.' Ella moved back into the food preparation area. 'I'll make some sandwiches.'

'Better make enough for Aaron and Kiri—they should be back any minute.'

For the barest moment Ella paused. Then she opened the fridge and rummaged inside it. 'Where are they?'

'The park. Aaron's teaching Kiri how to play cricket.'

'Ah,' Ella said meaninglessly, and started slapping various things between slices of bread like she was in a trance.

'Yeah, I think that's enough for the entire Australian and English cricket teams,' Tina said eventually.

'Oh. Sorry. Got carried away.'

Breathe, Ella ordered herself when she heard Aaron calling out to Tina from somewhere in the house as she was positioning the platter of sandwiches on the table.

'In the kitchen,' Tina called back.

Tina turned to Ella. 'And I guess you'll tell me later about last night. Probably not fit for children's ears, anyway.'

Ella froze, appalled. Tina *knew*?

'I mean, come on, your mouth,' Tina teased. 'Or are you going to tell me you got stung by a bee?'

'Who got stung by a bee?' Aaron asked, walking in.

CHAPTER TEN

'OH, NOBODY,' TINA said airily.

But Aaron wasn't looking at Tina. He was looking at Ella.

And from the heat in his eyes Ella figured he was remembering last night in Technicolor detail. Ella felt her pulse kick in response. *Insane.*

'Nice to see you again, Ella,' he said.

Could Tina hear that caress in his voice? Ella frowned fiercely at him.

He winked at her. Winked!

'Kiri can't wait to see you,' he continued. 'He's got a present for you—he's just getting it.'

'Oh, that's— Oh.' She gave up the effort of conversation. She was out of her depth. Shouldn't Aaron be keeping Kiri *away* from her? Ella wondered if Aaron had taken a cricket ball to the head. They were deadly, cricket balls.

Ella was aware a phone was ringing. She noted, dimly, Tina speaking. Sensed Tina leaving the room.

And then Aaron was beside her, taking her hand, lifting it to his mouth, kissing it. The back, the palm. His tongue on her fingers.

'Stop,' she whispered, but the air seemed to have been sucked out of the room and she wasn't really sure the word had left her mouth.

Aaron touched one finger to her swollen bottom lip. 'I'm sorry. Is it sore?'

Ella knocked his hand away. 'What's gotten into you?'

The next moment she found herself pulled into Aaron's arms. 'I've got a solution,' he said, as though she would have *any* idea what he was talking about! Yep, cricket ball to the head.

'A solution for what?'

'You and me. It's based on the KISS principle.'

'The what?'

'KISS: keep it simple, stupid.'

'*Simple* would be to forget last night happened.'

Ella started to pull away, but he tightened his arms.

He rested his forehead on hers. 'Let me. Just for a moment.'

Somehow she found her arms around his waist, and she was just standing there, letting him hold her as though it were any everyday occurrence. *Uh-oh. Dangerous.*

'There's no solution needed for a one-night stand,' she said.

He released her, stepped back. 'I don't want a one-night stand.'

'Um—I think you're a little late to that party.'

'Why?'

'Because we've already had one.'

'So tonight will make it a two-night stand. And tomorrow night a three-night stand, and so on.'

'We agreed, in Cambodia—'

'Cambodia-shmodia.'

'Huh?'

'That was then. This is now.'

'Did you get hit in the head with a cricket ball?'

'What?'

'You're talking like you've got a head injury.'

'It's relief. It's making me light-headed. Because for the

first time since Tina and Brand's wedding I know what I'm doing.'

'Well, I don't know what you're doing. I don't think I want to know. I mean, the *KISS* principle?'

'I want you. You want me. We get to have each other. Simple.'

'Um, *not* simple. Kiri? Rebecca? The fact you don't like me? That you don't even know me?'

'Kiri and Rebecca—they're for me to worry about, not you.'

'You're wrong. Tina wants me to help her look after Kiri. Surely you don't want that? Aren't you scared I'll corrupt him or something?'

'Ella, if I know one thing, it's that you would never do anything to hurt Kiri. I've always known it. What I said, in Cambodia...' He shrugged. 'I was being a moron. Projecting, you called it, and you were right. There. I'm denouncing myself.'

'I don't want to play happy families.'

'Neither do I. That's why your relationship with Kiri is separate from my relationship with Kiri, which is separate from my relationship with you. And before you throw Rebecca at me—it's the same deal. You don't even have a relationship with her, so that's purely my issue, not yours.'

'You said the R word. I don't want a relationship—and neither do you.'

Aaron took her hand and lifted it so that it rested on his chest, over his heart. 'Our relationship is going to be purely sexual. Casual sex, that's what you said you wanted. All you were interested in. Well, I can do casual sex.'

'You're not a casual kind of guy, Aaron,' she said.

He smiled, shrugged. 'I'll *make* myself that kind of guy. I said last night I would take you any way I could get you. We're two adults seeking mutual satisfaction and nothing more. An emotion-free zone, which means we can keep it strictly between us—Tina and Brand don't need to know, it's none of Rebecca's business, and Kiri is…well, protected, because your relationship with him is nothing to do with your relationship with me. Simple. Agreed?'

Ella hesitated—not saying yes, but not the automatic 'no' she should be rapping out either. Before she could get her brain into gear, the kitchen door opened.

As Ella pulled her hand free from where, she'd just realised, it was still being held against Aaron's heart, Kiri ran in, saw her, stopped, ran again. Straight at her.

'Kiri, my darling,' she said, and picked him up.

She kissed his forehead. He hugged her, his arms tight around her neck, and didn't seem to want to let go. So she simply moved backwards, with him in her arms, until she felt a chair behind her legs and sat with him on her lap.

Kiri kissed her cheek and Ella's chest tightened dangerously. Kiri removed one arm from around Ella's neck and held out his hand to her. His fist was closed around something.

'What's this?' Ella asked.

Kiri opened his fingers to reveal an unremarkable rock. 'From the beach where you live,' he said. 'Monica.'

Ella smiled at him. 'You remembered?'

Kiri nodded and Ella hugged him close. Santa Monica. He'd been to Santa Monica, and remembered it was where she lived.

She felt a hand on her shoulder and looked up. Aaron was beside her, looking down at her, and she couldn't breathe.

The door opened and Tina breezed in. She paused—an infinitesimal pause—as she took in Aaron's hand on Ella's shoulder, Kiri on her lap.

Aaron slowly removed his hand, but stayed where he was.

'So,' Tina said brightly, 'let's eat.'

* * *

Lunch was dreadful.

Kiri was at least normal, chattering away about Cambodia, about Disneyland, about Sydney, completely at ease.

But Tina was giving off enough gobsmacked vibes to freak Ella out completely.

And Aaron was high-beaming Ella across the table as though he could get her on board with the force of his eyes alone—and if they were really going to carry on a secret affair, he'd have to find his poker face pretty damned fast.

If? Was she really going the 'if' route? Not the 'no way' route?

Casual sex.

Could she do it? She'd liked having someone close to her last night. She'd felt alive in a way she hadn't for such a long time. And she hadn't had the dreaded nightmares with Aaron beside her. So. A chance to feel alive again. With no strings attached. No emotions, which she couldn't offer him anyway.

But, ironic though it was, Aaron James seemed to have the ability to make her want to clean up her act. Maybe it was the way he was with Kiri, or that he cared so much about an ex-wife who clearly made his life a misery, or his general tendency to turn into Sir Galahad at regular intervals and save damsels in distress—his sisters, ex-wife, Tina, her.

Whatever the reason, if she wanted to rehabilitate her self-image, was an affair the way to start? Every time she'd let a guy pick her up, determined to do it, just do it and move on, she'd hated herself. Now that she'd gone the whole nine yards, wouldn't she end up hating herself even more? Especially if it became a regular arrangement?

'I'll clear up,' Tina said, when lunch couldn't be stretched out any more.

'Ella and I can manage,' Aaron said quickly.

'No, *Ella and I* can manage,' Tina insisted. She stood and arched her back, grimaced.

Ella got to her feet. 'You should rest,' she told her sister. 'And you...' with an almost fierce look at Aaron '...should get Kiri into bed for a nap. He's sleepy.' She started gathering empty plates.

Aaron looked like he was about to argue so Ella simply turned her back on him and took an armload of plates to the sink. She stayed there, clattering away, refusing to look up, willing him to leave.

And then, at last, Tina spoke. 'The coast is clear. You can come up for air.'

Ella raised her head cautiously and waited for the inevitable.

'What's going on?' Tina asked simply.

'If you mean between me and Aaron, nothing.'

'Of course I mean you and Aaron. He's gaga. It's so obvious.'

'He's not *gaga*.'

'Oh, I beg to differ.'

'We just... We just got to know each other in Cambodia. I called in to check on Kiri a few times when he was ill with dengue fever and Aaron was out in the field, so he's...grateful. I guess.'

Tina snorted out a laugh. 'If that's gratitude, I'd like to get me a piece of it. I'm going to remind Brand tonight just how grateful he is that he met me.'

Ella had stayed out as long as public transport allowed but Aaron was nevertheless waiting for her when she got back, leaning against the library door.

No reprieve.

She'd three-quarters expected this, though, so she had a plan.

She would be *that* Ella—the cool, calm, untouchable one—so he knew exactly what he'd get if he pursued this insanity that she couldn't quite bring herself to reject. With luck, he would run a mile away from her, the way he'd run in Cambodia, and spare them both the heartache she feared would be inevitable if they went down this path.

If not...well, they'd see.

'Are you going to wait up for me every night?' she asked, in the amused tone that had infuriated him in the past.

'I can wait in your bed if you prefer.'

The wind having effectively been taken out of her sails, Ella headed slowly up the stairs without another word. Aaron followed her into her room, reached for her.

'Wait,' she said, stepping back. 'You really want to do this?'

'Yes.'

'One hundred per cent sure?'

'Yes.'

She sighed. 'It's going to end in tears, you know.'

'I'll take my chances.'

Another sigh. 'Okay, then—but, first, ground rules.'

He nodded, deadly serious.

'No PDAs,' she said. 'If this is casual sex, it stays in my bedroom—or your bedroom. No touchy-feely stuff beyond bed. And *absolutely* nothing in front of Tina or Brand or Kiri.'

'Agreed.'

'When one or the other of us decides the arrangement is over there will be no questions, no comments, no recriminations, no clinging. I will let you go as easily as that...' she clicked her fingers '...if you're the one ending things. And I expect you to do the same.'

He narrowed his eyes. 'Agreed.'

'No prying into my private life.'

He looked at her.

'Agreed?' she asked impatiently.

'I don't know what "prying" means to you—you're supersensitive about things other people consider normal conversation, and I don't want you taking a machete to my head if I ask what any reasonable person would think is an innocuous question.'

'If you think I'm unreasonable, why do you want to go down this path?'

He smiled, a smile that held the promise of hot, steamy sex. 'Oh, I think you know why, Ella.'

She was blushing again.

'What about if I agree that you are under no obligation to tell me anything that makes you uncomfortable?' he asked.

She digested that. 'Fair enough. Agreed. And ditto for you.'

'No need. You can ask me anything you want, and I'll answer you.'

That threw her, but she nodded. 'But I won't ask. Any conditions from your side?'

'One. Monogamy. Nobody else, while you're sleeping with me.'

'Agreed,' she said, but she tinkled out a little laugh to suggest she thought that was quaint. 'Anything else?'

'No. So take off your clothes.'

CHAPTER ELEVEN

'I DO LIKE a masterful man,' Ella said. And then she reached for the hem of her dress.

But Aaron stopped her. 'I've changed my mind,' he said. 'Come here.'

Ella stepped towards him, her eyebrows raised in that practised, disdainful way that seemed to aggravate him.

When she reached him, he took the neckline of her cotton dress in his hands, and ripped the dress down the front.

A surprised 'Oh...' whooshed out of her. There went the practised disdain.

She looked up at him. His face was stark as he dragged her bra down her arms, imprisoning her with the straps, and bent his head to her breasts. He sucked one nipple, hard, into his mouth, and she gasped. Moved to the other. He eased back to look into her eyes as he pushed her tattered dress almost casually over her hips until it dropped to the floor. 'I'll buy you another,' he said.

She couldn't speak, couldn't raise her defensive shield of indifference. Could only wait and watch. Her arms were still trapped, and he made no move to free them. Instead, he brought his hands up to cup her breasts, thumbs smoothing across her nipples, and then lowered his mouth again.

How much time had passed—a minute? Ten? Longer? He wouldn't let her move, just kept up that steady pressure, hands and lips, until she was almost weeping with pleasure. Ella was desperate to touch him, but every time she tried to reach around to unhook her bra and free herself, he stymied her.

At last he stepped back, examined her with one long, lascivious look from her head to her toes. Then his hands went to the front of her panties and she felt, heard, the fine cotton tear. 'I'll replace those too,' he said softly, and then her breath shuddered out, rough and choppy, as one of his hands reached between her legs. Within moments she was shuddering as the pleasure tore through her like a monsoon. Hot, wet, wild.

He spun her, unhooking her bra with a swift efficiency that seemed to scorn his earlier languorous attention to her body. With the same speed, he stripped off his own clothes. Then his hands were on her again, arousing her, preparing her, as he backed the two of them towards the bed.

He fell onto the bed, on his back, and dragged her on top of him. 'Here, let me.' His voice was hoarse and urgent as he positioned her over him, moving her legs so that they fell on either side of his and thrusting blindly towards her centre.

'Wait,' she said.

It took only moments for her to raise herself, straddling him with her knees on each side of his straining body. She reached over him, grabbed a condom from the drawer. She ripped the package open with her teeth, slid the sheath onto him with slow, steady movements. Smoothing it as he jumped against her hand. And then she took him inside her with one undulating swirl of her hips. Stilled, keeping him there, not letting him move, deep inside her.

'No,' she said, as he started to buck upwards against her. 'Let me.' And, rising and falling in smooth, steady waves, she tightened herself around him until he gasped her name. Clutching her hips, he jammed her down on top of him and exploded.

Ella, following him into ecstasy, collapsed on top of him.

She stayed there, spent, as his hands threaded through her hair, stroking and sliding.

She wanted to stay like that all night, with Aaron inside her, his hands in her hair, his mouth close enough to kiss.

Except that he hadn't kissed her. Not once.

For some reason, she didn't like that.

It's just casual sex, she reminded herself.

On that thought, she disengaged herself from his body and got off the bed. Pulling her hair back over her shoulders, she smiled serenely down at him. 'Excellent, thank you,' she said. 'But there's no need for you to stay. I'll see you tomorrow night.'

Tina had assorted chores to do the next day, so she left Kiri in Ella's sole company.

Ella had taken him to the park to practise catching the cricket ball. Was that the hardest, unkindest ball in international sport? Ella thought so, as she looked at her bruised shin.

So for the afternoon she'd chosen a more intellectual pursuit—painting. It was a challenge to keep Kiri's paint set in the vicinity of the special child-sized activity table Tina had moved into the library for him, but they'd accomplished it.

As assorted paintings, laid out across every available surface, were drying, she and Kiri curled up together in one of the massive leather chairs, where she entertained him by letting him play with her cellphone.

She was laughing at Kiri's attempt at an emoticon-only text message when Aaron walked in.

'Shouldn't you be on set?' she asked, sitting up straighter.

'I'm on a break so thought I'd come back to the house. What happened to your leg?'

'Cricket-ball injury. That's a sport I am never going to figure out.' She gestured around the room. 'Check out Kiri's paintings while you're here. Which one's for Dad, Kiri?'

Kiri scrambled out of the chair. 'Two of them. Here's Mum...' He was pointing out a painting of a black-haired woman in an orange dress. 'And here's Ella.' In her nursing uniform.

Ella felt her stomach drop with a heavy thud. Just what the man needed; his ex-wife and his current lover, as depicted by his son, who knew nothing of the tension in either relationship.

But Aaron was smiling like it was the most wonderful gift in the world. 'Fabbo. One day, when you're famous, these are going to be worth a fortune.'

Kiri giggled, and then went to perch back with Ella. 'Ella's teaching me the phone,' he confided. 'I called Tina.'

'You're not international roaming, are you?' Aaron asked. 'That will cost you a fortune.'

Ella shrugged, not having the heart to deny Kiri. 'They're only short calls.' She smiled at Kiri as she scrolled through her contact list.

'See, Kiri, there's Dad's number. If you hit this, it will call him. Yes, perfect.'

Aaron's phone rang, and he dutifully answered it and had a moment's conversation with Kiri.

And then Aaron tossed metaphorical hands in the air. He asked Ella for her phone number, punched it into his contact list, then handed his phone to Kiri, showed him the entry and let him call her.

She and Kiri chatted for a while, as though they were on opposite sides of the world instead of sitting together.

Then Kiri looked pleadingly at his father. 'Dad, can I have a phone?'

Aaron laughed. 'Who do you need to call, mate?' he asked.

'You. Mum. Tina. Jenny. And Ella.'

'Well, calling Ella might be tricky,' Aaron explained,

and lifted Kiri into his arms. 'Because we'll never know where in the world she is. And we don't want to wake her up at midnight!'

An excellent reminder, Ella thought, of the transience of their current arrangement—because at some point in the near future she would indeed be somewhere else in the world, far away from Aaron and Kiri.

When Aaron took his leave a short while later, she felt ill at ease.

It had been a strange interlude. Why had he even come? Maybe he didn't trust her with Kiri after all, and was checking up on her.

But it hadn't felt like that. In fact, he'd seemed delighted at her obviously close relationship with Kiri. And not at all freaked out at having a painting of her presented to him as a gift, which must have been awkward.

Knowing how much Aaron adored Kiri, and how keen he'd been to keep the two parts of this London life separate, well, it didn't make sense.

And Ella didn't like it.

Ella spent the next three days in a kind of hellish heaven.

Taking care of Kiri during the day and spending her nights with Aaron.

She adored her time with Kiri. She took him to Madame Tussaud's and to see the changing of the guard at Buckingham Palace, toy shopping for the baby, and for him. In the process, falling a little more in love with him every day.

She longed for her nights with Aaron. The pleasure that made her want to sigh and scream, the roughness and gentleness, the speed and languor, and everything in between.

But the arrangement was playing havoc with her emotions. Kiri's innocent stories about his father were making her feel altogether too soppy about a casual sex partner. And there were moments during the steamy nights when she and Aaron seemed to forget their agreed roles, becoming almost like real parents having the whole family chat.

Minus the kissing.

An omission that should have reassured her that this was just sex...but didn't.

And then, after five consecutive nights of lovemaking, Ella opened the morning paper and the sordidness of her current situation was thrown into sudden, sharp relief.

Only one half-column of words, not even a photo. But, still, the wreck of her life came crashing back.

It was an article about Javier, full of platitudes from various authorities with no actual news of his fate. But it felt like an omen, and it savaged Ella's conscience. Because she realised that since being with Aaron, not only had she been free of nightmares but she hadn't had any thoughts about Javier either.

So when Aaron came to her room that night, carrying a bag, she pleaded a migraine, knowing she looked ill enough for him to believe her.

'Can I get you anything?' he asked, concern creasing his forehead as he dumped the bag carelessly on her bed.

She forced a strained smile. 'Hey, I'm a nurse, remember?'

He nodded, and then completely disarmed her by drawing her against him and just holding her. 'Sleep well, angel,' he said, and left her.

Angel?

That was going to have to be nipped in the bud.

She approached the bag with some trepidation. Pulled out a raspberry-coloured dress that even she could see was something special, and a bra and panties set in a matching shade that was really too beautiful to wear. The replacements for the things Aaron had ripped off her, obviously—although, strictly speaking, he didn't owe her a bra.

She stared at them, spread on the bed, and tried to shrug off the sense of doom that gripped her.

* * *

Aaron was dragged out of a deep slumber by a kind of screeching wail, abruptly cut off.

He sat up, perfectly still, perfectly silent, and listened. Nothing.

He shook his head to clear it.

Nothing. Imagination.

So—back to sleep. He gave his pillow a thump and lay back down.

Sat back up. Nope—something was wrong. He could feel it.

He got out of bed, padded out of the room, shirtless and in his shorts.

He opened the door to Kiri's room opposite and peered in. He was sleeping soundly.

So…Ella? He opened the door to her room quietly.

She was lying perfectly still, her eyes wide and staring, her hands jammed against her mouth.

He didn't think. Just slid into bed beside her, took her in his arms and arranged her limbs for maximum sleeping comfort.

She said nothing, but she didn't kick him away, which had to be a good sign.

'Just to be clear,' he said, 'I'm not asking questions. So don't even think of telling me to leave.'

She looked at him for one heartbeat, two, three. Then she closed her eyes, and eventually he felt her ease into sleep.

It wasn't going to be easy to not ask at some point. He'd better wear his thermal underwear to ward off the frostbite during that moment. Hmm. Oddly enough, it didn't daunt him. He snuggled her a little closer, kissed the top of her head. *One day, Ella, I'll know it all.*

Damn Aaron James.

It was his fault she was in a dingy hotel room that wasn't big enough to swing a rodent in, let alone a cat.

Not that she hadn't slept in an array of substandard places over the years, though none had ever cost her a staggering hundred and twenty pounds per night.

He'd had to come into her room last night when she'd been at her most vulnerable. And sneaked out this morning without waking her, without having the decency to talk about it so she could slap him down.

So here she was. Hiding out. Staying away until she could find the best way to end things with him. Because things were just not quite casual enough to make this arrangement work.

Aaron was moving house tomorrow. That should signal the end of their liaison. She shouldn't have let Aaron persuade her in the first place. Because look where it had landed her. She was confused about Aaron, guilt-stricken about Javier, miserable about everything—and in a shoe-box-sized room that was costing her a bomb.

Ella sighed heavily, and sat dispiritedly on the bed. It was kind of slippery, as if the mattress protector was plastic. She popped into the bathroom to splash some water on her face and the *eau de* public toilet aroma jammed into her nostrils.

Well, that settled one thing: she might have to sleep here, but she wasn't going to breathe in that smell until she had to. She was going out for the evening.

In fact, for this one night she was going to rediscover the excesses she'd left behind in Cambodia. And when she was sozzled enough, she would return to face the room.

She would *not* run headlong to Tina's and one last night with Aaron.

Which was how Ella found herself playing pool with Harry, Neal and Jerome; three gorgeous, safely gay guys.

She was hot. Sweaty. Dishevelled. A little bit drunk.

Just how you wanted to look for a surprise visit from your lover.

Because that was definitely Aaron James, entering the

pub just as she hit the white ball so awkwardly it jumped off the table.

Aaron James, who was standing there, glaring at her. Fate. It really wasn't working for her.

CHAPTER TWELVE

HE'D BEEN WORKING his way through the pubs in the vicinity of Tina and Brand's because he'd known Ella wasn't staying with friends, as she'd told Tina, and he suspected she wouldn't stray too far, given Tina's advanced pregnancy. So it wasn't exactly fate that he'd found her, because this was the seventh pub he'd tried. But it sure felt like it.

He should go, leave her to it. She didn't *have* to see him every night. Didn't have to get his permission to stay out all night. Didn't have to explain why she was laughing over a pool table with three handsome men.

Except that she kind of *did* have to.

And it would have been stupid to search through the pubs of Mayfair for her and then turn tail the moment he found her.

She was wearing a skin-tight black skirt that would give a corpse a wet dream. A clingy silver singlet top just covering those perfect breasts. Black high heels—that was a first, and a very sexy one. Her hair was piled on her head, who knew how it was staying up there? In fact, not all of it was. Her messy hair made him think of having her in bed.

Aaron watched as she bounced the white ball off the table. As all four of them chortled. He seethed as the blond guy kissed her. Felt murderous as the other two hugged her, one each side.

She knew he was here. He'd seen the flare in her eyes,

the infinitesimal toss of her head as she'd directed her eyes away.

Oh no you don't, Ella. Oh, no. You. Don't.

Ella decided the best thing to do was carry on with her evening as though she hadn't seen Aaron standing on the other side of the pub with his hands fisted at his sides like he was trying not to punch something. She was not going to be made to feel guilty about this.

The guys started hunting in their pockets for beer money. Ella dug into her handbag. 'Don't think so,' she said mournfully, as she scrabbled around inside. And then her eyes widened. 'Hang on,' she said, and triumphantly drew a ten-pound note from the depths, along with one old mint and a paper clip.

'Hooray!' Jerome exclaimed with great enthusiasm. 'Off you go, my girl—to the bar.'

'Or maybe not.'

The voice came from behind Ella but she knew to whom it belonged. That accent.

She'd known he would come to her. Had expected it. Was she happy about it? Yes, unbelievably, given she'd intended to avoid him tonight, she was happy. *A bad sign.*

She looked over her shoulder at him. 'Hello, Aaron.'

'You and pool tables, what's up with that?' Aaron asked mildly. He tucked a strand of loose hair behind one of Ella's ears. 'Run out of money, sweetheart?'

'Yes,' she said, looking at him carefully as she turned fully towards him. He wasn't giving off *sweetheart* vibes. Aaron dug into his jeans pocket, pulled out a fifty-pound note and handed it to her.

'Are you going to introduce me to your friends?' he asked, as she stared at the cash as though she couldn't believe she was holding it.

'Huh?' she said eloquently.

'Your friends?' he prompted.

Ella looked around as though she'd forgotten their existence. Pulled herself together as she noted her three new drinking buddies gazing at her with avid interest.

'Oh. Yes,' she said, and hastily performed the introductions.

'And do you really want another drink, or shall we hand that money over to the guys and head off?'

Ella was torn.

'Ella? Are we staying or going?' Aaron asked, steel in his voice.

She *should* tell him to go to hell. But she found she didn't want to fight with Aaron. Not here. Didn't want to fight with him, period.

'I guess we're going,' she said. 'So here you go, boys, thanks for buying my drinks all night and I hope this covers it.' She smiled at them. 'I had a brilliant time. And remember what I said about LA. If you're ever there…'

Assorted hugs and kisses later, Ella did her slow walk out of the pub.

'You're not fooling me with the slow walk, Ella,' Aaron said as they reached the footpath.

She stopped. Turned to him. 'I don't know what you m—'

He pulled her into his arms sharply, shocking that sentence right out of her head.

He moved to kiss her but Ella put her hands up, pushing against his chest. 'You don't kiss me any more.'

'Is that so?' Aaron asked. Purely rhetorical—she had no time to answer as he planted his mouth on hers like a heat-seeking missile hitting its target. His hands went to her bottom and he pulled her against him, pelvis to pelvis.

Ella gasped as he released her, and her fingers came up to touch her mouth. 'Why are you so angry with me?'

Aaron looked down at her, unapologetic. 'Because you left me.'

Ella couldn't help herself—she touched his cheek.

She went to pull her hand away but Aaron caught it, held it against his face. 'And because I'm jealous,' he said.

'Jealous?'

Aaron nodded towards the pub.

Ella was stunned. 'But they're gay.'

He didn't miss a beat. 'I don't care if they're eunuchs. Because it's not sex I'm talking about. We're monogamous, you and I, and I trust you with that.'

That certainty shook her. She swallowed hard. 'Then what?'

'It's the whole deal. Being with you. In the moment. In public. *That* smile. That's what I'm talking about.'

That smile? Huh? 'We're in the moment in public now,' she said. 'Which I hope you don't regret.' She tilted her head towards a small group of women as she tugged her hand free. They were staring at Aaron as they walked past. 'I think they know you. I keep forgetting you're a celebrity.'

'I don't care.'

'You're *supposed* to care. Just sex, on the quiet—no scandal. Look, let's be honest. It's not working out, this casual sex thing.'

'No, it's not.'

She couldn't think straight for a moment. Because he'd agreed with her. Which meant it was over. Just what she'd wanted.

'Right,' she said. And then, because she still couldn't think straight, 'Right.'

'We're going to have to renegotiate.'

'There doesn't seem to be much point to that, or much to negotiate *with*,' Ella said, as her brain finally engaged. 'Given you're moving out tomorrow, let's just call it quits.'

Aaron pursed his lips. 'Um—no.'

'No?'

'No.'

'Remember our agreement? No questions, no—'

'I don't give a toss about our agreement. We are not

going to go our separate ways because you decided to click your fingers on a public street.'

'See? I told you it's not working. The casual sex deal meant no messy endings. And you're making it messy.'

'But it's not casual, is it, Ella? And I don't want to let you go.'

Her heart did that stuttering thing. She forced herself to ignore it. 'You knew there couldn't be anything except sex. And it will be too hard to keep even that going once we're living in different places.' Swallow. 'And I—I have an extra complication.'

'Which is?' he asked flatly.

'I have—I have…someone.'

'Look at me, Ella.'

She faced him squarely, threw back her head, eyes glittering with defiance.

'No, you don't,' Aaron said.

'Oh, for goodness' sake, I do! I do, I do!'

'If you had someone, you couldn't be with me the way you have been.'

She gasped. He couldn't have hurt her more if he'd stabbed her.

Because he was right.

How could she love Javier if she could pour herself into sex with Aaron in the no-holds-barred way that had become their signature? It had never happened before—only drunken fumbling that she'd run away from every single time. The antithesis of what she did with Aaron.

Aaron was looking at her with almost savage intensity. 'We need to settle this, and not here. Come with me.'

'Where are we going?'

'I don't know—a hotel.'

She laughed, but there was no softness in it. 'I have a hotel room. It stinks like a public toilet and has a plastic mattress protector. That sounds about right. Let's go there. And don't flinch like that.'

'I think we can do better than that, Ella.'

Ella wanted to scream. But she also wanted to cry. And instead of doing either, she was goading him, making everything ugly and tawdry, turning it into the one-night stand it should have always been. 'All right, then. Let's "settle" this,' she said. 'One last time. I'm up for it. You can use my body any way you want, and I will show you there is nothing romantic about an orgasm—it's just technique.'

'Is that so?'

'Let's find out. But if I'm going to play the mistress, I warn you now that I'm going to want access to the mini-bar.'

'Any way I can get you, Ella,' he said, unperturbed. 'You can devour everything in the mini-bar, order everything off the room-service menu, steal the fluffy robe, take the towels—anything you want.'

'I've always wanted to steal the fluffy robe,' Ella said, and took his arm.

CHAPTER THIRTEEN

AARON HAILED A cab and asked to be taken to the closest five-star hotel. On the way, he called to check on Kiri and let Jenny, who'd arrived in the early evening, know he wouldn't be home that night.

Ella waited through the call, clearly still furious with him. Well, too damned bad.

Aaron hastily secured them a room for the night and as they headed for the hotel elevator, he drew Ella close to him, holding her rigid hand. He breathed in the slightly stale pub scent of her. But he couldn't have cared less whether she came to him straight from the shower or after running a marathon through the city sewers.

The elevator doors opened and then they were inside. Alone. The second the doors closed, he was kissing her, sliding his hands under her top. One hand moved up to cover her breast, moulding it to his palm, teasing the nipple to maddening hardness with unsteady fingers. He'd thought she might push him away but, no, she kissed him back, straining against him. He broke the kiss, his breath coming fast and hard now, and bent his mouth to her shoulder, biting her there.

The elevator stopped and they broke apart, staring at each other. Without a word, Aaron grabbed her hand and pulled her quickly out and along the corridor. His hands were shaking so much he almost couldn't work the door mechanism to their suite. And then they were inside and Aaron reached for her again. Wordless. Driven. Desperate.

But so was Ella.

She yanked his T-shirt up his chest and over his head. 'Ah,' she breathed, as her hands went to his hips and she pulled him toward her. She put her mouth on one of his nipples and held tight to his hips as he bucked against her.

'Ella,' he groaned, hands moving restlessly to try to hold onto her as her tongue flicked out. 'Let me touch you.'

'Not yet,' she said, and moved her mouth to his other nipple. As she did so, she started to undo the button fly of his jeans.

He groaned again but couldn't speak as her hands slid inside his underwear.

'Do you like me to touch you like this?' she asked.

'You know I— Ahh, Ella, you're killing me.'

Laughing throatily, Ella stepped back, started to undress.

'Hurry up,' she said, as he stood watching as she wriggled out of her skirt.

It was all the encouragement Aaron needed. In record time, he'd stripped.

Ella, naked except for her high heels, turned to drape her clothes over the back of a handily positioned chair. Aaron came up behind her and caught her against his chest. His arms circled her, hands reaching for her breasts.

She dropped her clothes and leaned back against him, thrusting her breasts into his hands. She moaned as he kissed the side of her neck, gasped as one questing hand dived between her thighs.

'Oh, you're good at this,' Ella said, as she felt her orgasm start to build.

'You can still talk,' Aaron said against her ear. 'So not good enough.'

With that, he bent her forward at the waist until she was clinging to the chair, and thrust inside her. His hands were on her hips as he continued to move inside her, pulling all the way out after each thrust before slamming into her again.

The feel of her bottom against him, the intoxicating sounds of her pleasure as she orgasmed, clenching around him until he thought he'd faint from desire, the exquisite friction of his movements in and out of her built together until the blood was roaring in his head and demanding he take her harder, harder, harder.

Ella. This was Ella.

His.

Ella slumped against Aaron. After that explosive orgasm, he'd turned her around to face him, kissed her for the longest time, and now he was holding her with every bit of gentleness his lovemaking had lacked.

What she'd meant to do was give him a clinical experience. Instead, she'd drenched herself in soul-deep, emotionally fraught lust. Her anger was gone. And the bitterness. She felt purged, almost. Which wasn't the way it was supposed to be.

Nothing had changed. Nothing that could open the way for her to have what she wanted with a clear conscience. Sex couldn't cure things. Even phenomenal sex. Life couldn't be that simple.

Javier was still out there, the uncertainty of his fate tying her to him. Aaron still had a problematic ex-wife and a little boy whose inevitable loss, when they went their separate ways, would devastate her.

'Did I hurt you?' he asked, kissing the top of her head.

'This really is a regular post-coital question of yours, isn't it?'

'No. It's just that I've only ever lost control with you.'

There was a lump in her throat. 'Well, stop asking,' she said, when she trusted herself to speak. 'You didn't hurt me.' *Not in that way.*

'I didn't even think about a condom,' Aaron said.

Ella shrugged restlessly, eased out of his arms. 'I know. I wasn't thinking straight either. And me a nurse.'

'I'm sorry.'

'Me too, but it's done. Not that it's really the point, but I'm on the Pill. So if that worries you, at least—'

'No. No—I'm not worried about that. At least, not for myself. I wish I *could* have a child with you, Ella. Not to replace Sann but for you.'

That lump was in her throat again. She turned away. 'Complicating as all hell, though, pregnancy, for casual sex partners,' she said, trying for light and airy and not quite making it. She remembered ordering him to never say Sann's name again. But it didn't hurt to hear the name now. Not from him.

Aaron—what an unlikely confidant. The only one who knew her pain.

She cleared her throat, 'But now, do you think we could actually move out of this hallway? And where are those fluffy robes?'

Aaron obligingly guided Ella into the lounge area of the suite. He fetched a robe for each of them, and watched as Ella belted hers on, then sat on the sofa to remove her shoes.

He came to sit beside her, slipped an arm around her shoulders and drew her back against him so that her head was against his shoulder.

'You know, don't you, that I'm not a nice person?' she said.

'No, I don't know that. I've watched you work. Seen how much you care. The way you are with Kiri. I know how protective you are of your family. I know you wanted to adopt an orphan from Cambodia, and I've seen what the grief of that did to you. These things don't add up to "not nice".'

'I've been jealous of my sister, of the baby. That's not nice.'

'It doesn't look to me like Tina's had her eyes scratched out,' Aaron said calmly.

'Well, I'm over it now,' she admitted. 'But it took some soul searching.'

'I'm thinking soul searching is a bit of a hobby of yours.'

'And I— Over the past year I've done things. Things I'm not proud of.'

'You've had a lot to deal with. Cut yourself some slack, Ella.'

'You stopped kissing me.'

'And you think that was some kind of judgement?' He broke off, laughed softly. 'That was a defence mechanism. That's all.'

'What?'

'Casual sex? Just sex—no kissing, because kissing is not casual.'

'Oh.'

They stayed sitting in silence, his arm around her, for a long moment.

Now what? Ella wondered.

But then Aaron broke the silence. 'So tell me, Ella, about the "someone". The someone I know you don't have. The someone I think you once *had*. Past tense. Right?'

'Had *and* have.'

'Hmm, I'm going to need a little more.'

'His name is Javier. He's a doctor. Spanish. He was kidnapped in Somalia.' *Whew.* 'There was an article in the paper this morning.' She looked up at him briefly. 'Hence my need to go a little off the rails tonight.'

Aaron nodded, saying nothing. And somehow it was easy to relax against him and continue. Aaron, her confidant. 'We were in love. Very newly in love, so new that nobody else knew about it, which was a blessing the way things turned out, because I couldn't have borne the questions, the sympathy.' Pause. 'I should have been with him that day. It was my twenty-fifth birthday, two years ago. I was supposed to be in the jeep with him.'

Long pause. She could almost hear her own pulse. 'You've got no idea how awful it was. The conditions. The soul-sapping struggle to provide healthcare to people who desperately needed it. Because even before you think about treating illnesses like malaria and TB and pneumonia and HIV, you know that the drought, the violence, the poverty, the poor harvests have made malnutrition a force that simply can't be reckoned with. The kids are starving. Sometimes walking hundreds of kilometres just to drop dead in front of you. And ten thousand people a day are dying.

'And your colleagues are being kidnapped or even murdered, and armed opposition groups make it almost impossible to reach people in need, even though everyone *knows* the suffering, and even hiring a vehicle to get to people is a tense negotiation with clans in constant conflict, and the very people who are providing the tiny bit of security you can get are okay with the deaths and the kidnappings.'

She stopped again. 'Sorry I'm so emotional.' She shook her head. 'No, I'm not sorry. It needs emotion. When you're resuscitating a one-year-old girl, and there is a tiny boy next to her so frail that only a stethoscope over his heart tells you he's alive, and two more critically ill children are waiting behind you, why *not* get emotional?'

His hand was in her hair, stroking, soothing. 'Go on, Ella. I'm here.'

'Anyway. Javier and I were heading to one of the refugee camps in Kenya. But I got malaria and I couldn't go. So I'm here and he's somewhere. Alive, dead, injured, safe? I don't know.' Ella drew in a shuddering breath. 'And I feel guilty, about having a normal life while he's lost. And guilty that I can be with you like this when I should be waiting for him. And just plain guilty. I'm a wreck.'

'Ah, Ella.' He eased her out from under his arm and turned her to face him. 'I'd tell you it's not your fault, that you have a right to go on with your life, that anyone who loved you would want that for you, that you wouldn't want Javier to be trapped in the past if your situations were reversed; but that's not going to set you free, is it?' He ran his fingers down her cheek. 'You have to be ready to let it go.'

'The thing is I don't know what he'd want me to do, or what he'd do in my place.'

'That says something, doesn't it? You were only twenty-five, and in a very new relationship. If you're really going to keep a candle burning in the window for the rest of your life, I'm going to have to find the guy and make sure he's worth it, and I don't really want to do that. Somalia is scary!'

Ella smiled. 'You really do have that heroic thing going on, don't you? I think you *would* go there if you thought it would help me.'

'Nah. It's not heroic, it's self-interest. Memories can bring on rose-tinted-glasses syndrome. Which, in this case, makes it really hard for a mere actor to measure up to a Spanish doctor kidnapped while saving lives in Africa. Even with the malaria documentary under my belt, I'm coming in a poor second.' He kissed her forehead. 'But it's just possible, in a real flesh-and-blood contest, I could edge past him. Unless he happens to be devastatingly attractive as well.'

'As a matter of fact...' Ella trailed off with a laugh.

'Well, that sucks. Maybe I *won't* go and find him after all.'

'Yeah, well, Somalia really *is* scary, so I wouldn't let you go. I wouldn't like to lose you too.' Ella resettled her head on his shoulder. 'Okay—now you know all the salient bits about my past. So, let's talk about you. You said I could ask you anything, and you'd answer.'

'Ask away.'

'I'll start with something easy. Tina told me you raised your sisters after your parents died.'

'Easy? Ha! It was like a brother-sister version of *The Taming of the Shrew*, but in triplicate.'

Ella smiled. 'And you love them very much.'

'Oh, yes. Lucinda, Gabriella and Nicola. My parents were killed in a boating accident when I was eighteen. The girls were fifteen, twelve and ten. I was old enough to look after them, so I did. End of story, really. Two of them are married with kids now, one is married to her job—she's an actuary but she looks like a fashion designer—and all of them are happy.'

'It can't have been easy.'

'We had some nail-biting moments over the years, no doubt about it. But I won't go into the scary boyfriend stories or the fights over schoolwork and curfews. We just belonged together. Simple.'

Pause. And then, 'Is it okay to ask about Rebecca? Like, how you met?'

'Sure. I met her through Brand. The way I meet all my women.'

Ella pinched his thigh.

'All right, not *all* of them,' he amended, laughing. 'Let me give you the abridged version. We met at one of Brand's parties. He was living in Los Angeles back then and I was over there, trying to make the big time— unsuccessfully. Rebecca was doing the same, equally unsuccessfully.'

'So you drowned your sorrows together?'

'Something like that. We were an item in pretty short order. Happily ever after. For a while at least.'

'What went wrong?'

'Nothing. That's what I thought, anyway.' He sighed. 'But looking back, it was all about work. When we returned to Australia I started getting steady jobs. We adopted Kiri and everything seemed fine. But I got more work. Better work. And more work. Making a fortune, no worries. But Rebecca's career stalled. She wasn't happy, and I was too busy to notice. Until it was too late. She started doing a few outrageous things to get publicity in the mistaken belief it would help things along. And before I knew it, it was party, party, party. Drugs. Booze. More drugs. I know Tina told you about the rehab. Well, Rebecca's been to rehab before. Twice.' He shrugged. 'I'm praying this time it will work. This place, it's called Trust, it really seems good.'

'Oh, Trust—I know it, and it is good. She's in safe hands there.'

'Thanks, Ella.'

Ella brought his hand to her lips and kissed it. 'So I guess you've been trying to make up for being too busy to notice when things started to go wrong.'

'That's about the sum of it.'

'Am I going to do the "not your fault" routine?'

Aaron touched her hair. 'No. I'm as bad as you are when it comes to guilt, I think.'

'And Kiri? Why adopt? And why do you have full custody?'

'The adoption? We'd always planned to adopt a child in need and that just happened to come before trying for our own. The custody thing? Well, no matter what's between Rebecca and me, she wants only the best for Kiri, and she recognised that that was living with me, because although she likes to pretend she's in control, she knows she's not.'

She touched his hand. 'You love her. Rebecca.'

'Yes, I do,' Aaron said. 'But it's no longer *that* love. I care about her, as a friend and as the mother of my son.'

'It sounds very mature.'

'Hmm, well, don't be thinking it's all sugar plums and fairy cakes, far from it. She likes to get what she wants.' He laughed. 'I suppose we all do, if it comes to that. But when she needs something, she tends to forget we're divorced and she's not above a bit of manipulation. That can make it hard for us to move on.'

'She wouldn't like it? The fact that I'm here with you.'

'Probably not,' he admitted. 'Unless she had someone first.'

'So you won't tell her.'

'That depends, Ella. On whether we're sticking to our initial arrangement.'

Silence.

Ella wasn't ready to face that.

She got to her feet, headed for the mini-bar and started looking through the contents. 'So,' she said, moving various bottles around without any real interest, 'getting back to the important stuff. Condoms. Or the lack of them. Pregnancy we've covered. But I can also reassure you that I was checked before I left Cambodia and am disease-free. It's something I do regularly, because of my work with AIDS patients.'

'Me too, disease-free, I mean. I've been an avid fan of the condom for a long, long time.'

She turned. 'But weren't you and Rebecca starting to try for…?'

'Trying for a baby? No. For the last year we weren't trying *anything*. You see, along with the drugs came other problems—new experiences Rebecca wanted, such as sex with a variety of men. Including two of my friends. *Ex*-friends,' he clarified. 'I could forgive her for that. I *did* forgive her, knowing what was going on with her. But I couldn't…well, I just couldn't after that.'

'I don't know what to say to that.'

'Not much *to* say. I did try to keep my marriage together, because commitments are important to me. But some things just…change.'

Ella thought about that. What a lovely thing to accept. *Some things just change.*

'Anyway, enough gloom.' He walked over to her, gave her a quick, hard kiss. 'Come and have a bath with me.'

Aaron grabbed the scented crystals beside the deep bath and threw them in as the tub filled. Then he lifted her in his arms and kissed her as he stepped into the water, settled. Kept kissing her until the bath was full. He took the soap from her and washed her, kissing, touching, until she was gasping for air. But he wouldn't take her. Not this time. 'Condoms, so you don't have to wonder,' he said, by way of explanation.

'I have some in my bag,' she said, shivering with desire.

'Monogamy, remember?' Aaron said. 'I don't think roaming around London with a bag full of condoms fits the principle.'

'Just handbag history—like the expired bus tickets in there. I wasn't going to use them.'

'It's okay, Ella. I know that. Somehow, I really do know that.' He got to his feet, streaming water, but before he could leave the tub Ella got to her knees. 'Not yet,' she said, and looked up at him as she took him in her mouth.

The next morning Aaron ordered a veritable banquet for breakfast.

He was whistling as he opened the door, as the food was laid out in the living room. The robe he'd purchased for Ella was in its neat drawstring bag, positioned on one of the chairs.

He'd left Ella in bed with the television remote control, and was halfway to the bedroom to fetch her for their lovers' feast, mid-whistle, when he heard it. A sound between a choke and a gasp.

'Ella, what is it?' he asked, hurrying into the room.

She was pale. Deathly so. Like the life had drained out of her. She looked up at him, and then, like she couldn't help herself, back at the television.

There was a man being interviewed. A gaunt man. Beautiful—not handsome, beautiful.

'It's him,' Ella said.

CHAPTER FOURTEEN

'HIM?' AARON ASKED. But he knew.

The news moved onto the next item and it was like a signal had been transmitted directly to Ella's brain.

She got out of bed. 'I have to go,' she said. But then she simply stood there, shivering.

'Go where?'

'Africa.'

'You can't go anywhere in that state, and certainly not Africa.'

'Don't tell me what to do,' she said, and started dressing. It took her less than a minute.

'Ella, you have to talk to me.'

'I did enough talking last night.'

'For God's sake Ella, I—'

'No,' she cried, and then raced to her bag. She looked up, wild-eyed. 'Money. I don't have money for a cab.'

'Calm down, Ella. I'll take you where you need to go.'

'I don't want you to take me anywhere. I want—I want—' She stopped, looked at him, then burst into tears.

Aaron tried to take her in his arms but she wrenched away from him, turned aside to hide her face and walked to the window. She cried as she looked out at the world. Cried as though her soul was shattering.

And just watching her, helpless, Aaron felt his life start to disintegrate.

Gradually, her sobs subsided. She stood leaning her forehead against the window.

Aaron came up behind her, touched her gently on the shoulder. She stiffened but didn't pull away.

'You're going to him,' he said.

'Of course.'

'You're still in love with him, then.'

Pause. And then, 'I have to be. And I have to go.' She turned to face him. 'I know I already owe you money but will you lend me enough for a cab?'

'You don't owe me anything, Ella.'

Aaron grabbed her by her upper arms and drew her forward. 'I'll wait for you to sort this out, Ella. I'll be here, waiting.'

'I don't deserve for anyone to wait for me,' she said, and her voice was colourless. 'Because *I* didn't wait. I *should* have been waiting for him. I *intended* to wait for him. But I didn't. Instead I—I was...' A breath shuddered in. Out. 'I can't stand it. I have to go. Now. I have to go.'

'All right.' Aaron grabbed his jeans and pulled out a handful of notes. 'Take this. And here...' He grabbed the hotel notepad and pen from beside the phone and scribbled a few lines. 'It's my address in London. We'll be there from today. And this...' he dashed another line on the paper '...is the phone number for the house. You've already got my mobile number. Whatever you need, Ella, whenever.'

'Thank you,' Ella said, and raced from the room without another word or glance.

Aaron looked at the sumptuous breakfast, at the robe he'd bought for Ella just because she'd joked about wanting to steal one. She hadn't seen it, wouldn't have taken it if she had.

Javier was back. And that was that.

And then, two days later, Rebecca disappeared from rehab in the company of a fellow addict, a film producer, and he knew he was going to have to fly to LA at some point to bail her out of some heinous situation.

Yep. That really was that.

Ella felt weird, being with Javier, even after a week together.

He was the same and yet not the same.

Every time she broached the subject of the past two years he closed the discussion down. He simply thought they would pick up exactly where they'd left off, as though those two years had never happened, but Ella couldn't get her head into the same space.

She couldn't bear to sleep with him, for one thing.

She told *him* it was to give them a chance to get to know each other again. She told *herself* it was because she'd been stupid enough to forget the condom with Aaron—that meant she had to wait and see, because things *did* go wrong with the Pill.

But, really, she just didn't want to.

She tried, desperately, to remember what it had been like, that one time with Javier, but the only images that formed were of Aaron.

So it would have been disloyal somehow. To Javier, who didn't deserve for her to be thinking about another man. And, bizarrely, to Aaron, who was now effectively out of her life.

Ella sighed and got out of bed in her tiny hotel room. Padded into the bathroom and looked in the cabinet mirror. What did Aaron see that made him fall on her like he was starving for the taste of her? She was beautiful, she'd been told that often enough to believe it, but had never thought it important. Until now. Because maybe Aaron wouldn't have wanted her so much if she'd looked different.

Was it shallow to be glad that something as insignificant as the shape of her mouth made Aaron kiss her as though it was the only thing in the world he needed?

Ella gave herself a mental shake. She had to stop thinking about Aaron. Javier was her future. Javier, who'd been
returned to her, like a miracle.

Today, they would fly to London so she could introduce
Javier to Tina, who'd had the Javier story thrown at her like
a dart as Ella had packed her bags. He would be there with
her for the baby's birth. Even her parents would be coming
in a month, to meet their grandchild…and the strange man
who'd been kept a secret from them. And wouldn't *that* be
interesting, after her mother's blistering phone soliloquy
on the subject of Ella keeping her in the dark?

Out of control, the whole thing. A runaway train, speed-
ing her into an alien future.

Ella closed her eyes.

Did I hurt you? Aaron's voice whispered through her
memory.

Yes, she answered silently. *Yes, you did.*

Heathrow was bedlam, but Ella almost dreaded exiting
the airport.

She was so nervous.

About introducing Javier to Tina and Brand.

And about the inevitable meeting between Javier and
Aaron.

Javier, she'd discovered, was the jealous type. Not the
cute, huggable kind of jealous Aaron had been that night
outside the pub in Mayfair. Sort of *scary* jealous. The prospect of him and Aaron in the same room was enough to
make her break into a cold sweat.

She welcomed the flash of cameras as they emerged
from Customs. Javier was whisked away for a quick photo
op, and she was glad. It meant she would have a moment
to herself.

Or not.

Because, groan-inducingly, Aaron was there, waiting for her. In his T-shirt and jeans. Looking desperately unhappy.

He strode forward. 'Tina sent me instead of a limo. Sorry. I tried to get out of it, but nobody's allowed to say no to her at the moment, she's been so worried about you.'

'Everyone must hate me.'

'Nobody hates you, Ella. Everyone just wants things to work out.'

Ella could feel one of those awful blushes racing up her neck. 'I'm sorry. For running out like that, I mean. I should have explained, I should have—'

'Ella, don't. I know you. I know what you went through. I know why you had to go. I should have just stood aside. Please don't cry.'

Ella blinked hard, managed to gain her composure. 'You always seem to know. I wish... Oh, he's coming.'

Javier, unsmiling, put his arm around Ella the moment he reached them.

Aaron held out his hand, just as unsmiling.

It was like an old cowboy movie, trigger fingers at the ready, Ella thought, a little hysterically.

'Javier,' Aaron said. His hand was still out, ignored.

Ella took Javier's elbow. 'Javier, this is a friend of Tina and Brand's. And mine. Aaron James. He's very kindly giving us a ride.' Ugh, was that a *wheedle* in her voice? Disgusting.

'I'm pleased to meet you,' Javier said solemnly, at last taking Aaron's proffered hand for a single jerking shake.

Aaron gave him a narrow-eyed look. There was a small uncomfortable pause and then, taking their baggage cart, Aaron said, 'Follow me.'

Javier held Ella back for a moment. 'I don't like the way he looks at you,' he said.

Ella gritted her teeth. This was the fifth time in a week Javier had taken exception to the way a man had looked at her. She would have loved to tell him to get over it, but this particular time he had a right to be suspicious.

Aaron looked over his shoulder, no doubt wondering what was keeping them.

Looking straight ahead, Ella took Javier's arm and followed Aaron.

It was always going to be an uncomfortable drive, but this was ridiculous.

Aaron was fuming, relegated to the role of chauffer.

Javier spoke only to Ella, and only in Spanish.

Charming!

Ella answered him in English, but the agonised looks he was catching in the rear-view mirror told Aaron she knew her Spaniard was behaving like a jackass.

Okay—so maybe jackass was his word, not Ella's, but he stood by it. *Nice choice, Ella.*

It was a relief to pull up at the house. After he helped hoist their luggage out of the boot, Aaron drew Ella a little aside. 'Ella, so you know, Tina's insisting I come to dinner tonight,' he said softly.

'That…that's fine,' Ella said, glancing nervously at Javier, who was giving her a very dark look as he picked up their bags. With a poor attempt at a smile Ella hurried back to Javier, took his arm and ushered him quickly into the house.

Aaron sighed, wondered why he'd even bothered warning her about him being at dinner. However prepared any of them were, when you parcelled it all up—Ella's uncharacteristically submissive demeanour, Javier's haughty unfriendliness, the prospect of witnessing the reunited lovebirds cooing at each other all evening, and his own desire to do some kind of violence to Javier that would ruin at least one perfect cheekbone—dinner was going to be a fiasco of epic proportions.

* * *

Aaron had been braced ever since he'd got to Tina's, but he still couldn't help the way his eyes darted to the door of the living room when it opened for the final two guests.

Ella looked like a deer caught in the headlights. She was wearing a dress. Dark grey. Silky. Simple. Classy. She was wearing her black high heels. He wanted to run his hands up her legs. He could drool at any moment.

Their eyes met for one sharp, tense moment and she blushed.

Javier said something and Aaron shifted his gaze.

Javier was everything Aaron wasn't. It was more pronounced tonight than it had been at the airport. Javier was elegant and sophisticated. Stylish in that way Europeans seemed to manage so effortlessly. Javier's hair was jet black, lying against his perfect skull in well-behaved waves. His eyes were equally black—dramatically moody. He was dressed in black pants and a pale pinkish-purple shirt that not many men could carry off.

And since when had Aaron ever noticed, let alone cared about, what other men were wearing?

He tore his eyes away, took a bracing sip of his Scotch.

Hellos were said. A drink pressed into Javier's hand, another into Ella's. Tina kissed Javier on the cheek. Javier touched Tina's ringlets as though entranced.

Tina laughed. 'A curse, this hair. Only Brand likes it.'

Javier smiled. 'Not only Brand. I like it too. Lively hair.'

Tina laughed again, shaking her head until her curls danced a little.

Great, Aaron thought. Javier was going to be adored by Ella's sister. Just great.

Brand, who was standing beside him, made a disgusted sound and rolled his eyes. He'd always known Brand was an excellent judge of character.

Tina was saying something about the need to fatten Ella up.

'It's her work,' Javier said, pulling Ella very close. 'She worked too hard in Cambodia.'

'Getting any information out of Ella about her work is like pulling teeth, but Aaron told us a little about the conditions there.'

Javier looked straight at Aaron. Hostile.

Not that he could work out the whole backstory of Aaron's obsession with Ella from one glancing look.

Could he?

'And what were *you* doing, Aaron? In Cambodia?' Javier's voice was perfectly polite, and chilling.

'I was filming a documentary on malaria.' *And fantasising about your girlfriend.*

Tina was starting to take on a little of Ella's deer-in-the-headlights look. Sensing the undercurrents, no doubt. 'So, Javier,' Tina said, 'are you able to share with us a little about…about…your experience?'

Javier smiled at her, but to Aaron it looked almost dismissive.

'I was not badly treated,' Javier said. 'Just not free. But not, perhaps, a subject for tonight. Tonight is a celebration, you see. Ella and I…' He stopped, smiled again, drew Ella nearer.

How much closer could he *get* her, anyway? Aaron wondered furiously as he watched Ella. But she wouldn't meet his eyes. Wouldn't meet anyone's eyes.

'Ella and I would like to share our news,' Javier said, and raised Ella's hand to kiss the palm. 'Ella has done me the honour of accepting my proposal of marriage.'

Aaron caught the sparkle on Ella's finger, and turning away, swallowed the rest of his Scotch in one swig.

Aaron hadn't come looking for Ella.

Didn't want to be alone with her. Not now. When he felt so raw.

And yet there she was, in the kitchen, straightening up after putting something in the fridge.

And there he was. In the kitchen. Forgetting why.

He must have made some sound because she straightened. Turned. The fridge door swung closed behind her.

For a moment Aaron couldn't breathe.

'How are you, Aaron?' she asked quietly.

'Fine.' The word sounded as though it had been bounced into an airless room.

'And Kiri?'

'Fine. He misses you.'

He saw her swallow. She said nothing. Well, what did he expect her to say?

Aaron took a step closer to her. 'There were no consequences? I mean as a...a result of—'

'I know what you mean. I told you I was on the Pill. But just in case, I'm waiting...' Stop. Another swallow. 'I mean, I'm not doing anything... I'm not...with...' She drew an audible breath. 'Until I know.'

'That's good,' Aaron said, miraculously understanding. 'I mean, is it good? Yes, I guess it's good. I guess it's...' Nope. He couldn't finish that.

Silence.

Ella was turning the engagement ring round and round on her finger. 'How's Rebecca? Rehab? How's it going?'

'It's not. She left early; with a drug-addicted film producer. Never anything mundane for Rebecca.'

'Oh, I'm so sorry.'

He rubbed a hand behind his neck. 'Just one thing. I told her about you, about us. In case...'

Ella was fidgeting—which he'd never seen her do. Playing with the damned ring. 'Does that mean...? Does everyone know about us?' she asked.

'No. Nobody else. And Rebecca isn't talking—except to her publicist, who's working out how to go public with the film producer.'

'It's just…Javier's the jealous type. I don't want him to… You know what I mean.'

'I'll fix it so nothing rebounds on you, I promise. And I guess there's nothing to say, anyway. You're engaged.'

Another awful silence.

Aaron took one step closer. 'Have you picked a date? For the wedding?'

'No. Not yet.'

'Why are you doing it, Ella?'

She held out her hands. Imploring. 'How could I say no? How could I refuse him anything after what he's been through?'

He had a few pithy answers for that—but found he couldn't voice them, not when she looked so tormented. 'I'm glad you're not sleeping with him,' he said instead.

He took one more step, close enough now to take her hands, hold them. 'And I know that's unworthy, Ella, but I've discovered I'm not good at giving in gracefully.'

'This is not doing us any good, Aaron.' Ella tried to pull her hands free, but Aaron held on. 'Let me go. If you don't, I don't know how I'll bear it.'

He pulled her hands against his chest, held them there. 'Ella, we need to talk.'

'We are talking.'

'Not here, not like this.'

'I can't. I need to get back in there.' She pulled her hands free. '*Please*, Aaron. It's very difficult just now. Please.'

'*Porque estas tardano tanto?*'

Both Aaron and Ella turned towards the doorway, where a frowning Javier was standing.

'I'm coming now,' she said in English, and walked out of the room, pausing just outside the kitchen door to wait for Javier to join her.

'*Andante, te seguire pronto,*' he said.

Ella looked at Aaron quickly, nervously, then as quickly away. 'All right,' she said.

Javier moved further into the kitchen. He looked Aaron over and seemed to find nothing there to worry about if his slight sneer was anything to go by.

'You know Ella well.' Statement, not question.

'Yes. I do.'

'You watch her.'

The comment surprised Aaron; he'd been conscious of *not* looking at her all night. 'Do I?'

'I can understand. She is beautiful.'

Aaron was silent.

Javier smiled, but it wasn't a friendly smile. 'She is beautiful, and she is mine.'

'If she's yours, what's your problem?'

'I just want it to be clear. So, I think you were bringing the cheese? I'm here to help.'

Cheese. Of course. He had offered to go to the kitchen and get the cheese.

When the two men returned to the dining room, Ella smiled blindingly at her fiancé—the mouth-only version, ha!—put her hand over Javier's when he paused by her chair and touched her shoulder, then moved her chair a smidgeon closer to his when he sat beside her.

Ella's hand kept disappearing under the table and Aaron guessed she was giving Javier's thigh an intermittent pat. Probably reassuring him that she was not remotely attracted to the brooding thug at the other end of the table who now, perversely, couldn't seem to keep his eyes off her.

Which word was stronger—disaster or catastrophe?

Because he was designating this dinner party a catastrophic disaster or a disastrous catastrophe—whichever was worse.

CHAPTER FIFTEEN

WHEN ELLA'S CELLPHONE trilled the next morning and Aaron's name flashed, she felt a wash of emotion that was a weird hybrid of joy and anxiety.

'Hello? Ella?'

Ella gasped. *Not* Aaron. 'Kiri! Is everything all right?'

'Where are you, Ella?'

'I'm at Tina's darling, why?'

'We're going to see Mum, and I want to say goodbye. But Dad says you're too busy.'

'Where's Dad?'

'Filming.' Giggle. 'He forgot his phone.'

Her heart swelled with longing. 'When do you leave, Kiri?'

'Soon.'

Which was kid-speak for any time. Tomorrow. Next week. An hour.

Ella bit her lip, thinking. Aaron was on set so the coast was clear. Javier was out, and he didn't have to know. The apartment was within walking distance. Could she do this? See Kiri once more? 'What about if I come over now?' Ella found herself asking.

'Yes!' Kiri said, excited. 'I painted you a picture. Of you and me.'

'Well, I have to see that!' she exclaimed. 'I'll be there soon.'

* * *

It didn't take long for Aaron to realise he'd left his phone at home. He felt guilty that he'd be late to the set, because Brand had to head to York in the afternoon to check out locations for an evening shoot, and the schedule was already tight, but he just had to turn back for it. After Kiri's dengue fever episode Aaron liked to be instantly contactable at all times.

Aaron raced into the apartment. 'Jenny?' He called out, and hurried into the living room. 'I forgot my phone, so—' He broke off, and his heart leapt so savagely he couldn't catch his breath.

Ella. Here.

She was sitting with Jenny and Kiri, one of Kiri's paintings in her hands, but she seemed to be holding her breath as her beautiful violet eyes rose to his and stuck there.

Jenny, looking from one to the other of them, murmured something about Kiri needing something. She took Kiri by the hand, led him from the room.

Ella shrugged awkwardly. 'Sorry,' she said, putting down the painting and getting to her feet. 'But he called and I... He said you were leaving?'

'We are—in a few days. Rebecca overdosed. I've got to make sure she's okay.'

'Oh, Aaron.'

'But there's a bright side. It scared her. She's heading back to Trust.'

'That's good. Great.'

'And I'm going to meet Scott too.'

'Scott?'

'The film producer. He's with her. Thank heavens he seems to be on track. She says it's serious between them, and I need to think about what that means for Kiri.'

He could smell her. His heart was aching. He couldn't seem to stop his hand moving up to rub his chest, not that it ever made a difference to the pain.

'We're going to move to LA once the film is done,' he said. 'To support her. I had an audition there a while back, and I've got a callback, so hopefully…'

'That's great.' Ella smiled—that infuriating smile that didn't reach her eyes. She picked up her bag, preparing to leave. 'I'll be moving, too. Spain.'

'Not LA?'

She shook her head vehemently. 'Not LA. So maybe this time fate will do the right thing and keep us out of each other's way, huh?'

She laughed, but Aaron had never felt less like laughing, and her own dwindled away until she was staring at him, equally silent.

Aaron watched her closely. 'So, we're going to stand here, are we, Ella, and smile and laugh and pretend we don't mean anything to each other? Because I don't think I can do it.'

Her eyes widened. 'Don't,' she said. 'You and Rebecca and Kiri have a long path ahead of you. You need to concentrate on that.'

'And you have to concentrate on martyring yourself, is that it?'

'Stop it, Aaron. Loyalty is not martyrdom. I *owe* Javier this.'

'Two years apart, and then suddenly you get engaged? What do we even know about him?'

'*We* don't need to know anything. Only I do.'

'I told you I'd be waiting for you. And then—'

'Waiting for what? Don't throw Rebecca's new man in my teeth as though that's supposed to make a difference. You've just told me you're following her to America. Where does that leave me? Where?'

He crossed the floor to her. 'I *hoped* in LA. Close to me. Where we could work it out.'

'Oh, spare me. I'd just be carrying two loads of guilt—leaving Javier when he needs me, and being your bit on the side. Well, I'm not doing it.' She paced. One step. Two. Three. Back. 'I knew this would happen. Keep it simple, you said. Casual. And then you proceeded to make it anything but. I tried to make you leave me alone. Sydney, Cambodia, London—every time. Why couldn't you? Why?'

'Because.' *Oh, great answer. Who wouldn't buy that?*

She looked, rightly, incredulous. 'That's an answer?' She turned away, tearing her hands through her hair as though her head was aching.

'All right, I'll tell you why. Because I'm in love with you.'

She spun back to face him. Her mouth formed a silent 'O'. She seemed incapable of speech.

'It's true,' Aaron said, and felt a sense of wonder himself. 'I couldn't leave you alone, because I loved you. I *love* you.'

'I don't want you to.'

'You don't get to dictate to me on this, Ella. If I could have dictated *myself* out of it, I would have. Because, I can assure you, it's not something I wanted either.'

She backed away a step. 'It's just proximity. Because I'm here. And I threw myself at you.'

He laughed harshly. 'Except that I've been lugging it around since Cambodia.' It was true. True! Since *Cambodia*. Why hadn't he realised it before? 'And I'm the one who was doing the throwing,' he continued. 'Always, always me. You were the one running. And I'll tell you this: it's a pain in the butt. *You're* a pain in the butt most of the time, with your bad-girl routine and your secrets. But...' he shook his head '...I love you.'

'Well, stop it. This is a mess. We're a mess. Just as predicted.' Her breath hitched. 'And I—' She broke off, rubbed her hands over her face again. 'This is so frustrating. Why do we do this to each other? Why can't we ever have a normal discussion?'

'I think it's because I love you, Ella.'

'Stop saying that.'

'And I think it's because you don't want to hear it, so you prefer to fight.'

She did that thing where she got herself together, visibly changing from distraught to pale and blank and cool. 'Remember what I said about Disneyland? That it's a blast as long as you remember it isn't real? Let's just say we've had too many turns on the teacups. Your head will stop spinning soon.'

'No, it won't, Ella. My head will still be spinning. My heart will still be aching. And I will still be in love with you.'

She looked at him coldly. 'Then just be happy I'm refusing to help you mess up your life.'

CHAPTER SIXTEEN

ELLA HAD AN uncomfortable night.

Aaron loved her. *Loved* her.

But it didn't change anything. Because with Brand stuck in York and Tina needing a distraction from her constant back pains, it was *Javier* who took her and her sister out for dinner. It was *Javier* stopping outside Ella's bedroom door when they got home, kissing her, urging her with that sharp, impatient edge to his voice, *'Let me in, Ella. It's time, Ella. Why not, Ella?'*

Why not, Ella? Because Aaron loved her. How was she supposed to sleep with anyone else, knowing that?

It was a relief when Javier left the house after breakfast the next morning, so she didn't have to feel the heavy weight of his dark eyes on her, silently accusing her, questioning her, beseeching her.

Tina was restless, and irritable, and uncomfortable. Demanding a cappuccino from a particular café, which Ella took herself off to buy and bring back so Tina didn't have to get out of her nightgown. Ella hoped Brand's train was on time. She had a nervous feeling Tina's persistent backache meant the baby was preparing to introduce itself to its parents, and Tina would make Brand's life hell if he missed even a second of her labour.

The thought made her laugh as she walked into the house, takeaway coffee in hand. It always amused her to think of Brand—for whom the term alpha male could have been coined—as putty in her sister's hands. Because that's what—

The coffee cup slipped through Ella's fingers. 'Tina!' she cried, and ran towards her sister's crumpled form at the foot of the stairs.

Tina groaned.

Ella closed her eyes, silently thanking every deity she could think of. And then she crouched beside her sister. 'How many times do you have to fall down the stairs before you learn that you do *not* hurry when you're about to give birth?' Ella demanded. 'Brand is going to maim everyone in sight if anything happens to you.'

'It was only the last couple of stairs. I was feeling so awful, and I'm having those horrible Braxton-Hicks things, and I thought I'd go back to bed. So shut up, Ella, and just help me up.'

'Let me check you out first,' Ella said, but Tina was already struggling to her feet—only to slump back down again with a sharp cry.

'I can't get up, Ella. I think I sprained my ankle. And I…' She stopped, and her eyes widened as she looked down at herself, at the floor beneath her. 'Ella!'

She sounded scared. And Ella, seeing the puddle pooling around her sister, understood. Tina's waters had broken.

'But Brand's not here,' Tina wailed, and then she gasped and grabbed Ella's hand. A long, keening moan slipped out between her clenched teeth. 'Oh, no, oh, no,' she whimpered, as her hand loosened after a long moment. 'Ella, I can't do this without Brand. I promised him I wouldn't. He's going to kill me.'

Ella gave a shaky laugh. 'Tina, my darling, the only way he's going to kill you is by kissing you to death. Now, there will be ages to go, but if you're okay to stay there for a moment, I'll go and call the hospital and tell them we're coming in. And I'll call Aaron—he's on standby to drive you to the hospital, right?'

'Okay. Good. No!' Tina grabbed Ella's hand again and held on so tightly Ella wondered if her phalanges were about to snapped in two. Instinctively, she timed the hold. Counting down, counting, counting.

Seventy seconds. The contractions were coming close together. *Uh-oh.*

Tina let go, took a shaky breath.

'Right,' Ella said again, super-calm despite a finger of unease trailing a line down her spine. 'I have to let you go, okay? Just for a moment, to call the hospital.'

Tina, white-faced, nodded. 'And Brand. You have to call Brand. Oh, what's the time? He told me this morning he was trying for an earlier train.'

'I'll try. Just wait, okay?'

Ella raced for the phone and let the private hospital where Ella and Brand had chosen to deliver their baby know they were on their way in. She tried to call Brand but got his voicemail. Assuming he was out of range, she opted not to leave a message; if he got a message about Tina going into labour the moment he switched on his phone, he'd likely hijack the train and make the driver go faster!

She came haring back to Tina, who was in the throes of another contraction—*way* too soon. She allowed both her hands to be grabbed, the knuckles crunched, for the duration, but said, 'Try not to hold your breath, Tina. Just breathe, nice and deep and slow.'

Tina gave her a look that promised her a slow death, but she gave it a gasping try. At the end of the contraction Tina looked up at her. 'Did you get Brand?'

'He must be out of range, Tina. But I'm sure he'll be here soon.'

Tina started to cry, and Ella hugged her. 'Shh,' she said, kissing the top of Tina's head. 'Everything's going to be fine. But we need to get you off these hard tiles and clean you up, and I still need to call Aaron— Oh, hang on, someone's at the door.'

Praying it would be someone useful, Ella raced to the door, tugged it open. Aaron—in the process of knocking again—almost fell inside, and slipped on the spilled coffee. 'Whoa,' he said.

'Thank goodness!' Ella said, and dragged him further into the hall.

'Before you say anything, Ella, I'm not stalking you. I promised Brand I'd look in on Tina, so—' He broke off. 'What's happening?'

'It's Tina, she's in full-on labour!' Ella whispered.

At the same time Tina threw out a wobbly, wailing, 'I know, it *suuuucks*,' from the floor at the base of the stairs.

Ella gave Aaron a warning look. 'It does not suck,' she said, all brisk and professional. 'Because the hospital is expecting us and Aaron is going to get the car and Brand is going to arrive, and everything is going to go according to plan.' She smiled brightly at Tina as she hurried back to her—just in time to take her sister's hands as a scream, followed by a string of graphic curses, tore from Tina's throat.

When the contraction finally stopped, Tina was incoherent, so Ella quickly pulled Aaron aside. 'We're not going to make it to the hospital,' she told him.

'What's wrong?' he asked, sharp and serious.

'Her contractions are too close together, they're too intense, and they're lasting too long. I'm thinking precipitous labour.'

'That sounds bad! *Is* that bad?'

'Well, it's fast, and it's going to be very painful.'

'But if we get her into the car straight away?'

Ella was shaking her head before he'd finished. 'No, the way things are heading, we'll be delivering the baby by the side of the road, and that's *not* happening with this baby. I'm calling an ambulance, but childbirth isn't the highest condition on the triage list. So I'm going to get ready here, just in case. And I'm going to need you to help me.'

Aaron looked completely appalled, but he nodded. 'Just tell me what to do.'

'She's twisted her ankle so—'

A scream from Tina interrupted her. Another contraction.

Ella hurried back to her sister, Aaron beside her. Ella gripped her sister's hand, uttering useless, placating nothings, until the contraction passed. Then she brushed Tina's sweat-damp hair off her face. 'Right, darling, we're not taking any chances with an Aussie driving in London. I'm calling an ambulance instead, and then we're going to make you comfortable while we wait for it to get here, okay?'

Tina nodded, white with stress and pain and terror.

'Aaron's going to stay with you while I'm gone—just for a minute, okay?'

'Okay,' Tina said, sounding pitiful.

Ella drew Aaron aside again. 'Just keep her calm. Encourage her to breathe, deep and slow, deep and slow, but get ready for some screaming.'

'I can take it,' he said.

Tina, eyes glazed, wasted no time in grabbing Aaron's hand as he dropped beside her, squeezing tightly through another fierce contraction. Ella waited, roughly timing through a scream, scream, scream, to the whimper and slump. Ninety seconds.

'Hello, Hercules!' Aaron said admiringly. 'I need to get me some of whatever it is you're eating, bruiser.'

As Ella raced for the phone, she heard Tina give a strangled laugh. She gave another silent prayer of thanks, for Aaron's arrival. Aaron would look after her sister in every way possible—her health, her spirits, her dignity. What more could you ask for at a time like this?

Three calls later, the ambulance, Tina's private obstetrician and another fruitless try for Brand, and she raced up the stairs as another agonising contraction ripped through her sister, with Aaron encouraging her to scream her lungs out if that's what she felt like doing. Not exactly keeping her calm, but Ella had the felling Aaron had the right of it. If Tina wanted to scream her way through, let her!

Ella grabbed an armload of sheets, towels and blankets. She added a fresh nightgown. She then picked up several pairs of sterile surgical gloves from her ever-ready supply, a bandage for Tina's ankle, scissors, rubbing alcohol and an assortment of cotton wool and gauze pads. She winced as she heard Tina's wailing cry as another contraction hit her.

She juggled the goods into a semi-manageable pile in her arms and descended the stairs again. Halfway down, when Tina was silent again, she heard Aaron say, 'You know, Tina, women have been giving birth for thousands of years—and *you're* the one who gets to have Ella personally presiding over the action. How cool is that?'

'Very cool,' Tina gasped out, and met Ella's eyes as she arrived at the bottom of the stairs. 'Very, very cool.' She mouthed, 'I love you,' at Ella, and Ella almost cried.

'Love you too,' she mouthed back. And then she took a deep breath and hurried into the library. She shifted the couch so she had room to stand at the end of it, then quickly put down a thick layer of towels, covered them with a sheet, spread more towels where Tina's hips and thighs would go. She propped cushions, stacking more towels close by, and prepared blankets for when they'd be needed. Over the sounds of her sister screaming, she quickly used the rubbing alcohol to clean the surface of Kiri's activity table, then laid out on it everything else she'd brought from upstairs.

By the time she was back at the stairs, Tina was lying on her side, half on Aaron, abusing him for not massaging her in the right spot.

Aaron, accepting the abuse with equanimity, merely looked up at Ella and asked, 'Ready?'

'Ready,' Ella said.

'Tina,' he said, 'I'm going to lift you now, okay?'

Tina, distressed and almost incoherent, shook her head. 'I'm too messy. Look! I can walk. Or hop. Arm. Just your arm.'

'Tina, when did you start being such a girl?' he asked. 'Get over it and put your arms around my neck.' And then he effortlessly gathered Tina close and lifted her. He carried her into the library, oblivious to the amniotic fluid soaking his T-shirt and jeans.

'Can you balance her while I get her changed?' Ella asked.

'Sure, if you promise not to tell Brand I saw her naked,' Aaron said, and that gave Tina a much-needed laugh—quickly choked off as another contraction hit her.

Somehow, Ella and Aaron managed to get her stripped, freshly nightgowned and settled on the couch.

Ella stroked Tina's sodden hair off her face again. 'Shall I tie your hair back?' she asked,

'Yes, it's really annoying me.'

Ella whipped the elastic from her own hair and bundled Tina's heavy mass of ringlets into a ponytail high on her head. 'And now,' she said, 'I'm going to go and wash my hands, while Aaron waits with you.'

Five minutes later she was back. 'Tina, I need to check how dilated you are, okay?'

Tina cast a look in Aaron's direction.

Ella smiled, understanding. 'While I do that, Aaron is going to go and get me an ice pack for your ankle.' She looked quickly at Aaron. 'And I need some string or twine—I think I saw some in the kitchen drawer. And I need bowls and a plastic bag. Oh, and warm water, but you can get that next trip.'

'On it,' he said, and bolted from the room as Tina went mindless with another contraction, her painful, guttural cries making Ella wish she could take the pain for her.

'Ella. Ambulance. Not…going…to get…here,' Tina gasped as the contraction eased.

'I don't think so, darling,' Ella said 'My niece or nephew seems particularly impatient. Like you, always in a damned hurry.'

'Okay, so let's get onto the important question,' Tina panted out. 'Do you…th-think Brand…is going to be upset…when he finds out I'm in love…with Aaron?'

Ella forced a laugh as she snapped on her sterile gloves, marvelling that her sister could crack a joke at such a time—her precious, amazing sister! 'I think Brand is going to be in love with Aaron himself once all this is over,' Ella said, and searched her head for a distraction. 'So, names. I'm thinking Boadicea, Thorberta and Nathene for a girl. Burford, Lindberg and Ogelsby for a boy. Nice, huh?'

But Tina's strained chuckle was cut off by another moaning scream. 'Ella, Ella, I need to push.'

'Just hang on, hang on, darling. Try to breathe through it.'

'Breathe? Don't be so stupid, Ella. I need to push!'

Tina was sprawled, spread-eagled, with one leg off the couch. Ella positioned herself between her sister's thighs as Tina pushed, pushed hard. She lifted the sheet she'd draped over her sister's legs and, as soon as the contraction eased, inserted her fingers to find—

Oh, no. 'Tina, darling, I can feel the baby's head,' she said.

'What? What?' Tina panted.

'The baby's well and truly on the way. I think we can assume all those back pains you had yesterday weren't back pains, they were labour pains, so…'

But Tina was having another contraction, so Ella shut up, caught her sister as she surged up off the couch, held her and let her yell.

'You were saying?' Tina asked weakly, as she sagged back limply. But almost immediately another contraction hit her, and Ella held onto her again and simply breathed, hoping to calm her.

'I'm going to kill Brand. Kill him!' Tina screamed.

Aaron, coming back into the room loaded up with everything Ella had asked for, said, 'Let me do it for you.'

Tina's laugh turned into another screech, and then it was roller-coaster time.

The contractions had Tina in their vicious grip and wouldn't let her go. She was sweating gallons, and Aaron stayed by her side, hanging onto her hand when she needed it, wiping her brow, occasionally leaning over to wipe Ella's too.

Ella had gloved up again, and this time when Tina said she had to push she told Tina to go ahead, because nothing was going to slow this baby down.

All modesty had fled. Tina just wanted the baby out, even if Aaron had to reach in and yank it through the birth canal—which Aaron pronounced himself ready to do, only to be punched and to be told not to be such an idiot.

Ella was staring between her sister's legs. 'The head is crowning,' she said, very calmly. 'Not long now.'

The house phone was ringing. Then Ella's. Then Aaron's. All were ignored.

More contractions. 'Now push, Tina, push now.'

Phones ringing again. One after the other. Once again ignored.

Another contraction. Pushing, pushing, panting, pushing. Tina was shaking. 'Here comes the baby's head,' Ella said. 'Try to stop pushing now, Tina. Stop, the head is here. It's here, Tina.' Ella checked quickly to ensure there was no cord wrapped around the baby's neck. Breathed a sigh of relief. 'Beautiful. Oh, Tina, so beautiful.'

Aaron was holding a weeping Tina's hand, whispering encouragement, kissing her forehead, tears in his eyes, while Ella was supporting the baby's head.

Phones. Ignored.

'One more push and it will all be over,' Ella said, as the baby's head rotated to one side as though it knew what it was doing. And then one shoulder emerged, and the other, and the baby shot into Ella's hands like a bullet. Ella was crying, Tina was crying, Aaron was crying.

'It's a girl,' Ella announced, and, supporting the tiny baby's head and neck carefully, she tilted her to enable any fluids to drain from her nose and mouth.

The baby, eyes wide open like she was completely outraged, gave a strong, angry cry, and Ella quickly checked that she was pink right down to her extremities, her limbs were strong and flexed and that basically she was alert and perfect and gorgeous. Tina held out her arms, and Ella laid the baby on her mother's chest.

Ella checked the wall clock as she took off her gloves. Forty-five minutes from the time she'd spilled that coffee in the hall to the birth of her niece. Incredible! 'Aaron, just pull Tina's nightgown down a little, off her shoulders. Tina, that will let you be skin to skin with the baby. It will help release oxytocin in your body, which will make the placenta slip out faster.'

Judging by the delirious look on Tina's face, Aaron could have done anything just then and she wouldn't have known it. As Aaron adjusted Tina's nightdress, Ella drew a blanket up over the baby's back, making sure Tina, who was shivering, was covered too.

'What can I do next?' Aaron asked, looking at the blood soaking the towels underneath Tina.

'The blood's nothing to worry about, Aaron.'

He passed a shaking hand over his eyes. 'Thank goodness.'

'There is just the placenta to go, if you can pass me that bowl,' she said.

'And then do we get to cut the cord?' Aaron asked.

We. Such a little word, but it made Ella want to kiss him. 'When it's stopped pulsing, if the ambulance isn't here.'

She ran a tired hand across her forehead. 'But first—the phones, Aaron. I'll bet it was Brand. Can you—?'

But Aaron didn't have to do anything, because Brand erupted into the room, wild-eyed, followed by two paramedics. 'What the hell—?' he started, and then came to a dead stop. His mouth dropped open as he stared at Tina. Then he rushed forward, fell to his knees on the floor beside the couch. 'Tina?' He sounded awed and shaken. 'How did this happen?'

Teary, exhausted, but smiling, Tina reached out a hand, and touched his cheek. Ella and Aaron shared a look as Brand grabbed Tina's hand, pressed a kiss to the palm—just a simple kiss and yet it was so intimate.

One of the paramedics came over to confer with Ella, who quickly provided details of the morning's drama.

And then Ella realised she and Aaron were *de trop*.

The baby was being checked; the placenta would be delivered and bagged; Tina would be taken care of. Brand was cooing at his wife and daughter.

With a smile at Aaron Ella inclined her head towards the door, and the two of them left the library. The stood in the hall, looking at each other. And then Aaron said, 'I never did get the warm water.'

Ella started to laugh.

'And where the hell did I put the ice pack?' he asked.

And then they were both laughing. They laughed, laughed, laughed, as Aaron—covered in dried amniotic fluid—pulled Ella—covered in blood—into his arms. He buried his face in her loose hair. They clung together for a long moment, before drawing apart slowly.

Euphoric, shaken, exhausted, they stared at each other. Ella's heart was aching, her breath jammed in her throat with a lurching, desperate need to touch him. To huddle against him and weep and sigh and just *have*.

Brand broke the spell, exploding out of the library with

the same energy with which he'd entered it. 'I cut the cord,' he announced proudly.

Next moment, he was grabbing Ella, hugging her. Ella could feel him shaking. 'I love you,' he whispered in her ear.

'I love you too, Brand,' Ella whispered back, and kissed his cheek. 'And your beautiful wife, and your adorable baby girl.'

'Audrey Ella McIntyre—that's her name,' he said. And then he freed one arm and reached for Aaron, dragged him in. 'Mate,' he said. Just one word, but it said everything, because in it was joy and love and excitement and gratitude.

'Do we get to smoke a cigar now?' Aaron joked, and was dragged closer still.

'You're an uncle now—no smoking,' Brand said, in a suspiciously husky voice.

Then Tina and the baby were being wheeled out of the library, and Brand, laughing maniacally, was off like an arrow as he followed his wife and daughter out of the house.

Aaron cocked an eyebrow at Ella. 'So, can I clean up that spilled coffee over there and make you a new one?' he asked.

He was very conscious of the butterflies swooping in his gut, now he was alone with her.

Butterflies? Did a grown man even *get* butterflies?

He *never* got butterflies.

Ella looked at him, biting her bottom lip. Was she going to say no?

'It wasn't my coffee. It was Tina's.'

'So I *can't* make you one?'

'Yes, yes, of course you can,' she said, but she looked nervous. 'I'll clean the spill later, though.' She took a deep breath. 'Right now, I really, really do need coffee. Just as soon as I wash myself up.'

Aaron did what he could to clean himself up, then made

his way to the kitchen. He wondered what kind of conversation they could have after delivering a baby together. And after yesterday's conversation, when he'd told her he loved her.

So, Ella, how's it going? Decided you love me yet?

His smile twisted. Maybe not.

Aaron realised he was standing there in a trance, looking at her while he rubbed his hand over his heart. He hated it that he did that when he looked at her, whenever he even *thought* of her. His T-shirts were all going to start showing wear and tear in that one spot.

He busied himself with boiling water, setting out cups, spooning instant coffee. Ella came in and took a seat at the kitchen counter.

Aaron handed her a mug. 'So, Ella, do you need…do you need…anything? From me? Now? Do you need…' *Me? Me, me, me? Do you need me, Ella?* 'Um…anything?'

'No. It's just…'

Just her voice. Her husky Yankee voice was enough to make him melt. 'Just?'

'I can't believe I was jealous—of my own sister, of this baby. Because now…' She stopped, shook her head. 'It's just so perfect. Isn't it? Perfect!'

'Yes it's perfect, so take off the hair shirt for a while, Ella, hmm?' He reached over, touched her hair, just once. 'Funny, isn't it? Brand had every specialist in Europe on speed dial, and all it took was you.'

'I was so scared,' she said, and he heard the steadying breath she dragged in. 'I don't know what I would have done if you weren't here.'

'Nobody would have known you were scared. You're just amazing, Ella. But, hey, if you want to fall apart now it's all over, here I am,' he said. 'You can cry all over me.'

Ella looked at him and smiled—that glorious smile, with her mouth and her eyes and her heart and her soul.

That smile.

It told him that, regardless of what they wanted or didn't want, they were connected.

It was fate.

'Oh, Aaron,' she said.

He thought she would say more, but then, outside the room, there was a quick burst of Spanish.

'I'd better go,' Ella said, and leaving her coffee, untouched, on the counter, she rushed from the kitchen.

Hmm. Fate had a lousy sense of timing, all things considered.

When Aaron and Kiri walked into Tina's hospital room that night, Ella was there, holding the sleeping baby.

Her eyes lit up when she saw him and his heart felt like it was doing a triple back somersault with a full twist. He caught himself doing that hand-rubbing thing over it again and had a bad feeling it wasn't a habit he was going to kick any time soon.

'Hello, Kiri,' she said. 'Aaron.' She looked kind of shy. It was entrancing. 'Recovered from today's high drama, then?'

'Yes,' he said. Not exactly a scintillating conversationalist tonight, but after the intimacy they'd shared at Audrey's birth—even though they'd been so focused on Tina they'd barely spoken to each other through the experience—he found himself tongue-tied. He was just so in love with her. He wondered how he hadn't seen his obsession with her for what it was sooner.

Love. If he'd admitted it to himself in Cambodia, they'd be married and she'd be pregnant by now; although, after today, how he'd actually *live* through Ella in labour he didn't know, and nobody would have the power to keep her from him—not even her.

'Ah, Kiri, my favourite boy,' Tina said. 'Did you come to see me or Audrey?'

'You *and* Audrey,' Kiri said, approaching the bed. His eyes were huge, staring at the baby.

'Smooth talker,' Tina said, laughing. 'Ella, let Kiri see her properly.'

Ella settled herself in the chair next to Tina's bed and beckoned Kiri closer.

When Kiri was beside her he asked, 'Can I touch her?'

'Yes,' Ella said. 'In fact…' She shot Tina a questioning look and waited for Tina to nod. 'You can hold her. But you'll have to sit very still in this chair. Can you do that?'

'Give Tina the picture first, mate,' Aaron told him, and Kiri handed it to his father without taking his eyes off the baby.

Aaron laughed as he presented it to Tina. 'I think we know where his priorities lie, Tina, and they're not with you or me—or even Ella, who used to be his favourite up until two minutes ago.'

Ella settled Audrey on Kiri's lap and positioned his arm so that it was firmly under her head. 'She doesn't have a strong neck yet, so you need to be careful that you hold her head like this. All right?'

Kiri nodded. Audrey didn't fret, just accepted this little boy who was holding her as though it was the biggest adventure of his life. Then Kiri leaned his face down to the baby and softly kissed her forehead.

Ella looked at Aaron. Aaron looked at Ella. Aaron reckoned an outsider could have mistaken them for the parents of both children.

Tina cleared her throat. 'Ella,' Tina said, 'why don't you take those flowers from Aaron?'

'Sure,' Ella said, and there was relief in her voice. 'I'll go and cajole another vase out of the nursing staff.'

Aaron perched on the edge of Tina's bed, watching Kiri with the baby.

'I'm so grateful, Aaron, for what you did today,' Tina said.

'I didn't do anything.'

'You kept me calm, you rubbed my aching back, you let me squeeze your fingers, you took more verbal abuse than any man should have to.' Slight pause. 'And you gave my sister strength, just by being there.'

Aaron shook his head. 'Ella didn't need me, Tina.'

Tina looked at him, like he was a puzzle. 'Men really are stupid, aren't they?' she asked. 'Look, Aaron, now that you've seen my lady bits being stretched to oblivion, I feel I know you well enough to be blunt with you. So I'm just going to come right out and ask you: what are you going to do about Ella?'

Aaron jerked so suddenly his leg slipped off the bed. 'I—I— She—'

'Yes, you're as articulate on the subject as she is. Look— you're divorced. Can you make like you really, really mean that, Aaron? And then get my sister away from that man.'

'I thought you liked him?'

'And that's what's stopping you, is it? The way you think I feel?'

'Ella doesn't feel that way about me.'

She fixed him with an incredulous stare. 'Don't be an imbecile. She won't *admit* to feeling that way about you while you've got a wounded animal to look after. Apologies to Rebecca, but you get the picture.'

'She won't leave Javier.'

Tina gave an exaggerated sigh. 'Stupid and so damned *aggravating*. All right, then, forget Ella. Stay in your rut, juggling all your balls and making sure none of them accidentally hits another while they're in the air, and let Javier have her. Because she will marry him, you know. She has a greater capacity for pity than Mother Teresa ever did. Oh, well, at least they'll have good-looking kids.' She turned to Kiri. 'Kiri, sweetheart, I think Daddy wants a turn. You come and tell me about this lovely painting.'

Aaron took that to mean she couldn't bear to speak to him.

He lifted Audrey out of Kiri's arms and stood there, staring down at the newborn and rocking her in his arms. And wondering...

Ella smiled at him as she came back into the room. 'Got a vase,' she announced, and positioned it, flowers already arranged, on the window ledge.

'I think Audrey's smiling at me,' Aaron said.

'If she is, Brand will beat you to a pulp,' Tina said, sounding like she was relishing the thought.

Ouch. 'All right, maybe she's not smiling,' he said. Her tiny mouth opened and closed a few times. 'Is that what you'd call gurgling, maybe?'

Ella laughed. 'No,' she said.

'Hmm. Man, she smells good,' he said after a moment.

'Yes. Babies always smell delicious.' She made a last adjustment to the flowers and then held out her arms for Audrey. 'Time for her to go back to bed,' she said. Aaron gently laid the baby in her arms so she could place her in her bassinette.

Oh, Lord, he thought as that mesmerising scent of Ella's hit his nostrils. She smelled more delicious than a thousand babies.

'Where's Javier tonight?' Tina asked, all innocence.

'He's out with some of his friends. There's a new medical mission in Ethiopia and...' She shrugged.

Tina raised her eyebrows. The picture of disapproval. 'So he's going back to Africa. Would that be before or after you're married, Ella?'

'I don't know, Tina. I guess he'll tell me when he tells me.'

A snort from the bed. 'Very wifely of you, waiting to be told. But not very Ella.'

'It's not like that.'

Another snort.

Aaron judged it time to step into the breach. 'I have

something to talk to Ella about.' he said to Tina. 'Can we leave Kiri with you for a few minutes?'

Tina gave him a beaming smile. 'Go. Please. Go.'

'I guess we'll go, then,' Ella said dryly.

Ella and Aaron paused outside the room. And then Ella burst out laughing. 'Is it hormones, or did I miss something?'

'You missed something. I don't know how to break this to you, but I don't think she's crazy about your fiancé.'

'Oh, I know that. Subtle, she isn't.'

'What happened?'

'Just a vibe, I think.' She looked hesitant. 'Do you think we can grab that coffee, without launching World War Three across the table?'

'I'm game if you are. I'll try to keep it at skirmish level rather than a heavy mortar attack.'

'Then I'll keep my grenade pins just half-pulled. Cafeteria, then? The coffee will be awful, but—'

'Cafeteria,' he agreed.

Ella wondered what the hell she was doing.

In a cafeteria, with Aaron, on purpose. Aaron, whose last attempt at drinking a cup of coffee with her had ended with her running to Javier. Aaron, whom she'd basically ordered not to love her.

'So what's the vibe?' Aaron asked, sliding a cup of coffee across the table to her.

Her mind went momentarily blank.

'Javier, Tina?' Aaron prompted. 'The vibe?'

'Oh. Well.' She stalled, taking a sip of coffee. 'She says he's too controlling.'

'Is she right?'

'He…' Another sip of coffee.

'What's wrong, Ella?'

'Huh?'

'If you can take two sips of that coffee and not make an

icky face, then you're not tasting it. Which means you're distracted. So, what's wrong?'

What was *wrong* was having this conversation with Aaron. But somehow, bizarrely, it was *right* too.

'Javier is…different,' she started, hesitantly. 'From what I remember, I mean.'

Aaron leaned back in his chair. 'And we're not talking good different.'

It wasn't a question, but Ella answered anyway. 'I think, no. But I don't really know yet. He won't talk about what happened. It makes it…hard.'

She watched as he absorbed that. His fists had clenched. And there was something in his eyes that urged caution.

'Go on,' he said.

She shook her head. 'This is a bad idea, talking to you about this. After…well, after—'

'After I declared my undying love and you threw it back in my face?'

'Yes, definitely a mistake.' She started to get to her feet.

He reached across the table, gripped her wrist. 'Sorry, Ella. If I promise to not let my skyrocketing testosterone get in the way, will you tell me?'

She relaxed into her seat. Nodded. Then she licked her lips, nervous. 'I told you he's the jealous type. Well, he *really* is.'

'You mean, of me?'

'Oh, yes. Even the thought of you helping me today with the baby? Well, let's just say it didn't go down well.'

'But that's insane.'

'And it's not just that. Not just you. He's jealous of everyone. Every man I talk to. Every man who looks at me.'

'Frankly, he's an insecure dirtbag.'

That surprised a laugh out of her. 'That's your testosterone not getting in the way, is it?'

'But he really *is* a dirtbag. Jealous of me? I get it. Because I want you. You know it. I know it. Tina and Brand know it. Tinkerbelle the neighbour's Chihuahua knows it. But, Ella, he does realise you're Hollywood-gorgeous, doesn't he? Every heterosexual man on the planet would take a second look at you. Come on! He's going to be living in hell if he can't cope with that—or he's going to make *you* live in hell because you won't be able to stop it. If he knew you, he'd trust you. So you're basically telling me he doesn't know you.'

Coffee. Sip. Ghastly. Okay, tasting the coffee was a good sign. 'You're so sure you know me that well?'

'I know that much about you. In fact, I'm wishing you were a little *less* faithful the way things are panning out. So, we're back to him being a dirtbag.'

'I haven't exactly been the poster girl for virtue, though, have I?'

'People do all kinds of things to get through tough times. They drink. They play pool with strange men.' Smile. 'They have sex with hunky Australian television stars.' Bigger smile. 'So what? Last time I looked, it wasn't the twelfth century. Nobody expects a twenty-seven-year-old woman to be a virgin, or to enter a convent to wait until her man rises from the dead.' He took her hand. 'Here's the sales pitch for me, just in case you ever end up interested: I wouldn't care if you'd had sex with a thousand men before me, Ella.'

She wanted to both smile and cry, but did neither. 'It wasn't like that, ever. In fact—'

He cut her off with a sharp, 'Hey, stop.'

'Stop?'

'Yes, stop. Don't tell me. And it's not because I'm squeamish either. Or *jealous*. It's just none of my business. As long as it was *before*. Now, after? Well, that's another story.'

'But it wasn't before, was it?' she said. 'It was after. I had the option of waiting for him and I didn't. I was with you.'

'You are *not* serious, Ella! He was missing for two years; maybe dead. And in my book you *were* waiting. You certainly weren't living.' He squeezed her hand. 'You're not really going all hair shirt on me, are you?'

'I don't think you're the right person to be lecturing me on excessive conscience, Mr Married-Not-Married.' Her shoulders slumped. 'I wish he was more like...' She cleared her throat. 'Nothing.'

'It's "not married". *Not* married. Just to be clear, in case that's what's stopping you from leaving him and throwing yourself at me.' Pause. 'And it's not nothing, I think.'

She smiled. 'It's just...well, you're very different from Javier. And I think he *would* care that I'd been with you. And I think...' Pause, swallow. 'I think I have to tell him. Don't you?'

He let go of her hand, sat back abruptly. 'How did we end up here? One minute we're talking about your sister's excellent intuition when it comes to fiancés and the next you're getting ready to throw yourself on your sword and confess something that's *none of his business*. Shall I say that again? *None of his business.*'

'But what if he finds out? *After* we're married?'

'Who's going to tell him?' Then Aaron seemed to catch himself. He shook his head, bemused. 'I can't believe I'm saying this! If it sounds like I'm talking you into marrying him, don't listen to me.'

'It just seems dishonest. Knowing how he feels about other men even looking at me, telling him is the honourable thing to do.' She looked Aaron straight in the eye. 'It's what you would do, isn't it?'

'I'd break up with him. That's what I'd do.'

'Be serious.'

'I am. Serious as a sudden home birth.'

'You told Rebecca about us.'

'Rebecca and I are divorced, remember?'

'And when you found out about Rebecca being unfaithful, you forgave her.'

He sighed. 'It's not the same, Ella. It's not as simple as

admitting you've been unfaithful—although in your case I'll dispute that to my dying day—and getting a blessing in return for being honest.'

'*You'd* forgive me.'

'As far as I'm concerned, there's nothing to forgive. But that's me. If he's the jealous type, and controlling...' He paused, seemed to be weighing his words. 'Who knows how he'll react?'

She looked at her watch. 'Anyway, we'd better get back to Tina. It's late and you need to get Kiri home.'

They left the cafeteria and walked in silence back to Tina's room.

'Thank you for listening,' she said, stopping him just outside. 'You know, don't you, that I've never been able to talk to anyone the way I talk to you? I *don't* talk to anyone like this. Only you. Do you know how much it means to me to have this?'

She reached up, cupped his cheek, and he pressed his hand over hers.

'You don't need to do this, Ella,' he said.

She removed her hand. 'I do,' she insisted. 'And I have to believe he'll forgive me.'

He blew out a breath. 'He will, if he's not a complete idiot. And, for the record, I'd forgive you anything shy of genocide.' He pursed his lips. 'Nah—I'd forgive you that as well.' He frowned down at her. 'And if he *is* a complete idiot, you've got my number. I told you I loved you and I meant it. And I told you I'd wait for you. I will, Ella.'

His hand was over his heart, rubbing. Ella, noticing it, frowned. 'Are you all right?'

'What?' He looked down, stopped the movement straight away. She was surprised to see a slight flush stain his cheekbones. 'Oh, yes,' he said.

Long pause. 'It's hopeless for us, you know that, Aaron.'

'No, I don't,' he answered. 'And I hope you realise I'm

in deep trouble with your sister. She thinks I'm out here convincing you to run away with me.'

'You don't want that, Aaron. Not really. Rebecca needs you. Kiri needs Rebecca. And Javier needs me. That's our lives.'

'You left out who you need, Ella. And who I need. I don't accept that our lives are about what everyone *except* us needs. If you could be a little less martyr-like about it—'

'I am not a martyr.'

'Maybe not all the time, but you're in training. Inconveniently, right after meeting me.' He took her hands in his, forestalling any more protestations. 'Anyway, just don't get married too soon. Make sure you get to know the man a little better first.'

'Ella?'

They broke apart and Ella whirled in the direction of Javier's voice.

Ella hurried towards Javier. 'I'm glad you made it.'

He made no move to touch her. 'Are you?' he asked, keeping his flashing black eyes trained on Aaron, who nodded at him and stayed exactly where he was.

Like he was on sentry duty.

Ella was torn between wanting to thump Aaron and wanting to kiss him. Here he was, protecting her from her fiancé in case Javier didn't like what he'd seen—when, really, what was there to like about it? Seeing your future wife holding another man's hands and gazing at him.

There was going to be an argument. And it wasn't going to be pleasant. But not here.

'Yes, I am,' Ella said, determinedly cheerful. 'Visiting hours are over but they're not too strict. Let's go and see Audrey. She looks just like Tina.' She looked at Aaron. 'Doesn't she?'

'Yes,' Aaron agreed. 'It was good to see you, Ella. I'll just pop in for a moment to say goodbye and collect Kiri, then leave you to it.' With what Ella could only describe as a warning look at Javier, Aaron walked into Tina's room, saying, 'Kiri, time to make tracks.'

Ella started to follow Aaron in but Javier stopped her with a hard grip on her arm. 'First, I think you had better tell me what is going on with you and him,' he said.

'Not in a hospital corridor.' Ella eased her arm free. 'Now, come in and see my sister. See the baby. Then we'll go home. And we'll talk.'

Javier didn't touch her on the way home. Didn't speak to her. Didn't look at her.

Ella dreaded the impending argument. But she longed for it too. Because they had to deal with everything—their pasts, their fears, their insecurities, their hopes—before they took another step towards marriage.

Having Aaron to talk to had made her realise she should never have kept her grief locked in for so long. Being able to talk to someone, confide in someone would have eased two long years of heartache.

So now she was going to talk to *this* man. She was preparing to share her life with him, and she couldn't do that without sharing how the past two years had changed her. And if Javier wouldn't confide in her in return, tell her how he'd stayed sane during two years of captivity...well, she didn't know what she'd do. Because she needed that knowledge. The insight. The trust.

They entered the house, went to Javier's room.

'So talk,' he said, and closed the door.

'I—I guess I should start with—'

'Start with what is going on with Aaron James. Why was he holding your hands?'

Ella stayed calm. 'He was comforting me. That's all.'

'Comforting you *why*?'

Still calm. But she licked her lips. 'Because I had just made a difficult decision.'

'What decision? And why were you with him when you made it? Why not me?'

Okay, not so calm. 'I was with him because the decision concerns you.'

His eyes narrowed. He said nothing. Just waited.

'To explain, I need to go back. To when you were kidnapped, and I tried so hard to find out what happened to you, and nobody could—or would—tell me anything. I wasn't a wife, I wasn't a sister. Nobody knew I was even a girlfriend. I'm not sure anyone would have helped me anyway. Because nobody knew anything. All I could do was wait. And wait. And…wait.'

He hadn't moved a muscle.

'It does something to you, the waiting,' she said, drowning. 'And I know you must know what I mean, because you were waiting too.'

'This is about you, Ella, not me.'

'But you never talk about it. You never—'

'You. Not me,' he rapped out.

She jumped. 'Right. Yes. Well…I—I—'

'Waited for me,' he finished for her, and it was more of a taunt than a statement.

'Yes, I did.'

'And you kept waiting, and waiting, and waiting.'

'Y-yes.'

'Until Aaron James came along.'

She sucked in a breath. Sudden. 'No. At least, yes but…no.'

He looked at her. Utterly, utterly cold. 'Yes but no?'

The snap in his voice had her stomach rioting.

'You slept with Aaron James. Just say it.'

She jumped, jolted. 'I thought you were dead.'

He had started pacing the room. 'You wished I was.'

'No!' she cried. 'Never, ever, ever.' She felt like she was running at a brick wall. It wouldn't yield; only she could.

Or try, at least. 'It's over between me and Aaron. He is no threat to you.'

Javier stopped, looked at her, incredulous. 'No threat to me? No *threat*?'

'I will be living in Barcelona, with you. He will be on the other side of the world.'

He shoved her against the wall. 'He is your sister's friend. He will be there, always.' He punched his fist into the wall beside her head. 'You have been denying me what you gave *him*. You introduced him to me. You made a fool of me.'

Ella stayed ultra-still, scared to move. 'I wanted to tell you. I am telling you. Now.'

'Now!' He looked into her face. He was only just holding his fury in check. 'Two years I survived, to come back and learn that you have slept around.'

'Don't say that,' Ella said.

'How do I know that you weren't sleeping with who knows how many men from the moment I was gone? We'd only known each other a few weeks when you slept with me. A woman like you would sleep with anyone. That's what I think you have spent the last two years doing. Now, just admit it, Ella.'

Ella thought of all the things she had planned to tell him tonight. The confession about Aaron, yes, but also about Sann, about her life in despairing limbo. And this is what it had come down to. 'No,' she said quietly. 'I will not admit to that.'

He raised his hand as if to hit her.

Her eyes blazed. 'If you touch me, I will make you sorry you're not still in Somalia,' she said.

'No, I won't hit you,' he said. 'You're not worth it, Ella.'

It took all of Ella's courage to turn from Javier. To walk slowly out of the room, not run, as his curses continued to rain on her.

She sat in her bedroom, shaking. She could hear drawers and cupboard doors slamming. Curses. Wheels on the floor—his bag. There was a pause outside her door. She imagined him coming in...

She held her breath, realised she was trembling like a leaf.

Then another inarticulate curse. Footsteps going down the stairs.

Out of her life.

Even three floors up she heard the front door slam.

'Some things just change,' she whispered to herself, and remembered Aaron saying exactly that to her.

She'd thought it would be comforting to accept that.

Instead, it made her cry.

CHAPTER SEVENTEEN

ELLA? ELLA PICK up. It's me.

Hellooo? Ella? Why didn't you return my call?

Ella, pick up! Come on, pick up!

Yeah, three messages were probably enough, Aaron decided, catching himself before he could leave a fourth.

He contemplated calling Brand to do some back-door sleuthing—but pictured his lifeless body sporting a variety of blunt and sharp force injuries should Ella get wind of that, and opted to spend the night tossing and turning instead as he wondered how the confession had gone. Whether Javier and Ella were in bed, burying the infidelity hatchet in a lusty bout of lovemaking.

No!

He would *not* imagine that.

He would, instead, plan what he would say, how he would act, tomorrow, when he made a last-ditch effort to woo Ella, regardless of what had happened between her sheets tonight.

And screw the best-buddy routine the two of them had enacted at the hospital; he should have whisked her off into the night instead of letting her saunter off with the darkly brooding doctor.

Anyway, enough dwelling on what he should have done. More important was the future.

So, back to what he was going to say to Ella.

And it was suddenly so clear! Why did it have to be three o'clock in the morning when he realised that keeping things simple was not about compartmentalising things to death? Ella in one corner, Rebecca in another, Kiri in a third. Him in the fourth, sashaying back and forth between them. Tina had put it best—he was juggling balls to make sure they didn't ever connect.

Dumb, dumb, dumb.

Because who wanted to juggle for eternity? It was exhausting. You had to stop some time and hold all the balls together in your hands, if you didn't want your arms to fall off.

Yep, it was crystal clear at three o'clock.

He was getting quite poetic.

And perhaps a little maudlin. Because he couldn't help revisiting every stupid argument he and Ella had ever had, wishing he could go back and fix every single one of them to get the right ending.

How arrogant he'd been, to insist they couldn't have a relationship because of his complicated life. Who *didn't* have a complicated life? Ella's was worthy of its own miniseries! All he'd managed to do was give Ella every argument she'd ever need to keep him at arm's length for the rest of their natural lives.

And she knew how to use them.

One. What was good for Rebecca. Well, if Rebecca knew she was the main obstacle to his relationship with Ella, she'd laugh herself sick.

Two. What was good for Kiri. As if being around Ella could ever be bad for him!

Three. His own initial disapproval of her. Short-lived it may have been, but Ella had turned out to be an expert at hurling that at his head.

He wanted to slap himself in the head when he thought back to how he'd made Ella feel like she wasn't good enough to be near his son. Except that he couldn't hit himself hard enough; he'd need some kind of mediaeval mace with all the spiky protuberances to do his self-disgust justice.

Just how was he going to fix the situation?

He could do better. He *would* do better. He would be sane, articulate, charming, passionate, clever. He would convince her that she belonged with him.

Tomorrow he would prove that love was really simple. Just being in it and grabbing it when it hits you and making your life fit around it, not it fit around your life. *Very* simple.

What time was a decent time to arrive at Brand's, given Tina and Audrey were coming home from the hospital? Just after lunch? That seemed good timing. For a sane, reasonable man who was insanely, unreasonably in love with a woman who held all the cards.

He found that he was rubbing his chest over his heart again.

Man, he hated that.

One look in the mirror the next day had Ella raiding Tina's store of make-up.

She couldn't look like one of the undead for Tina's return from the hospital.

And she would have to handle the news of her break-up with Javier carefully, with no mention of last night's awful showdown, if she didn't want Tina packing the electrical wires and blowtorch in a backpack and going off to hunt Javier down.

But she would, at last, tell her sister everything about the past two years, including what had happened with Sann. She would let her into her pain and grief the way she should have done all along.

And then she would go back to Los Angeles. And she would tell her parents.

And then it would be time for her to move on, and make new memories.

No guilt, no shame.

'She's not here, Aaron.'

Aaron heard the words come out of Brand's mouth but couldn't quite compute.

'Not here?' His eyes widened. 'Then where is she? *How* is she?'

'If it's the break-up with Javier you're talking about, she's fine. I'd go so far as to say she's relieved.'

Aaron felt a wave of intense happiness, until the look on Brand's face registered. 'So when will she be back?' he asked.

And then Brand put his arm around Aaron's shoulder, steered him into the library.

Not promising.

Brand poured Scotch into a glass, held it out for Aaron. 'Her flight home took off about half an hour ago,' he said.

Aaron took the glass, almost mechanically sipped.

Brand walked over to his desk, plucked a small envelope off it, handed it to Aaron.

Aaron.
I think we've all had enough upheavals for a while so let's not add any more drama. Good luck with Rebecca. And hug Kiri for me.
Ella

He looked up and caught Brand's eye.

'That's it?' he demanded.

'That's it.'

He reread the note.

'Yeah, screw that,' he said. 'When do we wrap up filming?'

'Four weeks.'

'Then that's how long she's got before I go after her.'

'Princess Tina will be pleased,' Brand said, and slapped him on the shoulder.

CHAPTER EIGHTEEN

ELLA WASN'T HOME.

Aaron almost laughed as he recalled the way he'd played this scene out in his head. He would knock on the door of her apartment. She would open the door, stare at him, smile that dazzling smile—the one that had her heart and soul in it—and then she would leap into his arms and kiss him. She would tell him she loved him, that she couldn't live without him. That she'd been waiting for him.

Very satisfactory.

Except that she wasn't home.

The only romance he'd had so far had involved charming Ella's young gay doorman into letting him into the building.

Well, he'd told Ella more than once he would wait for her. And here he was, waiting.

It had been four weeks. Enough time for Ella to miss him desperately. Enough time for him to get all the elements in place to counteract Ella's martyrish inclinations: Rebecca was doing brilliantly at Trust; her new love affair was steaming ahead and Aaron liked the guy; custody arrangements had been sorted; and Aaron had even managed to nab that lead role in the LA-based detective series he'd auditioned for.

Fate was lining up for him at last.

Now he just had to pray that Ella wasn't about to head

off to the Congo or float herself down the Amazon, and life would be perfect.

If he could just get her to say three little words.

He didn't really know if she could say those words. Or feel them.

He heard the elevator, and scrambled to his feet. He'd done this four times already—all false alarms—but, hey, he wasn't about to be found by the love of his life sitting on the floor.

Then he saw her. She was wearing the dress he'd bought her in London. That *had* to be a sign.

He felt those blasted butterflies again. Actually, forget butterflies; these were more like bats. Humongous bats.

He knew the moment she saw him. The hitch in her stride. Then the slow, gliding tread towards him.

'Well,' Ella said inadequately, with the smile that didn't reach her eyes.

All Aaron's optimism dropped through his gut to the floor. 'Don't,' he said. 'Don't smile like that. Not like that. Not now.'

'I don't—'

'And don't say you don't know what I mean. Because you do. Aren't you happy to see me, Ella?'

He heard her suck in a breath. And then she said, 'Is everything...? Is everything okay? Rebecca...'

'In rehab. Taking control. Doing great. But even if her life were off the rails, I'd still be here, Ella. What I would have told you, if you hadn't left London when you did, was that I was going to make things work for us come hell or high water. No matter what was happening with anyone else. Rebecca, Kiri, your family, even Javier—I'd still want you with me. All right, to be honest, I still want to damage one of Javier's cheekbones, so having him in our lives might take a little work.'

'Javier just couldn't forgive. Couldn't even accept. And I realised either he'd changed or I never really knew him.

But if you'd seen him, so heroic and caring and brilliant in Somalia, you—'

'Yeah, yeah, don't expect me to get all misty-eyed over his good doctor deeds, Ella. And he had nothing to forgive. I don't want to talk about him. I don't care about him. I only care about you.'

He stepped closer to her. 'I don't know what I'll do if I can't have you. You and I, we're supposed to be together. Can't you feel it? We've learned, both of us, that life isn't about hanging on the sidelines, waiting for things to get better. Or worse. Waiting for fate to come and toss a grenade or a bouquet or a wet fish. I'll catch every grenade, Ella, and I'll still love you. I'll navigate any difficulty to have you.'

She blinked hard. Again. 'Oh.'

'I'll follow you to Sierra Leone or Chad or Somalia or Laos.'

She shook her head. 'It's good old America for a long time to come, so you'll have to think of something else.'

'Hmm. So, what about…?' He held up his hands. They were shaking. 'What about this? Nobody else has ever made me shake just because they were near me, Ella.'

'Are you sure? Are you really sure, Aaron?'

He waved his hands at her. 'Look at them! Like a leaf in a gale.'

'I don't mean— I mean I don't want you to regret me. I don't want to become one more responsibility to bear. And you know, better than most, I've hardly been a saint, so I'd understand—'

'Stop talking like that!' He started undoing his shirt.

'What about Kiri? How will Rebecca take it?'

'Kiri loves you, and as for Rebecca—was I just talking about not caring? But if it will get you over the line, I swear I'll get her blessing in writing. My sisters—they've posted an embarrassing video on YouTube begging you to take me—wait until you see it. And I've already gone and—'

'What are you doing?' she asked, seeming to notice at last that he was removing his shirt. 'I'm not— I don't— I— Oh!'

'Do you like it?'

Ella came forward, put her hands on his chest. He'd had her name tattooed across his chest. Her name. Bold and beautiful.

And something else.

Dropping from the A over his left pectoral muscle was a gold ring that looked like it was entering his skin where his heart was, anchoring her name there. Her fingers traced it. 'Oh, Aaron. Yes, I like it.'

'I'll ink my whole body for you Ella, if you want.'

'No, just this,' she said. 'It looks…permanent.' She put her head on one side, querying him. 'Is it?'

'The things I'll do to get a green card,' Aaron quipped, and then gathered her in, held her against his chest, tilted her face up to his. 'Yes, it's permanent. And so are you. Are you ready, Ella, my darling? You know I want you. You know I'm obsessed, besotted, madly and wildly in love with you. Tell me you feel the same. Tell me you're ready. Come on, Ella. Say it. Say it.'

'I love you. And, yes,' she breathed. And then she smiled and her face lit up like the sun. Bright and gold and glowing. His smile. Just for him. 'I'm ready.'

He closed his eyes. Breathed in. Out. Opened his eyes. 'Then let's get inside. I want to have my way with you— No, wait! I want you to have your way with me. Hang on, I want— Oh, Ella, just open the door.'

* * * * *

LET'S TALK
Romance

For exclusive extracts, competitions
and special offers, find us online:

- **f** facebook.com/millsandboon
- **⊙** @millsandboonuk
- **𝕐** @millsandboon

Or get in touch on 0844 844 1351*

For all the latest titles coming soon, visit
millsandboon.co.uk/nextmonth